BUILT ON BROKEN PIECES

LAMARTZ BROWN

Built On
Broken Pieces
Lamartz Brown

This book is a work of fiction. Names, characters, businesses, organizations, places, events, and incidents are the product of the Author's imagination or are used fictionally. Any resemblance of actual persons, living or dead, events, or locales are entirely coincidental.

Library of Congress Control Number: 2021907443

ISBN: 978-1-7368347-0-1 (Paperback)
ISBN: 978-1-7368347-1-8 (E-Book)

Cover Design: TSPUBCreative, LLC
First Edition
Printed in the United States of America

Website: www.lifelyricsentertainment.com

PROLOGUE

"*I* will kill you right where you stand!"

"You betta go 'head wit' all that!" Mason barked, irritated that he had to even go through this.

"I'm going to ask you one more time. Why was she calling here crying she couldn't do this no more? Do what no more, Mason?"

An angry cry smacked Mason over the face right along with Linda's long fingernails. She couldn't believe what she heard. This girl sounded desperate, almost as if she was in love, pleading for her lover to love her back. Her gut told her it was more than what Mason was letting on. He was too defensive for it to be anything other than how she was feeling.

"Don't question me. I gotta go see about something really quick, and we can handle this when I get back."

"Do I look dumb to you?" A lamp flew past him, hitting the wall. He ducked in time as it shattered to pieces, sending a loud thunder through the apartment.

"Let that shit would've hit—" Another lamp shattered inches away from the first one.

"You ain't gonna do nothing but answer my question, or

1

everything in this bitch will be on fire if you keep playing with me."

"Linda, don't make me put hands on you."

"If you think I'm about to let you walk out of here, you got another thing coming. Where are you going, Mason?" Linda calmly spoke, daring him to think she was playing. All of her anger seethed through the words that proceeded from her mouth.

Mason hesitated. "I'm going to handle some business. Get your feelings hurt if you want to. We can talk about this when I get back… like adults."

Today, people were testing his patience, and he didn't like it. First, he had his team getting out of pocket, now things weren't right at home.

"Didn't I promise you I'll kill you the next time you hurt me?" Linda ran in the kitchen and grabbed a knife. She moved so fast, yet Mason couldn't move fast enough. He grabbed her hands in time to catch her before she got to slicing his skin.

"What are you doing?" Grabbing her wrist to gain control of the situation, Mason thought quick. He let go of one of her arms and focused on the hand with the knife. He was able to knock the knife to the floor and kick it away.

"I told you! I fucking told you! You did it again anyway! With her though?" Mason may have taken the weapon out of her hand, but he didn't take the fight out of her misery.

"I'm sorry, Sweets. I'm sorry." That was all Mason could get out while receiving blow after blow.

"I'm going to pay this bitch a visit." Linda pushed Mason away, kneeing him in the balls. It folded him as pain shot through his body. She grabbed her things and rushed out of the apartment. Mason wasn't too far behind her after he collected himself. The elevator had already taken off, so he was left taking the stairs. Linda had taken the keys to the car, so he had to get to her before she pulled off.

Ten flights of stairs later, Mason grabbed the car door handle as Linda was backing out the park. He was able to jump in the car in the seconds it took her to shift gears from reverse to drive. Linda sped out the parking lot of Grand Street Projects, doing eighty miles per hour, on a hunt to find the low down, dirty skank who appeared to have something going on with her husband. This time it was personal, and she wasn't going out like no fool. The stop sign fed her anger as she blew right past it.

"Linda, slow down! You are about to kill us."

"You already kilt us…"

BANG! BANG! BANG!

"Mason, why are you banging like that? Dang, I'm coming!" *He has a lot of nerve, had me waiting, and now rushing me to get to the door*, Jane thought to herself.

Jane swung the door open only to find Jax in tears. "Jax, what happened?"

"You didn't hear? They gone, Jane." Jax rubbed his head. He looked to have been crying.

"Who's gone?" Jane looked on, confused and worried. Tears built up in her eyes before getting the news. The pit of her stomach was telling her one thing, but she was hoping like hell that it wasn't true. This grown man was crying. Where they were from, gangsters didn't cry. The ball in the pit of her stomach grew bigger.

"Mason and Linda… they… they got in a car accident. They didn't make it. They were pronounced dead on the scene."

PRESENT DAY

Joe - I Wanna Know

I want to know what turns you on
I'd like to know (So I can be all that and more)
I'd like to know (I'd like to know what makes you cry)
So I can be the one who always makes you smile

"*I*s everything okay in here?" Jeda's nosy neighbor peeked through the door that was still open from what unfolded between her apartment's frame and walkway. We both jumped out of our skin, pushing us further to the edge of our anxiety.

"Yes, everything is okay. Thanks for checking. It's nothing for you to report; everything has been handled and taken care of." Not wanting to pull away from the strides we'd made but having to, we needed privacy. Without being rude, I grabbed the door handle, closing the door on the outside world as we stayed in our world that we created.

Our world. Happy or sad, we created it, so it was worth

staying in, right? Even in our own world, we couldn't live the way we outlined it for ourselves.

Our hands entangled as I led the way back to the couch, the therapy couch, where I was her therapist and she was my patient. I wanted her to pour out her heart, but I wanted her to do it in her own way. She couldn't put it off in hopes that we could move past it without talking about it. Jeda needed to let it all out, something she hadn't done in a long time. All of this pent-up aggression caused more problems than just dealing with it.

Most times, words were nothing but words; when there was no action, there was no result, but I think I continued to prove that my actions spoke louder than my words. As words started to leave my lips, it opened with an uneasiness, searching for terms to drop from the ceiling of where we were seated.

"All I ever wanted to do is take away the burdens you carry and free you of the heaviness of things I knew for sure you couldn't control. I'm your safe haven, helping you navigate through this thing called life. Talk to me, Jeda. I wanna know all of you. Seeing you like this, it's… it's breaking me."

I found her eyes pulling the words out of the sky to express how she was feeling. Her eyes grew darker at the pouring out of my soul. We'd always tried our best to be up front with each other. We built on the present; her past turned her into another person almost. My house was our getaway. I never even questioned why we never went to her house. Grammy was cool with it, so I didn't care as long as I got to spend time with her. I remember days where Jeda would shut completely down. I thought maybe she was battling depression. I had to look it up because she had all the symptoms. We fell into a routine. I wouldn't ask questions, but I would hold her until she was ready to come back to life.

"I… I don't know, Cash. I don't think you're ready to

accept the real me and all that I went through before meeting you. A part of me believes you, but the other part is scared as hell. Being completely naked leaves a type of vulnerability that can make or break a relationship, no matter how solid the foundation."

I wiped the tears that escaped from her eyes, letting her know that she could continue. I pulled her into a tight hug, squeezing all of her uncertainty. My hug made it a little easier to get to the root; I could tell by the way she melted in my arms. I hoped like hell it transformed into confidence to tell her truth. She pulled from my embrace, ready to start. She tilted her head back, trying to stop the tears and trying to gather her thoughts in the process.

"When I was younger, my sister and me..."

She took a deep breath, trying to find her words.

"My sister and I were playing in our parents' room while they were entertaining adult company. My sister Jasmine always was wild and adventurous, always willing to do something she knew we didn't have any business doing. I was the oldest, but that didn't stop Jasmine from testing the boundaries of our childhood.

"Let's play school." I always wanted to be the teacher while Jasmine was the student. Typically, I could get her to play along, but today she was on a mission to have more fun than the adults sitting in the kitchen, playing spades, and having a few drinks while listening to some good ole music.

"'No. I'm tired of playing school. You won't let me be the teacher, and I hate doing schoolwork anyway." Jasmine's voice was so innocent and convincing it would cause anybody to change their mind. She always brought more light to an already lit room.

"What do you want to play then? It's too late to go outside, and we can't mess up the room. We are not even supposed to be in here anyway. I don't understand why you wanted to come here. Our room has all of our toys.'"

9

"'Let's play cops and robbers like Daddy does every day. I'll be the cop, and you be the robber.' Jasmine giggled while making her way to our parents' closet, grabbing the police hat our dad wore proudly to work every day. She put the cap on and stood tall like a superhero, flashing her baby teeth, ready to take on the world.

"She started looking for something else, and when she couldn't find it, she proceeded to the closet. Jasmine asked me to help her climb a few boxes to get whatever she felt would complete her role as a police officer. Once she reached the top shelf, she pulled out a massive trunk that almost dropped on my head, but I caught it in time, using all my strength. Once I made sure Jasmine got down safely, I quickly examined the box of her choice.

"My heart leapt with fear as our dad's gun shined like it was on display at a jewelry store and we were there to make a purchase. I quickly closed the box back, not wanting to play the game anymore. If we got caught, I knew I wouldn't be able to sit down for weeks from the beating I would receive from our mother.

"No, Jasmine. We can't play with Daddy's gun." Jasmine began to cry, and I didn't want our parents to come in and catch us, so I agreed to let her hold it for a few minutes. I uncovered the box, unsure if this was the right thing to do, but it was only supposed to be for a minute. The gun was kind of too heavy for me to hold, and before I could get a good grip on it, it slipped through my adolescent hands and hit the floor with a thump.

"A crack of thunder filled the room as the gun hit the carpet. Jasmine gripped her stomach as red started to cover her white t-shirt like someone was pouring cherry Kool-Aid on her. Time slowed down, and I was stuck in place, not knowing what to do next.

"Our parents ran to the room, not anticipating what they saw before them. A scream erupted from our mother's mouth as our dad ran past me to Jasmine.

"'Come on, baby. Come on, baby, please,' was all I could remember our dad saying, before our mom started shaking me, wondering what happened.

"'What did you do? What did you do?' our mother repeated while shaking my brains out of my head. She must have factory reset me until I was on 'off' mode. I couldn't even whisper a word. My visual cortex couldn't put together the sentence needed to explain what happened. It's a time in history I want to take back. It's a moment that I'd record over if this was a VHS tape with the movie of my life."

Jeda was baring her soul. A sob erupted from a woman who had been through the fire and back. Wise beyond her years lay a little girl stuck, remembered by her past transgressions. She was bleeding from the hands of a mistake that changed her life forever. It grew louder. The neighbor would surely call the cops if she continued; if he listened closely, he should be able to tell this was a soul cry.

I reached out my arms to embrace her, but she stopped me.

"No! Let me finish!" Her hand collided with my chest, putting me back in my original spot.

"I wanted to die! Why me?"

She wiped her eyes, mustered up some strength, and kept talking.

"That's what I used to ask God every day. Why couldn't I be like normal? Why couldn't I have a happy ending like we see in movies? Yes, it's a fairytale, but why couldn't it be that easy?

She wiped the snot that was making its way down her lips, with her shirt, chuckling like a woman possessed. It was something in the way she laughed that caught my attention, wondering if this was her breaking point.

"Dip, we don't—" She cut me off.

"She turned me into a prostitute!"

"She did what?" This time, I didn't allow her to push me away. I wrapped my whole life, my entire existence, in my embrace with her. I wish there was a way to go back in time and be there to save her so that she never had to speak those words. Rhetorical question or not, Jeda continued.

"Two weeks after my sister's funeral, my father went back to work and got killed in the line of duty. He wasn't supposed to have gone back to work. Being in the house with my mother was driving him crazy. She wouldn't stop crying, cursing him out for stupid things. Her anger was directed at the wrong person. Her hate for me drove him out the house, but my mother blamed me for that too. Everything was my fault." Jeda shrugged her shoulders.

"I never even got a chance to mourn before she had these creepy, nasty old men on top of me. You would have thought she didn't even love my father. She became the biggest whore on this side of New Jersey.

"Each time, my virginity was ripped, taken in the middle of the night. A thief that was sent by my mother to feed her hatred for me. I became numb to it; it became my life, and it was nothing I could do about it until I met you." Attentively, I listened. Her release was causing her to seem lighter, like she was shedding weight right in front of me. She showed signs that it was a good thing that we met. It shifted the mood a little bit.

"You made me feel like we were in movies. You were a character in a book sent as my knight in shining armor. Never have I ever experienced the love and attention you showed me. You reminded me of my dad, a love so pure that it made me want to do and be better. You helped me realize I wasn't who my mother made me out to be."

"I bet he was a great man. He would be so proud of you. You're in college, you're writing and getting major attention. You're doing right with the money he left you, and you are not out here sleeping around. He's smiling, knowing his baby girl is doing her thing and leaving her mark on the world."

A smile slowly appeared on her face. It was like God lifted

a boulder off her shoulder. Her voice even changed to the sweet tone she used when dealing with me. Mase and Kareem always said that she used another voice when she talked to me, but I hadn't noticed it until now. I now understood her tone for life; it was a language translation into the struggle.

"Please don't judge me, Cash. I never told anybody what I told you. I need you to give me a couple of days. I have to work through a lot." She made me look into her eyes, searching for doubt, searching for a sign that would tell her something other than what she was feeling.

My lips met the softness of her doubt. It was a kiss that sealed the deal of the next stage of our relationship. Sharing this type of information was top tier; it was secret service information that only a few knew. A different responsibility now bound us. We lay on the couch and drifted into a deep sleep, both not knowing what was on the other side of the day.

Defensive Stance

The players on defense should always be in a defensive stance. This involves keeping the knees bent and arms out wide. This puts a defender in the best position to react quickly and steal the basketball.

"*J*hope you can handle this pussy like you handled that ball tonight." Those words teleported through the particles of the air, causing my dick to enlarge immediately. My dick was always ready to make me proud by standing to the occasion.

I chuckled, caressing my shaped-up beard as my tongue wet my lips to perfection like I was LL Cool J in the '80s. Tonight's win had all the ladies jockeying my teammates like we were already in the league, making millions. Winning was something that I became accustomed to in my line of work. This lifestyle afforded me plenty of opportunities that most guys my age only dreamed of having.

The welcoming energy that radiated from this thick shawty was so engaging that every guy wanted some of her time and attention, but her eyes stalked me. Her eyes were smiling as they traveled from my lips to the sleeping lion in my basketball shorts. She approached me with confidence, so bold that it caused the crowd around us to stop and take a look. The roar from my sweatpants gave her the green light to proceed without caution. The caution went out the window when she realized she had one of our attention.

"Shawty, you bold!" Keeping my eyes on her face, I felt all over her body. If I kept touching, I knew I'd be back to my old ways. Body stacked like pancakes, and I had the sweet syrup ready to pour. If she kept it up, I'd eat it like the last meal on earth. She could be my last meal and breakfast, making it brunch to keep me full for the rest of the day.

We were face to face now, enjoying each other's breathing patterns as we took in the summer night. The Summer League wasn't like my college games; it was a way to play ball how I was raised, without all the technical stuff. We played street ball. Those bragging rights went a long way where I was from. It was my five-ten physical physique that kept my name on the lips of all the ladies. My late nights in the gym paid off. I had to stay in shape because it went along with my image. The worship my body received from the ladies when I was naked kept me doing sit ups to keep the V leading to my pipe that the women loved so much.

"You think that was bold…" She grabbed my dick through my sweatpants as I leaned on my Nissan Maxima, enjoying the attention my dick was getting. By this time, everybody was back to their regularly scheduled program, which gave her some time to slide her hands down my six-pack into my shorts.

Attention was something granted to me at an early age. Nothing was off-limits in the life of a basketball star. I allowed her to rub on my dick. It was feeling amazing, but unfortunately, I was gonna have to pass. Before you knew it, we were going to be shooting a whole porno video outside. I rested my hand on her quest to make me bust, and stopped her.

"Shawty, not today, but if you catch me again, I'll be sure to make it worth your while." She tried to keep going, but this time I had to get a little forceful so she would release my golden ticket. She looked around to make sure she didn't get busted being turned down. I knew our interaction was more for attention than it was about me. I noticed that when her words left her plump, pink lips, but I played along to see how far she was going to take it.

Bold women always intrigued me. It was something about their approach that caused the man to rise and take charge. Women were still my second love. They gave me a high that basketball couldn't provide. It gave me something to focus on other than basketball, but lately, I wanted more. I had to admit that it felt like my player days were coming to an end.

She walked away confidently but not with the same confidence that she approached me with upon arrival. I watched her walk away as the lady did in the movie *Waiting to Exhale* that my mom used to watch. My head shook, not believing I let that fine shawty get off, but I had better things to get into tonight.

My boy Quincy ran up with a confused look on his face like he couldn't believe I turned down pussy.

"Shawty went to get her car or something, or you turned down some cutty? Please tell me you ain't turned down no cutty, bro? What's good with you? You usually don't turn down a good nut."

"I don't have to sleep with every girl that comes on to me, Quincy. I'm getting too old for this shit. As long as my dick is still getting wet, that's all that matters."

"Yeah, wet with that Jergens lotion." The way his voice

carried his laugh is what had me. It opened the door for my laughter to follow.

"Get out of here with all that. I don't have to beat my meat. I'm not you, playa. The flood gates are always open compared to the desert you continue to experience." I mocked his laugh.

"Whatever. What are you getting into tonight since you let shawty find her next mark?"

"Stop trying to keep up with my moves, and focus on your plans for the night." I dapped him up while pulling the handle of my car door, with one person in mind. As much as I tried to push her to the back of my mind, I couldn't.

Am I falling in love?

Love wasn't something that I felt comfortable with expressing. It was a foreign country that I didn't want to take a flight to experience. It was a destination that I thought I would never reach, but it was a journey that I was finding myself on.

How could I fall for someone who had all the love she ever wanted? She was married, I had to keep telling myself. To me, marriage meant a genuine commitment to your partner, your lover, and your friend. Qwana's actions showed something different. Never one to be soft, I tried my best to change the narrative, but it was almost impossible at this point. I was in too deep.

I started seeing Qwana during my freshman year in college, not realizing that she would be a staple in my life. Three years later, we were still sneaking around like we were high school kids. It was great at first. I leveled up by sexing a married woman, but somewhere down the line, shit changed. I started to yearn for her, every part of her and not only the sexual encounters—which were mind-blowing, by the way—but her company. I didn't know what it was about her, but she opened up a portal to an unknown place of comfortability that I never felt with anyone else. She didn't want me for my NBA contract or my looks, but she wanted me for me. Yes, my appearance reeled her in, but once she saw what was behind the walls of fame, she fell in love.

And so did I… I guess.

Before I pulled out of the park, I sent a text message confirming our loving-making session scheduled at our favorite spot.

Are you ready for me, Q?

Q: I'm more than ready for you! I'm waiting for you in our room.

I wanted her in our house!

Q: Don't keep me waiting too long, Mason

Nobody called me by my government but her, and it made my dick jump.

I got you, Q!

That was all I needed to hear, or should I say see. It made me put a little more pedal to the metal while riding out to "Slow Down" by Bobby Valentino. There wasn't anything slow about our relationship. It was on like Donkey Kong once I saw her. I never knew I had a chance until she picked up the first time I called her.

The first part was getting her number, the second part was her picking up. I knew if she picked up, I had her. That wasn't arrogance; that was just facts. I let Bobby talk his ish while I drove.

Slow down

I just wanna get to know you
But don't turn around
'Cause that pretty round thing looks good to me
Slow down

Never seen anything so lovely
Now turn around
And bless me with your beauty, cutie

ROOM 2669 WAS OUR ROOM OF CHOICE WHEN WE GATHERED for hours of steamy sex. It was the first room we got at The W in Hoboken, New Jersey, which wasn't too far from where I lived. I still wasn't sure where Qwana lived; she kept that to herself all these years. I didn't press her about it. I understood her situation, but things were about to change. This hotel life wasn't about nothing. I needed and wanted more.

My post-game routine was always to have a Hennessy shot before long stroking the hell out some pussy. It was a cycle that I knew all too well. I familiarized myself with the inner workings of a female. It was a gift given to me right along with the reward of basketball. I was a winner on the court and in the bedroom.

As my Nikes hit the pavement of the W's marble floors, I strolled right past the check-in counter and headed to a night of much-needed release. Sex was a release, but kicking it with Q for a few relaxed me so much more.

The elevator doors opened to a couple sexing with their lips as they enjoyed the embrace of each other. They immediately felt embarrassed as they rushed off the elevator, holding hands, skipping from the love in the air. My fingertips tapped the twenty-sixth-floor button, ready to match the same energy that their residue had left in their wake.

It wasn't long before I reached my place of peace, my getaway from being myself. As my fist was about to knock on the door, it opened with a swift motion. It was like walking through the automatic doors at Walmart. Her body was covered with milk chocolate skin, her nipples watching from a distance.

Her stilettos, I admired from the doorway. The things I was about to do to her body played like a vivid picture playing on a Hollywood screen. Her energy radiated a sense of fulfillment as she looked me over. The view from her lace see-through Victoria's Secret underwear invited me in to take my rightful place. For Qwana to be twelve years my senior, her body was better than most girls my age.

I closed the door behind me, shutting out the world, ready to relax, relate, and release. My glass of Hennessy was waiting for me by my chair that was fit for a king. Although a regular chair, the vibe she was giving me by waiting for a nigga turned it into a king's furniture.

I threw my belongings on the couch, sitting down with my eyes stalking her every move, loving the sparkle in her smile that made me feel like I was the only man in the world. It was far from the truth; she was married. I let the taste of the henny dog accompany the stare of her sexy walk. Qwana found a comfortable position on the bed after coming out her panties. One less thing I had to do. She laid on her back, giving me an ocean front view of her private island. I was a guest about to check-in to stay for a few hours. These days, I wished it was longer, a never-ending vacation.

I battled with my feelings; they were foreign.

My pep talks to myself hadn't been working. I needed more time with her; not wanting her to leave had become a thing. Always wondering what she was doing, I hated it when she texted me one-word answers; that always meant she was with that nigga. The thought of them together infuriated me. It wasn't always like that though. Once I got to know her, it proved that she deserved better than what this dude was giving her.

This headspace was something I thought I would never

occupy. Professional basketball players were not supposed to be faithful or settle down. I was supposed to be living a life of the young, rich, and famous. Even if I wanted more with Q, it wasn't possible. She belonged to someone else.

I poured another glass of Hennessy, and the burn of it hitting my tongue relaxed me a little more. Qwana's hands made her way down to her pussy lips, gently sliding them apart and finding her clit. A low moan left her lips as she found her rhythm, adding slight pressure before adding another finger to help. The next moan was louder, and her fingers were now adding their own penetration. These two shots, the view before me, and the moans had me ready to pull my dick out and get to work. Tonight, I wanted to take my time. Her nut seemed like it was overdue, another reason I knew her husband didn't deserve the sweet pussy goddess that was his wife.

Her body greeted me with satisfaction as my lips met her belly button. A whimper escaped her lips, almost as if she was holding it in all day. Stream rose with every kiss that I planted across her stomach. My head rested for a minute, taking in the scent of her Thousand Wishes Bath & Body Works lotion. My favorite.

"What are we doing, Q?" The words left my mouth and collided with her toned abdomen, blocking all hope. I didn't sign a permission slip for my feelings to go on this trip. It was in the way it was uttered that disappointed me. It was like I was begging for an answer. I was always sure, never unsure, but my words meant something different.

I wouldn't let her move. I wanted her to speak, and if I had to listen from this place or level of vulnerability, so be it. I caressed her body, waiting for her to answer. I was hoping that my hands would make her change her mind. I was a craftsman working overtime to win the contract for lifetime placement.

"Mason, please don't do this. Let's enjoy the few hours we do have." Her soft, manicured hands met both sides of my beard, lifting my head to meet her for a kiss. Her lips never got a chance to connect before I turned my head, wanting answers. She slowly but forcibly shifted her way from between my legs.

Qwana wasn't supposed to be the one I fell for, but I did.

I was a young boy looking to bone an older woman, to fulfill a fantasy. Once I found out she was married, that was another trophy on my shelf. Not only did I bag an older woman, but I bagged a married, successful one as well. College girls were average; while it was fun with them, they didn't make me feel like a man. Qwana challenged me. She talked business, investing, and creating generational wealth. Our brief intermissions turned into documentaries of our past, present, and future everything.

"You mean to tell me you don't feel what I feel?" I poured myself another glass of Hennessy, ready for this conversation.

"I don't know what happened to you, but this sentimental shit is not what I signed up for. I'm married, Mason!"

"You ain't happily married, so stop trying to play me like I'm some weak ass nigga!" My anger took the front seat as I drove my feelings to an empty lot. My mind did not understand why someone would stay in a marriage that they knew wasn't healthy.

"Let me worry about my marriage, and you worry about the young girls you entertain after your games. I don't have time to be playing with you, Mason. I want to enjoy our time together. I had a long day, and this conversation is making it even longer. I came to de-stress and not get stressed. So please, let's move on. Take all your frustrations out on this pussy. I need to cum and cum hard." I guess that was a failed attempt of changing the mood.

"I say when you get this dick. I control how hard you cum.

Don't you ever forget that. Remember, you need me. If you were getting it at home, you wouldn't be here. Yet you're sitting here begging for me to make you cum hard. While you worry about your marriage, you better worry about losing this good dick and conversation that I give you when you come calling. Women always yell there ain't no good men in the world. I'm the whole package, and you keep screaming about your husband this and that. Man, forget all that."

"Listen, Mason, what we are doing right now is enjoying each other's company. In a perfect world, I would be with you. But guess what? We live in the real fucking world! We met at the wrong time; I already belonged to someone else. If I could turn back the hands of time, I would've waited for you. All that matters is making the best of what we have now. It will work out the way it's supposed to work out."

Her stiletto lifted off the couch like she was a model in a Victoria's Secret photoshoot. Her steps toward me had a purpose. She wanted the conversation to be over, so her seductiveness indicated the topic was not up for discussion any longer. She bent over in front of me, giving me a whiff of her garden. My mouth watered, ready to show her how much my tongue missed the taste of her inner woman. Feasting on Qwana made a Thanksgiving meal incomparable to how full I got off her juices.

Her remaining steps were all I needed to move past my feelings and enjoy this hurting I was about to put on her pussy. Her husband was going to know that I was all up in it. It was gonna have my signature written all over it. If he was hitting it at all, he couldn't have been hitting it like me. The way her pussy responded to my stroke told me so. Her pussy talked to me and told me all about her problems. And this conversation I was about to have with it would be a long one since she wanted to shut me up.

I stood her up, grabbing her around her neck, biting the

back of her earlobe. Her back arched as she felt my dick making an imprint on her soft ass. I reached to free her breasts from her bra as our bodies waited in anticipation. I turned her around, picked her up, and put her on the table like she was an all you can eat buffet. I played with her clit while roaming parts of her body that I wanted to target first. My fingers were now doing the work, bringing her to her second nut of the night.

The tip of my tongue found her two perfectly round breasts for an appetizer, and I ordered my drink from the fountain pouring between her legs. I wouldn't have to worry about a refill; they kept *cumming* on the house. The tip of my tongue finally met the opening of her pussy lips as I rotated between kissing and using my language as pressure.

Eating pussy was my specialty, yet not a lot of girls got to experience this attraction. It only operated on special occasions, and this was always one of them. The table was rocking in sync with the movement of my tongue. She held my head in place, reaching her first orgasm of the night. Those other two nuts were just setting her up for what was to come. My tongue had her in space working for NASA, transferring her from labor to reward. I slowed the pace of my weapon of choice, letting her ride it, till the wheels fell off.

I picked her up and carried her to the bed, making my way back up to suck on each of her nipples. I threw her on the bed playfully as I came out of my shirt, sweatpants, and Calvin Klein boxers. I pulled her to the edge of the bed, sliding my dick through the slippery slopes of paradise. I wasn't playing nice. I wanted her to dream about me, calling out my name in her sleep so her husband could hear her. I tried to deep stroke her into a coma so that she would stay with me forever.

The sex didn't stop me from how I was feeling. Qwana's juices flowed like a tsunami, leaving a puddle up under us. If I didn't slow down, I was one pump away from letting loose. I wasn't trying to go down like that, so I activated the slow, meaningful stroke. That stroke that showed her who was boss. My dick was the key, and I was about to lock the door to this pussy. I couldn't have her husband experiencing this. If she didn't understand that, then I didn't know what to tell her.

"We all choose our destiny in life.
Hopefully, our choices don't end in destruction."
- Kareem

y Jordan 1's hit the concrete. The fire hydrant had the sidewalk wet, and if I didn't pay attention, my kicks would have ended up right in a puddle. You could tell the kids had been playing in it earlier. I surveyed the area, enjoying what summer had to offer. I couldn't walk around looking goofy, so I played it cool. Music blasted from the roof of someone's ride, echoing "Drop It Like It's Hot" by Snoop Dogg and Pharrell. Vill City was live; the hustlers were hustling, and the people were out doing their own thing. I welcomed the ganga in the air and appreciated the love that was always shown when I came through. I couldn't wait to roll up, I hadn't smoked since this morning.

"What's good, Reem?"

"What up, Reem?"

My head nodded, acknowledging the love while strolling through the middle section, taking in the scene. Everyone was in their own world, enjoying the actions of the people surrounding them. Say what you want about the hood, we knew how to enjoy ourselves. The hood was freedom, freedom from a world that didn't understand the fight. Vill City was my getaway from everyday life's pressures. It's where I came to chill with my boys, smoke some bud, shoot some dice, and have a good time. My guilty pleasure so to speak.

These days, my dreams had become something that I no longer enjoyed. I'd been needing more days in my element, hence why I was giving the Vill most of my time lately. When Mase talked about basketball, you could tell he was in love with the sport. When Cash sang, you could tell he was invested by the passion in his vocals. I wanted to have that feeling again. Becoming a doctor, at one point, did that for me. I used to be excited for class, ready to learn about the human body and what it took to save lives through whichever service I would provide. I still remember my brain connecting the dots to what I wanted to be when I got older.

My young eyes scanned the waiting room, sensing the anxiety of the people around. My grandmother's leg shook as she held my hand tight. Sweat started to build in the palm of my hand from her death grip. I wasn't sure why we were in a hospital, but I could tell it wasn't for the joy of a brand-new baby. Mase and Cashmere stayed behind, not ready to face another minute in the hospital waiting room. They had lost their mother and father to a car accident, months earlier. If I had to guess, we had to be here for my mother. She hadn't been doing good since my aunt and uncle died.

"Mrs. Harris."

"Yes." My grandmother stood up on shaky legs, voice cracking from the lack of hydration from waiting. A woman so strong but yet so fragile standing before the doctors yet again, this time, hoping and praying that it was a different outcome.

"My name is Dr. Jamison. Your daughter overdosed on heroin, but we caught it in time to save her life. She was fortunate that the ambulance was able to get her here in time. She is resting right now; we are going to keep her overnight for observation. She's going to need to hear some familiar voices for encouragement. Follow me."
The doctor rested his hand on my head, and we followed him through the magical white doors.

I didn't know what overdosed meant, but I knew it was terrible. The tears that erupted from my grandmother's eyes confirmed it. Before we entered the room, she kneeled down, meeting me on my level to share the mystery of our visit. Her words stuck in the heart of a mother who was tired of crying, trying to understand why her family? Her kids?

"Kareem, I need you to be strong for your mother. She is very sick and needs your help, baby." She meant every word; it was laced with an emotion unexplainable.

Instantly, tears released from my eyes without being invited. I didn't know why I was crying, but I pulled from the strength that I didn't think I had. That strength transformed me into the fixer, the person that put together things that were broken.

"I'm going to be her doctor and help fix her.". Before I could see my mom, I made up my mind that I would be her savior, truly believing what my young mind could imagine. If only I was a doctor at the time to save Aunt Linda and Uncle Mason. Young in wisdom but mature in intentions, I put an S on my chest, ready to save the world.

"You can't help everybody, baby," were the words that crushed my world not too long after I made that declaration. It wasn't as easy as the little boy in me made it look years earlier. It was a constant reminder that the person has to work harder no matter how hard you work. We all choose our destiny in life; hopefully, our choices don't end in destruction.

The Vill was live as always. The bright lights illuminated the middle section like a red-carpet interview for an award show. This was the nightlife; the summer had the kids still in play mode. They ran up and down, playing the many games we did as kids. This didn't stop the adults from learning life lessons, enjoying themselves in the process. I remember as a kid always wanting to experience what happened at night when we went to sleep.

My stride came alive as I looked for my boys Rick and Reese, who I grew up with since our days in Public School #6. They always kept me in trouble, but they held me down. If I wasn't with Mase and Cash, I was with them. They were like my extended family. Their house was the hot spot, the place to be. Ever since Ms. Yvette started having relations with Harvey Davis, they moved on up like the Jeffersons. He was the right-hand man to Dom, one of the most ruthless hustlers that ever hit the east coast. His name was brought up with the Ricky Porters, Frank Lucas, and Akbar Pray of the world. He swept Ms. Yvette off her feet and started grooming Rick and Reese for the streets right away.

It was tempting, very tempting. My boys were making significant moves. Knowing what drugs did to my mom was the only reason I hadn't taken Harvey up on his offer. It turned her into this person that almost hated life; it was like she wanted to die slowly. It was something I would never understand. I tried everything I could do to get her to quit, but the monkey kept crawling up her back. My mom would go weeks without doing drugs, but someone or something would always trigger her next nodding episodes. She would disappear into the day, searching for her answer.

I should have been her answer. I should have been the medicine that was the cure to her disease, but somehow, I felt like I was the infection.

The wind from the opening of the door blew the cloud of thoughts from above my head. Rick's body took up the door's inside frame; you could tell the food was his best friend. The sandwich in his hand was the other evidence needed to prove that he was overweight. The Fat Boys would have cast him in their movie as the fourth member. He fit the bill.

"You always got something in your mouth, with your fat ass." I pushed past him, grabbing his stomach that was hanging over his sweatpants.

"Fuck you, you built ass slim jim. My shawty loves my belly; she needs something to rub on, not something to write with, you colored pencil. Are you mad that nobody ever colors with a black pencil? He almost choked on his sandwich, laughing at his own joke, nearly missing the step down out the door.

"That's what you get, punk."

The white tiled floors led me into the living room where the rest of the fam was. I was met with Ms. Yvette's laughs echoing off the tan walls that went well with the brown couch that Reese was sitting on watching the game. Ms. Yvette waved to me as the hood gossip flowed between puffs of her Newport 100.

"What's good, Reese?"

Dap.

Fist bump.

Handshake.

Salute.

We greeted each other with our handshake that we made up when we were in the fifth grade. I had always been closer to Reese. Out of the two brothers, Reese was the smart one. He was the brains behind the operation, whereas Rick was the enforcer. They worked well as a team. They made up for each other's weakness, which meant it almost made them an unstoppable tag team. They were so different in personality, but their loyalty was the same.

His attention was on Major League Baseball. I didn't understand how he could watch this boring sport. He was always betting on the game, trying to hustle the people out of their money. It was a close game, and Reese's team was losing, so he was sweating bullets, and I enjoyed every minute of it. It was hilarious. We were so engrossed in the game that we didn't even hear Harvey come in. It wasn't until he cleared his throat that we all took notice. I should have known it was him from his Brut cologne that always visited before he appeared.

"Girl, let me go. Harvey here, and I ain't even dressed." Ms. Yvette hung up the phone and rushed past Harvey. He smacked her ass on her way upstairs, excitedly.

"Reese, it's money to be made, and it's not going to get made with you in here on this dusty ass couch.

"I got money on this game; what are you talking 'bout?" Reese mumbled, not taking his eyes off of the big TV sitting in the wall unit.

"You better stop getting comfortable. Your spot will get taken with the quickness. I need soldiers on my team that put in work twenty-four/seven. This ain't no game. This real-life out here, and we gotta eat. You hungry? You worrying about the wrong thing. Fuck that game."

Harvey looked at me.

Reese looked at me and sucked his teeth. Throwing his hands in the air, he brushed past Harvey, almost bumping shoulders but knowing that wouldn't be best. Harvey watched him walk out, shaking the house with the slam of the front door. Harvey called the shots around here, and it was nothing Reese could do about it. "That's what I thought," Harvey offered to no one in particular.

A smile and a hardy giggle occupied the respect I had for Harvey. He wasn't their real father, but he made life much easier for them when he started to come around. He was the one who put the food on the table and paid the bills in the house. Harvey was their ticket to the big leagues. Anybody could tell that he was participating in illegal activity; that didn't stop Ms. Yvette from moving him right in. He treated her somewhat good. All she cared about was that money which afforded her a life of luxury.

"What up, Kareem?" My eyes took in his navy-blue Stacy Adams and his creased Armani dress pants as he walked toward the closet right off the living room.

"Nothing, just chillin'." I could hear him moving around something in the closet.

"What you 'bout to get into? I'm about to make a run. You trying to ride?" Whatever he was searching for had him out of breath. He came back into view with a duffle bag of white wraps of what had to be coke. A black pistol was now added to his getup, tucked away by the covering of his button-up shirt.

Bssp! Bssp!

My cell phone buzzed in my pocket, letting me know I had a call coming in. By the ringtone, I could tell it was Jax calling on a three-way from his sister's house; he was in jail. Jax was an old friend of my mother's, who made sure to take care of me when he was home. Jail didn't stop him from checking up on me. I could tell he loved my mom, but he never admitted it, and every time I asked my mom what their deal was back in the day, she would always say they were just friends.

Jax was like the father I never had. Yes, he was in jail, but every time we talked, he always shared great wisdom. Jax was one of the reasons why I was still in school to become a doctor. He reminded me of my dreams frequently; it was like he always knew when I was up to no good. The streets talked, so I was pretty sure he still had his ear to the streets and probably had somebody following my every move. That's how overprotective he was. Oftentimes, he forgot that I was older now. He wouldn't like that I was sitting up here chopping it up with Harvey. He hated everything that came with the streets; his motto was the streets didn't love no one.

"Hold up, Harvey. Let me take this call."

"Cool, let me go upstairs and try to get a quickie from Yvette's fine ass."

I laughed, making my way out the back door. The back wasn't as poppin' as the middle section, but you could still feel the effects of the night in the air. The darkness hovered over me as the light from my cell phone gave me access to view my surroundings.

"What's up, Jax? I thought you were done with your rounds for the night. Who you had to jack for they spot on the phones?"

"Don't worry about all that, youngblood. You better answer when I call. What are you up to? Are you ready for that test tomorrow?"

"Oh, that's why you called me? You're always trying to keep tabs on me. I'm gonna study tonight when I get home. I stopped at The Vill after the class tonight to check Rick and Reese. I blew out a breath, ready for the lecture that would come.

"What did I tell you about hangin' down there, Kareem? You know that is not a place for an intelligent man like your-self. Rick and Reese is nothing but bad influences. Do you remember these are the same boys that got you kicked out of School 6, and your grandmother had to put you in School 4?"

"I know, Jax, but that was so long ago. You keep bringing that up like we weren't kids having fun, doing what kids do. We are older now. I know how to handle myself. I think you continue to forget that I'm twenty now; I'm about to be twenty-one in a few months. I'm practically an adult."

"Youngblood, you don't know what it takes to be an adult. You are still wet behind the ears. You getting a little pussy here and there, are a little more mature than the rest, but that don't make you grown. I'm about this life, so if I'm telling you

The Vill is not where you need to be, you need to hear me clearly. I'm talking to the grown man, not the little boy.

"Jax, listen—"

"No, I'm not going to listen. You have all the time in the world to relax and chill with your friends. It can't be the night before a big test. You've been complaining about not understanding the material, so you have to study to gain the knowledge needed to succeed in your field. What's the point of taking summer classes if you not going to take it serious?"

I didn't need this right now. I wanted to enjoy my night and not have to stress over college for once. My eyes met the sky as Jax continued on his Malcom X lecture.

"Lately, you've been down in the Vill a lot more. What's up with that? Do I have to make some calls, youngblood? You testin' my gangsta?"

"Nobody testing your gangsta, old man." The operator let us know we only had three minutes left on the call.

"I got your old man. Get home and study for that test so when I call you tomorrow, you can let me know you passed. Remember, we have a deal. You're going to graduate and then go off to medical school and make something of your life. The Vill will always be there. Rick and Reese will always be there, but you have a goal in mind. Remember?"

My head nodded yes like he could see my gesture, but before I could verbally say yes, the operator let us know that we had two minutes left.

"Youngblood, you got this. Let me know how everything goes. One love."

The phone hung up, signaling that the call was over. Jax had me weighing my options. I guess he was trying to protect me, from what, I wasn't sure. Things were different than when he was in the jungle we called P-Town. I walked back into the house with a different mindset than when I left out.

Harvey had made his way back downstairs. Our eyes met; he knew that I'd had to catch him on the next offering.

"Are you ready?" Already knowing the answer, clarification was needed.

"Nah. I'm gonna go home and study. I have a big test tomorrow."

"I respect that. Maybe next time. Hit me up when you want to make this money, Kareem. It's enough money out here for all of us, and it could be you who's making it. He unzipped the bag and took out a stack of cash, smacking me in my chest with a thump. I never saw this much cash all at once. I had a few jobs here and there but never received a thick ass amount of money. I didn't want no handouts; it came with a debt that I wasn't trying to owe. Nothing was ever free.

"I can't take this!" Picking it up off of the couch, I tried to hand it back to him. He pushed my hand back, picked up the duffle bag, and proceeded toward the door.

"Don't tell nobody I gave you that. That's between you and me. Spend it on yourself; you deserve it, college boy."

I looked at the stack of twenties, tempted to make the trip with him. I knew it would be more where that came from. I toiled between chasing Harvey down or studying, but ultimately, learning won. After all, that was the right thing to do. Or was it? Money had never been an issue for me. I had all that I needed; it was the stories of the things that went down on the block that caused me to rethink every time Harvey pitched for me to join his team. My boys were having a grand ole time; I wanted some of that. Not only were they bringing in good money, but they were respected for running with legends.

CASHMERE

Usher - My Way

You make me wanna leave the one I'm with
Start a new relationship with you
This is what you do

I hadn't spoken to Jeda in three days, and it was killing me inside. She wanted her space. I got it, but I needed to smell her, feel her, and get lost on the island of her penny-colored eyes that matched the glow of her skin. The first day I was okay with it; I understood. I needed to work through my feelings as well. I texted her on day two... nothing. When day three came, I was calling her off the hook. At this point, I was worried. After all, her mother came, almost setting off a detonator killing a whole country.

My taupe brown skin was covered with freckles that could only be seen if you were directly in my face. Not too many people noticed that feature about me. The fresh line-up my boy Jose gave me went well with the wet curls on the top of my head. That good hair ran in my family. My father had good hair; I inherited his genes, and I was glad I did. The ladies fell in love with my curls; it was the first thing I would get compliments on. Even when my haircut wasn't fresh, people would stop and admire my hair texture.

My towel hugged my midsection, holding on to every muscle, being sure not to expose what God has blessed me with. Mase and Kareem were my motivation to stay in the gym, and vocal strength came from breathing. Working out helped with that. Sex sells, and my female fans were going to be in love with my body. I wasn't as ripped as my brother and Kareem, but I was rock solid and in shape. People thought I was an athlete; I told them I only trained with one. Kareem wasn't into sports but stayed on the bench press during our early morning sessions.

I didn't get my dad's height like Mase, but all five feet six of me was proud to be a strong young black man. My bare feet touched the floors of the house I grew up in after my parents died. I passed by Kareem's door to see if he was home but realized he had a test today. I was used to sharing a room with Kareem, but he gladly accepted his privacy when Mase moved out two years ago to start his college career. My grandmother's room was on the first floor, right off the kitchen. Rarely did she take the stairs to see what we were up to. It was our own little space of comfort.

I wouldn't say we lived in a great area, but it wasn't the hood. We lived on the east side of Paterson. Governor Street was houses of families trying to do better than the poverty they were born in. It was far better than the projects, but we still lived in one of the worst wards in Paterson. We made do with what we had. My grandmother worked at Allendale Nursing Home to make ends meet. It wasn't much, but it got us through. Nowadays, we made sure to step up and take care of her. She could retire, but she was so loyal to that place that she refused. I don't know how she did it, but she did.

The sound of Donnell Jones "Where I Wanna Be" blasted through my speakers as lotion hit my body, making sure not to miss a spot. I was mentally preparing myself for my mission of finding out what was going on with Jeda. When we weren't right, I wasn't right. If I wasn't straight, everything around me crumbled. It was like she had a hold on me, on my every move. Her mood dictated my response to everyday life. I doubted she was doing it on purpose, but Lord knows I wished she loved me enough to notice. Sometimes putting your feelings aside made for a great relationship. What she failed to realize was that I had feelings too.

I got dressed in my Rocawear jean shorts with my clean white low-top Air Force Ones that were right for the sunshine that made it a hot summer day. It was a must to have a pair every year. As a singer, I took pride in the way I threw together my getup. It had to match my mood, my energy, and today I felt like thuggin' it out. I went to Kareem's room and looked in the full-length mirror that Mase left on his departure. He stayed in the mirror like it paid him. Mase had enough skills on the court that he didn't have to worry about looks, but he took it as seriously as me, a trait we inherited from our father, my grammy would say.

You could tell that my mom and dad were among the most fly couples that ever touched hood soil; their many pictures told that story. They screamed royalty; they were legends in the streets. They could have made a movie with Mason "The Major" Cotton as the lead character and it would have sold out. My dad was well respected, and my mom's name didn't follow too far behind. If you needed a picture of Bonnie and Clyde, you could steal one off 262 Governor Street walls.

We had to represent our name; it had to live on. We had big shoes to fill. My father's reputation superseded an avenge size shoe. That is why I think Mase was the way he was. He felt like he had to live up to our father's legacy. When my dad ruled over the streets, every man, boy, woman, and girl wanted to be in his company. There were so many pictures of my dad and mom giving out food and gifts during the holidays. You would've thought they were politicians doing things to get a vote.

I turned off the music, ready to get my day started. I had enough time to eat, take my grandmother to work, and use her car to meet Jeda when she got out of class. Today was my day off, but I'd do anything to see her, even if it was for a brief second. Even if she turned me away, I'd get to witness her state of mind. I'd get to see her alive; while that didn't matter to her, it was what kept me going. Her safety and wellbeing were my first priority. I already felt like I failed her.

How didn't I know what she was going through when we were in high school? I was her boyfriend, someone who was supposed to protect and cover her. Nights she was left to fend for herself, her secret place was no longer a secret; it was infiltrated by an army so strong that it caused Post Traumatic Stress Disorder. Her mission, compromised by the government that oversaw her world. Her life was a dictatorship, not a democracy, and it caused her to look at everything else that way.

I didn't want to control her life; I wanted her to prosper and succeed the way my grandmother told us the bible taught. I believed you could still thrive and go through some rough times; it was how you handled it that unlocked the next progression level. All I knew was I had to be patient and wait to see how everything would unfold.

"Boy, you better get down here and take me to work if you

want to keep this car here." My grandmother's sweet voice projected to the second floor of the house.

"Grammy, I'm coming. You know I had to make sure I was stepping out right."

"No, you're trying to impress Jeda, who doesn't care anything about how you look. That girl loves you for you."

I walked down the stairs as my grandmother looked off the second-floor porch into the mid-morning light. Summer always woke the average person up early; it was something about the summer air that brought out the best in people. As I made my way to the last step, I realized I needed to grab some breakfast or snacks to hold me over this morning while I checked on the love of my life.

"Grammy, you're going to be super early if we leave now."

"Boy, hush! I'm always early. I don't like to rush. Stop worrying about stuff I'm not worried about. I should be worried about you. I heard you up there playing those sad love songs. You can't sing your way through this one, son. This is where you have to put in work, baby. Love ain't built on nothing but compromise."

My embrace caught her off guard, it was so sudden. I held tight, needing the transfer that came with the strength from being in her arms. Her hugs had gotten me through plenty of days. She always knew what to say and when to say it. She was definitely sent by God, no lie. She cleared her throat. "Listen, it won't always last, but know what's meant to be will be. Now, come on and drop me off so you can go handle your business. Grammy ain't got time to be caught up in your melodramas. I watched the stories for that."

Boog!

She smacked me in my forehead and marched her short, sweet self to her room, I guess, to gather her things. I closed the porch door and made my way downstairs to the car. My grandmother's '95 Buick Century got us to games, talent shows, and everywhere else we had to be. Lately, her ride had been giving her problems, and she'd been against getting a new car. We all promised to put in to purchase her a car, but she refused.

I could probably get a car if I wanted to, but between paying for studio time and spending money to create a brand, it left me with nothing. My hustle was real, but I'd be glad when the real money started rolling in. I did what I did so one day I'd be able to give her everything her heart desired. My grandmother worked hard to raise three boys by herself.

"It's hot out here, but they be having my unit freezing cold. I should have grabbed a coat how cold it be." She scooted in the seat like her back was hurting her.

"Are you alright, old lady?"

"I got your old lady. I'll still make you go get a switch off the tree and whoop your little behind like I used to do ya momma. That girl sho' got a lot of beatings; her mouth was terrible. Back then, I didn't know better. I was knocking her clean upside her head. She knew how to test me, boy. I sho' miss her."

"Me too, Grammy, me too."

As I drove, I sang my grandmother some songs that I was thinking about recording. She was always someone who would tell me the truth. She said she knew her rhythm and blues. For her, it was how a song was sung, not so much about the lyrics. Lyrics could be relatable. It should be captivating, but it was in your raw vocals that brought those lyrics to life. She didn't like the music of today, but she understood the art.

Cruising through the streets, I was able to get my mind right after dropping off my grandmother. For me, it wasn't about the car; it was about the story behind it. I was grinding to get this career jumped off so I could drive in foreigns when I made it. I was low key working toward a come up. I was on the right track with my music; I needed my love life to fall in line. I had to get to this studio tonight; a brotha had a lot to say. My grandmother loved the song and told me to let her hear it once it was done. The medley for "Sincerely, Love" kept building traction in the studio of my brain, so I had to lay the track down. I think the best songs were birthed from real-life experiences; this one sure would tell it.

I hummed the lyrics the whole way to the campus to wait for Jeda. I parked in the parking lot where I knew she had to walk by to go home. William Paterson University was in Wayne, so she usually took the bus to school. It was her escape, she said. It was her time to write and get inspiration from the people around her. It was her freelance pieces that were born on NJ Transit.

Jeda always wrote; she became the head editor when she transferred to our school junior year. She lived in Fort Lee, New Jersey before her mom lost their family house. It was like she came to Rosa Parks High School and had something to prove with her writing skills. Mr. Gilman made her in charge right away, but to be fair, he took a class vote, and she won. Maribeth was mad, but my girl had skills. I was only on the committee; I wanted to be a photographer back then.

I parked with a few minutes to spare. Jeda's class should've been getting out soon. I knew my baby's schedule like clock-work. I felt like our communication had always been on point, but I wasn't so sure after her confession. Every time I thought about it, I struggled. I felt like my man card had been revoked. If you weren't a protector, how could you call yourself a man? How could you have a relationship period? It was a part of the job description. Obviously, it wasn't something I was high-lighting on my resume for boyfriend of the year.

How could I have not known what was going on?

My eyes caught the very essence of her beauty as I watched her from the glass on the inside of my grandmother's old, well-kept Buick. Her frame detached from every emotion, but her body had the shape of a goddess. Her Juicy sweat suit hugged her toned body from all that track we ran in high school. Her hair was pulled up in a sloppy ponytail, but it was still sitting tall on her honey brown skin. She was determined to get to her destination, but I planned to stop her from her bus stop journey.

"Ayo, honey dip, can I talk to you, beautiful? I couldn't let you pass by without trying to get your number." I caught her off guard. She jumped a little, trying not to get caught up in what I had to offer. *Was that a smile?* I was hoping it was.

"You ain't trying to give a brother no play, huh?" My laugh was stifled in the uneasiness of not knowing if she would slow down a little to give me the time of day. My feet danced, trying to catch up with her like in a 90's R&B video. The only difference was the song was playing from my heart, and the leading lady wasn't happy to see me.

I caught up with her and gripped her hand as she struggled to pull away. I wrapped my arms around her and hugged the doubt out of her body. She rested on my chest like she'd been waiting all day for me. The smell of her hair and the cherry almond lotion sent electricity through my body.

I appreciated the here and now. Jeda was meant to be in my arms.

"Why are you here?" she whispered in defeat.

I rested my chin on her forehead. My baby was tiny in stature but had the presence of the ninth wonder of the world. It was in the way she spoke, in the way she carried herself. People always thought she was a teenager until she opened her mouth and commanded the room. She was still quiet, but around the right people, she wouldn't shut up.

This was not who was standing before me. My hug was holding Jeda up; it was as if she didn't have any strength. She always needed time, especially in high school, but she always bounced back. I never saw her down for the count like she was at this moment. It was like her mother flipped a switch, and the whole fuse blew. I wasn't a handyman, but I was willing to fix this by any means.

My lips met her forehead, and I lifted her head so our eyes could meet.

"What do you mean, why am I here? Why can't I check on my future wife? Let me take you home. We don't even have to talk if you don't want to. I want to make sure you get in the house safely, and I'll be on my merry little way. Deal?"

"So you're going to act like nothing happened?"

Her eyes found comfort in everything else around us, avoiding the vulnerability of what was put into the universe. How was I supposed to act? Yes, she confessed something heavy, but she was worth the weight. I had to show some normalcy; that was the only way I knew how to be. My love for her didn't waver. Her confession made me love her more. It showed me she was strong and resilient, reclaiming her power each and every time she chose to wake up.

Most people would have folded in her seat; they would have given up or given in, but she didn't. Many nights she cried, but many mornings she got up praying for a better day. Some days might have been better than others, but she kept pushing. If that wasn't strength, I didn't know what else was. She was one of the strongest women I knew, besides my grandmother.

"Something did happen, Dip, and I'm furious that it happened to you. I cried, and I asked God why. I did. I haven't slept in three days. Three days! Thinking about different ways to go back in time and kill each and every one who hurt you. One by one, making them pay. I'm hurting too, Dip."

I don't know where these tears came from, but I caught them before they slid down my face with the destination of my lips. The man in me wouldn't let me cry, I had to be strong for her. So with everything in me, I took her hand and led her to the car, not accepting no for an answer. I lifted the door handle; only my grandmother could get it to work on the first try. I jigged it a little more, and it opened for her to occupy my space. I closed the door and proceeded to take my place as the driver.

I backed up into college traffic as Jeda looked out the window. Her chin rested in her hands, and her body was a magnet to the door, leaving space between our two worlds. The drive to her apartment complex wasn't far at all, but it gave me a few minutes to soak up her aura. The drive from Wayne to Haledon was quiet, but that didn't stop me from realizing that this roadblock we hit was severe.

Was this what they meant when they said for better or for worse? Although not married, had we reached our worse? Not knowing the answer to that sent my mind in overdrive, almost passing the turn for her apartment complex. I pulled into the park, turned off the engine, and we sat on our private islands for a minute. My lifeboat floated to her island first.

"Please look at me," I pleaded.

Her head turned slowly. I couldn't make out how she felt, but I did see that my petition was heard. She folded her arms over her breasts. Even in her distress, I saw how beautiful she was inside and out. An imperfect beauty shadowed with the mascara of life as makeup.

"Let me take you on a date. Me and you, enjoying a night of laughter and fun. You know when we get together how we do."

"I don't know about that. I think I need some time, Cash. My mom showing up really messed me up, as you can see. No telling if she's coming back. She wants some of the money that my father left me, and I'm not giving it to her. Her only ammunition was writing *Life Magazine*, exposing me for the whore she labeled me to be. She recorded me; she has tapes. I don't believe her, but what if she did?"

"Why now, though?"

"She messed up her social security somehow. It's in review or something. She was supposedly coming to collect on damages."

I couldn't believe what I was hearing. I was glad we were getting somewhere though. Now it all made sense. If Jeda didn't give her what she wanted, she was gonna try to kill her writing career before it started. If she did give in, she was giving her mom the power back, on top of all the other feelings she brought up by simply seeing her face.

"I don't condone you hitting your mom, but the next time she steps like that, go rogue on her, Dip, like Mrs. Smith. I'll be your Mr. Smith if you let me." I got a little smile.

"Trust me, if she comes at me again like she did, I will. I'm older now."

"Let's put all of that behind us and tackle it when it comes. You never know. Your mother might be bluffing, but we'll be ready for her if she strikes."

"You still love me? How can you love someone who has slept with multiple guys? They did stuff to me that I would probably never be able to put into words. I'm damaged, and you know what they do to damaged items? They throw them in the trash. I'm unfixable, Cash."

"I can show you better than I can tell you. This is only bringing us closer. I still worship the ground you walk on, girl. And you better believe when you can't walk, I'll be the ground for you to float on. Believe that."

I saw some hope with some sprinkle of doubt in her gaze resting on me. At this point, nothing I said would fix the turmoil fueling inside of her heart. It was better to show; action produces outcomes that talking won't. Jeda was a show-me kind of girl anyway. She didn't believe what I was spitting at first, but she gave in once she saw that I was consistent.

"I'll go on a date, but please don't push it."

"I won't, I promise."

I leaned over the middle console to give her a kiss, but she backed away, her head almost hitting the window. I was confused.

"I need some time in that area, Cash. I feel filthy. At the end of our junior year is when I stopped her from taking another piece of me. I had met you, and you changed my whole world. I wanted to be pure for you, clean from the impurity of someone else's demons. That's one of the reasons why we didn't have sex until we got to college."

"Sex wasn't a big deal for me."

"It was for me; it shows my love for you."

"Having sex doesn't prove you love someone."

"I know that now, but I'm still glad I stopped it; the terror of being tied to a pervert after they get their rocks off was numbing. But now you know that you weren't the first person I had sex with. I always wanted it to be you. I promise you."

"It was me, Dip. I was your first and only. Hear me loud and clear. Whenever you're ready, I'll be waiting. When you are finally ready, I'm going to make love to you and show you how much your past doesn't matter to me. Remember, no talk, only action. Take all the time you need."

"What time do you want me to be ready?"

"I'm about to go to this session; I should be back around like eight to take you out. Once I finish at the studio, I'm going to pick Grammy up, drop her off, then shoot and get you. Wear something nice. We haven't been out in a minute. It will be what we need, guaranteed!"

"I'll be ready by eight. Thank you, Cash, for understanding."

She exited the vehicle and reached the sidewalk to her

apartment, letting her feet direct her up the walkway. She walked through her door, which was her safe haven, leaving her scent behind in the aftermath. The heat from the conversation warmed the car a bit. I needed to blast this air. I drove off to go sing my soul out.

"YO, RUN THAT BACK." I NEEDED TO HEAR IT AGAIN. MY engineer Ru did what he was told.

I listened to the song's flow to see if I nailed the chorus the way I thought I did in my head. I closed my eyes, picturing the song playing on the radio during the Quiet Storm with Lenny Green. This ballad fit right on the playlist of nightly slow jams, matching Lenny's signature smooth and silky baritone voice. The lyrics to "Sincerely, Love" not only spoke to the lovers, it resonated with the singles wanting to be loved as well.

These early studio sessions allowed me to pay matinee prices. I had to fit in where I could. Living on the Credit Union check wasn't taking me far. I loved being a teller, but my dream was to be counting my own money, not somebody else's. Greater Alliance was grooming me for the head teller position, but little did they know this was not my final destination. I had big plans and big dreams for myself. They allowed me to create plan B in case it didn't work out, and I was grateful for that.

"Let me know where you want me to punch you in. Or you think we got it?"

"It sounds great, but it's missing something else. I can't put my finger on it. I'm coming out of the booth. I gotta think."

I laid the headphones on the music sheet stand that housed my little notebook of lyrics; I never erased anything. I played with the lyrics until it was right. My notebook was in a code that only I knew. I thought I had this song all figured out, but it was still missing the special ingredient needed to make it a number one hit. I took my seat at the boards, listening to the playback, trying to fill in the holes of a very personal song.

Mid thought, the wooden door to the studio opened behind us. As the song stripped down, vocals boomed through the speakers. Aonika Monroe walked in, her long legs preceding her. Her dark chocolate skin shone under the fluorescent lights of the studio mood. I hadn't seen her in a minute since her career took off. She was Paterson born, but she went to Eastside High; she didn't go to Rosa Parks Fine Arts like Jeda and me. I always knew she was going to make it. I'd be joining her soon.

"Wow, look at you, slumming it with us in Paterson. Wasn't you in L.A. shooting a video?"

"This will always be home, and you know it. Money doesn't define who I am; it helps me give back to the people who really rocked with me."

Aonika walked up to me, and I went in for a hug; she was always cool peoples. Her smooth skin met the side of my cheek, and I took her in. She was still slim-thick, but the celebrity life had her putting on pounds in all the right places. We used to do a lot of the same talent shows and events together. Her song "Never Let Go" was gaining notoriety from her Myspace followers. People were wondering who this African goddess was. Her foreign looks would have you mesmerized, and with a voice to match, it was the combination for success.

"You gotta let me take this song with me; it needs a female touch."

"Play this from the beginning, Ru, so Miss Aonika Monroe can get the whole feel of the song."

My eyes connected with her body as she swayed her hips to the bass knocking up against the riffs as they flowed with every syllable. She was enjoying the song more than I did while recording it. The light was lit, and she was creatively creating. I could tell it in the way she embodied the music as it played. It was a love song nonetheless, but the sexiness was produced in the way I sang it. Hopefully, she could tell me what is needed.

"Let me play around with it after I wrap up my other session. When I heard the receptionist say your name to my management team, I had to come and say hi and see how you were doing. It's been a minute, but I see you still here, grindin'. You still with what's her name?" She pointed at me, trying to find Jeda's name from the vault she had it in.

"Yes. I'm still with Jeda. I don't think that'll ever change." I wasn't sure that was true, but I couldn't let her know that.

"I always loved the way you loved her. It was like she made you float to Heaven every time she was around. I always wondered if a guy could ever love me like that." Her eyes weren't afraid to find mine.

"Of course you'll find somebody to love. You are an incredible woman who is doing big things. Your time will come."

"At this point, I'm married to my career, but if the right one comes along, I'll do anything to find true love."

Aonika got up from her seated position, ending the thought with a giggle and a hand wave. I admired her candidness and embraced her compliment of the type of guy I was. That didn't go unnoticed. I felt like Aonika had a thing for me, but I guess she respected that I was in a relationship. That didn't stop me from wanting to work with her. She got her big break before me, so I was trying to utilize her resources. Her big break might've just been my big break.

"Let me get your number and email so I can send you this track." I slid my Sidekick 2 out of my pocket, flipped the face, and started a new entry for her. I did it with so much skill;

you would have thought I was used to getting chicks' numbers. She called out her number and email for me to take. Our goodbyes were our final reassurance; we promised to talk soon. She knew what I needed to take my mind off of my current situation.

Fast Break

After a change of possession, a team advances the basketball as quickly as possible to attack the defense before they have been able to establish a good defensive position.

"Oh shit! No, no! How could I be so stupid!"

I jumped up out of my sleep, in time to catch Qwana in a full blown panic, trying to gather her things. I looked at the hotel clock—6:50 a.m. The sun shined in my face, confirming that it was indeed morning. The view that we had was amazing; you could see the New York skyline as the backdrop. It set the mood for whatever was about to occur in each room that enjoyed this very view. The balcony at night came to life, and it brought a whole other groove to the party. Qwana was killing my vibe by waking me up out of my sleep with this nonsense.

If my playback was anything to go by, I became champ after three rounds. Had her calling my name like a telemarketer collecting a debt. That pussy was owed to me—every last stroke. I didn't care if some of our time was wasted on sleep; it still was our time together, and I didn't regret it. Maybe this would teach her a lesson not to play with me. I got what I wanted when I wanted. Although she belonged to some else, I had my time with her.

I didn't care if I was selfish, and I damn sure didn't care that she missed her little curfew. This was the first time this had happened, and I was glad it did. Not only was I sending her home walking differently, but I was also sending her on my time. It wasn't planned, but it was calculated, confirming that the stars aligned in my favor.

She almost tripped over my sneaker, running to the shower after gathering her things. She slammed the door behind her, and I heard the water come alive. She was in there rushing to wash away all of her sins. No matter how much soap was applied to her silky smooth skin, it wouldn't wash away the adultery we committed. I played a role last night, and this morning my cast mate had to go back to her real life.

I didn't know how much more of this I could take. I guess I was on the flip side of the game, getting played like the shawties I had run through. It was all fun and games until your feelings were on display. This side of the L wasn't where it was at. I wasn't trying to lose, and I wasn't trying to love. It was team W for me. This shit was wack; this was one situation I couldn't control. A nigga had to figure out his next move. Whichever way you sliced it, I'd be straight.

When the shower shut off, the blood rushed to my head as I rested it on the dark blue and silver headboard that covered the back end of the wall. My eyes took in my surroundings; the floor-to-ceiling windows created a framed portrait of a postcard. The bathroom door swung open, and a fully dressed Qwana occupied this once empty space. It wasn't devoid of thought but empty of her presence that made the room come alive. People said she looked like Kelly Rowland from the group Destiny's Child, but I thought she looked better.

Her quick movement was met with fear as she made sure not to leave anything behind. She couldn't even look my way as I sat on the edge of the bed, now watching her every move. Why couldn't God save her for me? Naked like the day I came out of my mother's womb, I gathered my thoughts.

"For someone who wanted to enjoy their night, you sure are having a messed-up morning."

"Don't start!"

"I could say whatever I want! You are not going to ignore me like I'm not here. I play a lot of games, Qwana, and this not one. I'm the side nigga, but you not about to treat me any ole kind of way. You know how many girls I could have right now? And no, I'm not bragging; I'm telling you straight facts. I'm here with you and only you. You can't keep running from what we have been building."

She stopped in her tracks, caught by whatever she was running from. It zapped all of her power, and she broke. A bucket of big teardrops found its way to her perfectly mois-turized skin. It came out of nowhere, or did it? I was caught between consoling her or waiting for her to gather herself. Her cries wouldn't let me choose the latter. Fear invaded her lungs, and it was so strong it caused me to mentally put my body armor on, ready for war, not knowing the fight I was up against.

In all my nakedness, I met her at the edge of whatever cliff she was on. It didn't take me long to reach her; I covered her with my frame. Her arms made their way around me, embracing the possibility that I could save her. Save her from what, I wasn't sure. As we embraced, I was slow to speak but eager to find out what was going on.

"Yo, you good? Where did that come from? What did I say?"

She slightly pushed away from me, fanning herself like she had hot flashes.

"Trust me, it's not you. I'm tired too, Mason. I'm scared and not ready to deal with this. It's all I think about, but you know what else is hard to think about? What will my husband do to me if he finds out? You think he's gonna let me walk away into another man's arms? You must have had more than liquor. What drugs you on?"

"I dare him to step to me. He not ready for the ass whooping I'll put on him if he tries to do something crazy. I don't even know who this man is, and I'm confident that he ain't gonna have a choice. You don't have to worry about anything; I'll handle him. Let's drive over there right now and get your things. You can stay with me."

"Boy, have you lost your mind? I gotta go, Mason, and it's no way in hell I'm letting you come with me."

I tried grabbing her, but she pulled away, but not before coming back to kiss me on my lips. My naked exterior wouldn't let me chase her into the hallway. I didn't care if anyone saw my goods; I didn't want anyone to see me in despair. It was a flaw that I tried to keep hidden; it went against my lifestyle. Deep down, I knew that this was my karma for all the hearts I broke. Who knew that it would come around so fast?

I looked around the hotel room, not knowing what to do next. I still had the room until eleven, which didn't mean anything. I needed to remove myself from this situation. Qwana walking out on me left me frustrated and irritable. What wasn't she telling me? I knew she loved me; I also knew she once loved the man she married. I heard a few people say that how you get them is how you lose them. She crossed the line with me almost four years ago.

We were closing out our season as the state champions, and Coach Patterson wanted to treat us for our victory. We've been the state champions for the third consecutive year, and it was such a great way to send me off to college. Still hyped up off the adrenaline, we all met up at Maggiano's Little Italy in Hackensack. It was a little spot that one of my teammates' parent owned. This night was special though; it was the last game of my high school career.

All bets were on me to make it to the big leagues and put New Jersey on the map. Tim Thomas was the last basketball phenomenon to make it out, and I planned to be the next. It was in the cards for me since I was a little boy. My dad used to always have me on the court shooting around. He reminded me of Denzel Washington in He Got Game; *he was tough. Denzel took a page out of my father's book. There were times where he would make me sleep in my uniform so that I could be up at 6 a.m. shooting hoops in Grand Street Projects.*

It prepared me for this day and this moment. I wished I could share it with him. He would be proud. Coach always made sure to tell me that. My pops was a street legend, one would say, so he knew my breed. I had big shoes to fill, and the streets wouldn't let me forget it. In all that I did, it was measured against my father's success. We were known for various reasons, but it all helped our community in the end. My dad was a street pharmacist, one that gave back from his profits. He gave back to his city the way I gave back by putting us on the map in sports.

"Dog, did you see Brenda tonight? I think I might slide through her crib later to see what's up. She was all over a nigga after the game." Rome slapped my hand like he knew he had that in the bag.

"Nobody ain't trying to look at Brenda kangaroo face but you. She's gonna put you right in her pouch, little baby." West was imitating a jumping kangaroo.

Laughter could be heard from the crew. It was a cold March night that was met between seasons. Winter wasn't upon us, but it wasn't spring weather either. My black slacks and black button-down shirt matched how successful I wanted to be. Whenever we went out as a team, we would show how professional and ready we were for the big leagues. That, and Coach Patterson made it mandatory.

Coach Patterson motioned for us, signaling that our table was ready. Me, Reese, and Rick were the seniors on the squad, so the whole team followed our lead as we migrated to our secluded area off from the other customers. The coach was confident that we'd bring the gold home, so it didn't surprise me that this was planned. Once I saw where we were being seated, I made my way to the bathroom.

"I'll be right back; order me a Sprite wit' light ice."

"You sound like one of those old ladies saying, light ice. Do you want a muffin with that?" Reese joked.

"With a little bit of Ms. Yvette on the side."

"Yeah, aight!"

People don't play about they momma, but Reese knew I had a love for Ms. Yvette. Nobody was exempt from these jokes, though. Laughter flowed with me as I made my way down a dimly lit hallway, hoping I was going in the right direction. I was coming up on a door; hopefully, it was for the ladies' room. In my mind, ladies were always first, or that's how I saw it.

There were people who thought like me. I was coming up on the door as it opened to the lady's room. Her short bob cut matched her almond brown eyes as they wrestled with mine. She continued to clean the spot on her miniskirt, not taking her eyes off me. Her pocketbook slipped off her shoulders and hit the floor. I hurried to her rescue.

"Let me get that for you. It looks like you're having a little trouble."

"You're trouble, trying to get a peek in the lady's room. I caught you."

"You caught me admiring that big sauce stain you trying to hide with paper towel and water. Let me help you get that out."

"What is your name, little boy? And why are you all up in grown folks' business?"

"You know I'm far from little. Don't play yourself, and my name is Mason. Take off your skirt and let me take it home to wash it. When you come to get it, I'll show you how much of a man I am."

I cracked up every time I thought of that story. Our first encounter became years of rendezvous, and with each visit, we got comfortable. We started to crave one another, establishing a connection through late nights and early mornings. What Qwana couldn't do with her husband, I fulfilled that, and what these other girls couldn't do for me, she fulfilled that. I needed to step out tonight and enjoy time with my fam. Cash and Kareem knew what to do to get my mind off this tornado that hit my life.

"I might not be God, but I work for him."
-Harvey

The 46 Lounge was the place to be tonight. When Mase called me to let me know he needed a night out, I knew the place. It had been a minute since we'd all been out together. Life had been taking us in different directions, but we always made sure to make time for each other. I jumped at the chance to go out. School had been taking most of my time. I needed another way to decompress from this learning institution. Tonight, I intended to get a drink with my two-step. I rolled me a blunt before I got here. I had one ready for when I left. My eyes were low, just how I liked them.

"Right Thurr" by Chingy boomed through the speakers as we surveyed the scene of potential. It seemed we all needed this time, not only Mase. Harvey really had me pondering on his many offerings to join his team. The way that Reese and

Rick were getting money had me rethinking my next move. My drink of choice tonight was the Incredible Hulk. A couple of sips had my mind floating. Between the weed and the mix of the drink, it was a combination for a good night.

"Yo, snap out of it. We came here to have a good time. Y'all look like y'all lost y'all best friend or something. Take a sip, roll a blunt, or do something." I laughed at these fools, and they laughed with me. They knew I was telling the truth.

"Man, shut up. We got girl problems. Don't be mad at us you can't get no pussy," Mase countered.

"See, that's where you wrong, playboy. After I fuck, I keep it moving; I prefer to keep my feelings in check. The females know this. That's why you would never know who I'm smashing. They keep their mouth closed, hoping that I'll be back for more."

"At some point, Reem, trust me, that's going to get old, cuz," Cash pointed out like he was old enough to understand being tired.

"I once thought like you, but somehow, I got caught up." Mase took a sip of his Hennessy like it was the remedy to his problems.

"She got you going through like that, bro?" Cashmere couldn't believe what he was hearing. I couldn't believe it either. Not Playboy Mase.

"It's cool; I got it under control. The question is do you have your situation with Jeda under control?" Mase wanted to take the spotlight off of him.

"Jeda has been running this dude ragged since she met him. You don't think it's time to move on? You're young, and you're about to get that big break soon, so why not weigh your options?" If I had talent like Cash, I'd be Mr. Worldwide, enjoying the company of multiple women, not only one.

"I wish it was that simple, Reem. Unfortunately, being a

player wasn't in the cards for me." Cash played with his straw to his Sprite, speaking what he figured to be true.

"Anything is possible, little cuz."

"I gotta agree with Reem on that. I thought I was going to always be a player, never settling down. I was married to the game. Somewhere, somehow, I lost my skill to hit it and quit it. It's like I lost a part of me. I'm going to get a drink." Mase got up and pimp walked his way to the bar.

Cash and I laughed. Growing up, Mase vowed never to fall in love once he got his heart broken by big booty Keisha. We definitely saw a change in him once he started messing with Qwana. He gradually began curving shawties, keeping his womanizing to a minimum. Relationships and situationships were not something that I gave much attention to. My dick got wet from time to time, but I didn't wake up thinking about it. I had a few chicks from around the way on deck, but all they got was some breathtaking pipe and the door. They knew their position, and they played it well. It was the only way they would get to lay with a king.

"You'll be alright, Cash. Don't let this situation imprison your mind. It will all work itself out. You're the good one, remember? The good guy always gets the stick's bad end, but not you; your story will end differently. You're going to find real love one day, whether it's with Jeda or not. I believe that."

We both watched Mase entertain a baddie at the bar. He commanded her attention like a bee to honey. It took him a couple of minutes to talk his shit, but before you know it, Mase walked past us, headed toward the bathroom. He mouthed, "Jackpot." The redbone didn't even notice or hear him over the loud music. She was so focused on getting him alone that it wouldn't have mattered if she did. Although sleeping with another female wouldn't fix his problems, it was a stress reliever and a much-needed distraction. Whatever made him happy, I was with it. I was hoping by the end of the night I'd find Cash a temporary distraction.

"I'm gonna go get me another drink. You want one?" Knowing he didn't drink, I offered anyway. Maybe the drink would lighten his mood.

"Nah, cuz. I'm good."

"What you not gonna do is sit here and look like you lost your best friend. Groove to this music and enjoy the scene. We don't go out anymore; let's make this a good night, cuz. You deserve at least that; you can deal with your relationship problems later."

My waves were spinning after I got my shape up; it brought my features to life. Under the lounge lights, you could see my brass-colored skin glow as I made my way to the bar. It sure was packed up in here. Crowds made me nervous, but I realized that I'd be missing out on life if I let that part of me rule. It was a couple things I did to make myself a little more comfortable, like making sure to get a table facing the door if someone walked in ready to pop off. I also needed a table closer to the exit. Paterson was known for fights and shootouts, so I had to be prepared at all times. We weren't in Paterson, but everybody from around the way was up in this joint.

I ordered my drink and waited for the bartender to return. I leaned my back on the bar, people watching as I waited for my potion so I could transform into the incredible hulk. I was glad we all drove in the same car. The way my night was going, I knew I would probably end up a little tipsier than usual. I needed something to ease the beast that was fighting to get out. Something was starting to wake up inside of me. I felt a change coming, and I didn't know how I felt about it.

The bartender returned with my drink, but as I was pulling out my money to pay, he stopped me.

"It's paid for."

"What you mean it's paid for?"

"It's on the house, courtesy of Mr. Harvey." He pointed to the second floor VIP area that Harvey and his crew occupied. The neon blue lights that encircled the VIP area lit up as I surveyed the place that everybody wanted to be in. VIP had always been overrated if you asked me. One thing about us, we brought VIP to whatever table we were seated at. We didn't need to pay all that money to get the same pussy we would get anyway.

Harvey peered over the enclosed banister with a drink in his hand, gesturing for me to come to join him. Harvey was too cool for school in his dress clothes. I never saw him in jeans or sneakers; his style was straight old school. He always rocked some Stacey Adams with slacks and a button-up. He ruled with an iron fist that kept the young dudes in line. You had to go through Harvey to get to the big men, and that was even a challenging task. Harvey's goons always made sure to keep niggas at arm's length. So it was an honor that he kept reaching out, and if I didn't give him an answer soon, it might turn deadly. The thing is, I wasn't any regular ole dude. I did what I wanted to do on my own terms.

I sipped my drink as I walked to the VIP section, being sure not to spill my drink as party-goers listened to "Bring 'Em Out" by Tip. The beat was sick, but I was more New York rap. Don't get me wrong; I'd play a couple of rappers from the south, but Biggie, Nas, and Jadakiss were what I grew up on. I needed lyrical flow with some hard bars, and only New York rappers gave me that energy.

For the elite, the VIP section was for the street hustlers and fools who wanted to look important. The only thing I liked about VIP was that it was secluded. You got to control who came in and out with extra security, and sometimes in a tightly packed club, that was needed. As soon as I walked up to the entrance, this scrawny looking dude was trying to get past the big black bouncer, but he had no luck.

"I told you if you go ask Harvey, he'll tell you to let me in. Tell him it's Percy."

"Get out of here before you get your ass beat. Percy is not on the list. I suggest you go find a corner and sober up."

Hopefully, I didn't have to go through the same thing. I didn't take threats lightly. I didn't care how big security was; dude better not talk to me like that. It was like I always prepared for the worst. I wanted to get in front of a problem before it became a problem. Disrespect was something that I didn't tolerate, and I didn't care who it was. I respect you, and you respect me was something that I lived by. Anybody who went against that felt my wrath.

My hands had been certified by the hood. I'd been known to knock a nigga out here and there. Cash wasn't the fighting type, and Mase was too pretty to fight, so I did the dirty work. I was sure that, if need be, they could scrap with the best of them, but they didn't have to. And I was cool with that. Fighting was a way to take all my frustrations on somebody; it always made me feel better.

As soon as I got a chance to move past Mr. Scrawny and his drunk and high behavior, I was surprised that the bouncer held up the rope for me to pass. My access was granted without any words being spoken. That was easy. Good thing I didn't have to get out of character. I was ready to wrestle with the WWE Mark Henry lookalike.

"You see this shit," Mr. Scrawny was saying to no one in particular.

I didn't even turn around to entertain his comment. I was where he wanted to be. I was asked to be here, not the other way around. I could have made an example of him off GP, but I had to put my fighting days behind me. All I had to do was hit this nigga with a one-two, and he'd become one with the

BUILT ON BROKEN PIECES

floor. This second drink had me feeling a little superior. I knew how to handle my liquor, so only I knew when I'd had a little too much to drink. My poker face was glued to my exterior. I finally made it upstairs and over to Harvey.

"What's good, Harvey? Thanks for the drink. I really appreciate it, but you know I could pay for my own drinks."

"You family. Don't worry about it. I was trying to show you one of the benefits of joining my team. We need someone like you who doesn't take no shit and is quick on their feet. I believe you fit that bill. I don't know what else you need me to say to convince you that you were made for this life."

"Tell me something I don't know; you've been telling me this for a minute. You know what I'm about, my education and my family, Harv. I don't have time to get caught up with what comes with the streets." It sounded good saying it. It wasn't how I really felt anymore though.

"The way you think and the way you move, you won't get caught up. Trust me."

"You ain't God, Harv."

"I might not be God, but I work for him. You join my team, you'll be unstoppable. Once Dom put his stamp on you, you better believe nobody will step to you. That includes the police and everybody else who has breath in their body. All of this could be yours and then some," he encouraged. He was referencing the VIP area and the cash that was spread on the table. "I've been talking to him about you."

"Sounds good," was all I could muster up.

"How you did on that test the other day?"

"I passed, but I didn't do as good as I hoped."

"I hope it gets better for you." He sipped his drink, taking in the view from the VIP area.

These days, it seemed the more I got bored with school, the more Harvey invited me into his world. It was like he was sensing that I wasn't getting the same fulfillment I once did learning what it took to be a great medical professional and the possibility of becoming a doctor. His sales pitch was honestly starting to become more appealing. Reese and Rick seemed like they were living their best life since linking up with Dom and Harvey. They became generals in the streets; their stock went up real quick. It wasn't all about the street fame; it was about what it took to run shit.

"I hope so too."

"What are you doing later? I want you to take a ride with me. Some punk-ass dude owes Dom some money, and I need some extra muscle to accompany me. This dude is nothing to worry about, but this is a perfect opportunity to see how easy your job would be. People respect you in these streets; you're feared by many by how you carry yourself. You're a silent killer, kid. For this job alone, you'll collect a G. How does that sound?"

It sounded good to me, but I couldn't let him know that. Not that I was playing hard to get. I didn't want him to think that I was open for money. I wasn't for sale, and my life was worth more than a thousand dollars. I could definitely use the money. *We* could definitely use the money. My grandmother didn't know that I saw the bank's letter threatening to take our house if she didn't pay up. It had been on my mind since I saw it. I didn't even tell Cash or Mase. They had enough going on. I knew what I had to do, but was I willing to pay the consequences if caught up?

"I'll ride with you, Harvey. Where you want me to meet you?"

"Meet me in The Vill when all this close up so we can go make this quick money. I'm trying to be in and out so I can get home to some wet pussy."

"I don't need to know what you and Ms. Yvette be doing." I laughed, trying to erase the picture of Ms. Yvette's pussy from my mind.

I agreed to meet him, and I dapped him up and made my way back to our section of this fine establishment. Mase was now seated back at the table, and he and Cash were engulfed in a laugh at somebody's expense. As I got closer to the table, I saw Mr. Scrawny on the floor knocked cleanout. Somebody had enough and almost sent him to his maker. I knew it was a matter of time before somebody got him right. I joined in on the laughter.

"Yo, who were you talking to in VIP?" Mase probed.

"I was talking with Reese and Rick's stepdad."

"What he wanted? Y'all look like y'all was in a serious conversation up there. What did he want with you?" Mase looked at me with suspicion.

"I'm a grown man, playa. You forgot? We were talking business, and that business has nothing to do with you. Comprende?"

"You know what? You are absolutely right. I'm gonna leave it alone."

"Please do."

The rest of the night was cool; we enjoyed music, drinks, and each other's company. Hopefully, our time spent helped them sort out what they had going on. Harvey's offer was in the front of my mind; I was weighing my options. A G wasn't a lot of money, but my grandmother needed it, and she needed me to solve her problem right now. It wasn't the $50,000 she needed, but it was a step in the right direction. I didn't know how I would pay it without her knowing, but I'd get there once I at least paid $10,000. Either way, I would save her from having to experience losing something she had worked so hard to keep.

ALL BLACK EVERYTHING WAS MY ATTIRE FOR THIS NIGHTCAP. I had to blend into the darkness as the summer chills of the early morning air. They say the freaks come out at night, but where we were from, so did the robbers. Don't get caught slipping or you were gonna get got if you didn't play your cards right. The Vill still was operating in the wee hours of the morning. We didn't stay until the club closed; we didn't like the commotion it caused. I had to go home and change into some more comfortable clothes. I finally was on my way to meet up with Harvey.

The closer I got to the Vill, the more my adrenaline gave me a second wave of energy for the job ahead. I was officially on my way to work, and I couldn't wait to cash this check. I didn't know how many hours I would have to put in, but I was up for the task. My walk matched the massive stride of my Timbs hitting the pavement. I threw on the cans in case I had to stomp a nigga out.

As soon as I got to the middle section, I saw lights flashing from the parking lot ahead. Harvey was waiting in his pearl white Cadillac CTS with rims to match. He motioned for me to get in the car so we could start our shift. Rick and Reese were in the back seat, which in turn gave me dibs on the front. I dapped my boys up, happy to see a familiar face on the heist. Harvey left that out, but I was glad I had my boys watching my back.

"You finally decided to join us, huh?" Reese reached up and slapped my chest, playing Tarzan for me.

"About time his scary ass did, looking like a built burnt hotdog with ya black ass. You almost the same color as the black you got on."

"You always got jokes, Rick. Don't get mad at me you can't see your hotdog over ya stomach."

Laughter erupted.

Tonight, we became debt collectors, collecting a debt owed

to a man who didn't play about his money or supply. Dom rarely came to Paterson; he had a whole team doing his work for him. He retired from the streets so long ago that most people forgot how he looked. When you did see him in the hood, Dom was there for blood, and most times, it was shed. That's the only time he really showed his face and the power that he possessed. He was a living legend but a ghost in his own right.

"Y'all ready to get this money? Playtime is over." Harvey started the car while asking his first question of the night.

"Hell yeah, I'm ready." Reese pounded his chest.

"You better believe," Rick followed up.

"I'm as ready as I'm going to be. This is going to be a quick, in-and-out job, right?"

"Yes, it will be. Let me do all the talking, and if I need y'all to throw hands or let that metal talk, I'll let y'all know. Hand me that bag back there."

Rick passed Harvey a large black duffle bag.

"You ever shot a gun before, Reem?"

An empty feeling hit the pit of my stomach, confirming that this was real. It was no turning back. The shiny Glock he handed me fit perfectly in my hand. It gave me a sense of power that I didn't know I needed. I changed into a super-hero, someone who was sent to save the day. My mentality from here on out was *let's get this money*. I'd never shot a gun before, but I knew I could do anything. This gave me the extra protection I needed.

"No, but you better believe I'll make it talk if need be. Don't worry about me; I got this, Harv."

"Look at the little baby growing up." Rick cocked his weapon that Harv gifted him with.

"These niggas better not step outta line." Reese sealed it.

Dap.

Fist bump.

Handshake.

Salute.

Harvey gave us the rundown of how we were going to execute the plan. Reese volunteered to get J. Baz to open the door. It was an easy operation, and I hoped it all went as planned. I didn't like it when my plans were interrupted and didn't go my way. My grandmother always shared her thoughts that I lived in an ideal world instead of the real world. I could hear her voice now. *"Everything can't go your way, baby; that's not how life works."* It was something that I guess I'd have to grow out of.

"Let's ride out." We pulled off, headed to collect some dead presidents. Hopefully, we didn't leave people dead in the aftermath.

We made our way up the hill to the Dog Pound. Alabama Projects was one of the major spots for Dom's operation. You had to be a bold individual to make your way through the Dog Pound if you didn't live there. Those grounds were covered by killers, drug dealers, and the fiends that would do anything to get another hit. Litter, trash, and everything else covered the streets before we pulled into one of the most dangerous neighborhoods, ready to start a war if necessary.

We pulled into the back lot and crept our way through the sleeping cars to get to the entrance. There were B-Boys on the post, but we fit right into the night, ambling, checking our surroundings. On an average day, I'm sure Dom and or Harvey would pull up and get the respect they deserved. This was different; he wanted to catch a nigga slipping. The smell of piss invaded my nostrils. Cans, bottles, and trash were the decor of the run-down buildings before us. We took the elevator up to the tenth floor.

Everyone was quiet on our way up. I guess this was our test, a test that Rick and Reese got to study for. They'd been watching Harvey since they met him. They were pushing weight, but nothing more than that. Ms. Yvette turned a blind eye to their dealings; they were now living better than most. Nothing but multiple streams of nontaxable income. She became hood famous, and that was enough to forgive her sons' indiscretions.

We crept off the elevator like a mini army, ready to reclaim our territory. Harvey led the charge down the long hallway to the last door. Reese knocked with force but not enough to alarm the neighbors. We all moved out of the sight of the peephole, waiting for the opening of the vault. What we wanted was waiting behind the grey steel door marked 10C. Whoever was behind the door took their time, frustrating us to the point that we were about to kick in the door.

"Who is it?" someone yelled.

"Rated R!" Reese shouted back.

"What you want?"

"Give me two eighths and a bad bitch if you got one."

"Aight, bet."

The door slowly slid open, revealing the culprit behind the voice that had us waiting. His eyes were low, his face ashy, and his clothes needed washing. We wasted no time running up in the apartment, closing the door behind us. He peed himself as soon as Harvey came into his view. It was like he saw a ghost and couldn't believe it was real. I wasn't sure if this was J. Baz, but if it wasn't, he'd better let us know where he was at. Rick covered the door while Reese and I stood on the side of this mystery dude.

"You thought you were going to continue waking up knowing you were playing with Dom's money?" An irritated laugh escaped from Harvey's tight lip.

"I don't know, please. I don't know what you are talking about, Harv."

"You had one job, J. Baz."

Bingo!

"One job and one job only," Harvey continued.

"Please don't kill me. I'll get Dom his money. Tell him to give me a few more days, and I'll pay him with interest."

"No, you're going to go get his money right now, with interest. We don't run a charity; this ain't layaway. You took the product. Now where is the cash? I'm going to ask you one more time, and if I don't hear where it's at, Reem here will show you what happens to weak niggas like you."

The sound of my Glock echoed through the apartment as I cocked it back for emphasis, showing him that I was wit' it. The smell from him peeing himself went right with his surroundings. I couldn't believe this dude peed himself. He was definitely weak; no man, no matter what, should see you sweat. If I was gonna go out, I was going to go out swinging. It could be with my fist or with the shiny piece that was ready to blow in my hands. My heart picked up pace as I waited to see what his next move was.

Thump.

A sound came from inside a closed door straight ahead to my right. I wasn't sure if it was a bedroom or bathroom, but someone else was in this joint. Reese ran from the front door, hearing the sound as well. We all looked at each other, trying to decide what to do. I thought, quick on my feet. I grabbed J. Baz up, pushing him toward the room where the noise came from. He was my shield. I kicked the door open, and three young boys were in there with weapons drawn. They had to be no more than fourteen or fifteen years old.

"Oh, I see. This was a setup, huh?"

My Glock now was pointed at J. Baz's apple head as the rest of the crew came in ready with their guns drawn. We weren't outnumbered; we had the upper hand. We had their boss held at gunpoint, and it wasn't anything they could do but give us what we came for. There were two tables inside the room, one with money all over it and a counting machine. The other one was where the drugs were being bagged, I guess. Weed smoke was in the air, and it did nothing to mask the pee smell coming from their fearless leader.

"You don't know who you little nigga are messing with. He pays you, but that money belongs to Dom. Then that makes you an employee of mine, so I suggest y'all put dem guns down, or it's going to be a situation up in here."

Before they could even move, Rick walked up and hit the biggest one with the butt of his gun. That caused the other two to drop their weapons.

"I smelled fear like an all you could eat buffet. Next time, cock the gun before you point it, youngin." Rick kicked the boy on the ground, not caring that he busted him open with one hit.

"Rick, grab a bag and get all this money and drugs off these tables. Check the whole apartment and take anything valuable. Reese, find something to tie these little niggas up. He's gonna pay one way or another." Harvey mushed J. Baz in his head, causing him to fall to the dirty floors.

He blended right in with the dirt and grime of his unkempt apartment. Reese found the tape in one of the kitchen drawers. After Reese taped the boys' arms and legs, he threw me the made-up handcuffs. I turned J. Baz around and taped his hands and feet together, matching his three henchmen.

"I got everything. We out."

Boom! Harvey pulled his trigger, leaving J. Baz lifeless. This was my first time seeing someone get killed. I wasn't too worried about me; it was the young boys that would have to live with this forever. Harvey had to make an example out of Baz to show these young niggas what happened when you stole somebody else's money. One day they might want to get put on; they needed to learn the laws of the streets. They didn't want to end up like their boss laying in a pool of his own blood.

"Next time, we won't be so nice."

We exited on Harvey's last words. There wasn't any need to run or walk swiftly. We didn't want anybody to tip J. Baz off when we were coming; that was the only reason we crept up the way we did. Now we could ride into the early morning, enjoying the fruits of our labor, watching the sunset as we ended our night but started our day.

Chaka Demus & Pliers - Murder She Wrote
I know this little girl, her name is Maxine
Her beauty is like a bunch of rose (betta know)
If I ever tell you 'bout Maxine
You would say I don't know what I know

*R*omantic dates and getaways were what held a relationship together. It was in those moments that you realized why you fell in love with a person in the first place. It reminded you of all the fun you could have if planned right. At the beginning of Jeda's and my relationship, that's what brought us closer; our intimate encounters built our foundation of love, or what I thought was love. Being young and in love, most people felt it was impossible. I wanted to show people otherwise, so I did what I thought would prove them wrong. I did everything in my power to figure out what love really meant.

Did I succeed? One would argue that I didn't, but at least I tried, I guess. I was on my way to go pick up this pure but broken beauty. I was confident that we would get back on track; this was my first attempt to make that statement accurate. The smell of my cologne boosted my confidence; you could smell it in the air of my grandmother's Buick as I voyaged to my destination. Tonight, I pulled out my Levi jeans and Tommy Hilfiger button-up shirt with Wallabees on my feet to complete my look. I was photo shoot fresh, looking like new money.

Hoboken, New Jersey was not too far from where we lived. Overlooking the water and enjoying a Ruth's Chris steak was my definition of a great night. I also wanted to go dancing at this little spot that played dope music. I had a little surprise for her at the end of our night that I hoped she would love. Jeda didn't ask for much, so I knew that she would love everything I had planned. I was ready to build more memories, which would transcend time and stay with us, even when the going got tough.

The car came to a rolling stop as I parked in my spot. It wasn't my spot per se, but it was the only place I occupied when I came to chill with or see about Jeda. I checked myself in the visor, making sure I was straight. I wanted to fit right in with this captivating, divine, and splendid statuesque that was Jeda. My sidekick buzzed with a text message.

Honey Dip: I'm ready.

We always seemed to be on the same wavelength. Little did she know, I was already outside waiting for her. We both had a thing with being late and not sticking to time. Time was money, and we had none to waste. Most people didn't care about time, but it was crucial for both of us. My inside was vibrating, awaiting what the night held in store for us. That text let me know we were on the right track and on the same page. My fingers slid across my sidekick, texting her back with urgency.

I'm outside Dip. I can't wait to see you.

I grabbed the flowers I had for her from the back seat. I pushed open my door, made my way to the front of the car, and slightly leaned on the hood for support. My breathing picked up when Jeda came into my eyes' view. I didn't tell her where we were going, but she would fit right into the night's plans. She sashayed toward me in her high-waisted Baby Phat jeans, convex brown blouse, and red russet high heel shoes. Her walkway became the runway for American's Next Top Model. I sat in awe, but as she got closer, I couldn't help it anymore; I had to hurry up and get to her.

She had a broad smile on her face, looking from my eyes to the dozen red roses I had for her. Her sweetish, insidious perfume made its way up my nostrils as she permeated the space between our bodies. I kissed her lips passionately on impact, hoping it would last forever. I missed her thick, sensual lips brushing up against mine. It was as if the world stopped around us, giving us space and opportunity to engage in gratification.

I didn't want to stop, but I knew we had to. I would end up between her legs and in her bed, which wasn't a terrible idea, but it had been a while since we had a chance to enjoy the nightlife. I knew Jeda wanted us to take our time getting back intimate, but by the way she kissed me back, I knew it was only a matter of time. I gave her one last peck on her lips before handing her the roses.

"These are so beautiful, Cash. I love them."

"They're beautiful like you, Dip. This night is about us and the resurgence of our relationship. I feel like every relationship has to go through a renewal every so often. People change, situations change, and so should relationships."

"I've been waiting for change all of my life, wondering if it would ever happen for me, and it started to look good until… never mind. Let's get our night started."

"I agree; let's choose tonight to forget about all we have going on and celebrate the victory of still being in love."

I grabbed her soft French manicured hands and led the way to the passenger side of the vehicle.

The gentleman in me opened her door, making sure she got in the car comfortably. I knocked on the window before I made my way around to the driver's seat.

"I love you, yo. And it's nothing you could do about it."

The glass window being our divider, her lips sitting at the top and bottom of her teeth presented a smile. That was all I wanted to see. It not only made me smile, but it warmed my inside. I'm not going to front; it got my dick hard too. I couldn't help it; Jeda had a way of stimulating my mind, body, and soul. Let me get my mind off her neatly shaved pink crush velvet anatomy part. If she only knew the things I would do to it right now. I was not trying to rush the night, so I pushed all thoughts of sexual behavior out for the time being.

As soon as I got in the car, I stopped and looked at my future wife, admiring the glow in her eyes. She was back to being herself, actually looking at me as if she loved me. We'd spent so much time together over the years, but this seemed different. It was like we were starting over, learning to love each other more profoundly. We were now seeing each other through another lens, magnifying our imperfections but bringing out the beauty in the painting we created.

"I got something for you." I reached in the back seat and grabbed her second gift.

"Why are you doing all of this?"

"Stop acting like I haven't always been like this. And open it."

Fireworks went off in her eyes as she laid her eyes on the diamond tennis bracelet that I bought her. It was a small investment needed to show how much I cared about making

Jeda happy. It wasn't in the material part of it; to me, it was the thought behind it. Jeda slowly looked from me to the box, not connecting the dots that this was real. She did share with me some time ago that gifts weren't something that she got. Not on her birthday or special holidays, so I always tried to change that narrative for her.

"OMG, you have outdone yourself, Cash. This looks expensive. How much did you pay for this?" She held up the piece, examining the sparkle of each diamond as it lit up the car.

"Don't worry about all of that; let me put it around your arm so it can shine like you."

"Boy, you really pulled out all the stops tonight, huh? I was a little skeptical at first, and I didn't know what would happen. I still have a lot on my mind, and I can't seem to get over this hump. You already proved tonight that I have someone in my corner to help me."

"I told you actions speak louder than words. That's what started our relationship. I had to show you that I was truly about this life. Nobody ever taught me how to love someone. My dad never got a chance to teach me that. Mase tried his best, but his actions didn't line up with his words. So I read about it, watched movies and TV shows about it, trying to understand how to love a woman."

"That says a lot about you, Cash. Who does things like that? Nobody I know or ever came in contact with took it to that level. You are a rare breed, babe. I don't know what I did to deserve you. I'm happy you're here."

I took the box from her and put the bracelet around her wrist, adding to her ensemble. Jeda was in a world of her own as she became one with her gift. I finally pulled off, ready to jump-start our night. The night sky was clear and peaceful as I made my way to the Garden State Parkway. One thing about Jeda and me, we loved to jam on the 1's and 2's while riding and tonight wasn't different. The Buick didn't have a CD player, but I bought a tape adapter for my Sony Walkman. Mario "Let Me Love You" was the first song from my mix CD I put together. It fit right along with our situation. We let the music do the talking as we enjoyed the ride, dancing, and singing like a duo on Apollo.

We zipped through lanes on the highway, enjoying our karaoke session. I kept watching Jeda, making sure she was invested as much as I was. We pulled up to Ruth's Chris and got in the valet parking. There were never any parks in Hoboken; it was a hot spot by the water. We didn't wait long; we exited the car looking like two celebrities. She most definitely fit the bill of a famous person's girlfriend or wife. Her hair blew with the wind as the night's air became her fan, making sure she didn't sweat out her Doobie.

"We have a reservation under Cotton for two."

"Good evening, Mr. Cotton; your table will be ready shortly."

"Thank You."

We waited for a little while they got our table ready. Jeda's body was pressed against mine as we took in our surroundings. I wrapped my arms around her waist, her Juicy Couture perfume airy but intoxicating.

"What you think about this spot so far?" I whispered in her ear.

"It's really nice; I still can't believe you doing all of this."

"It's all for you, Dip. All for you."

"Cotton, table for two."

"That's us."

We made our way to our table. The New York skyline lit up like Christmas. It was our view tonight; it was breathtaking, to say the least. We got comfortable and grabbed our menus to see what we would be ordering. This was our first time here, but we heard great things about this place. One thing about us, we were foodies, always looking for a great place to dine and do takeout. Hanging with Jeda had me putting in extra hours at the gym. We stayed stuffing our faces.

"What you thinking 'bout ordering? She never could make up her mind, so I wanted to make sure we were ready once the waiter came to our table.

"I'm looking at the bone-in New York strip. You?"

"I'm thinking about getting the stuffed chicken breast."

"That sounds so good." She licked her perfect set of lips, anticipating eating off my plate, I bet. No matter how much food she got, she always seemed to eat off my plate, sometimes more than she ate off her own. It was our thing that we always joked about.

"Are you guys ready to order?' The waiter, with his pen and notepad, awaited our response.

I motioned for Jeda to go first. He took our orders and disappeared into the busy establishment. It was a Friday night, so everybody wanted to forget about the work week and focus on the weekend. My weekend wasn't looking too shabby if it was going to be with this ravishing beauty before me. I wanted to put in the time now; being an entertainer didn't always buy you enough time to really enjoy your loved one. With Jeda's writing career taking off, I wasn't sure if we'd ever have time for each other.

"What's new in your world? Are you working on anything new for *Life Magazine*?

"Yes! They want me to write something for their Women's Lifestyle section. Something similar to the 'Woman to Woman' article I wrote. I'm excited but a little nervous. I wish I could fly to L.A. and meet the editor and team there so I can put faces to names."

"One day, you'll get a chance to meet whoever you want to meet. I also know for sure that your next article is about to be bomb. Do you have anything in mind that you want to write about?

"I'm playing with a few things. Nothing set in stone yet. They want it for their December issue, so I may add some holiday flavor to it. I wanted to write something as great as the 'Woman to Woman' article I wrote. If I never entered that contest, I probably would still be writing in my journal. It's still unreal to me."

"You got skills, Dip. Before you know it, you're going to be running your own magazine. Is that still your dream?"

"I mean, yeah, it is. Hopefully, one day it happens."

The shrug of her shoulders wasn't as convincing; it only added to her doubt. Somewhere along the way, she stopped believing that it was possible. It's funny how you can be so dead set on achieving something, and then something or someone comes to steal it from you. I bet money that the thief was her mother. It was like this lady took Jeda's confidence with her. Before I could counter, our waiter was here with our food.

We talked while we ate, but you could tell that my questioning dampened the mood a little. I wasn't trying to; we promised ourselves we were going to hold each other accountable. It was our way to make sure we were successful apart and successful together as a unit. Our goal was to create and leave a family legacy from our own blood, sweat, and tears.

Bill paid, stomachs full, and the rest of the night before us had me dancing out of the restaurant. Jeda's giggles kept me acting a fool; people watched on, laughing along with my stage act. The night kissed our skin; it was something about a summer night that set a mood for a night to remember. Jeda immediately grabbed my arm and got close. The drive to the Mad Hatter wasn't too far, and I was lucky that I got a park on the street. I swooped right in, and we walked a block, and the sounds of "Actions" by Terror Fabulous blared through the speakers.

The night sky was aglow with bright city lights. It was always good to make reservations. I walked right by the line. I knew it was going to be packed; it was Reggae night. And plus, my boy Reef was spinning the records tonight. I gave my name, and we were in there. As soon as we walked through the door, Jeda's hips started moving, and so did my body. We followed the waiter to our table.

It wasn't even eleven o'clock, and Reef had the place jumping. I gave him a fist pump, and he nodded. We got comfortable, ordered some drinks, and danced in our seats until "Murder She Wrote" came blaring through the baseboards of the Hatter. We came alive at the same time as soon as the beat dropped. We found our space on the dance floor and got lost in the move of our hips. Jeda's back rested on my chest as she swayed to the beat. I held on tight, not wanting to let go.

Our bodies became one with the beat; our rhythm radiated each move.

Have her cruise di corner where she jooks an' where she jam

We were caught in a daze, speaking with our movements.

She know about Lou, Crack an' every money man (ah true man)

My hands found Jeda's hips, and my pelvis got in sync with her soft booty cheeks.

Lost in a moment meant for us, nothing else mattered.

Murder she wrote, na na na

Murder she wrote

This was one for the books. Reggae night was what we needed. We danced for a few more songs, lost in each embrace. We were sweaty, but it was for a good cause. It was time for us to end the night, and I intended to add more perspiration to our bodies. I couldn't keep my hands off her; she had me aroused in every way. We exited the building, intoxicated from each other. I held her close as we made our way to the car.

"Something is vibrating, Cash. Is that your phone?"

I searched for my phone, and sure enough, it was ringing with an unknown number.

"Hello"

"I can't wait for you to hear what I did with the song!"

"Aonika?"

"Yes, I want to play it for you myself. You free? Come to the studio. I'll be here for a few more hours."

Jeda pulled away.

"Dang, I'm actually busy right now. When is the next time you'll be in town?" I looked at Jeda, asking her with my eyes to give me a minute. This was big for me, great exposure that can help launch my career.

"I'm leaving next week, but I won't be back on the East Coast until the New Year when my album drops. I can always send it to you, but I wanted to see your face fall in love with the song all over again."

"I can't right now."

"I understand; it's last minute, so I'll take a rain check, but come through next week Friday around the same time. Thanks for trusting me with your song."

"I got you. Thanks, Aonika. Talk to you soon."

With that, we ended the call.

SLAP!

"Aonika?"

"Why you—"

"Oh! You got your old bitches calling your phone? That's what we do now? I knew the moment I told you, you would turn on me. I trusted you! You and that bitch can go to hell."

"Dip, come here."

"Don't touch me! Take me home."

Her eyes were now dark, tears sitting at the brim of her

eyes. She wouldn't let a tear fall. She seemed more angry than hurt. I didn't know what to say, but I wasn't sure anything I had to offer would fix the problem. We were making strides forward but got knocked back ten. I watched her out of my peripheral, and if looks could kill, murder was what she wrote.

Beef

An acronym used often by coaches teaching players how to shoot with correct technique for the first time. B = Balance. E = Eyes. E = Elbow. F = Follow through.

She really thought this was a game. The only game that I wanted to play was B-ball. My phone kept going off, and I ignored it like it wasn't ringing. Qwana's text messages went unanswered. I had to teach her a lesson. It was hard, but I had to take back what was rightfully mine. I started to feel like I was being used for some gut-wrenching pipe. I had to use that to my advantage. Qwana was the first girl I ever loved, and she probably would be the last. Big booty Keisha didn't count.

Did I say love?

I couldn't believe I subconsciously admitted it. The more I had time to think about it, the more I came to that conclusion. I could no longer cage my thoughts; I thought about Qwana everyday all day. Her touch, the way she rubbed my feet after a tough and challenging game, her smell, the Romance perfume by Ralph Lauren she wore, the way she listened when I talked. She didn't want to hear about basketball; she wanted to know me for me. I couldn't shake my feelings for her if I tried.

Shawty from the club was a great distraction, but she didn't give me the same energy as Qwana did. The way club shawty took my dick in her mouth, you would have thought she went to school for it, studied for it and got a good grade. She had me about to collapse from the sloppy top she was giving so freely. I couldn't take females like her seriously; she was too easy. How many other dudes did she offer this service to? You can't turn a hoe into a housewife, and I wasn't trying. I dug the fact that we could be seen in public, and we didn't have to sneak.

"No Better Love" by the Young Gunz played as Qwana's name popped up on my sidekick screen for the third time today. I'd been ignoring her for a few days now. I wasn't sure when I was going to answer the phone, but I knew I had to. I had to either continue to deal with it or really throw in the towel. I'd been battling back and forth since her first unanswered call. I had to let her sweat a little, but I thought it was time to hear her out.

"Oh, now you want to talk."

"I know you saw me calling and texting your phone, Mason. You're acting really childish right now. Grow up."

"Grow up? You fucking grow up. I'm a grown ass man who doesn't have to sneak around. I make my own decisions, so stop trying to play me before I pull your card."

"Yes, I want you to stop acting the way you are and get out of your feelings. I wanna see you."

"Give me your address, and I'll come right away."

Silence.

"That's what I thought. You don't want to see me; you want this good dick that your husband not giving you to satisfy the fire between your legs. That pussy yearning for me, huh?" I chuckled, confident that her body was calling for me like a telegram of an R. Kelly song.

"Get us a room this weekend, and I'll show you how much my pussy misses you."

"I'll think about it. I'll hit you by the end of the week to confirm. Should I call your husband too? I'll tell him it's for training; he needs training on how to tame that pussy."

"I gotta go, Mason. Please think about what I said."

I hung up the phone, not even caring to say goodbye. When I said goodbye to Qwana, it would be for good if she didn't start acting right. At this point, I had the upper hand, and I planned to use that to my advantage. Eventually, she was going to have to choose between her old life or her future with me. Age was nothing but a number, so I didn't see that being an issue. Right now, it was getting her husband out of the picture.

My focus had to be redirected to the task at hand. I always put my best foot forward at practice like NBA scouts were there. I was in my last year of college, and I was determined to finish strong. This season, I felt I had more to prove. I turned down quite a few offers over the years. College was my backup plan in case ball didn't work out for me. My mother always told me to have a plan B. Her advice still echoed in my ear, reminding me that basketball was not the only thing I was good at. If I didn't know better, I would have put my eggs all in one basket. I wouldn't be young forever, and I couldn't control injuries, so I needed something more. In this profession, you didn't know who was in your corner. Everybody had a motive; they saw dollar signs when they saw me. So I had to be careful in this next stage of my life. It was another added stress to my list.

I'd been surrounded by love all of my life, but everybody around me had their own thing going on. Cash was one hit away from achieving his dreams, and Kareem was a few years from enrolling in medical school. We were now grown and going in different directions. This was the most we had been apart since before we were born. It was cool, though; they were doing their thing, and I was proud of them. I had to figure out what was next for me.

I showed my skills and kicked it for a few, and I was on my way. Basketball came easy; I put no effort into it. I was nice on the court, and nobody could tell me different. I didn't know why I was wrestling inside. I pulled in and released a slow deep breath. It was time for me to visit the one person I knew could help me sort out my problems. I had to go see my Grammy; she could put so much stuff in perspective. If no one else could, she indeed could. I took my shower, got dressed, and jumped on the highway, headed down I-95 North.

EVERY TIME I CAME BACK HOME, I ALWAYS FELT A SENSE OF peace. It was as if it was waiting for me to show up. I would still be living here with my grandmother if she didn't kick me out. She told me to go live my life and don't stop on the count of her. It was so hard initially; I used to show up to the house every day to check on her. She still had Cash and Kareem there, but I always was her protector. I was the oldest, and I made sure the house ran smoothly.

I unlocked the door to my childhood home where I grew up, and laid the groceries on the table. We had a lot of fun in this house, but we also got in some trouble behind these four walls. It still smelled the same, the smell of clean linen was my grandmother's favorite scent, and she still had it invade the nose hairs of everyone that walked in. The house was pretty quiet; nothing had changed. She probably hadn't changed a thing since the first day she moved in here. Making minor changes here and there when something broke and could no longer be fixed was how she got by.

"Look who came to check in with an old lady. Hey, my big baby."

Making her way into the kitchen from her room, her voice calmed me instantly. Her voice was so sweet, soft, and filled with wisdom. I smiled so hard that it hurt, she always brought light to a dark situation. Don't get her mad, though, she'd let you have it if she had to.

"Hey, Grammy!" I wrapped her tight in my arms, not wanting to let go. My tall frame towered over her, but I still felt smaller. I felt like a kid again, looking for her to make things right for me, even if I was the one who messed up.

"Hey, baby. What brings you by on a Monday evening? Come on, take a seat. You didn't have to bring any groceries, Mason."

"I want to cook you something." I started taking everything out of the bags. "It's my way to show you I didn't forget about you." When I was gone for a long time, not able to visit, I always felt guilty. Between the summer league, messing with Qwana, and school, my days had been pretty full.

"Boy, hush. You are a grown man, and you have your own life to live. I'm straight."

I cracked up laughing.

"You straight? Grammy, what you mean you straight? You've been talking to Kareem a little too much. Unless you got a young boyfriend I would have to kill."

Now it was her turn to laugh. For a long time, it was hard for her to even smile after my parents died.

On top of that, she lost Aunt Jane, her only living daughter, to the streets. That left her with three boys to raise on a housekeeping salary. She made it look easy, but looking back as an adult, I knew it was far from it. Cash, Kareem, and I made a pact years ago that we were going to follow our dreams and make mad cash so we could take care of her. We were on the right track, but it was taking too long. Grammy was starting to age.

Her laugh was still caught in her breathing as she continued.

"Baby, if I tell you about my boyfriend, then I would have to kill you."

"Grammy, that's not funny." She found that to be extremely funny.

"I'm glad you came to see me, Mason. Something is on your mind. Talk to me."

"So I can't come home to see my old lady?" Playing with my beard, I looked down toward the floor. I didn't want her to think that I was using her; I honestly did want to see her but talk to her simultaneously.

"You know that's not what I meant, baby. I can feel you in turmoil, like when you were young. The only difference is I now have to allow you to sort things out on your own. It was something that your old lady had to get used to, but it was needed to help you mature from a young man to a man. That doesn't mean you can't talk to me."

"Grammy, what if I didn't want to play basketball for the rest of my life? Like, not go to the NBA but stay local and do something else? Would you be mad at me?"

"I would be mad if you were making this decision based off of somebody and not how you really feel. What do I always tell you?"

"Always do what makes you happy." She nodded her head, confirming that I was right.

"Correct. Too many times, we take other people's happiness over our own. While it's an excellent quality to have, we tend to lose ourselves to make other people happy. You have a big heart, son, and people with big hearts always try to find fulfillment in doing things for others."

"Basketball used to make me happy, but these days, it's merely something I know I need to do to make a better life for you guys."

"See. That's what I mean, son. What do you want to do? What makes you happy? Not what you can do to make others happy. Trust me, everybody will fall in line once you figure that out if they love you."

Silence.

What she was saying made sense, but I didn't think I was programmed like that. Since I could remember, basketball had been my only love outside of the sweet taste and feel of a woman's inner parts. I needed some advice on that as well, but I'd pass and figure that out on my own. That would be awkward. I still didn't feel comfortable talking to Grammy about that.

My dad drilled it in my head every morning and every chance he got that I was born to play ball. It was a dream he never got to pursue because of an injury, and I felt I owed it to him to follow in his footsteps. And plus, I was good at it. That was a win-win in my book.

Basketball was something that I'd been working on my whole life, but these days I was wondering could I be successful without it.

"Your silence is scaring me, son. You were always the one who had it figured out. Other than them fast tail girls, you had no issues. You're at a crossroads, and whatever decision you make, know that it will be the best decision. The hard decisions are often never made. We don't want to be wrong about them is one of the reasons that come to mind. How can one learn without taking the necessary steps?"

"Grammy—"

"Wait, baby. Let me finish. You lost the love for the game when your dad died; the glow that was once in your eyes was no longer there. Your ten-year-old mind couldn't process it. Playing ball is what made you and your dad close. You worked yourself harder than he ever could. You had to prove to him that you loved him through basketball. It was your way of coping, but I knew eventually it would catch up with you."

"Why you never spoke up?" This was getting a little too emotional for me, but I needed answers. I wiped my tears, determined not to cry, but they kept falling anyway.

Boys don't cry! My father's voice echoed throughout my brain.

"Some things, baby, you have to figure out on your own, and that was one of those times. If I had pulled you from basketball, you would have rebelled, and it wouldn't have been good. So I let you find your way, and I'm glad I did. Basketball was your counseling; it got you through the rough days of losing both of your parents. Without it, you would have surely gone down the wrong path."

"I wanted to make him proud."

"Each and every day you choose to wake up and do something with your life, that's making him proud, baby. You did what he couldn't do; you exceed his expectations, I bet. We can't hold onto things that weren't meant for us. Sometimes, we as parents put our shortcomings on our kids, expecting them to make up for what we lacked."

"So you saying I'm not good enough to make it in the NBA?" I had to understand. I worked hard for it.

"Now, you know better. What I'm saying is you need to do what's right for you. If you wanna play basketball, baby, play basketball. If you want to open a restaurant, baby, do it. Whatever you want to do, do it. You're going to be successful in whatever you put your mind to."

She got up on her feet and came over to me and hugged

me like she did the day my parents died. While this wasn't a sad moment, it showed me that somebody believed in me. I could never do wrong in her eyes, which gave me the courage to move forward. I didn't know what moving forward was, but I would soon have to figure it out.

They said nothing lasts forever, and good things must come to an end,
so this was only temporary.
- Kareem

I was still on a high from my nightcap the other night and the blunt I'd just had before getting to my day. The evidence in my hand was a clear indicator of my come up as I stood in line to pay the mortgage for the house. Cash worked at a bank, so I asked him a few questions, not giving away that it was for Grammy. Wachovia Bank wasn't taking our home, and I was going to make sure of that. I had to figure out how I was going to get the rest of the money up. I had a few things in mind. I exited the bank, satisfied that I could pay something. It wasn't much, but I'd have it all by the due date.

I thought about what took place the other night as I made my way from downtown Paterson. We could have gotten killed if those kids knew better. They probably didn't even know how to shoot a gun, but you'd do anything when you were in a panic and scared. The job was a walk in the park, but would it always be? I asked that question to myself the whole morning after. I couldn't sleep; my adrenaline was still pumping. I kept looking at the money on my nightstand, realizing I made that in less than thirty minutes.

Easy money was not always good money; as long as I wasn't killing nobody, we were good. To be honest, sometimes you had to do what you had to do, so I was prepared for that if it came. This wasn't one of those times. I had this mortgage to come up with; I also needed money to fund my lifestyle. Money gave you access to things you wanted; it unlocked many doors you didn't even know existed. People would do some crazy stuff for a little piece of change, and it was sad, but it was the way of the world, unfortunately.

"Money, Power, Respect" became my theme song years earlier. I finally understood the process. I was in the first stage of that, but the respect factor was something I never had a problem with. I had a dude here and there who wanted the smoke, but not too often did someone try me. I ran with the best of them. I became well known, the ones who hung around me did as well. Cash and Mase brought another level of respect than Rick and Reese. Two different worlds collided through me.

I was free to do whatever I wanted to do. I loved those days; it gave me a chance to relax or play catch up. Today was a relaxed day. I was all caught up thanks to Jax pushing me to finish my seven-page paper. He could sometimes come off as a hard ass, but it was coming from a sincere place. What he had to understand was I lived in the real world; he was living on a secluded island away from hard decisions.

It was still early enough for me to go grab some grub from DJ Deli on 21st Avenue. Man, I could go for their grits and cheese, eggs with cheese, and some slappin' turkey bacon. A roar from my stomach confirmed that we were on the same page. I rode through Paterson's streets, letting the summer air hit me, passing the run-down houses and buildings that made Paterson what it was. Summer was cool, but I couldn't wait till winter, my favorite season. That's when you hustled and planned so that when spring and summer came, you could execute.

I was a regular at DJ Deli, so I was greeted like family when I walked in. I ordered, took a seat, and scrolled through MySpace. My phone started ringing, and Harvey's name popped up. He did say he'd be in touch, but I didn't think it would be so soon. I was so used to seeing him at Reese's house I thought he would never use my number. He was calling, not chirping, so it had to be urgent.

"What up, Harv?"

"What's up with you, nightrider? What ya day looking like?"

I hated when people asked me that; being thrown off my schedule added to that hate. People always seemed to insert themselves when you said you had nothing to do. That question was a setup.

"I'm always on the move, Harv. There is always something to do, people to see, and money to make. I get in where I fit in. You feel me?"

"I feel you youngin, and I ain't mad at you. The boss wants to speak with you. You free in a few hours?"

"What does he want to talk to me for?"

"You never ask questions when the big man wants to see you. You should be honored; he doesn't meet with too many people. He hasn't even met Rick and Reese yet, so that says a lot about you, kid."

The street legend, the man behind the multi-million-dollar drug enterprise, wanted to talk with me? Dealing with Harv was one thing, but speaking with the head honcho was another. I always heard stories about Dom from the streets, never knowing if any of it was true. I think he is around the same age as my mom, so she could probably tell me if some of the stories were true. More than likely, she was somewhere now trying to find a vein; I doubt she'd remember anything.

"Aight, I'll get up with him. When and where?"

"Meet us on Bunker Hill, 2 East Eleventh Street at ten o'clock. When you get up to the gate, tell them you're there to see Dom."

"Bet."

I couldn't wait to see what this was about. A surge of fear shifted through my body, but then I asked why. I didn't know him, and he didn't know me. I'd heard the stories, but I never witnessed it myself. I'd have to come to my own conclusion, somebody else's might lead me down a road I didn't want to go. If Dom set up to meet with me, he knew what I was about. Hopefully, this meeting would bring me closer to the bands I needed. I was on a mission to get all the money I could get by any means.

BUNKER HILL WAS A PRIMARILY INDUSTRIAL AREA OFF OF RIVER Street, east of the Passaic River. The night cooled off a little from the blazing heat that August brought. Everybody and their momma was outside. I felt like a thief escaping the night. I pulled up to the gate, and security was on their post. There was one on each side, and they made it a point to let me know that they were packing heat. I rolled down my window and told them who I was and who I was there to see. I was granted access.

I parked next to two blacked-out 2005 Cadillac Escalades with tint and shiny black rims to match. If I had to guess, that would be what Dom was riding in. Harvey's ride was next to it. One of the guards met me as I was stepping out of the car. Before I could even close the door, he was up on me.

"You got any weapons on you?" He proceeded to pat me down without permission.

If this was some regular dude on the street, I would have cold-cocked him for violating my personal space. I was outnumbered, and I wasn't strapped like them, so I let him do what he was told to do. I had no choice anyway; I was in their territory, not knowing what I was up against. We were deep in Bunker Hill, surrounded by nothing but factories and warehouses. I never even knew that anything was back here.

"Follow me."

By this time, the other guard joined us. One walked before me, and the other walked behind me. I felt like a threat to national security, and I was being put away to never strike again. The walk into the warehouse created a thick, spine-chilling silence that was met with darkness upon arrival. I studied my surroundings, taking in everything my eyes came in contact with and mapping out my exit plan in case things didn't go as I wanted. I was always one to think of the worst, so that if it presented itself, it wouldn't surprise me. I hated surprises.

An inhumane screech reverberated, coming from the direction we were headed in. I didn't know whether to stop in my tracks or keep going. I couldn't show these guards that whatever that was kind of scared me. The tormented sound carried throughout the warehouse; it was one of utter distress and longing to be freed from pain. As we got closer, my curiosity was quenched with the gruesome scene before me.

Hands tied, crimson blood covering most of his body, a man sat beaten within an inch of his life. I thought he was dead until his swollen lips tried to plead his case. He tried talking through what had to be a broken jaw, his words were broken and muffled.

"Pleaseeee don't! Don't kill me, Dom! I'll pay back everything I owe."

Before I could even witness more of the horrendous criminality of death that loomed from every punch coming from this riotous demonic person, his voice, calm but authoritative, spewed out instruction without even looking back our way.

"Take him to my office."

That was all that was heard before I was snatched from the distinctly gray and disquieting area of action that was taking place. Was that Dom? His deep sinister voice stayed with me way after he was finished giving orders. I didn't even get a good look at him; his back was turned, sleeves rolled up, and he was doing his best Muhammad Ali boxing techniques. He was dressed professionally, not as pimpish as Harvey, a little more defined and put together.

We made our way up to Dom's office that overlooked the whole warehouse. If it wasn't for Thing One and Thing Two, I would be watching the action from the skybox of an office in which I was hesitant to take a seat. The vacant straight-backed chair that I chose kept me from running up out of here. I was seated, waiting for the boss, but it might be a waiting period; he had his hands full.

I admired his office, the black artistic paintings, the art pieces, and enough books to fill up a library. *Does a man of his status even read books?* I wondered. Most drug dealers I knew only cared about one thing and one thing only, and that was money. With money came pussy, so that was secondary but equally necessary for the hood hustlers. I felt like I was sitting in one of my professors' offices.

Footsteps could be heard coming down the hallway. One guard was at the door behind me, and the other was standing before me, awaiting the arrival of the HNIC. It was like they knew it was him; their whole demeanor changed when they realized that the boss was near. They stood taller, looked meaner, and braced themselves for their next task at hand, whatever that may be.

I didn't even turn around; his Tom Ford cologne met me before he did. His dark charcoal skin and grim expression added to his deep voice, echoing order after order. The scar on his chin moved with every syllable. His goatee couldn't cover the nasty scar, but he embraced it as a part of him. His men moved quickly after getting their next assignment for the night. His blood-stained hands were making one with the towel he had, removing the unholy reddish liquid from his exposed body parts.

I looked on, waiting for him to speak. His back was now turned to me. He was behind his desk looking from the skybox at the scene he created. More than likely, he was checking to make sure that everything was being handled the way he intended for it to. The silence was unbearable; it was sending chills up my body, waiting for an explanation of why I was here. He finally turned to face me, and his shiny bald head took a seat in his big presidential chair.

We made eye contact.

"I heard you stepped up the other night and helped Harvey retrieve my money. It was an easy task, but you had heart in the process. That's rare nowadays. Many people want power but don't know how to take it. Harvey tells me you do."

"I wouldn't say that. I was asked to help with a job, and I did it."

"You didn't have to, but you did. What changed? Harvey has been trying to get with you since he started fucking Yvette. He claimed to have seen a little bit of me in you, and there's only one me, so I had to see for myself."

"What changed? Nothing really. I had to start looking out for myself. There were many reasons I shouldn't have taken

Harvey up on his offer; none of them had to do with me directly. I do things on my terms, so it wasn't no disrespect to you or Harv, but I call the shots in my life. And I didn't see a benefit until now."

Dom stared right through me; it was like he was trying to read my mind or get a better feel of the man sitting before him. I wasn't your average twenty-year-old. I now saw firsthand what Dom was capable of, but it still didn't intimidate me. He could probably take me out at any time, but I had confidence that I wouldn't go down without a fight. I held the stare, showing him what he heard was true.

"You got heart, Kareem, and I appreciate that characteristic in anybody I meet on this side of the business. Real recognize real, and the more I talk to you, and the more you've been in my presence, I could see what Harvey was talking about. What's next for you?"

I didn't know if it was a trick question, but I had a few things in mind. My goal was to get this money and call the shots of how and when I would do it. I couldn't get caught up in anything else, so I had to make that clear. Dom wasn't someone who you could tell what you were and weren't doing, but he had to understand I wasn't either. I was the captain of this ship, and it didn't move until I said it did.

"I need some weed to sell at my school. With the connections I have, it would be very profitable for the both of us."

A sardonic laugh crept from his stomach up to his neck into the four walls of his office. I didn't know I was doing standup comedy tonight, and I didn't appreciate him mocking me. I had to keep my feelings at bay. One, I was outnumbered, but two, I needed the money and didn't want to mess up my long-term plans. I strategically thought through this, and it was the only way to get the cash in time for the bank to not sell our house.

"Are you sure that's what you want to do?"

"I'm positive."

"Since you helped me out, I'll help you out. It's the least I could do. What you trying to cop?"

"I can start out with an ounce and show you how well I could move it, and we can go from there."

"If you say you have the clientele that you do, and ounce not going to get you any money. The work you put in with Harvey, I'll give the rest for free as a show of appreciation. How does that sound?"

I never even thought about the start-up money. I put the whole thousand on the house, not knowing I would get a call from Harv to meet Dom. My thoughts lined up with what I had in mind, but it went quicker than I expected. I thought I would do more jobs with Harv to prove my worth, but that one job had me on the fast track to obtaining this dough. I brought it to him, so I couldn't back down; he upped the ante.

"Sounds like a plan."

"It's one thing I don't play with, and that is money. I'm doing you a favor. You did me one. The last time I did a favor for someone, dude ended up tied to a chair, getting the crap beat out of him. Don't let that be you."

His eyes turned darker at his comment; he was looking at me for a rebuttal, almost daring me to say something or challenge his warning. I didn't like the feeling that I was making a deal with the devil. This may not have been the best way to accomplish the task at hand, but it was the quickest. These college kids were about to put major funds in my pocket, and I was sure of that.

"Reap, take him to the greenhouse."

The greenhouse?

We were surrounded by nothing but factories and warehouses; I wondered where this greenhouse was located. I had to figure out how to move more product than I anticipated. It was many factors that played into this role, and I was about to find out how real it was. I had no doubt that I was capable; it was new to me, and with everything new, I had to process first.

"Let me know if you need anything. Reap will see you out." He turned his chair around, sifting through papers.

"Bet. Good looking."

I got up from my seat and proceeded to the greenhouse with Reap leading the way and his partner in crime not too far behind. I was going to do this until I came up with all the money, and once I was done, I'd evaluate if I should continue. They said nothing lasts forever, and good things must come to an end, so this was only temporary.

JANE

"*I*f you have a radio, Walkman, beeper, cell phone, camera, or any electronic equipment, you will not be allowed inside."

"Put all of your items in the bin and walk through."

Beep.

"Miss, please step to the side and raise your hands. Do you have any metal or items in your pocket that you didn't put in the bin?"

"No. I put everything inside."

This hairy, stink breath woman guard always tried to make a fool of me when I came here. She gave all the women a hard time. I wasn't sure what she had to prove or what message she wanted to get across, but every week was becoming a little bit too much. She waved her magic wand up and down my body, trying to waste more of my time and energy.

One by one, we were called into a private vestibule to open our mouths, raise our tongues, and fold down our waistband to ensure we were not bringing any contraband into the facility. Once I passed that test, I was let up the flight of stairs to the final waiting room. This part seemed to get longer and longer each week, waiting for the guard to begin calling our names for our visit.

Visiting Rikers Island became a way of release; it became something I looked forward to, and today wasn't any different. No matter what this guard was trying to do, I didn't care. I was used to her and her antics, and today it wouldn't work. When I first came here, I let her have it. Back then, my mind wasn't clear, but each day of sobriety got me closer to freedom in my reactions. I finally was able to make it through to go see my sponsor.

It had been a hard couple of months, but I'd been maintaining and making it through. This was the hardest thing I ever had to do in life, yet I was doing it this time. I'd gone months without doing drugs before, but this time it really felt different. I wasn't sure if it was Jax's involvement or I needed to show my son that his mother wasn't weak.

You're a weak excuse for a mother.

Kareem's words were a repeated reminder of who I was, but it also helped me finally get clean. Those were his last words before he finally gave up on me. That was almost seven months ago, but it played in my head like it happened yesterday. I wasn't always the greatest mom, but there was a time when I was. I guess all that was erased because of years of clouded judgment.

I sat at our table, awaiting the man who helped me get this far. Although Jax was locked behind bars, he did more for me than people who were free. If I hadn't stopped by his sister's house that day, I would have never gotten this far. That collect call came through right in time, and it changed my world for the better. At first, it was tough, but I took it one day at a time.

A loud sound went off in the visiting area, indicating that

the prisoners were on their way in. I sat up straight and made sure my clothes and hair were presentable. It had been a long time since I felt pretty or cared about my appearance, but somehow, Jax had a way of making me care. The way he looked at me always sent chills up my spine; even when I was skin and bones, he built my self-esteem. I often felt it was jail talk, but as I became myself again, I started to see the light.

I watched the inmates file in one by one, waiting to see his face. I looked on in anticipation. His palpable and oddly sensual frame was dressed in his orange jumpsuit, his protruding biceps went well with his effortless strides. John "Jax" Jacobs made his way over to me with a charming and crooked smile. He looked more handsome than the day I met him. For him to be in jail all these years, he hadn't aged a bit. If this was years earlier and we both were free from our situations, we most definitely would have been. Would have been what? I wasn't sure. It was something that I thought about all the time. What if?

"Look at you putting on some healthy weight. You starting to look like the girl I had a crush on back in the day, with ya sexy ass."

It was a compliment for sure, but it was a reminder that I lost my way.

Our hug and embrace were cut short by the clearing of the stink guard's throat with her hating ass. We took our seats, and at first, we sat in silence, trying to figure out where to start. I hadn't seen him in the last month; I was busy trying to rebuild my life. Looking for a job and an apartment had me on the move, keeping me alive in a society that didn't want to see me do better.

"You really are starting to look more and more like yourself. I was a little worried about you. I haven't seen you in a month and some change."

"I've been really out here trying, Jax. I have my days, but

for the most part, I've been progressing. That one day at a time matters, and I'm learning that. I might have a job at Nabisco in Fairlawn. My second interview is tomorrow."

"Look at you! I'm proud of you, Jane."

"It's not what I went to school for, but it's a step in the right direction. All I need is housing now, and then I'll be on my way."

"You know Mrs. Harris will let you stay with her until you get back on your feet."

"She's a trigger for me, Jax. My mother is a sweet lady, but she had some evil ways. She was the one who put Linda and me against each other, whether she did it on purpose or not. I don't need her help; I got this on my own."

"You definitely got this. I always knew that. I was waiting for you to catch up."

He always knew how to make me smile.

"It's happening again."

"The dreams?"

"Yes, and I can't stop them. It's like every time I start doing better, it haunts me like it never left."

My breathing started to increase, and clips of that day started playing like a preview before a movie. My leg started shaking, and my eyes almost released pints of tears, but I held it together. I hated talking about the dreams and about that day. That's when life went downhill for me. But I had to. I couldn't keep it locked inside; this time it might kill me.

"Did you go speak with somebody about it?"

"I ain't going to no shrink. I'm not crazy. I made some bad decisions in life that cost me more than I was worth. If I only would have changed one thing, this could have all been a figment of my imagination."

"And what is that?"

"I shouldn't have slept with my sister's husband."

As the words left my mouth, so did the need to hide.

Shame invaded my lungs and the pulse of my heart rate. If I only knew what I know now, things would have been much different. The fact that I couldn't change that outcome was what had me in bondage for so many years.

"Mason took advantage of you. Mason and I were cut from the same cloth, not bound by blood but bound by the streets. We never really disagreed until it came to you. I couldn't understand why you chose him."

"I didn't choose him, Jax. Shit just happened."

"If it was only one time, then I would understand, but having a full-blown affair is different."

"I know. I killed my sister."

"I didn't say that, Jane. Now don't do that. I wish like hell I was there to save my brother; I probably wouldn't be in here. He would have made sure of that. That's the type of dude he was. We all wish we can turn back the hands of time, but we gotta let it go."

"It's easy for you to say. You're not the one having the dreams. Linda wasn't supposed to be in the car, Jax!"

My hand slammed on the table, causing stink breath to put her hand on her gun like I was a threat. I calmed myself and had to realize where I was. That part always angered me. Why did she have to get in the car?

"You're absolutely right, but it's nothing we could do about that now. It happened, Jane, and you spent most of your life trying to change it. Why not try another way? You might get a better outcome."

"I was good until I started having the dreams again. Mason was on his way. We needed to talk through things. Come up with a plan. A way to solve this love triangle we were caught up in. She wasn't supposed to be home."

"Do you ever think what it would have been like if we were together? Like, really together?"

The question caught me off guard, but I was used to Jax

letting me know that he had mad love for me. He didn't hide it. Jax wasn't bad looking at all; his brown skin and hazel eyes drove all the girls wild. His soft, curly hair made him look kin to Chico Debarge and them. He was straight out of the '80s when light-skinned brothers were in.

"I do. I mean, I do now that you helped me get a second chance at life. And you did it from behind bars. You didn't look at me differently, as a failure or even a crackhead. You looked at me as Jane Harris."

I may have been the one who got away, but Jax didn't hold that over my head. No matter how many times I turned him down, he was there to pick me up, even in those moments where Mason continued to break my heart. Jax was the rebound, and he didn't mind being one either. As long as I showed him some type of attention, he was good with that.

"I could have given you the world, Jane. Mason knew that too, but he wanted the best of both worlds, and I couldn't blame him. Anyway, when was the last time you spoke with Kareem?"

"The last time he walked out on me, turning his back on me for good. He was tired, and so was I."

"You're clean now; he would be proud."

"For how long, Jax?"

"This time? Forever. Kareem's been hanging down in The Vill a lot lately, and you know Yvette's ghetto trifling ass is messing with Harvey now. He doesn't need to be around those brothers who stay in trouble. They are bad news, and so is Harvey."

"You think he's working for Harvey? This the same Harvey that works for Dom?"

"Yup, same old country ass Harvey. I'm not sure if Kareem's working for him, but knowing Harvey, he's probably trying his hardest."

"Kareem is not dumb enough to be selling drugs, knowing

BUILT ON BROKEN PIECES

what they did to me. He's too smart for that. My son is going to be a doctor, and he promised me that."

"I've been checking up on him, but something is definitely off. I can't put my fingers on it. These jailhouse walls didn't mean I couldn't get information on what was going on in the streets. I'll keep you posted, and I'll try my best to keep him in line the best I can."

"I really appreciate that, Jax. I really do."

The remainder of our visit was nothing but laugher and old stories from the good ole days. We were young and dumb but full of fun, and it didn't get any better. My life then was way better than what I had to experience after the accident, but it didn't make what I did right. I couldn't lose my son to the streets like he lost his mom to them.

Keyshia Cole - We Could Be

Oh, reality is taking control of me 'cause I know, baby
I know that you're not with me, Oh loving you boy
I wanna contradict my word
I belong with you, I do truly want to know (want to know)

"Yo, you did your thing with this song Aonika." Putting my hands over my mouth in surprise was how the song ended.

I couldn't believe that Aonika Monroe finished "Sincerely Love". I honestly thought she would get busy and put my song to the back of her to-do list, but she actually came through. Her Goddess locs went well with her chocolate features, and her smile showed me that she loved what she did. We sat at the boards basking in the aftermath of how great the song sounded.

"I told you. That's why I wanted you to hear it in person, with me, as we listened."

Her eyelashes were long, and it was the way she looked at me that created this feeling in my stomach. I couldn't pinpoint the sentiment, but I knew from our childhood encounters that I had to be careful. Our love for music always brought out the best in us; it was like it brought us closer together. On a level that most couldn't comprehend, creatives had a different way of looking at things.

"I'm glad I got the opportunity to hear it with you too. I think it was fate that you were at the studio that day. We haven't really kicked it since our senior year of high school when I beat you in the Who Got Next talent show."

"Oh, I see you bringing up old stuff. I actually let you win."

"Let me win? Are you serious? I had the crowd at my fingertips as I paid homage to one of the greatest who ever did it."

"I still can't believe you chose a Michael Jackson song. That wasn't even your style, but it worked. You got a standing ovation. It was your dancing skills that shocked me. You were always the slow jams type of guy, but you stepped out of your comfort zone to win that."

"Sure did." I got up from my chair and tried to remember some of the moves I practiced months for. We laughed until our stomachs were hurting.

"So, listen, I wanted to share something with you, Cash. This stays here until the official announcement. Okay?

"Okay."

"I signed with Interscope."

I couldn't help my excitement; I got up and grabbed Aonika in my arms, spinning her around, making both of us dizzy. If we were not on cloud nine before, we definitely were now. Where we came from, not too many people made it out. There was so much talent in Paterson that would never get the recognition they deserved. I was so happy that Aonika was getting her due.

"Oh, my God! I'm so happy for you, Aonika. I always knew you would make it."

"Come with me, Cash. I'll be going on the road soon, and maybe you can get some stage time and open up for me. You have a few songs recorded, right?"

"I have mad songs recorded, but I don't know, Aonika. This all seems so sudden. I'm so happy and proud of you, but I don't think I could leave yet."

"I wonder what's stopping you. Is it Jeda?"

"It's so many factors that play into it. She is not the only reason. You are asking me to move to L.A., on a whole 'nother coast. L.A. may have a lot to offer, but right now is not a good time for me."

The offer definitely caught me off guard, but it was a great wake up call for me. I had to grind harder. I hadn't put any music out yet; I'd been waiting on that right song to upload. Everybody in Paterson knew I could sing; they just never heard me sing anything original. It was always a cover. It was time for me to really start letting the world hear my music, and hopefully, it would pop off from there.

"Sometimes you have to seize the moment, Cash. Please think about it, and if you ever change your mind, you have my info. I will say this though. You need an up-tempo song to show how much of an entertainer you can be. Your dance moves got you that extra point; that's the only reason you won that talent show."

"Everybody loves a good slow jam that they could sway to, make love to, or reminisce to. You trying to say I can't show my dance moves on a slow jams track?"

"I'm not saying that, but I would like to see what dance moves you'll do to 'Sincerely Love' if we were to perform it."

It wasn't nothing but space and opportunity to show Aonika that I could still entertain, singing the hell out of a slow song. I never put much thought into dancing; it was

something that came along with singing. I had to be the ulti-
mate package these days; it took Aonika to make me realize
what I needed help with.

"Press play and get up; you gotta dance with me."

I grabbed her hands as the guitar and piano keys became
one. I didn't know what I was doing, but it felt right. I did a
little movement with my hips as she stood before me, never
letting go of my hand. My verse started, and I began to turn
the lyrics into dancing. It was slow, but it had a beat that was
defined by a one-two count. I rode the chorus proving to her
that I had what it takes. I was waiting for her verse to see what
she had to offer.

"We're grinding on bitches now?"

My heart almost ripped out of my chest. My whole foundation shook, and I couldn't believe I got caught in a misun-
derstanding. I quickly pressed pause on the song, realizing
that I dug myself into a deeper hole. It happened so swiftly
and unexpectedly that I didn't know what to do to diffuse the
situation. My head shot right to the door, and Jeda was
standing there with food in her hands.

"It's not what you think."

Why was that the first thing a person said when they get
caught? Maybe it was a distraction until they came up with
better reasoning. I don't know. It was all I could think to say. I
stood frozen; Aonika was now seated back in her chair,
playing word association with our words.

"What didn't you get? I don't want you around her. She
wanted you back then, and she still wants you now."

Jeda came rushing toward Aonika, ready for war. It was
like deja vu all over again. They never got along; they were
always at odds for whatever reason. I couldn't step between
them in time before Jeda threw the food she had in her
hands. It almost smacked Aonika in her face; she moved in
time for it to hit the floor. A second later, she would have

had curry chicken, rice, and cabbage all over her face and body.

I couldn't believe Jeda did that, but when a woman was mad, there was nothing they wouldn't do. It was built-up frustration, for many reasons, but this definitely didn't look good. Me trying to explain myself now wouldn't make a difference. I didn't have it in me to run after her; I was getting tired of always having to prove myself.

If we had communicated, she would know that I was doing a song with Aonika. Instead, she wanted to react before knowing the actual facts. Sometimes things were not always as they seemed. We no doubt were having a good time, caught up in a moment, but it was nothing. I'm not going to front; me and Aonika had chemistry, but I knew who I wanted to be with. That was where trust came in.

"Are you okay, Aonika?"

I grabbed some paper towels and tried to clean up the mess Jeda made. She had the whole studio smelling like some good ole Jamaican food. She showed up out of nowhere. I'd been calling Jeda with no answer, so I was surprised that she showed up at the studio. I looked back at my phone to see if I missed a phone call or a text message, and I had none. I looked at Aonika over, making sure that she was okay.

"I'm good. Why is she always so angry?" Aonika was making sure nothing got on her clothes. Her focus was on that, but she stopped eyeing me for an answer.

"She's not always angry; she has a different way of handling things. Is it the right way? Absolutely not, but that's her way, unfortunately. She is going to be alright; we're going to be alright. I'm going to give her some time to calm down."

"If you say so. I'm hungry now. Let's go grab something to eat. You down?"

I thought about it, and I concluded that grabbing some food wouldn't hurt if I knew I wasn't doing anything wrong. It was time for me to start stepping out of my comfort zone and enjoying what was around me. For years, I was chained to "what would Jeda think," but it got me nowhere. I missed out on a lot of things that could have prepared me for when I got signed.

"I'm hungry too. What you trying to eat?" I licked my lips, anticipating getting my grub on.

"Boy, you better stop licking your lips like that." A grin set on her face as she watched my lips, daring me to lick them again.

"You down for The Cheesecake Factory? Everything's on me."

"You must have forgotten what type of guy I am. I don't care if you're making money; I'm still a gentleman at the end of the day."

"So that means it's a date?"

This felt wrong, my mind trying to prove to Jeda that it really wasn't nothing. When you were in a relationship, you gave up a lot to make the other person happy. All this time, I was always the one sacrificing. Kareem's words resurfaced.

Jeda has been running this dude ragged since she met him.

What if that was a true statement, and I didn't notice I was caught up? Caught up loving someone who couldn't love me back or love me the way I was supposed to be loved? I honestly couldn't blame her. I now knew what her childhood was like, but it was only so much a person could take. I couldn't continue being a punching bag and the person she took all of her frustration out on. I needed more.

"You barely touched your food. I thought you were hungry?" Aonika looked from her side of the dimly lit booth we were sitting at.

The Cheesecake Factory was a dope spot with some banging food, but I wasn't in the mood. I thought my mind would be right to enjoy some good cuisine and good company, but of course, my mind was on Jeda. Wondering if she made it back home safely, I kept checking my phone. I did send her a text saying sorry. I didn't even know why I was apologizing. It probably was making me more guilty in her book.

"I lost my appetite, but I'm definitely taking this home to grub on later or tomorrow for lunch." I looked down at my chicken madeira and shrimp scampi and tried my best to eat some of it while it was at least warm.

"Can I ask you something?"

"Most definitely, you can."

"Why her?"

"What do you mean why her?"

"You could have any girl you wanted, both then and now, but you still continue to go through the same cycle with Jeda. Does she have something on you that you don't want anybody to know about?"

I chuckled.

"I love hard, Aonika. I don't give up on people; that's always been me. It may seem like Jeda and I are not compatible from the outside looking in, but Lord knows we are. Does she have a temper problem? Yeah, she does, but she's loyal, and I don't have to worry about her being with me for my talent. Every girl that I have come across had an agenda. They wanted the clout that came with me being a singer and family with two of the most well-known people in Paterson, Mase and Kareem.

"Not every girl."

Aonika's long eyelashes batted at that revelation. Her smile invited me to ask her what she meant by that.

I knew the underlying message she was trying to convey, and I couldn't leave her out there. So I entertained her.

I leaned up and called her bluff.

"Name one girl that showed me different, other than the one I'm with."

She leaned up and with a momentous smirk. She wet her lips and looked me straight in my eyes.

"You're looking at her."

I admired Aonika for not backing down and saying what was on her mind. She could have any guy she wanted. She was a rising star, beautiful, and successful in her own right. We never clicked like that. I enjoyed our conversation and our love for music; you never knew what we could build on another level. We had potential, but my focus was on Jeda.

"You're dope, Aonika, like really dope, and to have you on my arm and be my girl would be a boss move, but my heart belongs to Jeda. I would want to give you my full, undivided attention; that's what you deserve. Someone that is into you and only you."

"That's real nice of you, and I wouldn't want anything less. You're a great man, Cash, a talented one at that. We could be friends, but I can't wait forever."

She planted a soft kiss on my forehead before leaning back in the booth. Was that her way of telling me she'd wait until I sort out my lovers' quarrel? I had some things to really think about; my relationship was really falling apart. I didn't feel as optimistic as I did before; I was all out of ideas. What was a man to do?

Fadeaway

A basketball shot can be referred to as a 'fadeaway' when the shot is taken while the player is jumping away from the basket. This shot requires a high level of skill and is used to create space between the shooter and their defender.

J finally caved in and got our room, but I wasn't excited as I usually was. I was generally looking forward to some gushy, but not today. I had other things on my mind, but I had to deal with this to check this off my list. This was a big year for me, and I wasn't letting anyone ruin that for me. I knew what I wanted, and if I didn't get it, I had to be man enough to move on in hopes that one-day, Qwana would come to her senses before it was too late.

I made it to the hotel before her, so I had some time to think about what I was going to say and how I was going to approach the situation. I didn't want to sound like a little female, but anything I said would show my vulnerability. Who

125

was I kidding or trying to front for? Nobody knew my situation but my family. They might clown me, but they had my best interest at heart, so I had to stop playing myself.

I made my way onto the balcony; it was so peaceful. It was where I came to clear my head. It was a little cloudy, but the rain hadn't started yet. They called for a thunder warning throughout the city. I took it all in before I felt drops of water bounce off the railing, creating a sound so calming. I looked to the side, allowing the droplets to hit my face. My dad used to make me practice rain or shine; it brought me back to those days.

My phone vibrated, signaling that I had a text.

Q - *I'm here, where are you?*

I replied back.

I'm in the room.

Every time I referenced this room, I always wanted to say I was home. My mind made me believe that Qwana and I were actually together, together. Like we lived together, she was coming home from a long day of work or an outing with some of her friends. Would we ever be able to share those moments? Were these moments important to her? I wondered if her husband felt the same way I did when she told him she was on her way home.

My stomach tightened thinking about that last part. When mentioning Qwana, you had to bring up or think about her husband. They were one, tied together by holy matrimony and the consecration of their marriage. She never really talked about her marriage, and I really didn't care, but these days, I wondered, questioning how we got here, four years later.

Overlooking the city, I heard a knock letting me know that Qwana had made it to our room. I took in a little more of what the light drizzle had to offer. I took one last long, deep breath before I made my way to the door. Part of me was happy to see her, and another part had an agenda.

Qwana jumped straight in my arms when I opened the door. I caught her out of reflex, but the kisses she was giving me had my dick hard in a trice. I held her with one arm and closed the door with the other. I backed her up against the wall, still holding her plump ass. I kissed her slow but aggressively; her arms were around my shoulder as our lips wrestled.

"I... miss... you," Qwana expressed through kisses.

I carried her to the bed, set her right in the middle as she came out of her shoes, and I slowly pulled down her jeans. I admired her curves; she wasn't thick, but she had some meat on her bones. She was aging like fine wine, and her body was straight and tight. She had her shirt off before I was able to even get to that part.

I pulled her to the edge of the bed, kissing down her stomach. I kneeled down, lifting her legs. I found her clit, massaging it in a calculated rotation, sending her body into overdrive. I replaced my now wet fingers with my wet tongue and turned it up a notch. She was in a trance, and this was only the beginning. As my tongue played with her most sensitive area, my index finger found her pussy hole, and we got in sync.

It was time to talk my shit.

Qwana rode the wave as her orgasm was building up.

"If you keep playing around, you won't be getting none of this."

I could tell I had her right where I wanted her by the way she was meeting my tongue and finger with her own rhythm. Her pleas for me to keep going almost caused me to bust, and I wasn't even undressed. I continued.

"This my pussy, and I don't like sharing."

Her drip coated my finger and tongue concurrently, and a

sexy moan inched its way up her vertebrae. She couldn't even speak, and that was how I wanted it; I only needed her to listen. I was juggling Newton's three laws of motion. I wasn't missing a beat; the stroke of my tongue, the penetration of my finger, and the vibration of my words created a puddle on the edge of the bed.

"You promise not to give my pussy away?"

Qwana's moans grew louder, and her body came to life like she was being shocked by a defibrillator.

Hold. Clear.

Her body went limp, zapping her of all her energy. I heard sniffles like she was crying; I was smiling at first. I thought I was that dude, but as I stood to my feet and looked at Qwana's face, I knew that wasn't the case. I wasn't sure what I did wrong or if I violated her in any way. I thought she was enjoying it. I immediately went into panic mode.

"You good? Why are you crying?

"Give me a minute."

She scooted her way up to the top of the bed. She patted the space next to her so we both could lay down. I was confused, but I wanted to know why she had tears in her eyes. She wasn't crying hysterically, but she was dropping a few tears. We laid on the pillows, and I looked toward the ceiling, and she laid on her side, facing me. I awaited her answer.

"You make it seem so easy to up and leave my husband, and it's frustrating sometimes. You have in your head this fairytale life that you want, but that's not my reality. What I can say is you have me thinking. I never even thought about us having a life outside of these four walls. Not that I didn't want to, but I was already taken."

"Why can't we change that?"

"Change what, Mason?"

"Obviously, you're not happy in your marriage. If you were, it would have never gone past our first encounter. Stepping out here and there is one thing, but having a whole affair is another. Don't you want to be happy? What is he providing you that I can't?"

"Four years is a long time, so of course, feelings are going to grow. This was never supposed to happen. Nic and I were supposed to get back on track, but somehow, we stayed on the path to destruction. I had some of my best years with him."

I turned my attention to her damped eyes, making it a point to look at her.

"Your future could look so much brighter if you let it. Y'all relationship has been done. Give me my chance."

Silence.

Since she couldn't fill in her next words of dialogue, I continued.

"You're not saying why you can't leave him; you're not giving me a plan to leave him, so why am I wasting my time? This shit stops today, and that's on God!"

I sat up in the bed and looked her way, folding my arms across my chest. Was I ready for her to choose her husband over me? I wouldn't know until faced with it. It is hard making decisions that could change your life forever, but I needed to give her that extra push. If I didn't apply that pressure, she would never leave him.

"Like I told you, I've been thinking about what you've been saying. That's a step right there. I have to get all my ducks in a row as well, Mason. This is not only about you and what you want. This affects me as well; I have more to lose."

"But you have so much more to gain."

"Fearless Mason ready to take over the world. It's cute and sexy at the same time, but my wisdom tells me this won't be a walk in the park. Focus on your season, and I'll make sure we're good on this end."

"This time, that won't work. I told you how I felt, and I'm serious. To focus on my season, I have to get this straight, me and you. I need a clear mind and someone supportive, and if that's not you, you need to let me know."

"I hear you, and I'm working on it. Until then, let's enjoy the rest of this night. Let's go to Je's Restaurant in Newark."

"The soul food spot on Harsley?"

"Yup, let me go get—"

"Wait. You're going out in public with me? That's a first. Are you serious?"

A smile spread across my face. I couldn't believe it, but I'd take it. Hopefully, this played out the way I needed it to. I never really got to experience Qwana out, around people. Our personalities matched in the bedroom, but I wondered what her vibe was in public. I was hyped for it, actually, and I couldn't believe she volunteered.

I DIDN'T KNOW WHAT GOT INTO QWANA, BUT SHE EVEN WANTED to drive in the same car. We had the room for the night, so she left her car at the hotel while we went to Newark. We talked and laughed the whole ride. She had never been in my car, so she loved the smell of Little Trees Black Ice air freshener. It had my car smelling like a straight-up cologne shop, and the ladies fell in love each time.

There were never any parks by Je's Restaurant, and today I didn't want to get aggravated with looking for one, so I went right to the parking lot a few blocks over. I never took Qwana out on a date, so I had to show her I was a gentleman. We learned about each other through pillow talk, never really putting our words in action, never even fact-checking to see if our stories lined up with how we were living. I felt like I knew her, but only time would tell if I really did.

My arm rested around her shoulders as we walked in unison. The rain had stopped, making it damp and muggy. Je's was a little hole in the wall spot that served some bangin' soul food. It gave me a family feel; it was like you were eating right out of Grammy's kitchen. All your cousins and aunties were invited. We found a little booth in the back and got comfortable.

"Thank you for choosing Je's tonight. What would you like to drink?"

We ordered our drinks and looked over the menu some more. We settled on our meals, and the rest of the night was ours. We sat across from each other, ready for a night of good vibes and good conversation. They had the radio playing old school jams that my grammy and dem used to sing. "Lady" by The Whispers was playing in the background—grown folks' music for sure.

"Are you ready for the season? I won't be seeing much of you. When basketball is on your brain, nothing else matters."

Qwana was right about that. When the season started, I shut out everything else to focus on winning games. This year was personal for me; I was being thrust into my next level of life. Whether I was prepared or not, life would go on, and that was sometimes hard to wrap my mind around. I was ready for the season, but I wasn't sure if I was prepared for what was after.

"Yeah. I'm as ready as I'll ever be. We were 20-13 last year. It was one of my best years stat-wise. My scouting sheet is not looking too shabby."

"Where would you want to end up?

"What if I tell you I'm thinking about exploring other options outside of basketball?"

It felt funny coming out of my mouth, but it was an honest question. It was something that I was seeking answers to. I wanted to know how the ones closest to me felt about it. It was ultimately my decision, but I still cared what they thought. To have people around you pushing you to do and be your greatest was not something that everybody could say they had. I wasn't sure yet where Qwana fit, but I'd soon find out.

"This is not the first time I'm hearing this, Mason. You have alluded to it many times. Are you still thinking about going to culinary school?"

One of the many things I was going to invest in when I was getting that NBA money was restaurant chains. I'd always loved cooking. The only difference was I wasn't going to be the cook. Most people didn't know I had that talent; they didn't care to know. All they saw was me with a ball in my hand. For the past few years, I'd been cooking Thanksgiving dinner for my family without help from my grams.

"Yup. That's still a possibility. I would hire a chef until I finish school, and then once I'm done, I can take over. By then, hopefully, the restaurant will be ready to open up a second location. I want to call it Courtside, a sports bar atmosphere with flavorful food and top-notch drinks."

"That sounds super Do—"

"Mason, is that you over there with your sexy ass? With a body like yours, I didn't even know you ate food." I wasn't sure how that was even a compliment. My face fell in my hands, not ready for the foolishness that was about to take place.

Qwana and I both looked toward the payment corner to see Kima and Rhonda popping their gum. From the looks of it, they were waiting for their takeout. They were some freaks from around the way that I busted down a few years ago. They were down with the get down, and that was a night I'd always remember. They walked over to our table unannounced, completely ignoring that I didn't want to be bothered.

"I knew that was you over here. I haven't heard from you in a while. What, you forgot about us?"

"Kima, if you don't go ahead with all that. There wasn't anything to forget. Leave us be, and take your busted friend with you." I can't believe she was trying to showtime. She was mad that I acted as if they didn't exist after I nutted all over their faces. Seeing me out, enjoying a lady friend had her panties in a bunch. I looked from the hood boogas to make sure Qwana wasn't falling for their childish mind games. I couldn't tell, but at this point, they were irritating the hell out of me, standing there looking dumb.

"Boy, you ain't even all that; you better hope I never release our sex tape," Kima, the bold one, uttered and slapped her ghetto counterpart high five like she was doing something.

Even if she did have a tape of us, I didn't care. Did I want my goods plastered all over the place? Nope, but I wouldn't let her see me sweat. She wasn't even trying to get a rise out of me; she was trying to get Qwana's attention. Kima kept looking her way, waiting for Qwana to say something. And Rhonda was standing there next to Kima, egging her on like the hype man she'd always been.

"It's always young chicks like you who gave good women like me a bad name. I suggest you go back over there to get your food before we end up on a Smack DVD for reasons other than battle rap."

Qwana's words were surprising, but I guess it was needed. It made Kima get back on her feet after grabbing a chair from a table in front of us. Qwana's stare was bone chilling; she meant every word, and she didn't take her eyes off of the ghetto superstars. I couldn't believe this was happening. Now Kima was close enough for us to smell her cheap perfume that smelled like feet mixed with weed smoke. Probably wasn't even perfume now that I think about it.

"Listen, lady, nobody was talking to you with your wack ass bob. None of the older men wanted you, so you had to rob the cradle. Isn't it a law against you sitting back here hugged up with someone that could be your son? His dick ain't that great for you to be begging for some jail time."

"He must have given you the groupie dick; that's why you mad?" I chuckled at Qwana's remark. She was holding her composure very well. Mature, actually, and I was falling more in love. Most girls would have jumped up, ready to fight and make a scene, but Qwana played it super cool.

"Old lady, you better be glad I can't catch a case, or me and my girl would have dragged you up out of here. Today, I'm going to let you live. You best to believe once your dried-up pussy turns your head, somebody else will be on his dick. It might be me, it might be Kima, or the other hundreds of women who got to experience what little Mason is working with. You ain't special, trust me."

Kim and Rhonda laughed like Qwana was a comedy on Def Jam, super funny. Before she walked away for good, she came back to say one last thing. Apart from me wanting to get up and escort both of them out, Qwana handled her own until Kima walked back up to the table.

"If I were you, I'd keep an eye on him," Kima mouthed. She turned around in a swift motion knocking the Pepsi right on Qwana's shirt and pants. Before you know it, Qwana jumped up and socker bopped Kima right in her face. Before Rhonda was able to jump in and swing, I got right in front of Qwana, who didn't want me to hold her back.

The owner and some staff ran over while everybody looked on, entertained by what was taking place. This was not what I meant; I wanted to have a chill night. Kima had it coming, and I was kind of glad that Qwana knocked her off her feet. We didn't tolerate any type of disrespect. Voices were at a level of hostility, and it was hard to end until the owner grabbed Kima and Rhonda's food and escorted them to the door.

"I'm sorry. You guys have to go as well. I'll put your food in a to-go container." I didn't protest. I understood he had to run a business.

"Make sure you keep your bitches at bay next time, or it won't end so well." Qwana grabbed her pocketbook and stormed out of the restaurant, leaving me waiting for the food and wondering how she was supposed to get in the car when I had the key. I hurried and grabbed my things, shaking my head in the process. We were getting hit from all angles, but I was up for the challenge.

"Keep one's nose to the grindstone. Everything else will fall into place."

- Dom

I didn't know if I was a good salesperson or not, but I was done with what Dom had supplied me with. I pounded my chest as I made my way from the bathroom. I was home. Between school and chilling down in the Vill, I hadn't been home a lot. The house had been quiet; with Mase moving out and Cash on the run, it hadn't been much movement on the second floor. I was met with the smell of bacon as it invaded our area of the house. It reminded me how we would wake up on Saturdays and Sundays to a full breakfast spread as kids. It was a great way to start our morning, and today wouldn't be any different.

The sun from my room window told me that at least the sun was out. I wasn't too sure about the weather; it had been unpredictable. I threw on my Rocawear jean shorts, some fresh constructions, and made my way downstairs as the Anointed Pace Sisters sang about if God was in a building. It was a song I was all too familiar with; my grandmother played it like it was the number one gospel song in the country. She had her back to me as I entered the kitchen, humming the tune, believing every word.

"Hey, Grammy. You got it smelling good down here." I went over to the stove where she was and gave her a kiss on the cheek. I towered over her petite frame as I watched her work.

"Boy, if you don't have a seat and let me finish up this food." She giggled, and I obeyed her command, but not before grabbing me some Sunny Delight.

Growing up, I would love to see her off to work. I knew that was when I could cut up and run the streets. These days, I liked to see her off to make sure she was leaving safely and to pray for her return. She had some papers on the table with her glasses, probably paying the bills for the month. While she wasn't looking, I slipped $250 under the documents, hoping she didn't see me. My eyes caught the top letter, and it was another letter from the bank. I had to hold my composure. I didn't want her to know I was snooping.

"Kareem, what are you doing?"

Damn.

"Grammy, what's this?" I held up the letter, already knowing the answer. I wanted to see what she would say.

"I don't need you meddling in my business now. You boys are grown, but that's my business." She was grabbing up all the papers when the money dropped. She looked at me with wide eyes, surprised that it was there.

"Your business is our business. Remember you used to say that to us when we were younger? Don't try and change it up now. Why didn't you ask for help, Grammy?"

"Where did you get this money from? The last time I checked, you didn't have a job, Kareem." She slammed the money in front of me like it was evidence in a murder case.

I didn't want to lie, but what was I going to say? *Oh, I sold a little pot at my school so I can take care of you?* She probably would slap me for that sad truth, and I didn't need that type of fever. I did apply for a valet parking job a few weeks back, so maybe I could use that for my money trail.

"I'm doing valet at Garden State mall now. Only on the weekends when I don't have school."

"That's supposed to be your study time, baby. I can pick up some extra hours at the job. I want you to finish school and stop worrying about me."

"We want you to stop working and retire, so why would I want you to pick up extra hours, Grammy? I'm a man now, and it's only right that you allow me to chip in around here. It's no longer up for debate. You turned all of us down before, but I'm gonna talk with both Cash and Mase and tell them it's time."

"It's time for what?"

"It's time for us to fully start taking care of you. Yes, we are in school, and we need to focus on that, but you sacrifice for us, and that's exactly what we are going to do for you. We have listened long enough; we are about to do it our way."

It wasn't much she could say; she saw my face. One thing Grammy knew about me when I made up my mind about something, it was nothing anyone could do. She had to allow us to grow up; we were no longer the little boys she had to look after. I think a part of her wished that we were. I was probably the one who gave her the most problems. I was seeking the attention my mother should have provided me. I understood that after having a conversation with Jax, and he brought it to the surface.

"My bull-headed baby, you remind me so much of your

mother." She leaned over, kissing me on my forehead.
"Grammy appreciates everything you boys do for me. Mason
bringing in groceries, Cashmere making sure this house is
cleaned top to bottom, and now you are slipping me money.
You boys are not leaving me anything to do."

"Do the things you always wanted to do but you couldn't
because you raised us three knuckleheads."

The breath that she released from her body was of relief; I
didn't know if she meant for it to come out that way, but it
put a smile on my face knowing I could help her through this
next phase of her life. She cared about everybody else; now it
was time for her to care for herself. I knew what I had to do; I
had to put in a call to meet up with Dom.

"ALLURE" BY JAY-Z BLASTED THROUGH MY CRACKED WINDOW AS
I rode through Paterson, trying to get to my destination. The
seat was pushed back, and the heat stalked my face. I made my
way through the hood as I rapped along with the song. *Man,
I'm high off life. Fuck it, I'm wasted.* My adrenaline told me that
life was what you made it. Since I now knew what I had to do
and my grandmother accepted that I wasn't backing down,
money had to be made. It was now life or death for me. I had
to keep my word and show my grandmother that we could
take care of her.

I didn't have direct access to Dom, but Harvey was easy to
get ahold of. It was like he was waiting for my call. I didn't
know if that was a good thing or a bad thing, but as long as I
could get this money up, I didn't care. The five hundred that I
made off the ounce would be the down payment for another
round. I was already the man on campus, but now that I had
that Ooh Wee, I upped my celebrity. At Felician University,

word got out quickly; while it was a saturated market, the bud Dom gave me beat out the competition in no time.

Messing around with Rick and Reese, I sparked up every day, multiple times a day. At first, I was totally against it. I thought all drugs were the same until Jax schooled me some years back. My mother's sins haunted me so much that I was scared to live life at one point. Once I started to mature and understand the beast's nature, that was when I became a beast. I began to connect the dots and realize that we all chose our own path, and each day, that was what I did.

Caught in the matrix of my thoughts, I slowly pulled up to the warehouse gate to get my clearance. The night was kissing the sky, and if you didn't know better, you would have thought this block was deserted. There was minimal light at the entrance, but once you passed the threshold, it was clear that it was made like that. Driving up, you couldn't see the guards dressed in their all black with their assault rifles attached to their every move. I peeped that the first time I came through.

Dom's loyal guards were at my car door before I was able to even cut the car off. They moved like ghosts in the night, trying not to be seen but heard if necessary. Getting pat down was something I could do without, but that was the price I had to pay to get what I needed. Once the guard saw that I wasn't strapped and I wasn't a threat, they led me into the warehouse. I wondered what I would walk into today. Silence engulfed our footsteps as we made our way through the dark and gloomy warehouse with Dom's office as the destination.

We entered Dom's office threshold, and I followed the leading guard inside as the other guard stayed in the hallway. Dom's back was to me; he was overlooking the warehouse through his skybox window. I didn't want to take a seat without being invited to, but Dom didn't even acknowledge that I was there. His citrus-tobacco-woods cologne created the office scent and was an indicator of whose office it was. His attention was on whatever he was looking at while simultaneously rotating Baoding Balls in his left hand.

"Have a seat." He didn't even look back; he continued to relieve his stress as I took my seat, looking around his office.

Dom finally turned around in his fitted Giorgio Armani suit; he looked me directly in my eye, fishing for fear or any other trait that showed him I wasn't worthy of being in his presence. I held the eye contact, not backing down from his cold stare. He took a seat, freed his hands, and went in his drawer for a cigar. He didn't even have to say anything; one of the guards came with a lighter and lit the cigar as Dom pulled until it was fully lit. If this wasn't boss shit, I didn't know what was.

"You wanted to see me?" His deep voice carried a hard-edge bass between the tokes of his cigar.

"Yes, I wanted to see if I could get some more green to sell. I ran through what you gave me; it was so potent that it had everyone coming back for more. I can flip what you give me in no time with a great return on your investment."

"Is that right?" Smoke encircled around him as his shallow grin and deep, piercing eyes looked to me for an answer.

"Most def."

My confidence didn't waver by his lack of intuitiveness; it actually ignited a fire within me to show him better than I could tell him. I was pretty sure people came to Dom with offers all the time. He had the money and longevity, so people trusted his hustler's mentality. I felt like this was a business opportunity that he shouldn't pass up if he was all about his money. The cash flow was almost guaranteed. I waited for his answer as he caressed the scar on his chin, thinking.

"How much we talking?"

"A half ounce. I'll go through that in no time."

"The only way I'm letting you walk out of here with $2000 worth of product is if you work for me. We all got a dollar and a dream, and a dream is simply a dream without work. You understand me?"

I understood what he was trying to say, but he needed to run down more details. I wasn't pushing anything other than bud; I refused to have people out here strung out like my mother. I wanted no parts of that. Truth be told, my hand was itching to get ahold of some real cash. I always hustled, never wanting to be a burden on the back of my grandmother. The type of money that I could make could pay off the house debt, remodel, and get Grammy a new car. All while I still lived my best life.

"What exactly does working for you entail?" I was intrigued; I couldn't even front.

"Am I fronting you this work, or are you paying me my money up front is the question?" He leaned forward with a stone-faced stare, almost as if he was coming into the light from the darkness.

"I got five hundred."

"You're about fifteen hundred short, my man. So tell me how this benefits me again?

"Not only will it give you another stream of cash flow, but it's a new market that I can take over. My school is not the only school; I'm connected at Willy P, Kean University, and Rutgers. I can triple your investment and probably bring in more revenue than you have ever seen running the green machine."

Dom stood tall and came from behind his desk and leaned up against it not too far from where I sat. The only thing separating us was the smoke coming out of Dom's mouth and thoughts of the deal I pitched. With guys like Dom, you never knew what they were thinking. Powerful people like him couldn't afford to wear an expression on their face; he had to keep it neutral to keep people guessing.

"I like you. Most people would have folded or been scared to talk to me based on what they heard or what they've seen. But you wanted to find out yourself, and I respect that. I must reiterate how serious going into business with me is. I don't play about my money, and I expect nothing less of you."

I nodded my head in acknowledgment. He continued.

"So this is how it's going to go down. I will supply you with the product, a burner phone, and a few blocks to service. I've been having problems lately with a few of my blocks, and before I start dropping bodies, your job will be to fix it."

"Wait. My deal included selling at school. How is giving me blocks a part of that agreement?"

"You're using me for money, and I'm using you to clean up the mess that was made. That way, we both walk away with something. That little chump change is not enough to pay me for trusting you to be on my team. You gotta put in work, and that's my final offer."

He got up from his leaned position and went to his skybox window, almost dismissing me as if I didn't agree to his terms. A part of me was feeling disrespected, and another part of me thought the only way I could prove it to him was to show him. Running a few blocks was a big ask, and I didn't know if I wanted that responsibility. I most definitely could do it, but did I really want to take that chance?

"If I do that, then the revenue I get from the school goes straight to me. In turn, I'll keep the streets in check."

Dom's head turned slowly, digesting the counteroffer and realizing that I wasn't a youngin from the streets who didn't know their worth. Yes, I needed money, but he wasn't going to pimp me. My work would speak for itself; I always allowed my actions to speak louder than my words. I didn't know what would come of this, but I was willing to find out. I was excelling in my academics, and with the extra money coming in. I was sure to reach my fullest potential.

From his watchtower, Dom's gelid stare was fixated on his operation as his back offered parting words.

"Keep one's nose to the grindstone. Everything else will fall into place.

*J*f only I would have given Jax a chance back in the day, maybe I wouldn't be where I was today. He had all of the qualities of a good man, something I didn't realize he had back in the day. I was chasing after adventure; I wanted to have some fun. He was too soft; I needed a rough-neck, the one that MC Lyte rapped about in her song. I wanted someone who challenged me and not someone who did whatever I wanted. He definitely had that light-skinned, emotional behavior. That emotion now showed me he cared. It was the missing piece in my puzzle of affairs.

My mother had a tight leash on me. I was the oldest, so she expected more. Linda got away with everything, and it drove me crazy. Her freedom created a rebellion that tore apart a mother-daughter bond. Every chance she got, Linda taunted me. While I had to study, she got to run the streets. Linda was fearless, and I think my mother admired that about her. She did what she wanted and dealt with the consequences, and there was nothing anybody could do about it. I never had the guts.

"*Jane, you trying to go to Masonic with us tonight?*" *Linda proposed as she got ready in the mirror of her room. I sat on the edge of her bed as she got glammed up.*

Masonic Temple was a local bar in Paterson that we snuck into from time to time. We were only high school kids, but we always seemed to find a way to get in and party. The last time I was there, my mother found out and made an example out of me. The keyword in that sentence was me. She tried it with Linda but didn't have any luck putting fear in Linda's heart. That was why it was so easy for Linda to still sneak out and enjoy the nightlife. Not me. I had midterms coming up, and I needed to pass to get this scholarship for school.

"*Momma is not about to let us go anywhere. We have midterms this week, Linda. You crazy?*"

"*Momma ain't letting you go nowhere, but I'm going. Mason is waiting for me.*" *She got all giddy thinking about the good times she was about to have.*

I thought about it long and hard, but I knew it wouldn't be a great idea for me to skip out on studying. As much as I wanted to, I knew that I had more important things to do. I didn't have it in me to go toe to toe with my mother, so I tried my best to stay on her good side. I had one more year, and I was out of her grip. I was going away to college and never looking back.

"*What about studying, Linda? Don't you have midterms too?*"

"*You always worrying about school. You have to have some fun in between, Jane. You should come. You know Jax is going to be there looking for you.*" *She chortled. Everybody knew that Jax had a thing for me.*

"*Ewww, no. If I go, it wouldn't be for him. How are we going to sneak out? Mommy is still up.*"

"*She'll be knocked out before you know it. If anything, we'll have to go one by one and meet outside on the side of the house. Here, let me put you on some makeup and then go in my closet and pick out something. You ain't going with me looking like you straight out of Sunday service." She laughed; I didn't.*

"Mason brought them clothes for you; that's the only reason you got them."

"My point exactly. Get you a man like me. If you give Jax some play, he will buy you things too, but you're always mean to him."

"I'm not using that boy for his money, and I'm damn sure not using him to buy me clothes. Nope, I'm not doing it. I don't care how much he likes me." I was tired of her telling me to use what I had to get what I wanted. This wasn't The Player's Club; this was real life.

I always felt I lived vicariously through Linda, but that was the only way for me to have some type of fun. She pushed the limits in everything that she did. Not only was she dating a man older than her, but she also chose a street dude that went against everything our mother taught us. The more she got involved with Mason, the more she challenged my mother's authority. It was like she was trying to give my mother a heart attack.

"Girl, I don't know what to tell you then. You always say what you can't do and Mommy this and Mommy that. School this and school that. Those are excuses that keep you in fear, and that fear have you missing out on excitement and gratification, only to prove a point to our mother. For what?"

"For what? She's our mother, Linda. She wants nothing but the best for us."

"I don't want to be old and miserable like Mommy. I need a man, and I want to enjoy my life. All that lady does is work for those white people that don't care shit about her. I want more out of life than the repeated cycle of this fake American dream that she keeps trying to sell us."

"But—"

"Either you going or you not. I don't have time to be wasting on you. I have to make sure I'm looking good for my man."

I hated when she did that; she always made me regret following rules. It was like, why should I follow the rules if she didn't and was still living her best life? Her grades weren't bad, but it wasn't the 4.0 that I averaged. I had a lot more to lose than her, but that didn't stop me from wanting to go. I saw it Linda's way, but I wanted her to see it my way as well. She always saw things through her lens, but if only she would take a peek into mine.

"I'm staying."

"Awwww, look at the perfect daughter, doing perfect things to appease her perfect mother. You never want to have fun." Linda threw the makeup on the dresser and opened her room door to let me out. "I have to finish getting dressed."

"Have fun and be safe, Linda." She slammed the door in my face and turned up her music and got ready for her night.

That was so long ago, but it still was a reminder of the different lives we lived as teenagers. I excelled academically, and Linda excelled at doing whatever made her happy. In my quest to do the same, I stumbled upon the wrong attention. It wasn't wrong at the time, but as time progressed, it became more than wrong. I mustered up enough strength to pull myself from the car. On wobbly legs, my shoes met the dirt underneath as I made my way through the lifeless grounds of Laurel Grove Cemetery.

It had been twelve years since I'd been making this same journey on this same day to pour my heart out, never knowing if I had been forgiven for my past sins. The pounding of my heartbeat almost shook the ground as I made it to my destination. The coldness of the moment sent a chill from my toes to my dry throat as I held back tears. No matter how many times I did this, it never got easier. This day always brought me to my knees, but this time it wouldn't break me.

My hand traced the letters of the tombstone.

Linda Cotton | Mason "The Major" Cotton: Two Souls Connected Together Even in Death. I read it, always wondering why my mother chose to put those words when she hated

Mason. That and many questions that plagued my mind down through the years. Even in death, they got to be together. It angered me, but as I started to become myself again, I realized that they were meant for each other. As much as I wanted to believe that what Mason and I shared was special, it was clear as day that wasn't the case. We shouldn't have crossed those boundaries.

I let the tears fall; it would give me a fresh start. All through the year, these tears built up, waiting to be released. Pent up, in this bubble that I couldn't see myself getting out of. All these years I lived there, only making appearances on this day to bare my soul to two people I hoped were listening, praying that God let them see how sorry I was for the part I played in ending their gift of life. The early morning crisp air assisted me in allowing words to formulate from my mouth, each word coming from a place of growth, of a clear mind for once in my life.

"Linda, I... I really miss you, sister. Life hasn't been the same without you." I took a deep breath, relaxing a little. That was the feeling Linda always gave me when I was around her. She didn't have a care in the world. I continued.

"Mason, you better be taking care of my sister up there. Knowing you, you are. I'm not going to lie; a part of me still misses you too." I sucked my teeth, not believing after all these years, I still loved this fool. That part still angered me and brought me back to my indiscretion. It was my road map to destruction. Sometimes I wondered if I really knew what love was. Was it supposed to hurt so much?

"Linda, I know you're tired of hearing this, but I'm sorry, sister. The way you described Mason and how he made you feel made me long for his touch. I was chasing the same high you were. Never knew I would get to experience what he had to offer, and once I did, I couldn't get enough. The way he handled my body, I couldn't stand that he was making you feel the same. In the beginning, I felt bad, but when I left for college and came back and saw the life you guys built, it enraged me."

I wiped my face, erasing evidence that tears even existed.

This year I wouldn't leave here looking to mask my pain by shooting up and nodding off until it was time to do it again. I was one with my mistakes, but that didn't mean I didn't have my moments. I chose to move on these days, not staying stuck and entangled in a web of pessimism. The more I believed I could get clean and get better, the healthier I got. I had to get to the root of the problem, where it started. I had to have it in my head to understand what I could have done better. And the answer to that was nothing.

"You both will be proud of me; I got my strength back. I should be moving into my own apartment soon. I got a job, and I think I'm gonna go back to school. This time next year, I'll be telling you guys a different story. Shoot, maybe I'll even find me a man and get married!"

What if?

I had to get going. It was bittersweet, but I was looking forward to what was next for me. I had to prepare myself for this long road to see Jax; at least I'd be on the bus surrounded by people. That way, I could keep my emotions in check. I was determined to beat this, and being with Jax on the day he lost his friend, his brother as well, could help both of us, even if it was for an hour. We all had great memories together, and to be around someone who understood would go a long way.

———————

I WAITED FOR JAX'S ARRIVAL, NOT SURE HOW HE WAS HOLDING up. He told me this was always a tough day for him too. He felt he let his brother down by not being there to save him. We sorta shared the same sentiment, which continued to bring us closer than we ever were. I wasn't much of a junk food eater, but I had to get something out of the vending machine to keep my mind busy. I guess that's why I'd been gaining weight; that was all I'd been doing lately. I hadn't looked this thick since way back when.

The sirens went off, and the inmates started filing in one by one. I spotted him as soon as his frame made it through the doors. Jax had bags under his eyes, and it looked like he had been crying. I couldn't imagine being locked up and not sharing my feelings to stay alive. You couldn't show weakness in jail, and I always wondered how he handled this day for so many years behind bars. I guess you could say I was locked up too, but at least I was able to suppress my feeling with the drugs that flowed through my veins.

We embraced, this time not caring what the guards' rules were. We hugged strength into each other, speaking without words. One thing for sure, being in Jax's arms felt so good; I melted, wishing I could stay there forever, but the guard cleared his throat. We both took our seats, not making eye contact, avoiding the inevitable. We were trying to gauge where to start; we most definitely had to talk about this day, what it meant, and how it changed our lives the minute the coroner pronounced them dead.

Our eyes finally met.

"How are you holding up?" Jax's question was loaded, and I knew it. He had expressed on various occasions that he wanted me to stay clean; it looked good on me. He was fishing and didn't want to come out and ask me if I felt like using.

"I'm not sure, honestly. I never had anybody to talk through this day with. It was always me and the needle. Every year when I left the cemetery, I went searching for a way to quiet the demons that spoke to my broken state. It's like I'm waiting to fail, to fail you, to fail Kareem, and to fail myself. That's what I was used to." I took a deep breath, realizing how weak my mind used to be. I was so bright but yet so dumb at the same time. I couldn't study my way through this; this was real life.

"I didn't even get a chance to properly grieve. Couldn't even go to the funeral, they denied my bail and told me I couldn't get permission to attend, we weren't blood related. That was my brother!" Jax's voice declared at a volume that caused everybody to stop what they were doing to figure out what happened at our table.

"You know, I didn't get a chance to make it to their funeral either. It still haunts me to this day that I watched the hearse and limos pass me going up Godwin Ave. I could still see the look in my mother's eye when she spotted me. She turned her head like she didn't see me, like I didn't exist. Why didn't she stop for me? Why, Jax?" Jax's fingertip wiped the fresh tears that spilled over.

"I wish I could answer that for you, Jane, but I can't. Those are questions that we probably would never get an answer to, and we have to be okay with that. Sometimes we don't understand the things we do, but we do them. When we hurt, nothing else matters but that hurt. Some of us would do anything to make it right."

Jax's hands met mine. It was something that I couldn't explain, I couldn't put into words; it wasn't anything more. Before the haters on the sideline pulled us apart, we unlocked our hands, releasing better energy than when we started. The silent pause gave way to another subject, and I couldn't be happier. We were supposed to help each other through this day, not make it worse. Our visits were usually us reminiscing about the good ole days and helping each other get through these present days. But something told me that I wouldn't like the following conversation either.

"You remember the cat Percy from the Boulevard that used to steal cars for Dom back in the day? He used to have that garage over there on Montgomery Street, down the street from Montgomery Park. Everybody used to go to him to get their car fixed from the hood."

"Yeah. I know Percy. Why, he died? He used to be on the street with me. We never ran with the same people, though."

"Nah, he in here walking around here telling everybody we boys. Talking about he got set up, trying to prove his innocence to the wrong motherfucker. You can't believe no crackhead, thinking we got something in common."

My heart sunk; that was one thing people believed about me at one point in my life. It was going to be hard earning that level of trust back. But I had to trust myself first. He continued, catching himself and apologizing with his eyes.

"You know what I mean. Anyway, Percy still works for Dom. He came to my cell, asking for a favor and saw a picture of Kareem. He started babbling and told me before he got locked up, he saw Kareem a lot in the Vill. Harvey was trying to get Kareem to do a few jobs with him. He is not sure what happened, but he saw Kareem spend some time with Harvey in VIP at some club. You gotta go check up on him, Jane. I'm a little worried. It's not much I could do behind these walls."

"I think I'm ready to see Kareem anyway; he needs to know that I'm clean. Hopefully, he will not get caught up with Dom. He was one evil person. I used to hate the way he looked at me with his black ass. He creeped me out, but he knew not to say anything, Mason would have checked him. He wanted to be Mason so bad but never had the balls to stand up against the king. That's why he constantly challenged you.

"Don't remind me." Jax's eyes turned dark, and he became another person. "I should have killed him when I had the chance." He came back to life, realizing his surroundings. He looked around, making sure no one heard him.

We never talked about his case; his story was always that

he got caught slippin'. When Mason died, it clouded his vision; he couldn't think without his brother. Not even a couple days after Mason died, Jax got brought up on some murder charges and had been in jail ever since. I started visiting him like a year ago, and it had been my routine. Jax and his sister helped me through this whole journey. If he would have played his cards right, he would've probably been where Dom was. They say that it's two ways out the streets, and that's jail or death; I wonder if he was happy with his ending?

"I'll call Kareem when I leave here and tell him to come over to your sister's house so we can talk. I miss my baby. For the first four years of his life, it was him and me. I don't know how I did it, but I did. Hiding that I had a baby from my family while juggling school took a toll on me; I don't know how I kept it a secret that long. I cried almost every night."

"I thought you wanted to get away. Shoot, I didn't blame you. Everybody was so proud of you; you did what we couldn't, Jane. I missed you those four years, but it was so much going on that the time passed me. And then when they told me you were home, you came out on the porch with this dark chocolate skinned baby. He was all giggles and spit bubbles. Little baby Kareem jumped right into my arms, not even knowing who I was, and we've been cool ever since."

I was known as the girl who went to college and came back with a baby. I got humbled real quick. I don't think Linda ever forgave me for keeping that secret. Yes, we had our issues, but we still were close. When I came back from college, that was when we really started to grow apart. I chalked it up as we were getting older, we didn't like the same things, and plus, she didn't live at home like I did. That's when I started asking myself was blood really thicker than water.

"At that time, it felt right but felt so wrong in so many ways, but I was already caught up; it wasn't much I could do. I made do with what I had and made the best of it. I wouldn't change it. I would have actually still kept it a secret, but the only difference is I would have believed in myself a little bit more, giving myself credit for the things I still accomplished as a single mother and college student."

"You still got a degree, and that's what I was proud of you for. Most girls would have given up, but you stayed the course and completed what you started. You have to give yourself credit for that if nothing else. How many people from our era can say they have a bachelor's degree in early childhood education? You thought I forgot? I was wondering why you would settle for a Nabisco job when you love working with and teaching kids?"

"How can I teach somebody else kid when I can't even get mine to talk to me?"

"It's going to take some time; Kareem will come around. You have to show him consistency. That's one of his many layers of how he was built."

"Wrap it up. Five minutes and counting," the guards brought to our attention.

Our time was coming to an end. I assured Jax I would follow up with Kareem to see what he was up to. That didn't mean he would be open to talking with me, but I was willing to try. I missed him dearly. I felt it was more Jax wanted to tell me, but to keep me from jumping off the edge, he kept it to himself. One thing I did know; things left hidden could always be found, and if it was meant to come out, it would.

CASHMERE

Trey Songz - Gotta Make It (Feat Twista)
Shawty (Shawty), All I Got is a dollar and a dream
Is ya gonna roll wit' me? (roll wit' me)
You see I've tried a 9 to 5, and it just don't fit me
(Fit me) (No)
I can get us out the hood and have us livin' good
Ya feel me? (Oh do ya feel me)

"Bro, get up. I know you heard me calling you, telling you that the breakfast was almost ready."

I sat up in my bed, realizing who was terrorizing my sleep. It reminded me of when we were kids. Mase was always the first one who woke; he was on the court at 5 a.m. every morning, practicing and perfecting his craft. He wasn't the only one this time around putting in work in the wee hours of the morning. I came in not too long ago from my studio session. So while he was up shooting baskets, I was up trying to create timeless music.

"Dude, what time is it?" I wiped my eyes, waiting for Mase to answer. I guess he was holding out; he knew that would get me out of bed to look. My sidekick died last night, and I didn't bother to put it on the charger when I walked in. I was exhausted.

"It's time for you to get up; we're about to grub. Kareem jumped in the shower, and Grammy is watching her stories. I'm waiting for the biscuits, and I'm about to cook these eggs, and then we can eat, so get up."

Basketball season was due to start in a few months, so this was Mase's way of spending time with us before getting caught up in the game he loved. Around his neck was the apron Grammy brought him some years back. In white letters, it read "The Major Chef." Major was a nickname the streets called my dad when he played ball before getting hurt and changing professions. I remember when Mase first got it; it seemed like he never wanted to take it off. He cooked only to wear it and made sure nothing happened to it.

"Okay. I'll be down in a minute; I got in the house not too long ago. You messing up my sleep, bro."

"You and Jeda were up all night making me a little niece or nephew?" He laughed, knowing damn well he wasn't serious. He always told me he didn't care that I loved Jeda, that I still had to strap up. I couldn't afford to have kids so young. I guess this was my brother speaking now and not the father he always tried to be to me.

"Yeah, she told me she was pregnant last night. I don't know what I'm going to do." My hands met my face for the kill. Mase came to the side of the bed and forcefully moved my hands; he now was serious.

"You serious, yo?"

I couldn't even hold in my laugh; I guess my acting skills were A1.

"Nah, I'm messing with you, bro. I thought I would get a

little laugh of my own since you wanted to put that out in the universe. Jeda is still not rocking with me like that, so no cutty for me." This time it was the truth, and sometimes the truth hurt. I wished Jeda and I were slapping bodies and enjoying intimate time, but that wasn't my reality.

"Yo, y'all are off more than y'all are on. How is that even a relationship, Cash?" My brother was right, and I was trying to figure out the same thing. Was this the beginning to the ending of our relationship?

"I'm tired of fighting with her. I've been in the studio, putting all of my energy there. That's been the only consistent thing. Remember Aonika Monroe?"

"Yeah, the shawty you used to do those talent shows with that wanted you to bust her down? Doesn't she have a song that is blowing up all over MySpace?"

"I was always with Jeda; that's why I paid that no mind. But yeah, her. Anyway, she got signed to Interscope and is staying in Jersey to finish her album. And guess who she asked to help?" I was smiling hard. This would be the first paramount move of my career.

"Yo, that's super dope, bro. I knew your time was coming. I heard her song, and it doesn't sound bad. She repping for the chicks, but I can hear and see the star power that she has. What do you mean by 'help her' though?"

"She already has about five songs, but she needs ten more songs to close out her album. Label orders. She was supposed to fly to L.A. to finish, but she convinced them that it would be better to record where she started, and they agreed."

When Aonika broke the news she wanted to work with me, I was excited. She couldn't pay me right away, but once her album was done, the money would start flowing in. I believed in her, and I trusted her, so it wasn't about the money; it was the experience I was after. So far, it had been nothing but fun to be in a room full of creatives, creating what would soon be a platinum album, God willing. What I liked most, though, if she didn't like a beat, she always asked if I wanted it or if I saw myself writing to it for myself. I got a few beats from her, and the song I recorded last night in my session was thumping.

"This sounds like the break you needed to get your foot in the door, but I have to say, Aonika sounds like she is waiting for you and Jeda to call it quits so she can take her place. I ain't gonna lie; that would be a good look for you. People buy into celebrity couples, so that would most definitely sell records. That's called great marketing, playboy."

I never even thought about it like that. Aonika was cool peoples, and I wouldn't rule out a relationship with her. It wouldn't be for exposure; it would be because she is beautiful, talented, and sexy in every part of the words. I caught her a few times, staring at me in her studio sessions. I can't lie; the chemistry was definitely there. The more I was around her, the more it grew. Right now, I wanted to focus on her music, my music, and the possibility of my relationship with Jeda working out. I was not giving up yet.

"Bro, you know where my heart belongs." I finally got out of bed, now smelling the aroma of breakfast waiting.

"Make sure Jeda's heart still belongs to you too." Mase exited out of my room and down the stairs to check on the spread I knew he conjured up.

As my feet hit the hardwood floors, I let Mase's parting words marinate. I had minimum time to get ready. By this time, a low, ominous growl came from my stomach. One thing my grammy didn't play was coming to her table without brushing our teeth or washing our face. At least I could do that quickly and worry about getting dressed after. I might go back to sleep after eating to let my brain rest.

Last night's studio session woke me up creatively. I always felt comfortable with ballads, but I took Aonika's advice and gave music lovers something to dance to. I think that was my missing ingredient. This song was different for me, and I couldn't wait to hear what people thought. I had to figure out how to get feedback; hearing feedback from family was one thing, but I needed feedback from unbiased music lovers.

"What up, yo? Kareem peeked his head into my room on his way downstairs to Chef Mase's VIP breakfast.

"Reem, what up? I'm surprised to see you up. I guess Mase got to you first, huh?" I laughed, knowing Mase and Kareem's history. They always used to get into it as kids. Mase expected Kareem to do what he ordered him to do. Kareem wasn't having that by no means.

"He better be glad I had moves to make this morning. I was out late last night. I can't believe I beat you home. I looked in your room, figuring you stayed at Jeda's."

"Nah, she is still in her feelings. I was in the studio."

"I see you. Keep putting in them hours. They still got you in that run-down room of the recording studio?"

"That's all I could afford, and I'm cool with that. It gets the job done. My time coming, playa. I'll be in the main room soon." I believed that in my heart of hearts; it was levels, and I was almost to the next phase. It was time for me to stop talking about it and be about it. I even cut back my hours at the bank. It was time for me to take it full throttle while I had the momentum. Once the record label saw my work on Aonika's project, I almost guarantee they would see my worth.

"Respect. Let me know if you need some money; I got you." We bumped fists, and Kareem started to make his way downstairs. I didn't know where he was getting money from, but I knew his word was his bond, so he was a lifeline if ever needed. I went to the bathroom to get cleaned up and presentable to eat breakfast with the fam.

"Hey, baby." I kissed my grandmother on the forehead, passing her at the head of the table. My eyes landed on the spread before us; Mase went all out—fluffy French toast, scrambled eggs with cheese, turkey and pork bacon, and some grits with cheese. And then the biscuit was golden crisp. He topped that off with an array of fruit. He wasn't playing. One thing for sure; I was definitely going back to sleep after this.

"It feels like old times; I have all my babies here with me." Grammy was beaming with delight. She always wore a smile, even when life kept knocking her down. She played the hand she was dealt, and she played it well. I admired people like her who survived a time in history that we, as black people, would never get back. She saw the worst of it and still found reasons to smile.

"I'm happy we are all here too, Grammy." Loud chuckles and laughter filled the room after repeating the same words at different times, speeds, and tones. We were most definitely family. We grabbed hands to pray.

"God, we thank you for this beautiful day you have given us; without You, we are nothing. You are our life, health, and strength, and we want to say thank You. Continue to put Your hedge of protection upon these here boys, and keep them tucked in the center of Your perfect will. Bless this food we are about to receive. Let it be of nutrients to our bodies. Bless the great hands that prepared it, in Jesus' name, amen."

"Let's eat." Kareem rubbed his hands together, almost drooling over the food like a vulture. That boy knew he could eat; he was always in the refrigerator eating somebody's food. He never cared if it was a name on it or not. He probably was high, knowing him.

"How have my babies been, I mean boys been? I want to hear about school first and everything else after." She released a joyous low laugh, putting food on her plate, looking around for someone to answer. Her eyes landed on me.

"Everything has been going well, Grammy. School is coming along. I'm passing my current classes with A's. I got some good news the other day." Grammy couldn't wait for me to share, and it made me excited too.

"What is it, baby?" She put her fork down, waiting. Everybody gave me their full undivided attention.

"I was asked to work on Aonika Monroe's debut album; she got signed to Interscope Records." Grammy clapped her hands together; excitement overtook her. She jumped up out of her seat to give me a hug and congratulate me. I was super proud. She lit up a whole lot more at my news.

"You ain't tell me that. That's super big, Cash. I'm proud of you." Kareem joined in on the love.

"That girl always liked you, so be careful, Cashmere. Try to keep it about music. She was always sneaky to me, waiting in the shadows. I know a home wrecker when I see one. Don't put your eggs all in one basket, baby. Keep your options open. This is only one door, not *the* door." I was immersed in Grammy's wisdom, taking in all that I could. This industry was cutthroat, and I couldn't allow it to be the death of me as a person.

"I hear you, Grammy. I'm still working on my songs. I actually finished this song last night that I think could be my first single. That's if I get signed. I need some good feedback."

"Let us hear it," everybody agreed. I did transfer the raw and unmastered version to a CD; singing it without the track wouldn't do it any justice.

"I'll let you guys hear it, but this time I need other people's opinion as well. I need to start creating a fanbase. People know I can sing, but do people know I'm an all-around entertainer? Not yet, so I've been brainstorming on different ways I would get feedback before I could get it mixed and mastered to put on MySpace to gain notoriety."

A light went off in Kareem's head like he had the perfect marketing strategy.

"Jaquana and Grandpa are having a kickback tonight in

the Vill, and their parties are always jumpin'. I can have them spin your record to see what the crowd thinks. You ready for that?" Kareem rubbed his hands together, ready to let the world hear what I had to offer. The crazy part was he didn't even hear the song yet, and he was already backing it. That's love.

"I'm down; it's time." Deep down, how would I know if I was ready if I never tried? I had recorded plenty of songs this last year, trying to find my sound. The more I worked at it, the better I got. I had to take it to the next level, and working with Aonika was showing me that.

We enjoyed the rest of our breakfast with love, laughter, and the gift of family-ship. I now had a plan in motion. The kickback in the Vill was the perfect place; everybody who was somebody was going to be there. I went upstairs to grab the CD and put it in our stereo that was in the kitchen. We let the beat drop as we listened and ate and got lost in the song's mood. My head was down, as I dreamed about the day I would get to perform it in front of a live audience.

"YO, THIS SHIT JUMPIN." MASE DECLARED OVER FAT JOE telling the crowd to lean back. Mase, Kareem, and I surveyed the room, trying to decipher how our night would play out. It wasn't packed, but if the party from outside came in the red-lit living room, it would break the fire code. All of their furniture was moved out, and it wasn't nothing but space and opportunity. There was only one way in and out of the party, they were not using the back door, but Kareem made sure that we were by it in case something went down.

I didn't know when they would play my song, but I trusted Kareem to get the job done. I can't even lie; I was a little on edge, but it was no turning back. Tonight was only a taste of what I had to offer as an artist, so whatever the outcome was, it wouldn't stop me from recording until I got it right. I usually skipped out on local parties; Jeda always deemed them ghetto. Not in a bad way; she didn't like that every party ended in a fight or a shootout—the same reason Kareem had us guarding the backdoor like we were top-flight security.

"Hey, Mason. I see your babysitter let you out." Kima walked over and yelled over the music while her sidekick Rhonda followed. Kima snickered, slapping hands with her homegirl like they had one up on the competition.

"Kima, go 'head with all that. You better be glad my babysitter didn't stomp you and Mad Dog 20/20 over here out." Kareem and I looked on, not knowing what the exchange was about, but we chalked it up as another day in the life of a player.

"She wasn't going to do nothing but catch a beat down. Hopefully, we will meet again, but next time I won't be so nice. Come on, Rhonda. The party sure not with them." The two ladies stormed off, leaving dust on their departure. We all looked at each other and started laughing hysterically. This was nothing new for Mase; he always seemed to get caught up messing with these females. I didn't think he'd ever learn, but then again, he did slow down a lot. His women issues didn't happen as often as they used to, at least not when I was around.

"What was that about?" I had to know. That exchange was funny, and it seemed to have gotten under Mase's skin a little.

"Dem birds saw Qwana and me in Je's Soul Food last week, and they made a scene. Got us kicked out and messed up a night I was looking forward to, too. Kima was mad that I never gave her this dick again." Mase grabbed his crotch and stuck his middle finger up like Kima and Rhonda was right in front of us. We fell over laughing hard as the bass dropped to "Tipsy" by J-Kwon.

"Yo, let me go handle this," Like a game of charades, Kareem held his phone up. Mase and I both nodded our heads, signaling that we heard him. His rigid movements suggested that he was a little frustrated or irritated by whoever was calling.

Mase and I let him handle his handle while we continued to enjoy the party. A lot of people I went to high school with were in the place; it felt like old times. The only thing I was missing was my arm candy, Jeda; she always made me look better. It felt weird without her; I hadn't spoken to her since her food fight with herself last week. I still texted her good morning and I'm thinking about you texts, but they went ignored. At this point, I was used to it; this time I was letting her have her space. I tried avoiding thoughts of her, and I was mad as hell; I let myself go there, I shook it off, and continued with my two-step.

"Let's go get some air, bro. It got mad hot, real quick." This meant the real party was about to start. Mase read my mind. We made our way through the dancers and the different conversations going on. Everybody was enjoying themselves, and the night was still young. We stopped by this little cooler and got two bottles of water. House parties would always leave you thirsty. By this time, the party had moved mostly in the house with a few lingering needing air.

As we made our way outside, the coolness of the night hit our faces as we finally made it past the many people that were in our way. You could hear the music blasting from the inside, so we weren't missing too much of the party. The entrance was not too far from the party, so we slowly walked to get some much-needed air. It was live out here tonight, and I was happy to be able to get my mind off of things. I'd been working hard to keep my relationship intact with Jeda while also trying to jump-start my career, and it hadn't been easy. As Mase finished his water, I looked on as he was looking around, and I was trying to figure out what for.

"Bro, you good?" I mimicked his posture and became inspector gadget, trying to figure out what he was looking for or who he was looking for.

"Who are these Cadillac Escalades?" I didn't even peep the two rides, and I definitely didn't see the two guys standing outside of both vehicles not saying anything. You couldn't even look into their eyes; they were covered with dark black glasses. Could they even see? Were they secret service or something?

"That's a good question." It had to be somebody very important.

"Where's Reem?" It all made sense now. We didn't come out here to get fresh air; we came out here to keep an eye on Kareem. He had been acting weird, but what Mase had to understand was Kareem was his own man.

A loud, horrid scream stopped me from answering Mase but added more questions to the list of where the hell was Kareem. It was far in the distance, but the person's agony could be heard over the loud music and the different conversations held; everybody except Mase and I went back to what they were doing. I knew they heard it; it was still echoing in my ear. It gave me a funny feeling in the pit of my stomach. Mase and I both looked at each other, most likely thinking the same thing, but before we could exchange thoughts, we heard a door open and slam.

On cue and almost simultaneously, the dudes at the trucks pulled out their guns and cocked them. Our eyes focused on who came out the open door but were quickly redirected when we heard the ammo in the clip get positioned in the chamber. My heart rate sped up, almost running for cover but stopped when I saw who it was and who he was talking to. Mase's feet moved quickly; he saw who it was too. My eyes were now pleading with Mase not to make a scene; it wasn't the right place or time to play big cousin.

"Yo, Cash, they're playing your song." Kareem and his two suited friends slowed down as they took in the tune like they were hearing it for the first time on the radio. I watched the people outside bobbing their heads; they seemed to be feeling it, like the group of girls dancing to it outside the party door. They were souping each other up as they busted their move.

Kareem wasn't slick; he wanted to take our minds off the fact that something wasn't right. He did for a few seconds, but that was short-lived when they stopped in front of Mase and me. Once they were close enough to see in the night, I recognized one of the dudes. He was the same dude from the club that Mase asked Kareem about. It was something about the other guy that had our attention. He screamed money, power, and respect before he even opened his mouth. They stood before us, continuing to listen to my track.

"That's you singing?" His deep voice was now putting me on the edge. It was how it rumbled with the texture of his baritone. It was as if he was looking right through me as his dark eyes were waiting for an answer. I couldn't help but look at Kareem to see who this guy was, but his frustrated stare told me to answer the question.

"Yeah, that's me singing. I'm thinking about dropping it on my Myspace account to see if I could possibly get a record deal." He didn't even ask all that, but for some reason, he made me want to tell him everything. His presence intimidated me, his charcoal skin blended in with the night, and the way he towered over me had me wondering.

"You have potential; that's a no brainer, but the quality of your music needs work. You need a better studio and a better engineer. I have some connections that could help you out with that. Here's my business card; if you're ready to make some real moves, hit me up." He didn't even wait for my rebuttal or an answer. He walked away, and the dude from the club followed. He stopped before entering the opened door of the Cadillac.

"Kareem, remember what I told you. Make sure it doesn't happen again." He finally got in, and with that, he and his henchman were off.

I looked at the business card that he gave me, Dom Hardy of Hardy Enterprises. I wondered if this was my open door to getting the backing I needed for my career. I put it in my pocket for future consideration but wondered how Kareem knew Dom Hardy and what he demanded shouldn't happen again. Before I could even get out my line of questioning, Mase started with his.

"Yo, who was that, and why was he barking around orders like you his servant or something?" Mase's irritation was evident, and his protective traits were laced with every word.

"I don't have to answer to you; I do what the hell I want. It's my business, and it doesn't have anything to do with you. So lay off me, my nigga." Anger radiated off of Kareem, but it wasn't from what Mase said. It was more to the story.

"Kareem, is that blood on your shirt?" I walked up, trying to examine the red stains, but he pushed me away and made his way down the middle section back to the house they came out of. I had to hold Mase back; they definitely would have fought tonight. It wasn't the time or place to do so. It was something different about Kareem, and I wondered if it had anything to do with the mystery guy that just left.

Block (Foul)

A player can be called for a blocking foul if they impede an offensive player's path without having established legal defensive position.

For a long time, I was mad at my dad for dying; he was supposed to be Superman. Untouchable. Invincible Not only did he die, but he let my mother die with him. Knowing he didn't have superpowers built anger inside a world without my parents. If Coach Patterson didn't take me under his wing, giving me pieces of what my dad should have, I would have been mad at the world forever. He filled a void that most kids would never get to fill who were fatherless.

Coach Patterson was my high school coach but also my mentor when I needed answers about life. He was my soundboard when it came to things my dad should have been here to guide me through. With the season starting soon, I had to get my dose of wisdom from the man who kept me on track all these years. To this day, he still kept up with all my games and highlights and even attended some when he wasn't coaching.

The next couple of months, my mind would be preoccupied with our season, but today's conversation wasn't going to be about the game we loved; it was about business. I needed to make moves and make moves fast. I had a plan in mind, and coach was the right person to help me execute it. While I kept my head in the game, I needed someone working in the background, moving the pieces while I focused on being the standing king. It was time for me to stop playing checkers and move on to chess.

"Mase, it's good to see you. You're always on time, which means you are early, but I expected nothing less." Coach Patterson opened his house door, ecstatic to see me. We embraced, and we made our way to his man cave in the basement. When I was in high school, I couldn't wait to be invited to his house. He had everything a young boy only dreamed of. It still looked the same with a few upgrades over the years. Maroon and gold were his colors of choice, reppin' Paterson Catholic High School like he still went there.

"Coach, I still can't believe you framed my jersey." I traced the casing that he had it in and was proud that he put me on his wall with the greats. I didn't think I could be compared to Michael Jordan, Kareem Abdul-Jabbar, Magic Johnson, and Wilt Chamberlain. It was hanging right next to his jersey, the great Tommy Patterson. He believed in me that much.

"You belong up there, son, and you haven't even reached your fullest potential yet. Take a seat and make yourself at home." That wasn't hard to do; he and Mrs. Patterson always treated me like I was family.

"Where's Mrs. P. at? I haven't seen or spoken to her in a minute." I was a little disappointed. I wanted her in on this conversation as well.

"She had to run out and show a client a house. You know

she's always working, even on the weekends." He shook his head, knowing his wife was a workaholic. She made major dough showing houses to A-list celebrities. She had prime real estate, and everybody who was somebody came to her for the asking.

"She is actually who I came by to talk to." Coach now had a raised eyebrow, wondering what I wanted with his wife.

"Oh, really?" He was now intrigued, seeing that it was not only a social call, but I had something on my mind.

"Yeah, I wanted to talk to her about possibly opening a restaurant. I can almost guarantee she can point me in the right direction regarding property and location. I need her expertise on how to make that happen. I'm not sure where I'm getting the money yet, but I want to do my homework so when my chance comes, I can capitalize on it."

He looked confused. Not too many people knew I could cook, not even him. When people knew you for one thing, it was hard for them to see you doing something else. Our bond was based around basketball, so that was mainly what we talked about. Don't get me wrong; we talked about personal things, but he allowed me to start those conversations. I never felt it was important to disclose until now.

"I'm not understanding? Is it something you are looking into for your grandmother or family member?" He was very attentive, waiting for the answer to his question.

"Listen, Coach, I've been really thinking about the next stage of my life, and I'm trying to weigh my options. I'm not so sure anymore if I want to enter the draft. I want to live a normal life surrounded by family, and I wouldn't be able to do that in the league. I'll be on the road for half of the year. My grandmother is getting older, and I want to not only take care of her financially, but I want to be there with her." I pulled in and slowly released a breath.

This was the first time I told anyone my plans of what I

was thinking outside of Qwana, and I didn't even go into full details with her. I sort of came to terms with the conflict in my head and started to embrace it a little more each day. It wasn't only a conflict; I knew I'd be letting a lot of people down that believed in me, including Coach Patterson. This wasn't about them, though; for once, this was about me and what I wanted.

"You are a smart young man, and I know you will make the right decision. I'm here to help you with whatever you need. Like I believe in you when it comes to basketball, I'll believe in you to do what you feel is necessary for you and your family. You've always been different, Mason, and if basketball is no longer making you happy, do something that does."

That seemed to be the theme of my life. *Do whatever makes you happy.* One would think it would be an easy task, but I always thought of the people I loved before considering myself. It wasn't a bad quality, but it kept me from pursuing a lot of different things. I don't regret anything, but I understood that I would eventually regret it if I didn't start putting myself first. The more I talked about what could possibly be my future, the more the weight was lifted off my shoulder. I hadn't made up my mind, but at least I had options.

"See, that's why I came to you, Coach. I needed a male's perspective. Someone that came from where I came from and fought some of the same fights that I'm fighting now. Do you ever regret not playing in the league?" It was always something that I wondered about him. From the tapes and highlights that I had seen, Coach could have definitely made it all the way. We never talked about it much, and I didn't care until now.

"Man, I was so young and dumb back then; all I cared about was partying and how many women I could sleep with. I got caught up, and it was too late to undo the error of my ways."

"I thought you got hurt?" The lines on my forehead created a look of perplexity.

Coach Patterson sat up in his seat and took a long breath before getting into whatever it was that plagued his mind about the inside information he was about to give.

"I did get hurt, but it wasn't in a game. I got hurt running from the cops coming from a party. I guess it was my payback for living young and reckless. I was having so much fun that I broke the rules every chance I got."

This was a different story than what he told us, but I guess he kept it to himself; he was ashamed. I looked up to Coach Patterson, and this didn't change that. It showed me he was human, and he made mistakes like the rest of us. He was still thriving in my eyes; he had a loving wife, a big house, nice cars, and clothes to match. That was why I came to him. Although he didn't make it into the league, he was still doing good for himself.

"Why didn't you tell us the real story, Coach?" Knowing the real story wouldn't have changed the fact that he was good at what he did. Not only did he coach, but he mentored so many boys down through the years. When you got into his program, not only did you learn the art of basketball, but you did better in school and wanted to be better in life.

"That's another question I asked myself a lot; I don't know. I wanted my actions to line up with my words, if that makes sense." His eyes looked to me for understanding, and I was grateful that he trusted me enough to bare his soul.

"Coach, it doesn't even matter. You're still one of the greatest whoever did it, and it certainly doesn't take away the many lives you've transformed with your gift." He had nothing to prove to me, but you could tell it was a weight lifted off his shoulder, and I was glad I was the one to help.

"Listen, no matter what you decide to do, own it and never look back. I wouldn't change a thing about that night, honestly. I wouldn't have met Cynthia if I went to the league. I had no choice but to slow down and focus on what really mattered. It wasn't meant for me, and I'm cool with that. I gained so much more than money and clout. I finished school and created a family. I'm living the life that God intended for me."

After all of that, he was still proud of what he accomplished. My conversation with Coach taught me a few things. As long as you woke up every morning knowing you did the best you could do with what you had, you accomplished something. It also taught me that dreams don't always show you the full picture and that it may be more than meets the eye. Our conversation was much needed, and I couldn't wait to see what else I could learn.

HIGH OFF MY CONVERSATION WITH COACH PATTERSON, I HAD to address another part of my life that needed fixing. It had been almost a week since I told Qwana she needed to choose what she wanted to do. Yes, a monkey wrench was thrown our way after Qwana's little encounter with them messy hoes. She still had a decision to make, and I wasn't playing this time. This creep life wasn't what I wanted anymore; I was tired of going through the motions. It was time for me to experience that real love with or without her.

I was a little early for our session, but I wanted to get my mind right before learning the outcome. My steps weren't as excited as they hit the marble floors of the W Hotel. What if this was the last time? Part of me felt I was prepared, but was I? I wouldn't actually know until the words came out of her mouth. I checked in and made my way to the twenty-sixth floor with so many what-ifs on my brain that I started to feel drained. It was as if my body was telling me something; I didn't know what it was telling me, but I didn't like the feeling. My nerves and emotions were all over the place.

I made it to our room; the sun was setting over the skyline of New York. I stood as the orange skies morphed into the night. I dialed for room service to bring me a drink; I needed one to calm my nerves and enjoy my night, even if it was to go wrong. I also ordered Qwana her favorite wine, thinking she might need it as well. I knew this wasn't an easy decision, but she had a week to really think about what she wanted to do. This wasn't the first time I expressed my feelings, so she had more than a few weeks in reality.

I needed the September breeze to tell me something as I took a seat out on the balcony. I allowed the wind to blow around my thoughts as I awaited my fate. A slight knock on the door interrupted my decompression session. They announced themselves, letting me know that it was our drinks. When I opened the door, I was surprised that it wasn't room service, but Qwana was standing there looking so beautiful. My heart skipped a beat; there she stood with both of our drinks in her hand.

Neither of us mouthed a word; we stood there taking each other in. Qwana's dark chocolate skin radiated a glow that matched her perfect smile. She leaned in for a kiss, and I almost turned away, but I missed her. I let our kiss collide as we got lost in the here and now. I heard fireworks in the background, but I knew it wasn't the fourth of July. I pulled Qwana inside, not wanting to break our kiss, but I knew we had to handle our handle. As much as I wanted to move to the next base, I had to call a timeout to talk some sense into my teammate.

"Why do I love you?" Qwana was caught off guard by the question, but I continued. "You really came into my life and changed my perspective about relationships and commitment." I grabbed my drink and threw it back, letting the taste take over my body. "Who would have thought that meeting you in the hallway that day would lead to love?" Qwana stood speechless. I grabbed her hand and led her over to the couch.

The zephyr from the open balcony door did very little to cool us off from the topic that was in the air. So many words were unspoken, both of us trying our best to form the poetry of our connection. We never expressed ourselves; that wasn't what our relationship was built on. We spoke through sex, which, after a while, opened the door for pillow talk and laughs. It wasn't supposed to be anything more, but years invested created mountains of feelings we thought were locked in a cave. Somewhere, somehow, I found that cave and no longer wanted to live in it. I wondered if Qwana felt the same.

"Please tell me you feel the same. That I'm not making these feelings up in my head." I gently touched her smooth skin and turned her head, facing me so she could look into my eyes. "Do you love me?" It was always insinuated, and you could tell through the way we sexed, but I wanted to hear her say it. I needed to listen to her say it.

"What if I say I do? What does that change, Mason?" I could tell it frustrated her a little, but I couldn't let her run from this conversation.

"It changes a lot; I'm no guru on this love thing, but it should matter. When you love someone, you should do everything in your power to be with them. Or at least that is what I would do. Love should conquer all, right?" I was still trying to figure this all out, but logic and common sense told me that I was right.

Qwana released a nervous and unsure laugh. "I thought the same thing at one point, but that's not real life. If that was the case, I wouldn't be here with you; I'd be with my husband." My jaw tightened at that revelation. "Love is a tricky thing. Each relationship has its own definition of love, and unfortunately, this is ours. Our love was built on betrayal; it was built on a foundation that I knew would one day crumble." Her tears descended from the truth of her words.

"Do you still love him?" Qwana's words opened up a portal of emotion that I was not used to. My voice cracked, unsure of why she still loved him. What didn't I have? Why wasn't I good enough? Age was definitely a factor, but besides that, I was all the man she needed. I was working on becoming a good provider; our sex was out of this world, so I was confused.

"Yes, I love him. Am I still in love with him? Probably not, but again, what does that change? I took vows with this man, for better or worse. It's something you would never under-stand; my life is complicated." I got up from the couch and paced back and forth, listening to what Qwana was saying. It was so much more behind her words than what she was saying.

"So what you saying, Qwana?" This portal of feelings was leading me down a path that was breaking me down. Her words broke my heart; my palms were sweaty, and my temperature rising, but I wouldn't allow her to see my tears. Nope, she was not going to see how much this was hurting me.

"It's for our own good." Yup, I heard her loud and clear, and it angered me. She didn't want to say it, but I knew. How could she choose her husband over me? Qwana got up from the couch and met in the middle of our hotel room. She tried to touch me, but I wasn't hers anymore.

"Get out!" I couldn't even look at her. I didn't want to be around her.

"But Mason—"

"But Mason, nothing. You chose who you wanted to choose, so don't try and explain now. Get out!" I pointed to the door so she didn't forget where the door was.

"I'm sorry." She gathered her things and walked to the door slowly. My back was toward her, but I felt her eyes burning a hole in my back. "It's safer this way, Mason. I promise you it is." And with that, she closed the door on what could have been.

My anger wouldn't let me cry or drop a single tear. Trust me, they were fighting to be released, but I had something else in mind. Something I knew would take my mind off this whole situation. I needed some pussy. That would remind me of who I was. I would have traded it all for *her*, but *she* didn't want it. It's all good.

I searched for my phone and scrolled through my contacts, looking for my distraction for the night. Any female I called would be honored to not only be in my presence but to experience a hotel like the W. I really didn't do repeat offenders; I didn't want them to think they had me. Tonight would be a little bit different, and I didn't care. I landed on Kiara, and she would be the next contestant to get this dick.

"Hey, Mase." She was so excited to hear from me but trying to mask it; her voice made calling my name sound sexy.

"Meet me at the W Hotel in Hoboken; I want to have some fun. You down?"

"Of course I'm down. Give me like an hour, and I'll be there."

"Aight, bet. I'll meet you at the bar." It wasn't much more to say after that, so I ended the call.

This was only a temporary fix, but before you know it, I'd be over Qwana. You know how many beautiful women I came into contact with every day? One of them would be what I needed them to be. It would take me a long time to trust someone, but that was all a part of the process. It wasn't a process that I was familiar with, but I was a fast learner. I made my way down to the bar to drink my sorrows away while I waited for Qwana's replacement.

You would never catch me, catching feelings.
- Kareem

How did I get caught up almost killing somebody for disrespecting another man? My philosophy had always been to protect myself and my family. I thought my job with Dom would be peaches and cream, but I was mistaken. The streets saw me as the new cat and tested my gangsta. I was known, but these hustlers were a different breed. They respected me as a person but challenged my authority; they were mad they were not handpicked by Dom himself. Jealousy would make you do some crazy things, and I witnessed it firsthand.

When I got the call from Harvey to meet him at the stash house, I rushed out of the party and made my way to where we kept all of the product and guns. It was weird that I was getting a call. I had everything running smoothly since I took over, or so I thought. That sentiment changed when I walked out of the party and saw Dom had pulled up. The same Cadillacs were parked near the entrance. That only meant trouble. The hood knew that there would be blood-shed when Dom showed his face, and it wasn't anything anyone could do about it. Most people hoped it wasn't them losing the blood.

Rick and Reese, who were now my lieutenants, met me, scared for what they thought was about to occur. They never met Dom personally, and to see him pull up created a fear that I never saw in them. I couldn't even front; I was a little nervous too. I wasn't going to show them that, though. I was the leader, and the leader showed no fear, even when the boss was present. They started with their twenty-one questions, and it irritated me; I didn't know anything.

"Yo, why Dom here?" Rick was out of breath, trying to keep up with my long strides.

"Instead of asking me questions, make sure everybody on their post," I snapped. The last thing I needed was for something to jump off while Dom was here. Rick stopped walking; he couldn't believe I spoke to him like I did, but I didn't have time for feelings.

"I don't know what has gotten into you, but you trippin', Reem. I'm gonna let you handle this, but we're gonna talk about how you've been coming lately," Reese expressed through clenched teeth. I usually would check a nigga for that type of behavior, but I let it slide. He was my boy, and we were both in our feelings. I had bigger fish to fry.

I used my key to the apartment that was located in the basketball section and let myself in. A metallic smell invaded my nostrils as soon as I closed the door on the rundown apartment, hoping it wasn't what I thought it was but realizing it was as I crossed over into the living room. Blood was everywhere, but there wasn't no one in sight. I followed the blood to the upstairs level of the apartment, my heart beating with every step. For it to be so much blood, there wasn't any commotion anywhere in the house.

On the second level, I went to what they called the master bedroom, and there they were. One of the dealers from the 4th Ward, Red, was tied to the bedpost butt naked with blood as his clothes. His name suited him tonight. I looked toward Dom and Harvey sitting there without a care in the world. They were waiting, waiting like the predators they were.

"Next time we say come, you better run here like your life depends on it. I wait for no one." Dom was furious. I heard about his ruthlessness, but it was never directed at me. I didn't know how to take it.

"I came as soon as Harvey called me. I had everything handled; what happened?" I was still trying to figure out why they had Red tied and beaten up.

Dom stayed seated in the chair, looking at me, rubbing the scar under his chin. I wasn't sure if that was how he calmed himself down or if that was what he did when he was thinking. Dom didn't answer right away; Harvey was a blank folder with nothing in it; couldn't expect too much from him. When Dom was around, Harvey didn't talk much, but he had so much to say any other time. He was a pussy. I walked over to Red's body; Red was now waking from being unconscious from the blows I knew he received. He started going crazy, rocking the bed and trying to get loose.

"Won't you ask him yourself?" Dom finally got up and made his way out of the room, and Harvey got up and followed him like a little puppy. Dom stopped at the door, turned around, walked to the opposite side of the bed with his gun, and cracked Red in the mouth. "On the other hand, meet me downstairs now." That blow knocked Red right out; he wasn't dead, but he was on his way, probably fighting to not see the light.

They didn't move until I moved, following me downstairs to the living room. Both Dom and Harvey still had their heat in their hands. I didn't feel comfortable yet carrying mine, and I regretted it at this moment; I was exposed. I could do nothing about it now, but I made a mental note to stay strapped. Rick and Reese were always with me; they carried, but they were not granted access to this exhibit.

"I need you to handle that upstairs; I don't want him breathing another breath." Dom's dark eyes stalked me.

"I know I'm new to this, but you gotta tell me why I'm taking another man's life." I didn't mind putting in work, but Dom had to give me something. I knew I would be getting my hands dirty at one point; that was how the game worked. It had to be a method to my madness though; I had to know what I was dealing with. That way, it could be done correctly.

"You do whatever I tell you to do when I tell you to do it. The only reason I'm going to tell you is so that you don't make the same mistake that Red did," Dom's deep, dark voice threatened. "Anybody that talks to police can't be trusted; this snitching shit is getting out of hand with you youngins. It's a code we live by, and if you can't abide by it, your time is up. Point blank."

"Say no more." If it's one thing I learned, it was to never be a snitch. It was an oath you took when you entered the game. It was one of the ten commandments for the streets and one of the most important.

"The cleaning crew will be here by midnight," Dom made known. His words were the ending of his instructions. He meant it, and he wanted it done. I wasn't sure how I would complete the task, but I understood how important it was to get rid of the rat. My life went from nothing to something all in a month's time. I called Rick and Reese to meet me at the house while I saw Dom off.

From that day on, I became more and more focused on the streets. School was still a priority, but the money and life I was living were more fulfilling. I didn't expect Mase and Cash to be outside when I was walking Dom to his truck. They were supposed to be partying, but they caught me at the wrong time. I wasn't hiding anything; I didn't want to explain myself. It would have turned into this big thing. I didn't need that type of headache, so I kept my dealings to myself. I was keeping my distance while I got everything under control.

It was one person that I could no longer keep my distance

from. Jax had been telling me that my mother had been looking for me. I even had a few messages from her saying she wanted to see me. She sounded well, but I wouldn't take that check to the bank. Hearing her voice brought back my longing for her. I could go days, even months, without caring, but as soon as I saw her or heard her voice, it was like all my feelings came back to the surface. I'd go from being mad to anticipating my mother's touch. It was weird, but it was something I went through all of my life.

She was no longer staying with Jax's sister. She had her own apartment, and I was on my way to see her. This was the first time since I could remember that she had her own. I guess that counted for something. If it wasn't for Jax, I would not have wasted my time, but he seemed adamant that she had changed. The closer I got to her apartment, the more my heart rate sped up. I'd been down this road before, and the outcome destroyed me each time. I was older now, and I understood how hard it could be as an adult, but I would never abandon a child that never asked to be here.

I locked up and threw away the key to emotions a long time ago. My mother was the only one that could find the key and unlock what I thought was caged. Before I even made it to her doorstep, I had to take a couple deep breaths, bracing myself for what I knew would be a heavy conversation. My mom was always apologizing for not being who I needed her to be instead of purely being it. I looked at other people's relationships with their mom and wondered why I didn't have that same motherly love.

It felt as if she blamed me for something or resented me for that matter, but she never came out and really confirmed it. I didn't know if it was her own demons, but it hurt, and it turned my heart cold. I learned to live with it, but that didn't mean it wasn't a part of who I was as a person. My romantic relationships were nonexistent. I got pussy, but that was the only attention that the females got from me, nothing more. You would never catch me catching feelings. I left that to Mase and Cash; they were in tune with that type of shit. I saw what it did to them, and I didn't need that type of dramatic play.

I looked down at the paper that I wrote my mom's address on *335-337 5th Ave, Apt. LL.* I was definitely at the correct address, but I didn't see Apt. LL. I only saw apartments 1-8. I walked to the back of the garden apartments and saw apartments 9-12. I was now confused and getting frustrated. *Did she lie about having an apartment, thinking I wouldn't come?*

"Kareem, you came." I turned around to see my mom holding a few grocery bags. She looked good. This was the best I'd seen her look. I tried not to smile and fought to not want to give her a hug. I stood there. "Boy, these bags are not going to carry themselves." She let out a nervous laugh, trying to break the ice.

"My bad, Ma." I grabbed the bags and let her lead the way to this imaginary apartment that I hadn't been able to find.

"I can't wait for you to see my apartment. It's not special, but it's all mine. You can come over anytime you want." I followed her across the little parking lot and down a few stairs. To the right was a laundry area that she showed me, and we entered her apartment. "I'm so glad you came to see me." She hugged me so tight once I put the bags down.

A part of me didn't want to hug her back, but it felt so good to be in her arms. She wasn't going to let go until I did, so why not? I took a deep breath and focused on breathing slowly and calmly to help regain control. I knew this would happen, but I didn't think it would happen so soon. You don't know how much you miss somebody until you are in their arms. She let me go and started putting the food away. I took a seat at her kitchen table, looking around; it wasn't a bad spot to call home.

"Where did you find this place? I almost left. I didn't see an apartment LL."

"Nicole sister Tamika helped me get this apartment. She lives in the front. When I first came to see how it looked, I couldn't find it either, but LL stands for Lower Level. Who knew?"

This time her laugh was more confident. We were both making small talk, trying to feel each other out. We had to start somewhere, so why not start with an extensive accomplishment. I had never known my mom to have an apartment, so this was a big deal. Jax told me a while back that people like my mom needed affirmations to stay on the right path. They were always told the wrong they did but never celebrated for the strides they made.

"I'm proud of you, Ma; you seem to be doing good." She looked down as she fidgeted with her hands. To the outsiders, she was weak, but to me, she was my mom.

"I'm trying Kareem, like really, really trying." She finally took a seat at the table. "Every day, I wake up wondering if this is real. I was so used to waking up surrounded by people that I only knew when I got high. When that high came down, I had nothing in common with them."

"Why is this time any different?" I thought she should figure that out.

"This time is different. I'm no longer allowing my past transgressions to rule my life. I did what I did, and I've apologized a million times for it. The only thing I can do now is move forward. Jax has been very instrumental in that. The hospital after my detox assigned me a therapist, and that's helping as well. The only thing I need now is for you to forgive me, and I know this time I'll stay clean."

Me, forgive her? There were layers to this. I needed to understand a few things. I thought forgiveness was a process; how can one forgive years of trauma all in a few seconds? I didn't know if I could, but it would definitely take some time. I looked over at her and admired her strength for once in my life. She finally was picking up her broken pieces and putting them back together.

"Ma, you know forgiveness is a process, right?" She had to understand this; I didn't want her to get caught up again, thinking that I didn't care.

"I know. I want to start the process. Anything I can do, I will. I need you, Kareem. You were always the reason why I wanted to get clean. Not for anyone else but you."

"Ma, you should have wanted to get clean for yourself, and I think that's where you were going wrong." She was again fidgeting with her fingers with teary eyes. She hurried and wiped her eyes before tears fell.

"You're right, but I didn't want you to think I never thought about you." Her eyes were pleading for me to understand what she was saying.

"You always made me feel like I wasn't good enough to be your son. You would look at me in disgust before breaking down in tears. Did I remind you of my father that much?" I always felt like I looked like her and the rest of the family, but she seemed to see something different. It was like she blamed and resented me for something that I didn't have any control over. I didn't ask to be here.

"I always loved you, Kareem. You weren't the reason for my downward spiral, my choices were. When I went away to college, everybody was so proud of me. When I got pregnant with you, I felt like I let them down." She paused, took a deep breath, and wiped the tears that were now running down her face." Your grandmother still hasn't forgiven me for keeping you a secret those four years that I was away in college."

"Wait! You kept me away from Grammy?" I was all in, listening to this newfound information.

"It's a lot of things you don't know, Kareem. I wanted you

to have a normal life and not worry about what happened between adults. You were a kid, so I shielded you to protect you, but to answer your question, yes, I did." She waited for a response, but I wanted her to finish.

"I didn't want to disappoint my mother, so when I found out I was pregnant, I kept it to myself, still going to school and bearing this secret all by myself. I got a job right away to save money. I knew the campus wasn't going to allow me to stay with a baby. Mommy and Linda would call me all the time asking how everything was going, and I would lie telling them it was going good." She got up to get some tissue and came back.

"Those were some of the toughest years of my life. I couldn't go home; they would have known what I'd done. So on holidays, I would act like I couldn't come home for whatever reason, and they would believe it. Linda was too busy living as a hustler's wife, and your grandmother worked so much to compensate for being alone that they couldn't think about little ole me. Four years went by, and I struggled, but I still kept my head in the books, got my degree, and then it was time for me to head home." She waited to see if I had any questions; I was letting it all sink in.

My mind was blown; I didn't know she went through all of this. I didn't remember much from back then, so I couldn't piece together these events. I always thought I was born in New Jersey, but my mom revealed I was born in DC. She went to Howard University. I wanted her to continue. I wanted to know what happened when she went back home. "Why didn't you stay in DC?"

"I wanted to, but I knew that they would eventually find out. I missed my family; I needed their support. I put my big girl panties on and came back home. Not only was your grandmother mad and disappointed, but your Aunt Linda was also angry. The two most important people in my life looked at me with disgust. They felt betrayed by what I did, and it broke me. It hurt me to my core. The only reason I came back was so I could feel the love, and they showed me none." That last part angered her; I heard it in her voice. She was looking into space like she was right there in the moment.

I couldn't help but feel bad for her, honestly. She felt alone through it all, and that would make any person go crazy. That still doesn't excuse her from the many years of neglect, but it did show me a different side of her that I'd never seen. We never know what someone is battling inside; from the outside looking in, you would have thought she wasn't strong enough, but it was so much more she carried. I grabbed her hand without even realizing what I was doing; she couldn't believe it either.

"Those things you can now leave in the past and focus on this new life you have been granted. Not too many people make it out the streets."

"Speaking of the streets..." She held my hand tighter, not wanting to let go. Now being able to look me eye to eye. "What have you gotten yourself into, Kareem?"

"What you talking about, Ma?" Did she know? I felt like a little kid again being scolded by my mom for the wrong I knew I was doing.

"I got a bad feeling, and my intuition is kicking in. I've been dreaming about you, and it hasn't been good dreams. I had a couple of people tell me you've been down in the Vill a lot lately."

Jax. It had to be him; he had been on me about it for a few months now. "Ma, I'm good; you don't have to worry about me. Rick and Reese are still my best friends, and that's where they live. I'm not a kid anymore where everybody tries to keep me from them; they good peoples."

"If you say so. Please be safe for me. We have a lot of catching up to do." She patted my hand before getting up from the table. "Let me show you the bathroom and my room. I got my bedroom set from Rent-A-Center the other day."

I left the conversation alone. I didn't want to continue lying to my mother about my life in the streets. I wasn't up to explain myself yet, if at all. Plus, I didn't even know if she would stay clean, so I kept my dealings to myself and myself only. My mom wasn't ready for that part of me, and I didn't need her getting thrust back in the streets from something I did. "Ma, can you cook me some of your bangin' spaghetti?"

"I got you, son."

Jagged Edge - True Man
First came the lies, then came the pain
You know you hurt me so bad, baby
But now I see, and now I know
Now I see that you really wasn't ready for me

$\mathcal{E}$nough was enough; I missed my girl. I hadn't spoken to her in a few days, to give her the space she always claimed she needed. This time, I didn't even text her. I wanted her to realize on her own that I was a good catch. Jeda never wanted to talk through our problems; she always ran from them, and I was the total opposite. I liked to talk out my issues; it gave a different perspective into the mind of the person you love. It was not about how I felt all the time; I liked to take the other person's feelings into consideration. No matter how much I told Jeda this, she still didn't understand, and I'm not going to lie; it was starting to frustrate me.

Silly of me, devoted so much time, To find you unfaithful, boy, I nearly lost my mind, Drive past your house every night, In an unmarked car, Wondering what she had on me, To make you break my heart, yeah. "You've reached Jeda. I'm unable to answer my phone right now. Leave a message, and I'll get back to you." Beep.

Jeda knew I would call; that's why she added that song to her answering machine. The other day, it was that joint from Ciara and Ludacris, "Oh." I didn't know what game she was playing, but I was done playing it. I got dressed with the quickness; Jeda must have forgotten I knew her whole schedule. She should've been getting home soon from her classes, and I would be right there waiting for her. Every girl wanted to see their guy fight for them, but I was tired of fighting all the time. How much more did I have to prove that I wanted to be with her?

The drive was what I needed to calm me down a little. I never wanted to enter a situation mad; it wouldn't do me any good. When you are angry, all you want is for the other person to understand that they made you that way. It made the situation worse, and all I wanted to do was make it better. At this point, I was all out of ideas on how to improve our relationship. It had never been this bad. Hopefully, we could choose love over everything else. It was a stretch, but I was willing to try. I knocked on Jeda's door, and there wasn't an answer. I guess she was still at school.

I waited patiently in my car for Jeda to show up. I parked right in my spot to give me a view of who was coming in and out. I turned up my music and let it do the thinking for me. I wished I could create music in moments like this, but I couldn't; my mind was clouded. Everybody from the party talked about my song and how much they liked it, so I had to follow up with something better. They played it three more times, and each time the dance floor was jumpin'. People were asking me how they could find it. I needed management badly.

I looked at the clock and noticed that I now had been waiting for more than an hour. It wasn't like Jeda to not come straight home. The only other place she would be is The Underdog, a local bar that college students hung out at. We hadn't been there in a minute, but she probably was there with her girls with everything going on between us. Jeda didn't hang out much, but when she did, that was her spot. It wasn't but a hop, skip, and jump, so I was there before you knew it.

If Jeda was in here, I was praying she didn't make a scene; hopefully, we could talk like adults. I made my way through the doors and scanned the place. I wasn't even there but for a few seconds, and I heard Jeda's laugh. I followed it to the back, and I didn't like what I saw. My heart started racing, blood started boiling, and before you know it, I snatched her right up out of a dude's face.

"Yo, what's the beef?" the dude barked. He thought he was about to get some play.

"Cashmere, get off of me!" Jeda yelled. I only let go of her to deal with this dude who felt he had a right to question me. She stormed off.

"Playboy, this is not what you want; I suggest you sit down. This is between my girl and me." There wasn't anything left for me to say, so I followed Jeda out the door. If he felt it was a problem, he could follow, and we could handle it outside.

I got to Jeda before she was able to get far. "You really trying to play me?" I looked around. Haledon was a white town, and the cops didn't play, so I had to check myself really quick. Through clenched teeth, I followed up, "This is what it's come to, Jeda?" My adrenaline was in the speed lane on a highway to hell if I didn't slow down.

"So you could check me for having a friendly conversation, but it was okay for you to be smiling up in that bitch face? You gotta be kidding me. This shit works both ways! If you could do it, I could too. Don't dish shit out you can't take."

"You still in your feelings about me working with Aonika? You need to grow up. That's business, Jeda. You always told me to follow my dreams. Just because you envisioned me following my dreams differently, doesn't mean it's not a step in the right direction to building my career. Right now, Aonika has the resources and the experience. Why can't you understand that?"

"So you're fucking bitches to get ahead now?"

"Are you serious right now? I haven't done anything with that girl but vibe over our love for music. It's the experience I'm after; I don't even want her to help me. I want to get it on my own, and why not learn while I'm at it? Huh?"

"Do what you want to do, and I'm going to do what I'm going to do." I had to process that; it felt like a stab in my heart.

"What you trying to say? You don't want to be with me anymore?" My world started spinning. Never in a million years would I have thought we would be here. My life revolved around her. I didn't know what I would do without her.

"I'm moving to L.A."

"Wait, what?" I wasn't expecting that. "Where is all of this coming from?"

"I have to start thinking about myself. Obviously, you are. You're putting your career over how I feel, and I'm doing the same thing. *Life Magazine* presented me with an offer I can't pass up. They got countless emails from women worldwide, saying how much they enjoyed my written piece. *Life Magazine* provided me with a list of schools that have great journalism programs. This could really be my big break, and the only thing that was keeping me from going was you." Her emotions were building up, and she was trying her hardest not to cry; so was I.

This was a gut punch for sure. We both stood there trying to figure out a life decision that couldn't be decided in one conversation, especially a heated one. It was definitely a lot all at once. "So if I didn't come trying to fix this relationship, you would have dipped?" I started to get angry all over again.

"You wouldn't have cared either way. You were too busy worrying about yourself."

"Are you serious? You really believe that nonsense you saying? It's always me coming to you after we have an argument; you never do anything wrong. I'm always the one to blame. Yes, you saw me in the studio having a moment with Aonika, but if you had stopped and asked questions, you would have known what it was, but yet you took the easy way out. It's only so much I can take."

"Yeah, yeah. I know I'm too much. If you can't accept me for me, we most definitely don't need to be together."

"All I ever tried to do is be there for you, and this is how you repay me? I had to find out that my girl is thinking about moving to a whole other coast, and I'm the bad guy? Man, do whatever you want to do, but one thing you can't say is I wasn't a good man." I walked away, hurt that I spent all this time trying to love someone who didn't care to love me back when times got rough. It took two, and unfortunately, Jeda wasn't a willing participant.

I didn't know where we went wrong, but the turn we took, I wish we could do a U-turn. I felt lost, on the road to nowhere, and I wasn't talking about the Buick I pulled off in. As I rode past Jeda, she called out to me, but I wasn't feeling her. Everyone in my life seemed to have their whole life mapped out. Mase was on his way to the NBA, Kareem would soon be graduating college and going to medical school, and now the love of my life was off to do bigger and better things. I was stuck, trying to figure out this music thing without any direction.

Maybe it was time for me to make that call to Dom.

Switch

A defensive strategy usually occurring when a screen is set that involves two defensive players swapping which player they're guarding.

"Sir, Room 2628 is not available." The hotel concierge relayed.

"Who name is it under?" *It better not be Qwana, creeping with somebody else.*

"Sir, I can't tell you—"

"You know what, you don't have to." I stormed off toward the elevator to see who the hell was in our room. I promise you, if it was Qwana, I was going to jail. I tried not to think about her, but I couldn't help it. My whole mind and body were going through withdrawal. It had been two weeks, and this had been the longest I'd been without seeing her. I was getting ready for war as the elevator ascended to the twenty-sixth floor. My heart pounded like a drum in a drumline battle.

My fist met the door with a bang like I was the police looking for a wanted fugitive. I heard movement and waited for whoever was behind the door to reveal themselves. I banged again, this time almost taking the door off the hinges. "I hear someone in there; open the fucking door, now." If it was Qwana, I had now revealed myself, but I couldn't help it; they were taking too long. A male voice spoke from behind the door.

"How can I help you?"

"Open the door. That's how you could help me." Strike one, it was a dude.

"I don't know what this is about, but you got the wrong room. Nobody knows you here, and you are disrupting us." Strike two, he grouped whoever was behind those doors as *Us*, which meant he was not alone.

"If you don't open this door, I'll be waiting for you. You can't stay in there forever." I saw red at this point; I wanted answers.

I heard running down the hallway; hotel security was now on the scene, and I didn't care.

"Sir, we are going to have to ask you to leave. You are disturbing our guests. We have a strict policy that loud noise and commotion will not be tolerated.

"I need to know if my girl is behind those doors, and I'm not leaving until I'm sure."

The door swung open, and two guys were standing there with a confused look on their face. They looked like they were together, but I wasn't sure. I felt so stupid. I ran my hand across my face, not believing I stooped this low. This was a hotel, so many people came here from out of town to get away and hide if they needed to.

"It's no girl here, as you can see," the flamboyant of the two spoke. "You did all of that; why don't you come in and we can take your mind off her." They were no longer scared but had smiles on their faces.

"Nah, you buggin'. My bad though. Y'all continue to do y'all." I made a fool of myself. Was I missing Qwana that bad? I went against everything I believed in and chased a feeling that I couldn't explain. It was okay for me to bring another girl to the room, but I went ballistic as soon as I thought Qwana did the same thing. Does it count that nothing went down?

"Oh my God, this room is so nice, Mase. I know this had to cost you a pretty penny. Thank you for inviting me, with your sexy ass." I had one too many drinks at the bar before Kiara got here. I wanted to get the draws and take my mind off Qwana leaving me. I let Kiara feel special for a minute, but playtime was over.

"Come here wit' your sexy ass." Kiara sashayed over to where I was seated. I couldn't front; shawty had a body on her. She was chubby-thick and had enough ass to make any man fall in love. I couldn't take her seriously, though; she was easy. I didn't have to work for it; her pussy was given to me on a silver platter. Tonight, I didn't mind the company, so I appreciated every inch of her body.

"I like it when you call me sexy" Kiara ran her hands down my six pack, worshiping my body, and I let her. She climbed on top of me and almost kissed me on the lips, but I moved in time to block her attempt. I wasn't that drunk. I pulled her shirt over her head and kept the momentum going, putting her nipples in my mouth instead. Her moans reached the ceiling above as she threw her head back, giving me open access to her nakedness.

Flashes of Qwana stopped me from enjoying Kiara calling out my name when I wasn't even deep inside yet. Kiara felt me hesitate. She got off of me to get on her knees; she unbuttoned my pants and zipped down my zipper to take my mans and dem in her mouth. My head fell back on the couch as her wet mouth went to work.

It felt good, but I couldn't get my mans and dem to agree with my mind. Kiara was going to town, slurping and sucking like her life depended on it. She stopped, seeing her efforts weren't having the same effect as they once did. Kiara wasn't the best I ever had when it came to her mouth game, but she wasn't the worst. I had to try something else to get me working. This had never happened to me. I tried to stroke it myself while she played with my balls. Nothing.

Kiara looked at me with those sad puppy eyes, and I felt terrible. It wasn't her; it was me. It was something that I wasn't going to tell her, though. She didn't need to know my business that I was in love and the person I was in love with left me. I wouldn't give her the satisfaction to know those details.

"Am I doing something wrong?" She stopped once she noticed I was no longer stroking. I blew out a frustrated breath. I was no longer tipsy and feeling good. I hated myself for not being able to get an erection. The reason behind it frustrated me more.

"You did everything right. I think I had too much to drink. I'm tired now." I stood to my feet as she stayed on her knees, almost begging me to not do this to her.

"So what now?" Kiara wondered as she got up from her position and put back on her bra and shirt. Loving Qwana gave me a heart toward females, so I did something I didn't want to do.

"You can stay and enjoy the room. Order what you want, and I'll come back in the morning to check out. I need to make a run, and it's closer to my house, so I'll stay there," I lied, but at least I didn't waste all of her time. I was going home to sleep this off, and hopefully, in the morning, I'd have my mind right.

"So you're leaving me here?" The confused look on her face was the same as the thoughts in my head.

"Yes. Enjoy the time away from your regular. I appreciate you coming through. I'll see you in the morning. Check out is at noon." I didn't even leave her any room to protest or say another word. I was out the door with the quickness, still not believing my luck.

I hurried to my car, reliving the past week like it happened today. When I got to the hotel to check out the morning after my malfunction, Kiara was gone. I didn't even bother to call her; there wasn't anything to talk about. I was making a fool of myself, all in the name of love. If this was what it felt like, I didn't want it. Or did I?

Since I couldn't get our room to feel like I was around her, I went to the only restaurant we ate at, Je's Soul Food. Even though our date didn't end on a good note, I still took a chance to see if I felt close to her. After all, it was the only time we were able to eat together. I hoped the booth we sat at was empty; I didn't want to make another scene. I chuckled to myself. I was becoming a stalker instead of the one being stalked. How times had changed.

This grub was about to hit the spot. I couldn't wait to feel somewhat better. I had to find different ways to get over Qwana; the ways I had been trying weren't healthy. I had to think of something quickly. I couldn't bring this into the basketball season. I had to focus, and missing Qwana had me doing the opposite. I parked, and I walked in deep thought. I never ate anywhere alone. It was always me and somebody else, but today I was a loner. I thought about calling Cash or Kareem, but I didn't want them clowning me.

"Are you dining in or taking out?"

"I'm dining in, and I want that—" I stopped mid-sentence. I couldn't believe what I was seeing. A smile spread across my face, but then what if she was here with someone else? It was only one way to find out. "I'll dine with my friend over there." I pointed to Qwana as she was eating her food.

"Excuse me, miss, is this seat taken?" Everything I felt about her leaving her husband and choosing him went out the window. I was happy to see her, and it was evident in my speech. Qwana looked up, already knowing my voice, and had a smile wider than the Atlantic Ocean.

"Mason, I was thinking about you." Qwana jumped up

from the booth and latched her arms around me for a kiss. A kiss in public? She must've really missed me. We didn't want to move from our embrace, but we had to. I could have stayed in this moment forever, but that wasn't realistic. I took a seat and admired Qwana's beauty like I was seeing her for the first time.

"I miss you, yo. Like, really miss you." I got up from across the table and sat next to her. I hated that my feelings were on display, but at this point, I didn't know any other way to be.

"I miss you too, Mason. I couldn't stop thinking about you since the day I left you in the hotel. I wanted to turn back, but you made yourself clear. You were so angry that I didn't want to anger you anymore. Since then, I've been planning how I could leave my husband, but... it's... it's no way." Fear entered her eyes, and it was the kind that told a story that something wasn't right. I felt it in the pit of my stomach. Who was this guy, and why did he have so much power over her?

"Has he been abusing you, Qwana?" Something in my gut was telling me he was. I examined her body for any signs. Why else couldn't she leave? I never thought about it until now. Her body language got rigid; she slapped her hand over her mouth to silence an uncontrolled whimper. How could I miss that? I was so caught up in myself that I didn't realize what she probably had to fight in her marriage.

"You've been my safe space, and I hate not having you around. I feel empty and lost without you." She wiped the tears that were now falling. "I understand though. You deserve better than me." She looked down, picked up her fork, and started picking at her food.

Qwana needed me, and if I didn't know before, I learned today. I wasn't sure what the future held after tonight, but I couldn't think about that. I wanted to enjoy Qwana's company while I got the chance. When something was snatched away that you loved and you gained it back, you'd do everything in your power to keep it. Although Qwana wasn't mine to keep, I was going to appreciate the time we had. I ordered my dinner, and we continued to enjoy the night as friends.

KAREEM

I'd called the shots most of my life, and I'd be damned if I let another man intimidate me into changing that. Money changed people; it wasn't doing anything but making me better.

- Kareem

*L*ife was definitely a roller coaster these days. Being in charge of so much gave me the ability to feel like Superman. Not only was I still crushing school, but the blocks that I was graced with were making money. Other than the little hiccup with Red, things were looking up. I didn't even get my hands dirty; I let Rick and Reese handle that problem, and they were happy to do so. My team was solid, and I wouldn't want it any other way. It was hard for Rick to accept that Dom put me in charge at first, but he came around once he saw that nothing really changed in the Vill. I still let them run the show; I had other blocks that needed my attention anyway.

I had about 10 G's waiting to be dropped on my grammy's

account for the house, and I was proud of that. The bank gave her sixty days to come up with the money, and I was sure that I'd have all of it by then. The adrenaline my heart got every time I passed through each block to check it out was priceless. The money I was making was worth it. I didn't know this was what I needed. It gave me the same feeling that becoming a doctor did, and with them both, I would truly be living my best life.

Today, I was scheduled to re-up; I still was pushing bud at my school, but I also got the bud for the Vill. The other blocks, the lieutenants went through Harvey. Nobody spoke to Dom; I was the only one who had that privilege. I was sure Dom was proud of his decision to make me that offer. I'd been bringing in more money since I took over; at least that was what Harvey told me. Whenever he came home, he would always run his mouth, all of a sudden off mute. It was weak in my eyes that he couldn't be himself around Dom, but hey, if that's how he wanted to live his life, that was on him.

I had a big test today in school, so I made my way to campus. I was a student by day and a street pharmacist by night. I scanned the few notes I did take; pharmacology was kicking my behind. Usually, people took it when they entered medical school, but I was ahead of the curve. This allowed me some breathing room during the first two years of medical school. I honestly wouldn't have taken the class if I knew I would be where I am now, but hey, I had to do what I had to do. I'd always been intrigued by pharmacology; it's the study of how a drug works on the body, its side effects on the body, and the way the body uses the drug. It was a class I was looking forward to since I was a kid.

"Ma, wake up. Wake up, Ma." I was ten at the time and still trying to process the change in my mother. She didn't even know I was there; she never came to pick me up anymore, so as soon as my

grammy left for work, I searched for her. Lo and behold, she was on Godwin Ave in what appeared to be a crack house.

"Boy, leave her alone and get out of here." Some dusty bum looking dude tried shooing me away like my mother didn't look dead with a needle in her arm.

I ran to the nearest bathroom, looking for something to get to fill up with water to throw on my mother. I found a cup tucked away in a broken cabinet and hurried to put water in it. The water pressure was low, so it took longer than I wanted it to. I ran back over to her body and threw the whole cup of cold water in her face. She woke up, looking around.

Her words were a little slurred. "Kareem, what are you doing here?" She slowly tried to hide the needle and the remnants of her drug habit. I wasn't stupid, and I heard the people talking, so I knew what she was into. I didn't want to believe it, but it was now staring me right in my face. I found her in what was known as the crack house; that should have been my indicator, but I wanted to see it for myself.

"What are you doing here?" I started crying. What if I didn't find her in time? What if she was really dead when I saw her? My young mind was posing all of these questions in my brain while looking to my mother for answers.

"Please go home, Kareem. I'll pick you up tomorrow. Let Mommy sleep." She turned over and gave me her back.

"Boy, didn't I tell you to leave from up out of here?" The dusty guy got up and now had his little army of friends with him. I took one more look at my mommy and ran off. I didn't stop running until I made it home. That night, I cried myself to sleep, and the days following, I tried my best to understand what drugs did to the body.

The D.A.R.E program was designed to keep us off drugs, but they never explained what drugs did to the body. Back then, I was on a mission, and here I was years later, now putting those theories to use. I was self-taught about many things in the medical field, but I learned even more, when I got into college, making me an expert in my field. I wish I wasn't exposed to the harsh reality of having a crack addict as a mother. Then again, I was glad I was; it built character within me.

I pulled up to the campus, ready to get this test over with so I could go on about my day. I was working so hard that I felt it was time to reward myself with something. I didn't shop much, but it was always expensive when I did it, so that's why my spending was a few and far between. It was time for me to enjoy the fruits of my labor. I had a couple of things in mind.

I exited my hooptie I inherited from one of Jax's connections. It was a gift for my eighteenth birthday. It wasn't anything fancy, but it had been getting me around. Jax wanted to make sure I could get back and forth to college, so he arranged an even exchange. The favor the guy owed him for a car for me. The pull he still had from jail showed me what type of dude he was; it spoke volumes. I'd been missing his calls lately; he had been calling during my street hours. I wasn't in the mood for a lecture.

"Ayo, Kareem, my man, how you doing?" White Boy John who bought a hefty amount of bud shouted. I hated that he thought we were cool; he had yet to realize he was only a customer. Trust was not something I gave so easily. You were guilty until proven innocent, and most people didn't make it to the prove themselves stage. My family was my friends, and my boys Rick and Reese were considered family.

White boy John was cool, but he talked too much for me. He was always yapping his mouth; it was mad annoying. He reminded me of the dude Marky Mark from the Funky Bunch. He wanted to be down so bad, but he was cool, nonetheless. "What's good? I'm coolin'. About to finish this test really quick so I can get up out of here."

"Right on, brother." White Boy John and I had classes together in the past, but I never really talked with him until I had bud. He always smelled like weed, so it was easy for me to find my first customer. I was glad I did; he spent crazy cash on most of my stock.

White Boy John wasn't doing too bad for himself either; he drove in a brand new 2005 Audi A7, and that thing was clean. I wasn't sure if he was born into money or he was actually making it for himself. So far, I felt I could trust him. That was the only reason I was even walking and speaking with him right now.

"How you doing with what I gave you? You, straight?" I was about to re-up, so I wanted to know if I should get more.

"I probably got one more blunt left to roll from what you gave me. But, peep, I was talking with my dad the other day. He asked me where I was getting bud from. He stays trying to keep tabs on me, but I understand he doesn't want me to get caught up. He tries to shield me from the street life, but it's in my blood. Have you ever heard of the Blanco family?"

I hadn't. My eyebrows raised. "Nah, what about them?"

"Well, back in the day, my father used to run with one of the leaders of the Blanco Cartel. He was heavy in the streets. I told him about you, and he ran your name." White Boy John saw that I wasn't happy and tried to explain himself. "It's... it's nothing you have to worry about; my dad knew your family."

"What you mean he knew my family?" At this point, I had to stop walking to figure out where he was going with this. My family was everything to me, so I had to make sure they weren't a target.

"He knew your uncle Mason and some dude named Jax. He had nothing but great things to say about them. They did business together back in the day. If Mason was still alive and Jax was out of jail, they probably would still be making money together."

"Small world. What's your dad's name?" I had to check my sources, meaning with Jax, to see how legit this story was. It would be some time before I could; he would ask too many questions that I didn't care to answer right now.

"Word it is. They call him Scottie B. He was tight with Lenny Blanco, and from the stories, he tells me, they played no games. One day I'm going to invite you over so he could meet you so you could hear yourself." With that, we started back walking. I didn't need anybody I sold to knowing my personal business. I didn't know what kind of pull White Boy John's dad had, but he had to have some sort of reach if he found out that information. I created different scenarios in my head, trying to connect the dots of the business deals my uncle and Jax had with Scottie B. and the famous Blanco Family.

I spent the next two hours finishing up my test. Often zoning out about how to better run this operation. I never want to get caught up, and I didn't want to die, so I had to stay on top of things. Always being one step ahead of the game will keep you in the game. I had a lot on my plate, but I wasn't going to allow it to knock me off of this mountain I was climbing. My life always had a purpose, but this added on bonus made it worth it.

TRANSITIONING FROM SCHOOL LIFE TO STREET LIFE WAS relatively easy. I was smack dead in the heat of the night, eyes low, cruisin' the streets to my destination. I got a call from Harvey not too long ago that my shipment was ready for pick-up. I was politicking in the Vill until I got that call. Rick and Reese wanted to roll, but I received clear instructions to always come by myself. If I was the boss, my boys would be by my side. Always protected at any cost.

A creature of the night, the darkness became my best friend. It was when most of my planning and excitement happened. When I had to get right with school, I still studied and pursued that dream. I had to find a balance; the stash house was on lockdown days before a big test. I also set aside two hours out of the day to study with minimal distractions. My runners and my crew were gonna know their leader was book smart too. We hustled smart, with a plan in mind to help the ones coming up under us. I was trying to be that example.

I pulled up to the gate, and the guards did their usual. I had the black duffle bag filled with cash. The weight of the paper stacked inside changed over time; I was definitely putting in that work. Right now, Governor Street, Godwin Avenue, and Alburn Street were making major bread under my leadership. The Vill was no doubt bringing in that dough, and that was off weed alone. We became the hub, that's where I was stationed. My crew was starting to make names for ourselves.

"All my money there?" Dom's back was my view as he looked out his skybox window. Smoke battled between his words and the glass view before him as he awaited my answer.

"Do you want me to count it in front of you? You don't ever have to ask me that question again." Dom turned his head slowly, eyes burning a hole through my head. He remained calm, but his stare was deadly. He walked to his chair, the smoke moving with him.

"I can ask you what I want, when I want. You a bold little motherfucker, telling me what I can't ask you." He chuckled a little, but his laugh was far from funny. "You remind me of someone, and I don't know if I like it."

"We don't have to like each other; we have to do business. I respect you; you respect me. You won't have any trouble out of me. I'm here to put in work, nothing more. Nothing less. I don't want no problems." I had a plan in mind, and I couldn't let feelings get in the way of that. From what I could tell, and by the way Harvey acted, Dom wanted yes men around. I wasn't one of them.

"Your work is on the table. Dre and Compound will see you out." I looked a little longer at the man before me. The stories and even the evidence of his ruthlessness still didn't make me fear him. I'd called the shots most of my life, and I'd be damned if I let another man intimidate me into changing that. Money changed people; it wasn't doing anything but making me better.

"Why is it two bags?" Checking my inventory, I unzipped the big one, thinking it was bud. My eyes must have been playing tricks on me, or I had the wrong bag. I zipped back up the white powder and checked the other bag. The other bag was for me.

"They're both yours. I want you to start pushing that white boy in the Vill. I've heard the clientele has been asking, and you're going to deliver."

"I told you I wasn't pushing no powder; this wasn't in the agree—"

"When you work for me, you will sell what I give you in the timeframe I give, or there will be consequences. That's the agreement we made when you accepted our first term, and it's no renegotiating. Either you in or are you out." Before I could even answer, the two guards were standing in the doorway pointing their guns.

For the first time in a long time, I felt stupid. I lifted my hands for them not to shoot. This wasn't going to be as easy as I thought. I sold my heart to the devil, and he locked me into a contract I didn't read the fine print on before signing. I didn't know what he would gain for this, but there wasn't much time to find out. I was shook, but I couldn't show them that. I grabbed both bags, and the men in black put their guns back in their holsters.

"By no means is this a threat; it's to show you who's boss.

You young niggas wanna be about this life, but do you really have what it takes? If you were smart, you'd play nice. I'll make you millions. The game needs a nigga like you, but you gotta learn first. I understand I won't be around forever; it's going to take the right one to take my place." Dom was close enough that I could smell the mint cigar scent on his breath, along with the vibrations of being a stone-cold killer.

The guards pushed me toward the door. I gripped the bags tightly, fists itching to drop them and start swinging. I would have the advantage in a real fight, but I was no match for their AK47. I made it to my car and threw the bags in the trunk. As long as they didn't touch me again, we were good. I drove off; it wasn't until I got around the corner that I could breathe. I'd been in situations before but never feeling like I could lose my life.

I was going to do what was asked until I figured out how I would solve it. It wasn't the worst thing in the world. I didn't like that he felt the need to pull out guns. I wasn't strapped, but my hands were dangerous, so he felt threatened. It was cool though; it wouldn't be for long. He didn't know I was using him to get what I wanted. When he was no longer needed, he'd know, and there wouldn't be anything he could do about it. I wouldn't be who I was made to be if I didn't.

*J*t wasn't long before Jax and his cellmates made it to the visiting area. I always managed time waiting, looking at other families. The different walks of life, having one thing in common. Some didn't make it out, choosing the lifestyle over making a better life. Visiting Jax proved to me that not everybody behind bars was meant to be there. He still didn't think I knew the truth of his arrest. He wasn't a snitch, so he took his punishment like a man; they didn't make solid brothas like him anymore. I watched him approach the table in his orange jumpsuit, looking better than he did before he went in.

After years of not knowing how a man should treat a lady, I got rid of wanting a bad boy. I grew up, and life kicked my butt, but I was able to see how good of a man Jax would have been to me. I didn't know his infatuation ran so deep until our conversation when I visited him. I never paid him any attention. He was always there when I needed him. Then I went on my drug binge and lost touch, only to be reunited through his sister. I owed them my sobriety.

"Hey, beautiful lady. It's always good to see your face. Jax wasn't himself. He always had something slick to say when he first came out. Something was off. I played it off, seeing if he would play along. Eventually, I would find out.

"Trying to see how you are doing. You haven't called in a few days. Everything alright?" I'd been coming to see Jax less and less; my hours started picking up at work. I had to get used to having a job again; it was standing on my feet all day that I didn't like. I hoped he wasn't mad about that. I'd be tired. That wasn't the vibe I was getting though; he didn't seem angry. He was more sympathetic. I saw Jax mad when I ticked him off, and this wasn't that.

"I feel like I let you down again, Jane." There was a hint of anger attached to that. A boulder sat in the middle of my stomach. Always a gangsta and a gentleman, he had a soft spot for me. For him to confess that meant it would be something I wouldn't like.

"What are you talking about?" I sat back in my chair, waiting for the bomb to go off. Eye contact was important to men like Jax; he even taught Kareem to always look a person in their eye. He couldn't even connect with mine.

"I should've finished what I started years ago. I chalked it up to the game when I got set up. Don't get me wrong; I did some dirt in my day. But those murders wasn't me. My hands were clean; I was mourning my brother Mason's death. It's the only reason he snaked his way through."

"Who, Jax?" I was following but clueless at the same time. I was pretty sure Jax had many enemies in his line of work.

"Dom!" Jax shouted, alerting the guards of the agitation of his truth. He brought down his voice, but the sentiment was still the same. "He set me up, Jane. He was calculated, and I was too hurt to fight. All the money was gone, and I had no one to turn to. They all turned their backs on me for him. They were loyal to Mason; they only tolerated me to kiss his ring. I didn't care as long as they respected me."

"You always claimed your innocence, and I believe you, but you never went into details about your case. I heard a few things, but I didn't know what the truth was." I couldn't give away that his sister already spilled the beans.

"At the beginning of my bid, I used to replay the phone conversation I had with Mason before his accident. He and Dom were arguing over the moves Dom was making. He started giving orders without first consulting with Mason, and it was costing us money. We had got robbed at one of our 4th Ward stash houses. Dom sent a crew to Newark and started a war with the wrong crew. He was smart, though; while he wiped out their crew, he wiped out ours. Right up under our nose."

"That's how he expanded his empire?"

"He had the manpower and the iron fist to fake his way to power. He always envied Mason; no matter how many times I would tell Mason, he still kept him around. It cost him his life and my life too."

"He lucked up. If Mason had never got in that accident, he would have stopped it all." That was a sure thing. I thought Jax would agree, but he sunk further into whatever else he was holding on to.

"Mason was set up too." I never saw a gangsta cry; Jax was always good at holding his tears in. This wasn't a place where you showed those emotions. A pipe started leaking in the foundation of his reality. You wouldn't have even known he was crying if you weren't looking at him. It was a silent pain of regret.

"What you mean?" I had to sit up and rest my elbows on the table for support.

"Dom had Mason killed." My world started spinning as his words echoed loud like an inexperienced trumpet player.

"How when he died in a car accident?" I now needed answers!

"Percy was the missing piece."

"What does a crackhead like Percy have to do with this?"

"Dom had Percy mess with Mason's car. The week before Mason's accident, we were set to drive to Miami and meet a new connect out there. Mason always wanted to take road trips when we had enough money to fly. He had Percy check the truck at his garage to make sure we were good to go. The trap was based on his speed, and the day he left after getting into a heated conversation with Dom, with no brakes, he ran right into the Semi-trailer truck. Linda wasn't supposed to be driving. We were all supposed to be in that car, Dom knowing Mason liked to be a speed racer helped to his advantage."

"Wait, so you mean to tell me... that... that my sister got murdered by accident?" They may have to take me out of here on a stretcher. My limbs felt lifeless, gasping for air that I knew existed. *Murder?* Not my sister.

"He didn't know that Linda would be in the car."

"He murdered her." That's how I saw it.

"There's more. Kareem has been selling drugs for Dom." He leaned in after the next detonation to whisper. "Percy had a lot to say before he closed his eyes forever." I knew the type of man Jax was; he got the job done. I hoped that mother-fucker would rot in hell for helping shatter lives. Now I had to take care of it on my end. Dom had to get dealt with. On my sister!

"He fucked with the wrong family!"

"You better not do anything crazy." He looked around, making sure we weren't being watched.

"All these years, I blamed myself for thinking it was my call that lit fuel to the fire. I could still hear Linda's voice on the other phone as she yelled into their bedroom. *Why does my sister want to talk to you? Jane, Jane, why you calling here knowing I would be at work?* I hung up the phone. Then you busted through my doors telling me that Linda and Mason were in a bad accident."

"We gotta get to Kareem before he does. Talk some sense into that boy; he gotta know who he's in bed with." Not only did he kill my sister, but he also took away the only two guys I ever loved. He wouldn't get my son. I promise you that. Now that I had uncovered the truth, I would stop at nothing to make it right. If I owed my sister, even Mason, anything, it would be to avenge their death.

CASHMERE

Usher - You Make Me Wanna

At this point the situation's out of control
I never meant to hurt her
But I gotta let her go
And she may not understand it
While all of this is going on
I tried, I tried to fight it
But the feeling's just too strong

In your life, one thing could trigger a whole bunch of emotions you thought were either lying dormant or you didn't know even existed. After Jeda's confessions of a better life without me, it really had me on edge. It had me second-guessing everything I felt I worked so hard for. My relationship had been rocky before, but it had never been over. I didn't even bother to call her. I didn't know what to say. My hurt started to turn into anger, and regret began to settle in. I was always taught that you shouldn't regret the

225

choices you made. I wished that applied to my situation, but unfortunately, it didn't.

"Hey, get dressed. I'm on my way to get you."

"You are?" She sounded confused but excited that I called at the same time.

"Yes. I want to talk to you about something."

"Okay. Give me a few minutes." She smiled through the phone. It was all in the way she spoke each syllable.

Jeda wasn't the only one making moves; so was I. After I wrapped my mind around it all, it created a different type of grind. It unlocked the next level of what I knew would be my greatest. Maybe it was what I needed. I don't know, but it sure pushed me. While it was a weight lifted, it also left a void. Experiencing loss had a way of rearing its ugly head. I lost so many people in my lifetime that meant the world to me; Jeda was another to add to the list. This loss was different though; this was someone alive who knew what I'd been through and still chose herself to get back at me.

I left the house on a mission. I needed ammo to make noise in the music industry, and I think I found my supplier. If it wasn't for Aonika's management and someone taking a chance on her, she wouldn't be where she was today. That was my missing link; I needed someone to invest. Money wasn't everything, but it helped to do what had to be done on a larger scale. You had to spend money to make money had always been a hustler's motto, and it rang true for the music business.

"You called your glam squad over? You weren't playing. You needed that minute, huh?" I laughed. Aonika got in the car looking like she was going to an awards show. Her face was beat to perfection, her locs looked freshly done, and her ass was sitting perfectly in some Apple Bottom jeans. The sparkle in her eyes laughed along with me.

"Boy, get out of here. I stay ready; I can't get caught slipping in these streets. I have a reputation to uphold. I have always been a bad chick. Don't get it twisted." Aonika flipped her hanging locs behind her shoulders and posed. If I had a camera, I would definitely take a pic for my archives.

"Well, you look beautiful." She always was a pretty girl to me, but these days she was evolving into this woman right before my eyes. Our late nights in the studio helped me to understand her a little more. "I have a meeting with a potential manager, and I wanted you to come with me for support.

"Wow, that's exciting. Where did you meet this person?"

"I was at a party, and they were playing my song. This guy named Dom started asking questions about my record. This dude has money, and he claimed to have connections. I'm meeting him today to see what he could offer me. It's a lot of bullshit artists out here, so I needed some of your expertise." What Aonika didn't know was she'd been my distraction from my reality with Jeda. Between Aonika and music, that's all I needed to come to terms with ending a five-year relationship.

"I appreciate you trusting me." She leaned over the middle console and gave me a tight hug. "I'm so happy that you gained some interest. I remember when my management team reached out to me." Aonika's sweet-smelling perfume lingered in the air as she took her seat. "It changed everything."

"Let's go then." Aonika's rags to riches story was one that singers and musicians only dreamed about. Her positive energy was rubbing off on me; she was proof that anything could happen. While our paths may have been different, getting to our purpose all went back to it was all a dream.

I pulled off, not knowing what to expect. Aonika and I were lost in our thoughts as I drove to the address that Dom's secretary gave me. When I called him, he was out of the office, so his secretary took a message. She ended up calling me right back, giving me a time and date to meet with Dom. Thankfully, it didn't interfere with school or my hours in the studio with Aonika. I stole a glance looking Aonika's way; her attention was on whatever she was doing on her phone.

We pulled up to this building on River Street; I always wondered what was inside. I pulled up on the side of the building, facing the river that flowed through Paterson, Great Falls. I met Aonika on the passenger side, excited about the possibilities. They said good things came to those who waited. I'd waited long enough. We entered the building, not knowing where to go. It was quiet as if abandoned. We were about ten minutes early, but Dom didn't strike me as a guy that would be late.

Hushed tones were coming from the third floor of the building that was sitting on the riverfront. We checked each floor, admiring the work that was going into fixing it up. When we got in eye's view, Dom was conversing with two large men. They were the bodyguards that were protecting his trucks down in the Vill. They immediately stopped talking once we walked into the room. Dom's dark eyes and his sinister smile greeted me before words were even spoken. Aonika wrapped her arms around my waist, which made me feel a little better.

"Hello, Cashmere. You didn't tell me you were bringing company." He looked toward Aonika, checking her out.

"This is my friend Aonika. She actually got signed to Interscope, and I've been working on her project. Aonika, this is Dom, the guy I was telling you about."

She held out her hand. "Nice to meet you, sir." Dom's hand met hers; the smirk he had, I couldn't place. "Nice to meet you, young lady. Now, let's get down to business. We are looking to sign you to a management deal. With a signing bonus. How that sound?"

I tried holding my composure. "What will you offer as my manager?"

"It wouldn't be me directly; I have a few people in mind. I'll provide the capital. First, we are giving you a bonus of $25,000. I'll make sure you'll have money for your own studio. That way, all of your money doesn't go toward studio time. We will pay for radio play, music videos, and all marketing material. You will be a star before you know it, making us millions."

I liked the sound of that. Finally, somebody that believed in me enough to fund my dream. Some things were too good to be true, so I had to ask, "Why me?" I needed that question answered. He only met me one other time and didn't know anything about me. Heard my song only one time. Was Kareem talking about me with this stranger? Aonika was still holding on tight, probably figuring the same thing. She usually had a lot to say but was fixated on the power that radiated before us.

"I saw how the crowd reacted to your song; it doesn't take a genius to see you have talent." Dom started rubbing a scar on his chin. "It's my way of giving back to my community. Plus, your cousin Kareem is a hard worker; I pick up the same quality in you."

"How you know my cousin?" I've been meaning to ask Kareem the same question, but he hasn't been home.

"Let's say we do business. We not here to talk about Kareem. Let me show you where we would build your studio if you decide to take my offer." He showed us the second floor with his guards in tow. Dom painted a vivid picture of what the studio could become. Work had already started, and I was excited. He reached inside his pocket and pulled out an envelope and handed it to me.

I opened the envelope, and there was a check with my name on it for $25,000. My hand met my mouth in an oh shit motion. Aonika was even impressed looking on. I didn't know what to say. I was always wondering how I would get my start; it was now staring me right in my face. I looked around at what could be mine, envisioning the possibilities.

"I'll leave you guys to take it in. Gotta make a phone call." Dom and his goons left us on our own recognizance. I was speechless, not knowing what to say. I looked down at the check. I cashed other people's checks at the bank, but this one had my name on it. I never even had a check at work worth this amount. Dom was finally out of view, and we could no longer hear him talking on the phone.

Aonika jumped in my arms, excited for the possibilities. Her lips found mine, and the kiss was years of built-up passion, never reaching its full potential until now. "I'm... so... proud... of... you." Her words flicking my heart, opening the door a little to us becoming a possibility. Each word was met with a purpose in mind. Connecting on another level that we'd never been before, we entered what was new territory for us.

I was still gripping her butt with her legs wrapped around my waist. As I looked up at her with a bright smile on her face, my lips becoming one with hers. Aonika's body slid down until her legs were touching the floor, neither of us wanting to let each other go. I looked for the check to put it back in my pocket. It slipped out of my hands when Aonika wanted to get freaky. "What you think I should do, Aonika?"

"He's offering a lot; make sure you have someone look over the paperwork. With Dom's backing, you could finish your album and shop it around. The industry says that's the best way to do it. That way, you can kind of control some of the songs you want to release." She was jumping up and down, clapping her hands together. That made me smile even wider.

"My grammy told me a few weeks ago that a door would open for me! That lady knows everything." Thinking back on our family breakfast and conversation, I was hoping she wasn't right about Aonika.

"She was right. You deserve this. My album is almost done because of you. Now it's your turn, and we about to blaze that joint." Aonika started hitting the crip walk. "Right in your own state-of-the-art studio," she was mocking Dom's pitch. She almost peed herself at the clearing of his throat. She ran to me, attaching herself to me for safety.

"What did you decide?" Dom's dark eyes didn't blink. It was something about his charcoal skin and his stare that had everyone in any room pay attention. Obviously, he didn't want to share in our excitement, so I wanted to get straight to the point.

"Thanks for believing in me, Dom. Once I receive the paperwork, I'll sign on the dotted line. I look forward to working with you." I held out my hand for a firm handshake. My hand lingered there for a second.

"This handshake and that money in your pocket seals the deal." He then gripped my hand and got close. "Don't make me regret it." His sinister smile came into view once he stepped back. It was odd and a little intimidating, but as long as I did what I had to do, I didn't care. I was about to sing until I had a batch of songs that would launch me into stardom.

"When will the studio be ready?" The question wasn't even fully out before a whole construction crew walked in.

Dom didn't even answer; he let the arrival of the construction workers answer for him. "We'll be in touch." All three men made their exit. Aonika grabbed my hand and led the way as the workers got to work. I stopped in the doorway, looking back, picturing the setup. It was satisfying knowing I'd finally have a place to call home where history would be made, and classic music would be born. I stuck my chest out, proud.

Aonika and I made it back to the car. Words couldn't describe what I was feeling. I was floating with twenty-five G's in my pocket that I couldn't wait to put in the bank. We had a few hours before Aonika's session. "Let's go back to my crib and toast to this new endeavor." Aonika looked my way, pretty brown eyes pleading with me to take her up on her offer.

"I'm down." I wasn't even a drinker, but today I would indulge; it was worth celebrating. We joked and laughed all the way to her apartment in Elmwood Park. I parked in front of her house. Before I got my seat belt off, Aonika climbed over the middle console and started kissing me. Her butt was placed right on my tool; her grinding made it grow to its fullest potential.

"Come on. Let's go in the house." Aonika was able to come up for air, fixing herself for the walk to her apartment. I didn't even care that my dick was standing straight up. It was ready to bust out of these Enyce jeans. It had been a minute since I had sexual relations, and Aonika's body was calling, so I answered. I didn't know what waited on the other side of her door, but I was about to find out.

Crossover

A dribbling move involving a player passing the basketball from in front of their body from one hand to the other. This is the most common dribbling move and is great for quickly changing directions.

"You ain't got it in you."

"Watch me work." I lost him mid dribble, then I crossed him over. I made it to the three-point line and released the ball for the three, *Swish*. The crowd goes wild; well, at least in my head, they were.

"I let you win, remember that!"

"For an old man, you still got it, Coach P." I laughed. Coach Patterson hated to be called old. He sat down in his backyard, downing his water. The morning sun shined as I took a seat next to him. I was surprised when Mr. Patterson called me last night, telling me to come workout at his house this morning. I knew I had to come with my A-game if I were to do so, and I proved to him that he still couldn't beat me after all these years.

"I'm gonna show you an old man." Coach Patterson got up and started acting like he was Rocky, training for a fight. We laughed some more and fell back in our seats.

I'd been focused on working out and running drills; it was the only way to occupy my time. Qwana and I were only friends, but not having her how I wanted still aggravated me. All of the pent-up aggression went to good use; it caused me to be a beast on the court. Keeping myself busy made it a little easier to deal with the friendship title we put on our situationship. It wasn't what I wanted, but I needed her around. At least until I figured things out in my head.

"Mason, I wanted to talk to you about something."

"What's up, coach?" I looked his way, and he got serious, enjoying the breeze between his words.

"One of the reasons I wanted to become a coach is to give back to the young boys coming up after me. I've been coaching for twenty plus years, and I'm proud to have helped so many live their dreams. I was looking for ways to expand that outreach and help outside of basketball. These young boys need more."

"You've been doing a great job, Coach. You care, and not too many coaches and teachers can say that. Some of them are in it to collect a paycheck. You inspired so many, not only on the court but academically as well. A lot of us didn't have our fathers, but your guidance helped us focus." One thing for certain, I wouldn't be who I was today without the hard love and push of Coach P.

"I appreciate your words, Mason. Cynthia and I talked, and she was telling me how excited you were about this restaurant once she got to talk to you. I started thinking, really weighing my options about this business venture. I know you didn't ask for my help, but Cynthia and I would like to invest in you."

"I don't know what to say."

"If you choose not to go to the NBA, we'll be here to help build your restaurant business. We will be silent partners, letting you run it how you see fit. We would like to be included in all your decisions so you can have somebody to talk it through with. We believe in you and the plan you have laid out before us. You put a lot of thought into this plan. All you need now is a good location and a name."

Days after I spoke with Coach P, Mrs. P contacted me. She wanted to hear all about my plans to open up this restaurant. I didn't have all the details mapped out, but I knew where I wanted to start. She helped me brainstorm, and a few hours later, I had a much clearer picture. With Coach and Mrs. P willing to invest some of the money, I knew it would be a success. They were very successful in their own right and mature enough to guide me.

"Wow, Coach P. You really believe in me that much?" I never had anybody other than my immediate family care about me outside of basketball. Every conversation, every chance somebody got with me, that's all they wanted to talk about. I never paid attention to it until figuring out my next steps after college.

"You should know the answer to that already." Coach chuckled a little. "Take your time and think about it. In the meantime, Cynthia and I will start looking for some property. That way, you don't have to worry too much while you prepare for the season. Even if you decide to go make more history in the NBA, the offer still stands. Either way, you are getting your restaurant."

I had options, and I wasn't mad at it. I was honored that Coach P believed in me. This was shaping up to be a good day. It was a weight off my shoulder; I couldn't even lie. I could really focus now. I thought life had one up on me, but I rose to the occasion. It was like a perfect layup right in front of the defender. My morning was made. We finished up our conversation, mainly joking, him telling me about his player days. I laughed until I couldn't laugh no more.

"YOU MEAN THAT WE FINALLY GET TO MEET THE INFAMOUS Q?" Cash joked. He and Kareem laughed until they were out of breath. I didn't particularly see what was funny, but their laughter made me laugh.

"Man, forget y'all. Y'all better be on your best behavior. Remember she not one of these little hood boogas that y'all know. Don't try and play me." Now it was my turn to chuckle a little. I think I was a bit nervous, Qwana never met any of my people before. She'd been in the same room with them during games but never stayed after to meet them.

That was one of the hardest things I had to do when she came to one of my games. We had to act like we didn't know each other. Qwana always came up to me after the game as a fan to say good game and kept it moving like nothing. We would meet right after, and we would discuss the game once I released some tension. I tried a season where I wasn't having sex, but it didn't work for me; I needed a nut to play as hard as I played.

We rode to Palisades Mall in upstate New York, about thirty minutes from Paterson. It was a one-stop-shop for a night of fun. Our first stop was Dave & Buster's, a tight spot for food and games. Qwana would meet us there, and I couldn't wait. We'd been talking, but only as friends; we hadn't even been back to our hotel. Every chance she had, she'd steal away and give me a call to chop it up. It was weird. I wanted more with her, but I'd rather still have her around. I guess this was the price you paid when getting attached to a married woman.

"This a dope mall, but why does it feel like we hiding? Let me find out you still gotta watch your back. Is the pussy worth it?"

"Reem, it's about much more than that. Trust me."

"I never understood why y'all continue to get played by these females. That shit is soft to me."

His truth was killing my mood, but he did have a point. I did feel like a sucker for having to sneak around. In the beginning, I really didn't care; we got right up after our porn show, and we kept it moving. As the years went on, we started talking more, and that was where the feelings grew. When you started getting to know someone, it was bound to happen on top of good sex; it was a no brainer. When I was mad at Qwana, I regretted it, but I was happy I met her most days. I know it's mad weird.

"I used to think like you, Reem, that females were good for one thing, but then I met her. All that changed, and it showed me what I was missing. I used to hear Cash talk about Jeda, and you know their love is complicated." Cash playfully hit me on my arm. We busted out laughing. "But nah, for real though. Love always seemed like too much to handle. It wasn't until I started catching feelings that I understood why Cash fought so much to stay with Jeda.

"Yeah, yeah, y'all can have it. Will it ever happen to me? I won't bet on it, but it's going to take a strong girl to knock me out of that mindset."

"I'm the opposite of y'all; the sex is great, but to have someone hold you down, someone to call your own and share your heart with, that joint is priceless."

"Are you guys ready to be seated?" the hostess asked.

"We can be seated; we are waiting on one person who is on her way."

"Damn, everybody doesn't need to know you waiting on

your girl, playa," Kareem joked, making all of us laugh, including the hostess who had her lustful eyes on me.

"She's a lucky girl. Follow me." She sashayed to our table. "Let me know if you need anything." The hostess looked at me and me only before leaving the table.

"You really must be in love. The Mase I know would have either got her number or would have taken her in the bathroom after we were done eating. Which Mase is sitting here now? I need to know."

"Reem, why you keep bothering him? That's why y'all always used to get into fights when we were little."

"Ain't nobody messing with him. I'm fooling around; it's all for laughs, Cash. Damn, loosen up. What got your panties all in a bunch?"

"Every time y'all speak on Jeda, y'all make me feel like I was stupid for loving her or something. Like she ran me or something. Yeah, it's all jokes, but sometimes I feel like y'all be serious."

"Bingo, that's the real problem here." Kareem shook his head.

"What's on your mind, Cash?" Obviously, my brother needed to talk. I wanted to get this out the way before Qwana came through.

"Everything else seems to be going right but my relationship. A part of me feels it's over, and I can't stomach it. All those years down the drain."

Kareem spoke first. "Man, I always loved the relationship you had with Jeda. I personally couldn't do it. I wasn't judging you. I was telling you what I wouldn't put up with."

"I always admired what you had with Jeda. Y'all remind me of Mom and Dad, the power couple. We wouldn't be family if we didn't throw jokes. You know that's all we did growing up. Remember we had to laugh to keep from crying."

"Nah, y'all had to laugh to keep from crying. I'm a G, and

gangstas don't cry." We busted out laughing, and it broke the ice on that conversation.

My phone vibrated. *I'm here.* It was a text message from Qwana, letting me know she arrived. "Yo, I'll be back; Qwana here. Let me go get her."

"Awwww... Look at the lover boy running to go get his boo thang," Kareem teased, and of course, we laughed.

Qwana was looking down at her phone when I walked up behind her. I whispered in her ear, "Hello, friend. I've been waiting for you to grace us with your presence." My instinct was to wrap my arms around her waist, but I quickly thought against it. This creating boundaries shit was taking a toll on me. I was used to getting what I wanted, and plus, I was horny; I hadn't had sex since Qwana left me at the hotel. I could call any girl, but I couldn't risk what happened with Kiara to happen again. I had a reputation to uphold, and I was pretty sure she was running her mouth.

"Mason, you scared the crap out of me, boy. I was waiting for you to text me back."

"I wanted to come to grab you myself. Had to make sure you made it to me."

"What, you thought I was going to get lost and never come back?" Her laugh was so light and perfect.

"You almost did, so don't remind me." I gently gripped her hand and led the way to our table. "My brother and cousin are stupid. Don't listen to nothing they have to say. They haven't had their medicine yet, and it may show." We both laughed at that lie, but she got what I was saying.

"Thank you for finding Nemo; we lost him in a crowd of people. How can we ever repay you?" Kareem was on his feet, reaching in his pocket. He was trying so hard to have a serious face, but Qwana thought it was the funniest thing, so he couldn't hold it anymore.

"This is my stupid cousin Kareem, and the one over there

cleaning up the soda he spit on the table is my brother Cash-mere. Bro, it wasn't that funny."

"Nice to meet you, Qwana. We thought you were a made-up character from one of his English papers. I'm glad to see you are real." Kareem shook Qwana's hand. Cash slid out of the booth to greet her.

"We give hugs around here." Cashmere hugged Qwana, and as much as it was awkward to me, she didn't seem to mind. That made me smile, showing my pearly whites.

She slid inside the booth, and we all took our seats.

"How was your drive over?" I had to ease her into the conversation; Cash and Mase were sitting on go, ready to clown me in front of my *lady friend*.

"The drive over was great. Driving is a great way to think about everything and talk to yourself if need be. Y'all ever do that?"

"I know I do. I find myself in the car sometimes at my destination, not knowing how I got there. When you have a lot on your mind, that will do it. It also gives me alone time to run melodies through my head."

"I only like to drive at night. It's something about a night-time drive. The air, the lights, and the whispers of a quieter world."

"Interesting. I never looked at it like that." Qwana looked my way. "Mason, what do you say?"

"Wait, wait! She calls you Mason?" Here Kareem go. They both looked on in shock but with smirks on their faces. They knew my government was only used by the people I loved. I would always correct someone when they didn't call me Mase.

"Yeah, he must really like you," Cash confirmed. Qwana smiled.

"To answer your question, Q, I never put that much

thought into driving. I want to get to my destination and that's it."

"Since he wants to ignore my question. Let me tell you how he peed the bed when we were younger." The table erupted in laughter at Kareem's antics. The rest of the night was dope; we ate, played games, and enjoyed each other's company. My family had never seen me care for women, so it most definitely was new to them. They were either smiling or cracking jokes.

"You keep checking your phone." Cashmere and Kareem had gone back to the basketball court game, so we finally had some alone time. I noticed throughout the night, Qwana was checking her phone. I wanted to make sure she was good. I didn't want to cause any problems for her. I personally didn't care about her nigga.

"Nic is supposed to be home at a certain time, and I want to make sure I wasn't too far behind him. He's been up under me lately, staying home more. I don't want him asking questions. I'm tired of lying."

Her reality sent heat from the bottom of my feet to the top of my head. If I could guess, my face was probably red. The thought of her husband touching her was something I couldn't stomach but had to swallow. I hadn't been able to even get my dick wet, but yet she let her bum ass husband invade her privacy. I shook my head to get the thoughts out. *Friends* echoed in my head, but I didn't want to think about that either.

"So I'm one of your girlfriends now?" As much as I tried not to be pissed off, I was.

"You know you're more than that. I don't want us to keep lying to each other or withholding information. I want you to know all parts of me, and right now, my husband is a part of me. The foundation our relationship was built on is already shaky; why not build a firm foundation so that can stand the test of time?"

While she had a point and it made me look at it a little differently, it was still something that I didn't want to get used to. Mainly the fact that she was giving this nigga my pussy. I was getting used to our situationship. I now had to get used to being friends. It was going to take some time. Her confiding in me, basically telling me she was scared of her husband, kept us connected. If something was to happen to her, I would be devastated.

"We still have to set some boundaries. It's only so much I can take, Q. This is one of the hardest things I had to do in life. My heart pumps for you. The more I try to ignore it, the greater it grows. You have me waiting for your calls then wishing we never hung up. I don't know what you want me to do."

"I want you to trust me." Qwana's hands met my face as a sign that she understood. I always felt that Qwana loved me. She was stuck between being in love with me and loving her husband. I never knew the difference until she explained it to me. Loving someone is loving someone.

I leaned in for a hug, not caring if that wasn't what friends did. I had to have her in my arms, and if she kept it up, I was going to get a kiss too. When we were on the phone, I was straight, but it was when I saw her that was going to be the problem. Keeping my hands to myself was not a fun game. Flashbacks of me looking into her eyes while I stroked her pussy was a constant reminder of how much I missed the intimacy. It stopped being about sex a long time ago, but it was a connection that we'd lost.

"Get a room." Kareem was straight cock blockin'.

"Or at least go to the bathroom." Cash knew I was quick to take a girl in the bathroom that wanted the dick. Couldn't let Qwana know that, though.

"Y'all some haters for real. Let's get our things; we about to be out."

"Bet, I got some things to do and people to see anyway." Kareem walked ahead of us to get his things.

"It was nice meeting you Qwana. I was glad to put a face with a name." Cash pulled Qwana in for a hug. My brother approved. "Qwana, where you parked at? We're gonna pull the car wherever you are. Bro, we'll meet y'all outside."

"I'm parked by Modell's."

"Okay, I think we are parked around the same area."

"It was nice meeting you both; I'm glad you guys let me hang." Qwana shook Kareem's hand back at the table. Kareem wasn't a hugger; he barely showed any feelings, so that was his way of showing his approval, I guess.

They went ahead of us. Our walk was slow but steady; Qwana had to get home. I didn't want to let her go. I was contemplating kidnapping her, but I was sure her husband would come looking. My mind was in an uproar, trying to figure out how I could keep her with me for a little while longer. I would suggest we go back to our hotel, but I didn't want her to think all I wanted was sex. I was running out of options, and we had finally made it to her car. I never was good at goodbyes, but the quicker I let her go, the quicker she'd be back.

KAREEM

He must not know that it's niggas like me you don't play with!
-Kareem

"*K areem, I've been calling your phone, and you have yet to call me back. Don't make me come look for you.*"

This was the third message I received from my mom. The urgency in her voice told me she knew. I'd been avoiding her. If I knew one thing, more than likely, she kept her ears to the streets. She was clean for the time being, but it was hard to escape the confinements of the underworld. The streets had been talking, and my crew was making moves. I had to reposition Rick and Reese up top while I handled down the hill. Dom wanted me to put in work; I was gonna show him better than I could tell him that he needed me.

I didn't like the position I was in having to answer to somebody, but this was my situation right now. It wasn't the best situation, but it was very profitable in more ways than

245

one. I was making money and gaining respect all at once. One of my biggest accomplishments was seeing many young soldiers wanting to go back to school; they saw how serious college was for me. It was time out for breeding dumb street hustlers. It was more to life than slangin' and bangin'. I was trying to change the narrative that it was only two ways out, jail or death. Let's add moving on to bigger and better things.

I really felt bad about going MIA on my mom, but she did it to me all these years. Now I understood why she didn't want to be seen doing wrong. I felt like, in some way, that's what I was doing. I still hadn't told Cash or Mase, but I was pretty sure they'd heard too. If not, they would probably be finding out soon. I wasn't too worried about them; they'd understand once I told them why I did it. I needed two more big drops, and I'd have the money for Grammy's house. The return I was going to see with adding the coke would get me the remainder plus more.

"What's good, Cash?" He had music playing in the background but not too loud to where I couldn't hear him. If I had to guess, he was in the studio. Cash definitely had been putting in those hours.

"Yo, I want you to meet me on River St. You know that building across from the car wash by Lafayette Bridge?"

"Yeah, I know where that's at; you good though?" He didn't sound like anything was wrong. He actually was hyped about something. I knew my cousin.

"Yeah, I'm good. Man, be on your way. Call me when you are outside."

"Aight. Bet."

"*Ayo, turn that up.*" With that, he hung up.

One thing I could say about us, we always went after our dreams. We never wanted to be a burden to the people we loved. We wanted to be the ones quick to help; we cared. Hearing Cash's song and seeing the look in his eyes was a proud moment for me, knowing what he waited his whole life for. It was a lot transpiring at the time, but I did take in his shine. I got myself together and made my way to where the party was.

It didn't take me long before I was at the destination. I always wondered what was in this building. It always flooded down this way by the bridge, but somehow these businesses on this block always stayed afloat. I found myself a park and called Cash outside. I didn't know what floor or anything.

"Yo, Reem, you outside?"

"Yeah, I'm here. 237 River Street, right?

"Yup, aight. I'm going to meet you downstairs."

I made my way to the building entrance. As I was crossing the street, I could see Cash at the door. Mase had pulled up as if on cue. If I had known I could park in the dirt next to the building, I would have pulled in there. Mase and I walked up together, both ready to see what all the hype was about. It had to be something massive; Cash's greeting confirmed that.

"Yooooooo, thank y'all for coming. I can't wait to show you what I've been working on." Cash pulled the door to the building open and allowed us to walk through. We waited for him so that we could follow him to the big reveal. As we got closer to the second floor, you could hear the music blasting.

"This a new strip club or something?" We all laughed. "It better be some hoes in here that take quarters." We fell out laughing.

"You stupid, Reem. Close y'all eyes." Cash put his hand on the handle, not opening the door until we closed our eyes.

"Aight, yo, come on. You doing too much." I still did as I was told, I didn't want to take his shine. I was excited about whatever was behind the door, trying to match his happiness.

Cash slowly guided Mase and me through the door with our eyes closed. I wanted to peek, but I trusted my cousin.

The music blasting was definitely coming from this room. We walked in, and his song dropped. "You guys can open now."

Before I was able to take in my surroundings, both Mase and I looked at Aonika hanging on Cash, enjoying this moment with him. She was stuck to him like a girlfriend would be attached to their boyfriend. Her smile was bright, and her energy was intoxicating. She commanded the room, but more so, she wanted us to know that she was here to stay. She had nothing to prove to us but more to prove to herself. I ain't gonna lie; it caught us off guard, but we recovered quickly.

"I like, I like," was the first thing that came to mind to bring me back to why we were here. I meant to say it twice. I liked what I saw from a floor plan perspective, but I also liked that my cousin seemed happy without Jeda. Jeda had a way of wiping that joy away. I took everything in.

The layout was dope. You could tell it was unfinished but on its way to being done. We walked a little further into the open space, quietly. "This will be the sitting area. When this light is on," he pointed to a red light that read *In Session*, "nobody can enter the studio." He opened the door to a studio setup. When finished, it was going to look super badass, compared to the other studio I'd seen. I'd only seen the one Cash was recording out of and ones on TV. This was a straight step up from the hole in the wall studio he was at.

"Bro, this all you?" Mase posed the same question I was thinking. He got it out first.

"Yup, it's all me, bro. I found somebody to invest in my dream. This whole floor is me. It's not much, but it's better than the studio room I was in at the other spot. I could never afford the room that Ms. Aonika Monroe had, but I think this would do." Aonika blushed and fanned him away.

"Oh, stop."

I hadn't seen Aonika in a minute. Cash told us they were

working together, but it seemed they had been doing more than that. I never saw Cash with anybody but Jeda; this was super weird but welcomed. Anything or anybody that was going to make both my cousins happy, I was down for it. First Mase with Qwana, now Cash and Aonika were doing the thang. We all had somebody; my somebody was my money. It didn't talk back, and it did whatever I wanted it to do. That's the type of relationship I needed.

We did need to rap real quick without shawty hanging off his arm, though. We needed freedom to say whatever we wanted. My first question would be about her anyway. I needed details of this new love story unfolding. This was pure entertainment for me; Mase and Cashmere were on their way to winning an Oscar with the drama called their love life. I looked around again at what this could be, both the studio and the connection between Cash and Aonika. I needed answers.

"Aonika, do me a favor and play around with the soundboard in the studio. The rest of the equipment should be here sometime next week." She knew what it was; we needed our privacy.

"Okay." She kissed him on his cheek and went through the doors of the studio. We walked closer to the front door, where there were a few chairs to sit on. Of course, his big brother started first.

"You and Aonika together now? What happened with Jeda?" Cash shrugged it off like what Mase was asking wasn't a legit question. Maybe he was trying to figure it out himself.

"Can we focus on my new studio? I'll give y'all the details to that when I know." Jeda was his one and only, so it probably was hard for him to come to terms with it. I respected that and hoped Mase did as well. All Cash would do was shut down, and we didn't want that.

"So this all you? I'm proud of you, but where you get the money from?" Inquiring minds wanted to know.

"Dom invested—"

"Wait, Dom who?" My head started spinning; it felt like the wind was knocked out of my body at the mention of Dom's name coming out of my cousin's mouth.

"Dom, the dude I met at the party in the Vill that day you were acting weird. We still ain't talk 'bout that day."

"I don't know, Cash. Something seemed off about that Dom guy. What did he offer you?" Mase asked, curious.

"He offered me this studio and $25,000 for him to be a silent partner. He's going to help me look for management too."

"No... No... Please don't tell me you took his money?" Why Dom involved my family, I didn't know, but I didn't like it. I could handle anything he threw my way, but I wasn't sure Cash could. I got up and started pacing the floor.

"Yes, I did. Why you say it like that?" You could hear the nervousness in Cash's voice, piecing together that he might have made a mistake. That he did.

"Dom is someone you shouldn't be in business with; he plays dirty. I've experienced it firsthand." I knew the questions would start flying after, but I had to tell them so Cash could be careful. This shit pissed me off.

"I didn't want to believe what my mind was telling me that night, but I knew something was wrong. You dip out of the party, and the next time we see you, you with Dom and Harvey. This shit is now adding up. You work for them?" I wasn't in the mood for Mase to piss me off more.

"Yes, I do for the time being. What I'm doing is not up for discussion. Cash, I need you to return him his money. It will turn into something you can't handle. Trust me."

"So you selling drugs?" Mase wouldn't let up. He always was this way, so I wasn't surprised. The disappointment in his eyes triggered more anger within me. At this point, it wasn't about me; it was about saving Cash from making a huge mistake.

"I hope you're listening, Cash. Give him back his money. We'll find you another way. You gotta trust me."

"How can we trust you and you leaving out important details?" Mase, Mr. Prosecutor, still had his attention on me.

"Go ahead wit' all of that, Mason. Let up with all these questions. I don't have to explain my moves to nobody, and that's that. I'm trying to get in front of this before it takes a turn for the worst, but you beefing up on me like I'm the bad guy. I'm not going to say it again. I'm out."

I made my exit, furious that I allowed my family to get caught up in my mess. I could have stopped Cash from taking Dom's card at the party, but I didn't. I never thought Cash would call. Plus, I was too focused on what I was going to do with Red once Dom pulled off. Dom had a lot of balls; he must not have known that it was niggas like me you don't play with. It was one thing for Dom to have suckered me, but I'd be damn if I was going to let him dig his claws into Cash.

JANE

"*B*ingo!"
      I was desperate; I didn't know any other way. Since Jax told me about how my sister really died, I couldn't sleep. All I kept thinking about was how I was going to get to Dom. I went through different scenarios, and this was my best option. If I knew anything about Yvette, it was that she attended Friday night Bingo. I watched her from across the room as the person called off the numbers to confirm if they had bingo.

Yvette was always uppity and thought her shit didn't stink. We weren't friends or enemies, but we still kept it cute when we saw each other. Yvette's once knock-off brands were now replaced with the finer things in life. Her and Harvey must've really been hitting it off; she looked like a hustler's wife. That was supposed to be my sister; she was the glammed-up wife that everybody wanted to be like. Thinking about it made me angry. I had to keep my composure and put my plan in place.

Fearlessness was a trait I only inherited when I was high as a kite, but I took it right with me the day I put down the drugs. That was the only way I would survive in a world that only saw me as the crackhead. It was a past that most wouldn't forget; I was not what I once was. I'd continue to prove it, not to the world but to the ones who still loved me despite all that I'd done. I felt Kareem was on his way to forgiveness, but how would I know if he didn't answer his phone?

That made me hate Dom even more; he was keeping my son away from me like my mother used to do. My absence wasn't always my doing; after a while, I gave up. My mother's points were valid as to why she didn't want me to see him; I felt he was my only reason to get clean. And she took that away from me. That's why I hadn't been back to the house. This shit triggered a lot of things that usually would have sent me to the crack house, but not this time.

We were now on our break before the final game. I watched Yvette get up and followed her right into the bathroom. Yvette was yapping her mouth about something. That girl knew she could talk. "Girl, you know Lisa got caught messing with Tony the other night? It's about time she got caught, knowing that man married." I went into the stall next to hers, acting at its finest. Once she flushed, I waited until I heard the water running.

"Yes, girl, I heard," Yvette, gossip girl, replied.

I walked out of the stall, fixing myself, playing the role well. I looked up, and Yvette was looking at me through the mirror. She had to do a double take. She turned around quickly as I walked up to the sink. "I had to make sure that was you. Hey, Jane. I haven't seen you in so long; you look good, honey." I was gaining my confidence back each day at a time, so she didn't have to tell me. My weight was up, and the money flow coming from work had me looking extra cute.

"Hey, Yvette. Yes, it's been a minute. How have you been, girl?" I dried my hands, and we walked out of the bathroom together.

"I've been good. I see you in here trying to win that money too. I don't need it; I come here to have something to do." Like, did I really need to know that she didn't need the money? That was her insecurity talking; she didn't have much growing up, but she had more than most from around the way. That didn't stop her from belittling others to make herself feel better. She never tried it with Linda and me; we were the girls that everybody measured themselves to. Well, Linda, anyway. I came as a bonus.

"That's good to hear. Where are you working? I could use that extra money, girl." We were now at the snack counter grabbing something for this next round.

"Me, work? I have a man who takes care of me. You remember Harvey, right? He used to run with Mason and Jax back in the day." The mention of their names vexed me. Harvey used to be a low-level street hustler when they ruled the streets. He did petty stuff for niggas like Dom. I let her live in her fantasy, though.

"Of course I remember Harvey."

"Well, girl, he done swept me off my feet. The only work I have to clock is between them sheets, you feel me?" She held up her hand for a high five; I almost missed it but remembered I was playing a role. Yvette was the definition of a gold digger and someone who wanted to be hood famous so bad. Nothing had changed down through the years, I saw. We were all chasing that fast life at one point; I was glad I grew up.

"I know that's right." If fake was a person, it would be me right now. "Tell Harvey I said hey."

"Girl, you can tell him. He's picking me up. He always drives me around in his new Cadillac." I saw the sparkle in her eyes at her announcement of what he was driving. Dudes driving around in new cars didn't impress me. What did impress me was that after all these years, my reading of people was right. From what I could remember, Harvey was a very jealous and insecure man, so he wasn't about to let Yvette go anywhere without him. I was two for two.

I wasn't even paying attention to the game. I was more focused on my pitch to get Dom to meet me. We had history; Dom was the one that gave me my first hit, probably the first few. I thought at the time he was helping me cope, but now I looked back at it differently. It was like one day he was seen, and the next he was gone in the wind. It was all starting to add up now. He executed his plan well; he won the fight but not the war. He was not going to see me coming.

My plan had to be bulletproof. If Dom thought I needed drugs again, he would meet with me. The only difference was, he didn't make drug runs anymore; he was the king on the throne. I had a pile of thoughts and didn't know which way I would take, but I had to think quickly. I wanted to be prepared when I saw Harvey; I didn't want him to think anything was up. I needed this to go as smoothly as possible. My adrenaline was on a high as we got closer to the end of the game.

I made sure to meet Yvette at the door. As soon as I walked out, Harvey was glaring our way. He was parked right outside the entrance, leaning against the car, smoking a cigarette. His eyes traveled up my body to the glow in my face. He nodded his head, realizing it was me. Almost saying *Okay, I see you.* When he last saw me, I was begging him for some drugs. Now I was healthier than I ever was.

"Baby, remember Jane from around the way, Linda's sister?" It was always Linda's sister. A part of me hated it; it made me feel like I would forever live in her shadow. If I wasn't Linda's sister, it was crackhead Jane behind my back, so I'd take the first.

"Of course, I remember Linda's big sister. You look fine like wine."

"Harvey!"

"Yvette, get in the car. Now!" She stomped her way to the passenger side door, flung it open, and slammed it off the hinges.

"Slam my motherfucking door again and watch what I do to you." Through clenched teeth, the pimp in him spoke. That's who he reminded me of. With his creased dress pants and his matching button-down shirt, he took country cool to a new level. He screamed money but looked all types of wrong. His eyes met mine once more.

"Where you been? I ain't seen you in years."

"You wasn't looking for me either."

"Still got that mouth on you, huh?"

"Some things will never change, huh?"

"I always liked you, Jane. Hopefully, I'll see you around." I needed this not to end. Think quick, Jane. Think quick.

"How's Dom doing? You two were thick as thieves back in the day. You're still running with him?" He looked around at the mention of Don's name.

"He good. What, you miss him?"

"He really helped me get through losing Linda. I actually have some money saved up for him. I could never repay him for what he did for me, and he probably doesn't need my money; I owe him." I laid it on thick; Dom did help me out initially, so that wasn't a lie. He would sit around after giving me a hit to make sure I was good. Even held me many nights while I cried. I didn't know if that was a part of his plan to take over or if he really cared.

"Is that right?" It didn't look like Harvey was buying it, but hey, I tried.

"Yes. Tell him I want to meet with him. Now that I'm clean, I can see the value of his helping hand." I looked for a pen and paper in my purse. "Give him my number and tell him to call me." If Dom was still old school, he wasn't talking on the phone. "I would prefer to meet with him in private."

"I'll give him the information." Harvey looked me up and down one last time before opening the driver's side door. He turned up his music and pulled out the parking lot.

I didn't even realize I was holding my breath. I released it into the night, hoping I'd get that call. I hurried home to wait by the phone. I was confident Dom would accept; I saw something in his eyes when he used to supply me. A soft spot for little ole me; I even offered him sex once, but he turned it down, and I never saw him after. Back then, I didn't care; I was mad I had to find somewhere else to get my dope. He was another lost one amid my addiction.

I rushed home, anxiety kicking in. I had to get used to being alone. I was always around somebody in the streets, and it got lonely sometimes. Tonight wasn't one of those nights I could get in my head. I needed to get in touch with my son. I picked up the phone and dialed his number— voicemail. I tried three more times. The last time, I ended up leaving a voicemail.

I know I haven't been the best mother, but I have always loved you. I will never judge you or the decisions you make. Please call me, son. You can even stop by. I need to talk to you."

I hung up, disappointed that my son was avoiding me. I thought we were getting somewhere after his first visit. They say it would take some time for kids to trust parents who let them down, but he wasn't giving me a chance. He hadn't given me an opportunity based on the dirty deeds he was into. His lifestyle didn't matter; building a stable relationship did. I had to get to my son before Dom did.

The shrill scream of the telephone startled me. I hurried to pick it up. Not too many people knew my number. Kareem finally came to his senses.

"Hello."

"Meet Dom at the Bunker Hill warehouse. 2 East 11th Street at ten o'clock on Saturday." Harvey hung up.

CASHMERE

Mariah Carey - We Belong Together
When you left, I lost a part of me
It's still so hard to believe
Come back baby, please
'Cause we belong together

*A*s much as I loved creating music, I was happy that this session was over. I wanted to go home and go to sleep. I felt like I hadn't slept in days. We were at the end of recording the last few tracks for Aonika's debut album, and if I could say so myself, it was pure fire. We had twenty possible tracks that could make it on the final CD, but she was eyeing a 13-14 track set. I packed up my things and was on my way out. Aonika stopped me and wrapped her arms around my waist.

"Thank you, Cash, for all that you are contributing to this project." She looked up, still wrapped up in me.

"You got talent, and you got skills; I'm happy to be along

for the ride." I placed a tender kiss on her forehand. She closed her eyes, enjoying my wet lips connecting with her soft skin.

"Come by my place tonight? I should be leaving here in the next thirty minutes or so." She pulled back, looking for an answer.

"I might take you up on that offer. Let me go home and check on Grammy, and when you leave here, hit me, and we'll go from there. Cool?"

"Cool. I'll be leaving for L.A. soon, within the next few weeks. You better come and visit me." Aonika play punched me, feelings on display as she tried to cover up her vulnerability.

We hadn't really talked about what we were or what we were doing after our rendezvous. I had never been with anyone else but Jeda, so it was new to me but felt good all at the same time. I wasn't looking to jump right into another relationship right away, but having sex with Aonika probably gave her mixed signals. Her feelings were definitely starting to show more, and I felt terrible that I had to be that *guy*.

"You know I gotta come to LA." I gave her another hug, and I was gone.

I slowly walked to the car, enjoying the night's air. A car crept alongside me. At first, I thought they were going to stop. They kept right along with my footsteps, stalking my every move. I turned to see who it was, but the windows were tinted, shielding their identity. I made it to the parking lot on the side of the building. The car pulled in behind my car, and their driver side door opened.

"Can you keep your studio girl waiting for a few minutes so we can talk?"

"I see you came here to argue, and I'm not up for it tonight. I'm tired." My heart was no longer beating out of fear that something was about to go down.

"Cashmere, I'm sorry." Jeda's hoodie covered most of her face in the dark parking lot. Her apology did sound sincere, but I wasn't buying it.

I walked a little bit closer to her; it's like my body gravitated to her. I had to see her face, gauge her body language with the words that she spoke. I couldn't do that from where I stood, so I walked up to her.

"Cashmere, no!" I pulled off her hoodie, I needed to see her. I wasn't prepared for what I saw.

"What happened to your face Jeda?" I immediately went into panic mode, looking around, thinking her abuser was near. After the panic set in, I got angry. I wasn't even sure if we were together, but I was supposed to always protect her. That was my promise to her.

"My mother came back." She put her head down, ashamed that this was her reality, her truth. "This time, I wasn't going to let her get away with her words of war." Jeda started breathing hard. "She almost had me until she started talking about my father." Her father was her world, so I understood why she probably snapped.

I examined the bruising she had on the left side of her face. She was still a little sore by the way she kept flinching from my examination. I started checking out her body; if only I could pull off her clothes to kiss every inch to make it feel better. I pulled Jeda into my arms without words, and we stood there for a few minutes.

"I'm sorry. I've been in my own head about a lot of things. I shouldn't have shut you out or doubted you." My chin rested on her head as her words bounced off my chest to my ears. I was honestly over going back and forth apologizing, but this was a step in the right direction, so I embraced it.

"Shutting me out, Jeda, only pushes me further and further away. In the beginning, I dealt with it, and that probably was my fault. I never checked it. Both of our feelings matter at the end of the day. How is it that I can put my feelings aside to make you feel better, but you can't do the same for me?"

"I don't know. Before you, I had to protect myself by shutting out the world. I had to become numb to each situation I was thrown into. When my mother showed up this time, I could no longer ball up into a corner; I had to deal with it."

"What happened?"

"She came back, talking crazy. Calling me all types of hoes and bitches. She wasn't even in my apartment; she was banging on my door. She wouldn't let up. My tears weren't going to make her leave. So, I bit the bait." She pulled back, staring at me. "When I opened the door, she pushed her way through, knocking me off my feet. She must have been high. Her strength was unmatched."

"Why did you open the door?"

"She wouldn't go away, Cashmere. I didn't need my neighbors calling the office or hearing the foul things that could come out her mouth. I was already damaged in my head; I didn't need anyone else knowing that. It was when she started talking about my dad that everything changed. Can you believe he wasn't shot on duty? He was shot for being a dirty cop. After that, I lost it. Even if it was true, she shouldn't have told me that."

I didn't understand why this lady kept bothering Jeda, but by the sounds of it, she needed an ass whipping.

"Cashmere, I never had a fight before. I was close to it but never got to that point. I don't know what came over me, but this bruise on my face probably is nowhere near the bruises my mom has. I felt free after, no longer allowing her to hold things over my head. I went through the darkest times under her care; that's not a reflection of me. It was a reflection of her evil ways. I came to terms with that. If she wants to come back for more, let her. I'm not backing down anymore. I owe myself that."

A mother's hate shouldn't run that deep for someone that was born through them. "I'm so sorry you had to experience this yet again, but it sounds like it was needed to move forward." I pulled her to me to examine her face some more. She wouldn't look at me, probably ashamed. I couldn't help myself; I kissed her lips, gently pulling her chin up to meet the connection, enough to make contact. The second kiss was met with urgency. I knew I couldn't kiss all of our problems away or make us forget them; this was a start.

The words we couldn't express or didn't want to were translated through my lips, making out with hers. I pulled back, needing to collect myself; if not, I would have had Jeda bent over in my car. It wasn't about that, though. I picked her up and sat her on the trunk of my car. She played in my curls as my head rested on her breasts. I missed this; I missed us.

"I really thought I lost you." Jeda lifted my head. She was looking for some type of confirmation that she didn't. I didn't know if she could forgive me for sleeping with Aonika. Never officially calling it quits could play a factor. I was lost, and Aonika was there to soothe my temporary satisfaction. She was my distraction from the storm that was Jeda.

"On the real, Aonika was really holding me down by keeping me busy. It was still about you, though." I had to reassure her of the truth. "Even if you were right about Aonika, you gave way to her swooping right in to stake her claim. Never give someone that much power to take something you say you love. It's easier to run, but that's only letting the opposing side win. Love is a fight with different challengers waiting in the shadows."

"Wow. I'll take that."

"You still thinking about L.A.?" I looked up at her wanting to know.

"I have to go. I know I would regret it if I didn't. It's a great opportunity that will take me to where I need to go in my career. If you still want to be with me, we can make it work."

"If I want to be with you? Seriously, long-distance will be tough, so it's something to think about." I had so much invested in Jersey that it wasn't the right time for me to up and leave. Jeda knew that, so that's why she didn't ask me to come with her.

"Listen, let's think more on it; hit me up this weekend. We can talk and decide what we think is best. One thing I know is I can't be your friend. I can't watch you live life without me."

"That's where we agree." I wrapped my arms around her as she placed her head on top of mine. It was where I wanted to be. I was glad she gave us time to think it over. That meant we could tie up all loose ends. I picked Jeda up off the car, and she wrapped her legs around me as we leaned up on the vehicle she was driving.

"Wait, who car is this?"

"Boy, this a rental. I was so used to you driving me around. I only like taking the bus to school. I like having my own ride, so I think I'm going to definitely get one when I go to L.A."

Hearing her talk about L.A. crushed my heart. It was serious if it started to become something she looked forward to. If we continued or not, she would follow her dreams, which made me love her even more. It was something I would have to get used to. I held her tighter against her rental, her legs still wrapped around my waist. I made love to her lips, forgetting about L.A., forgetting about Aonika, enjoying every minute I had with her.

"You going to be able to drive? You look kind of drunk."

"Forget you." We laughed as she got in the car.

"This weekend."

"This weekend." I gave her one more kiss and watched as she backed out of the parking lot. She beeped her horn; I watched her until she disappeared.

"You still here?" Aonika brought me out of my daze, probably pondering why I was in the parking lot looking at a dark street. Jeda was long gone, yet I was still stuck on how much I loved her. After all that drama, after her darkest secrets, my heart always belonged to her. Nobody could tell me anything different.

"Was about to dip out, not before I came in to holla at you real quick. You saved me a trip." A nervous chuckle filled the air. I didn't know if she would want to work with me after this, but one had nothing to do with the other.

"I did all the work, and you're tired?" We both laughed. We always joked about who did the most work in our sessions. It made us work harder trying to outdo each other on a melody or verse that we were creating.

"You are really dope, Aonika... like really dope. The history that we make musically will live on forever. I have to end whatever else that's brewing between us." I paused before continuing. "Right now, let's focus on completing your project. I have to figure out what's going on between Jeda and me before getting to know somebody else. I don't want to hurt anyone."

"It was fun while it lasted." It was as if she already knew. I couldn't gauge if she was mad or hurt. "I always wondered why you didn't look at me like you look at her. I knew she would always have your heart." I couldn't even deny that, so I let my silence speak for me.

Foul

A violation of the rules, usually involving illegal contact with a player of the opposition.

"Yo, good shit out there today." Quincy threw his towel in his cubby next to me. We had finished the Scarlet-White scrimmage with a win. We were now back in school. I officially started my senior year in college.

My stats were looking good; I needed it to stay like that for the whole season. The crowd was what I needed; I played off of them. It wasn't the usual crowd, but at least people were there to see me kick ass. Fans made the game live; they turned up my adrenaline like it had a button. I was still trying to come down as the rest of the team did what they did. This was only the beginning. I was trying to take us all the way this year.

"Wait till our first game. We got Austin Peay State. We

gonna show them what we about." I fist bumped Quincy, and the rest of the locker room went up after my declaration. I was captain. This was my second year, so I had to outdo our record from last year. Last year we were 20-13, ninth in the Big East, which wasn't bad, but I needed to top that.

I had enough confidence in myself that I would get drafted as a first-round pick, whether my team went all the way or not. It wasn't about me this time. I wanted my teammates like Quincy to make it. A lot of these guys, that's all they ever dreamed about. I was guaranteed a spot, but not everybody could say that; one in seventy-five had the odds of making it to the NBA. I was blessed to be in that 1.3 percent.

It was still up in the air what I was going to do. I had time. I had a few agents who I was in talks with. Nothing was set in stone; I was weighing my options. I was straight on the court and looking at properties with Mr. and Mrs. Patterson. You could say I had the best of both worlds. A part of me felt that I could do both, honestly. If I went to the NBA, Mr. Patterson was willing to run the business while I made history. On the off season, I would come back to give him a break. Definitely something to think about.

"Where the shawtys at, Mase?" Quincy always used me as a magnet for his infatuation with women. I didn't mind being his wing man, but these days I had so much more to focus on.

"You tell me, playa." "No Better Love" by the Young Gunz started playing. Quincy looked at me surprised, seeing Q pop up on my screen.

"See, you know where the shawtys at. One calling you right now. Let me answer, bro." He cracked up laughing, trying to grab my phone. I didn't want to answer right away anyway. This friend shit was hard; it was taking a toll on my mental, but that's what I signed up for, I guess.

"Yeah, aight. Chill." I waved him off and went to a quieter area of the locker room to answer.

"What's good, Q?" Sniffling could be heard. "Q, you there?" I started to get a little nervous. I didn't know if she butt dialed me or dialed me by mistake. I listened on to see if I could get a glimpse in her world. I barely knew anything about Qwana. I knew she was the marketing manager for this big firm. She told me about work but never went into full details.

"If I ever called for you, would you come and get me?" Qwana's incredulous voice questioned.

Without a shadow of doubt, I would. I hesitated a little, trying to gauge where this was coming from. This was a first. Qwana always called me in good spirits, even when we were on the outs. "Of course, Q. You know I got you. You good?" There was silence. I couldn't contain my worry. "Qwana, you there? Where are you?" I looked at my phone; the call had ended.

I hit redial back-to-back. The call kept going to voicemail. I was out of options. I didn't know where Qwana lived or who she even hung out with. I felt defeated trying to trace the steps to any possible leads for me to get to her. I skipped on the shower and grabbed my things, headed to nowhere. I didn't have any idea where to start looking for her. I needed to think, but I couldn't do that in the locker room.

"Yo, you out?" Quincy threw his hands in the air with an unbelievable expression on his face. He was trying to hold in his laugh. He acted like he needed me to pull some pussy; he was bored and needed entertainment.

"I gotta handle something real quick. I'll hit you when I get back." Quincy was cool peoples. This was our last year together. I was pretty sure we'd see each other in the league; he already started his process.

"Aight, bet," was all I heard as I made my way to my car. I walked swiftly, sorta like my life depended on it. I wouldn't forgive myself if anything was to happen to Qwana. I needed her to be alright for my sanity. The thought of losing someone

I loved made my stomach turn. It brought me back to the day my grandmother set me down to tell us that my parents died.

"Mason, you and your brother come in here and sit down." We had come in from the park sweaty, which Grammy didn't like. I was hoping she wasn't calling us in the living room to scold us. We stopped in to get us some water, then we were back outside. It was Labor Day weekend; we were trying to enjoy these last few days of freedom before school started.

"Yes, Grammy?" Cashmere asked, catching his breath from chasing after me. He wasn't much of a baller, but he was very competitive. To make it fair, we always did stuff other than play ball. The intense game of tag we played had us tired, ready for more. When I saw the tears in her eyes, I knew something was wrong. Grammy was a tough cookie; I never saw her in this state.

"Grammy, you okay?" Cashmere took notice once he heard the panic-stricken tone of my voice. She wouldn't look at us once we noticed. My ten-year-old mind knew something terrible had happened. Cash started crying, which made my grandmother start weeping. I was holding mine in, waiting for whatever it was.

"Your... your... oh my God! No!" Grammy collapsed right on the living room floor, missing the edge of the coffee table that was in the middle of the room. We both rushed to her side.

"Cash, get her some water." He hesitated but came to his senses once I pushed him to go. "Grammy, please wake up. What happened?" Grammy... Grammy." Now I had tears running down my face. Whatever it was done kilt her. Please, Grammy, wake up." Cash came running back with water. He threw it right on my Grammy's face.

"What you doing?" I yelled.

"I thought that's what you wanted it for!" He was crying hysterically.

Grammy came to life, trying to catch her breath, almost probably drowning from the amount of water poured on her. "Cash, go get a towel, hurry!" He was fast as lightning as he made his way to the cabinet of towels. Cash rushed our way with a few towels. I wiped Grammy's face. I was on one side of her, and Cash was on the other side. After she gained her composure, we tried helping her to her feet.

Her recovery was met with whatever was plaguing her mind; her body gave out again. "No, No..." We were able to sit her on the couch. It took her a minute, but she finally got enough courage to fight through.

"Boys, I have something to tell you." Grammy scooted to the edge of the couch, leaning over, playing with her fingers.

"What's wrong?" Cash cried. Sensing that it was bad, which was the same feeling that I had in the pit of my stomach, I sobered right up once I realized I had to take charge. I wiped my tears; they both needed me. I couldn't show emotion. I had to get down to the bottom of what was ailing her.

"What happened, Grammy?" I needed answers.

"Your parents were in a bad accident, and... and they weren't able to save them." Her cries grew louder; everything went black. All I heard was loud crying in the background as I took flight. I ran out the door. I didn't know where I was running to, but I had to get away. I ran until I couldn't run anymore. I ended up at Montgomery Park, a few blocks from Grammy's house. I watched as the boys got busy on the court. The same court that my dad took me to on Saturdays to play the adults.

My tears met the silver metal of the gate overlooking the court. Resting my head against it left an imprint of being caged. If I heard my grandmother right, I had lost not one but two parents at once. From what, I didn't know. I shouldn't have left them in the state they were in; I didn't know what got into me. I let all my emotions speak with my body hitting the wind as I raced to uncertainty, to an invisible finish line.

My grandmother's words repeated in my head. They weren't able to save them. My dad was Superman; he got out of everything. It had to be a lie; it had to be a bad joke. We were still going to a *cookout this weekend; we had plans. I stayed until the last few people were making an exit. I couldn't go home and face what I was hoping was a dream. Jax found me and brought me back to what would be my new home.*

I was brought back to reality by the ringing of my phone. I smiled a little seeing Qwana's name pop up on my screen again. The other part of me was hoping I could get her location to come see her. I didn't care if she was home; I would take that chance to make sure that she was okay. I have to get some information on her at the end assessment. I couldn't be left in the dark, not knowing what to do.

"Qwana, you there? You had me worried for a minute. I was about to put a BOLO out on you, girl." Silence filled the phone. Movement could be heard, but no words were being expressed. "Q, why you not saying anything? Please tell me you are okay. Please!"

"Don't ever call this phone again!" A deep baritone echoed in anger. I looked at the phone, making sure I read the contact right. I couldn't even tell; they had hung up. As per my call log, it was definitely Qwana. If I had to bet, that was her husband.

When you do dirty deeds, you better be ready for the gardener to dispose of the dirty soil.
- Kareem

One thing about being the head nigga in charge was that people continued to test ya gangsta. The hood knew me for knocking a nigga out with the quickness. The streets didn't fight fair ones anymore. They played with guns, testing me as if I wasn't about that life. The same hands could pull the trigger if you acted crazy. I was speeding up top to one of our stash houses that got hit. Rick called me in rage. I didn't even understand him at first, but I was on my way.

"What's good?" I answered my phone, already knowing the line of questions I would receive.

"Where you at, Reem?" I was pretty sure Dom got the information as soon as it happened. "Some cats ran down on the spot on Godwin Ave." Harvey was collecting the information to report back. He needed an answer quickly, his words above the speeding limit.

"I'm on my way to handle it now. I'll call you when I know more." I hung up, not even caring to explain myself. Dom left me in charge, so let me be. I hadn't been in the game for long; I had to teach these niggas that it was the principle. I refused to be disrespected. When you took from another man without working for it, it became personal. If it was one thing they were going to remember about me, it was I didn't play about my money.

I pulled up, and the block was ghost. Only the everyday people, living their lives, were scattered about. I checked my surroundings, tapping the Glock attached to my hip. I had to get used to carrying, but like with anything else, I adapted well. I took the steps two at a time rushing right in. Ricky and Reese were standing before the runners and dealers that we helped eat and sleep at night. I slammed the door, ready to make a nigga pay. If I had to deal with Dom, somebody was going to have to deal with me.

"What the fuck happened?" Rick's cold stare stayed on the lineup as Reese ran it down.

"Yo, these niggas came out of nowhere. How they got on the block, that's what we trying to figure out now." Rick punched Scooby, the oldest of the lineup. Scooby was the one that was supposed to be the watchman for street activity. This wasn't a hangout spot. I stopped that as soon as I took over. Rick kept the money safe while Reese made sure the product was being replenished. This was our main stash house for the whole 4th Ward, therefore making it a big hit.

"They had to walk up or come from Twelfth Ave. side. I never even saw that car pull up." Scooby spoke through a bloody mouth, brave enough to say a word. He spit but didn't even bother to wipe his mouth. It was definitely more where that came from.

"Who was in the house?" If they didn't catch it on the street level, where was everybody that was in the house? Without putting Rick and Reese on the spot, I wanted to know their whereabouts. Rick was the heavy machinery. How did they get past him?

"Rick had left to go grab something to eat, and I was upstairs trying to get some pussy from Tasha." Reese paused for a minute, hearing, probably for the first time, where he fucked up. He kept on with the story. I hoped he knew we were going to deal with that when we got by ourselves. "I forgot I had some water boiling for some oodles and noodles. I slide out the pussy real quick, catching them niggas as they were leaving. They started shooting, silencer and everything. I wasn't even strapped; my shit was laying on the dresser upstairs." That was strike two. They were being careless, and it was unacceptable.

"Where Tasha at? For all we know, she could have set this whole thing up."

"I'm on it already. She downstairs tied up in the basement. We were waiting to see which one of these lames was going down there with her."

"Get these niggas talking. I don't want to hear they don't know either. Somebody knows something."

"Man, I told you I ain't know nothing." My walk to the basement door was halted. Before I was able to turn around, Rick held his gun pointed to the side of this little dude named Primey's head.

"Say that shit again. I dare you. Say it again." Rick's eyes were bloodshot red, maybe from the bud he smoked. He looked spacey.

Never one to let people handle my dirty work, I couldn't let Primey get away with his mouth, so I punched him in it— knocked him straight out. Reese threw a kick to his head for the finish. Primey now had a leaking nose and a leaking head, probably dreaming about his mommy. Reese followed behind me as I went to see Tasha down in the basement.

"How much did they take?" That was the main question and would determine how I would handle this situation. The basement was where we counted the money. That was where all our safes were, and we bagged up on the second floor. Nothing was done on the main level so that if we ever got raided, we could get rid of stuff quick. If they didn't have those silencers, the cops would have been here with the quickness.

"It wasn't much. They probably got away with fifty-five hundred the most. That's only because of what was left to count from yesterday."

"That's too fucking much either way. They shouldn't have been able to walk away with nothing, Reese." I stopped at the bottom step, really looking at this nigga. "Shit like this don't happen on my watch. That fifty-five hundred coming right out of you and Rick pockets, and that's each." I didn't want to hear shit. Tasha came into view. She was tied up, and once she saw me, she started to go buck crazy. Her mouth was sealed with thick gray tape. I stood there watching her, until eventually, she got tired. I needed her to answer a few questions.

"I'm not here to hurt you. This is what happens when things are out of the ordinary. The day you decide to give up some pussy, we get robbed. Tell me that ain't a coincidence?" I slowly released her lips from the bondage of not speaking.

"I swear, I don't know nothing. I was trying to have a good time. I swear, Reem." She was crying and shaking her head. "Please, I promise you."

I didn't know this girl, but she didn't have anything to do with it. She was now a liability though. Although no one was shot and killed, she witnessed our weakness. This whole setup was about to change; I needed a tighter reign. First, by dealing with the niggas I left in charge. I wasn't impulsive in thinking. For me, it had to make sense. If I was wrong, I'd have to deal with the consequences. Once I learned from it, trust, it wouldn't happen again. Fool a G like me once, but you wouldn't get me twice.

"Let her go." I moved in closer to Tasha so she could hear me and hear me clear. "Listen, this is not a pass go and collect your two hundred dollars in Monopoly. If we find out that the dots trace back to you, you're dead. It ain't worth it, trust me."

"Out the back." I made my way upstairs to handle the second issue. Rick was still staring these niggas down. That shit wasn't going to do anything. We had to make an example out of one of these little niggas. Scooby and Primey were now back on their feet. It wasn't willingly either. The other four were looking on with fear dripping from their stance.

"This is how it's going to go. Primey, since you want to run your mouth, I'm taking it old school on you." I pointed to all of them. "Take him outside and whoop his ass. I don't care if y'all boys; you better be glad I'm letting you keep your life. Starting with this..." I took my Glock out and split his shit with the butt of the gun. Blood leaked down his face as he hit the floor yet again. "Drag him outside and finish what I started. Until we find out who did it, all y'all guilty. You might live another day, but your days are numbered. Don't stop until I tell y'all to." Scooby was the first one to grab Primey up, and the others followed suit.

I was pissed as hell. Reese now joined me and Rick in the front room. I looked between the two of them. These were my brothers. Sometimes it was hard coming down on them. I didn't ask for this position; it was given to me, and rightfully so. The more I spent time out here, the more I realized I was built for this. It was a shady game that only a few could play, and with a little more time, I'd master it.

"I don't think any of them little niggas had nothing to do with it. Primey was a hot head that we had to get under control. He'll come around." Rick may have been on to something, but only time will tell if what he believed was true. It was two ways this Primey thing could play out, so it was my decision to make.

"Let's talk about the fact that you left your post to eat when handling business."

"I told that n—"

"Wait, you told him? You told him? You was in the house when them niggas was here? They still walked out with our bread. You couldn't even get a shot off. You know why? You had your dick in your hand. Both of y'all fucked up."

"It ain't our fault."

"We take accountability around here! That's what real men do. Don't let it happen again. Remember, y'all wanted this. We could have so much more if we do this shit right. Make sure the business is right, and the pleasure will come. We making millions or what? That's what we promised ourselves, right?"

"We making millions," Reese declared.

"Yes, sir," Rick followed up.

Dap.

Fist bump.

Handshake.

Salute.

"Hit these streets and find out who is responsible for this. I gotta go handle Dom. Clean up in here to. It gotta look like somebody live here. We don't want the cops snooping around. When you get it looking like something, find some spots to hide some guns. You should always have access to blast something if needed. If we gonna do this shit, we gonna do it right."

"Got you," was heard times two, working some of that twin power that was rarely seen. They were usually on two different planets.

"Handle that in the back too. He better need some emergency assistance. Keep him upstairs and let that nigga heal. When I get back, y'all better have some new information. We about to make the streets hear us!"

My phone started vibrating. This time, it was Dom. I blew out a breath. I had to put myself in his shoes. Rick and Reese had to answer to me, but I had someone to answer to as well. "Meet me at the warehouse now." There was nothing else needed. I was on my way anyway. I stormed out of the door and made my way to the man that was holding all the cards. I'd like to play my own hand.

I made it in record time, hating that everybody seemed to drive slower when you had somewhere to go. I made it to the gate. Never having come here during the day, it looked like a normal working factory, with workers and everything. A few workers were loading boxes into the back of some trucks. The two guards were still manning the gate, this time AK's hidden. One guard met me at my car. He had another dude with him that looked more like security than an armed killer.

"Please follow me," the security officer stated. At least he was polite and talked. The other two always grilled me without words.

We made our way through a busy warehouse. Normal regular working business hours was taking place. Workers were doing what was in their job description, waiting for payday. I always thought it was an abandoned warehouse used for illegal activity, but I was wrong. I was also wrong, thinking we were on our way to Dom's office. I was being led to a door that needed a code.

"Dre here will see you the rest of the way. It was nice meeting you. Have a great day." The security guard had turned around and left me with Mr. Mute as he entered his code into the mystery door.

I wanted to question him to see where we were going,

which would have stayed unanswered, so I didn't bother. I followed. We walked a long hallway to a steel door. The mute, Dre, knocked, and the door opened. Harvey was on the other side. Dre stayed put, I walked in, and the steel door closed. Two bodies hung from chains, and blood was everywhere to where I couldn't even identify whose bodies they were from first glance.

"Look hard. This is how you get stuff done." Dom didn't even look my way; he was looking at the bodies before us.

"I was working on it."

"Working on it and getting it done is two different things."

"See it how you want to see it. I put a BOLO out, and I had Rick and Reese putting their foot on the neck of the streets. I'm not sure what else it is you want me to do."

I didn't know when, but Dom got in my face, staring me down with his dark, cold eyes. His sleeves were pulled up on his light-blue dress shirt, and his tie was loosened with a few top buttons opened. He might have not been dressed for this type of labor, but that didn't stop him from turning around and punching one of the guys like he was a boxing bag. It woke up the guy, only to knock him back out from the blows he was taking. Harvey came up out of nowhere with a bat and cracked the guy hanging in the back, with five words... "You... got... us... fucked... up." This tag team was no match for the hanging bros.

"Let them down!" Dom barked orders. Harvey let them both down, letting their feet touch the ground. They couldn't stand. They looked dead but were surely breathing. "These two little motherfuckers thought they could get away with my money, and you let them."

"I let them?"

"I didn't ask you to speak. Listen." Dom pulled gloves out of his pocket, grabbed his gun, and put a silencer on it. He walked back over to me. Always when in Dom's presence, I prayed that I didn't go out like a sucker. He was the boss, no doubt, but there was a way to talk to me. I wasn't a little kid, and if I respected you, you were gonna respect me. I didn't care who you were. "You're going to do your job and what I pay you for. They gotta go. Both of them."

"Are you sure it was them?" I wasn't into killing innocent people. I never actually pulled the trigger on no one. I never had to, but I knew the day would come.

"I ask the questions around here. Why I keep having to tell you that is beyond me. If I said they did it, they did it. I did the work for you; all you have to do is clock out." Dom forcefully pushed the gun into my chest. If my balance wasn't strong, it would have knocked me off my feet. Boxers had to have that stance; if not, they'd lose the fight each time. I didn't like losing, so I learned that very important technique.

I grabbed the gun, examining it. I couldn't turn back now. It was either them or me, and I wasn't trying to leave here in a body bag. I walked over to both bodies and let them bullets loose without a thought. I stood over their bodies as new blood was added to the warehouse floor. I walked over to Dom and handed him his gun back, looking him right in his eyes. My job was done here; there wasn't anything else to talk about. I made my way to the steel door and knocked, and the door opened. I kept walking down the long hallway, back out the building to my car. My phone started ringing.

"Don't let it happen again." Dom's deep authoritative voice boomed through my phone speakers. "I killed niggas for less. Don't test me." It was a threat for sure, but it fell on deaf ears. If he was going to do something, he would have done it already. Dom was definitely slipping. If he kept it up, I'd really show him what I was about.

If it wasn't official before, it was official now. I was a part of this life. The day I was handed the keys to The Vill and most of the 4th Ward, I knew what I had to do. I knew both of the boys that were hanging. They were family members of Red. It was a possibility that somebody would care about their disappearances, but I didn't think they had it in them to run up and get buck. When you did dirty deeds, you'd better be ready for the gardener to dispose of the dirty soil.

I pulled off through the gates. It was only one person I wanted to talk to after I crossed over. My mother didn't live too far from the warehouse. She actually lived right down the street. I'd been avoiding her for too long, and it was about time I was real with her. I really didn't owe her anything, but if we were going to build some type of relationship, I needed to come clean. This was the life I chose, and it wasn't too much anyone could say. I was still going to go to medical school and finish what I started. Both areas were covered.

I cut my car off and sat in my ride for a little minute, trying to come down off the adrenaline of killing not one but two people. It kept replaying in my head, on top of the fact that I had to handle the streets. Getting robbed was one of the worst things that could happen. If people saw it was that easy, they would try it as well. I wasn't too worried, but I had to figure out how I was going to respond. A statement had to be made, or it would be a continued cycle; probably not right away but eventually.

I parted ways with my thoughts, making my way down to my mother's apartment. Being able to visit her in a safe place made some of my walls come down. I knocked, not knowing if she was home but hoping she was.

"Who is it?" her sweet voice asked. The tone in her voice even changed now that she'd been clean. It reminded me of before she let the streets become her best friend.

"It's Kareem," I answered back in an even tone. I'd learned

to hide my excitement with her; I didn't want to get my feelings hurt.

The door swung open, and before I was able to step through the threshold, she wrapped her arms around me, pulling me into a motherly hug that she didn't even know I needed. A part of me didn't want to embrace it, but the other part of me knew the killer in me needed to go back in hiding. My large frame rested in her arms, taking in all that she had to offer and wishing that she had expressed this same love down through the years. We both took deep breaths before releasing each other. "Boy, get in here."

Clean linen was always my mom's favorite scent, and you could tell by the aroma in the air that it still was. I plopped down on the couch, exhausted, not realizing how much I'd been doing these past couple months. Exhaustion was a weakness, so most times, I couldn't give in to the feeling. My mom came back from the kitchen with a bottle of water and a smile that I hadn't seen in a while. It made me smirk a little, remembering all the jokes she used to have when we used to hang tight in my childhood days.

"Kareem, I've been calling you. I thought you didn't want anything to do with me." She sat across from me on the loveseat. "I'm glad you are here, but that doesn't mean I'm not about to get in your ass." Her words were serious, but her expression showed empathy.

"I was busy, Ma." When being questioned, my guard always went up. I wasn't sure where that trait came from. Information was only given on a need-to-know basis. It was true though. I was busy. I had to figure out how I was going to tell her busy doing what. If most of her life wasn't spent on the streets, it would be much easier.

"How's school going, Kareem? I know college can be hard when you have a lot of distractions."

"School is actually going good. It's my last year before

medical school, so I'm progressing. I'll honestly be glad when I'm done."

"Why, so you can play in these streets?" Her stare confirmed that she knew. I could have a poker face with everyone else, but with my mom, she always saw right through me.

"I don't regret it, if that's what you want to hear. For so long, I kept you in mind as my reason not to. I had to do what I had to do. The only thing that I regret is coming up under Dom. He has no respect for the team that's keeping him a millionaire. It's not what I expected, and I may be in over my head." No one would ever see this part of me, the unsure part. It was a vulnerability reserved only for the woman who birthed me. For years, I had to keep most things bottled up. Yes, I had my cousins to talk to, even Jax, but I couldn't hand them my kryptonite. I definitely had trust issues, mainly from the woman sitting before me.

"Ugh, you sound like someone I knew. What I learned from that person is, the more I tell you not to, the more you're going to want to do it. You've always been your own person, living life at your own pace. Do I want you in the streets? Absolutely not, but you're grown now, and you have to deal with what comes with it. All you need to know is that I got your back. It's a dangerous game you playing, but I got the playbook. The streets in my ear too."

"Do you know Dom dragged Cash in this? I'm worried he's going to make the same horrible mistake of trusting Dom like I did." I put my head in my hands, not believing that my cousin had made a deal with the devil. I could definitely handle myself, but Cash wasn't built for this type of work. Hopefully, he did what I told him to.

"Don't even worry about it. Everything will be okay. You trust me?" Her line of questioning sent a chill up my back. The little angel was on my shoulder telling me to give her a chance. Her track record was evidence that I shouldn't, but the sense of peace that hit me from her words alone made me. She got up from the couch and extended her hand for a pound to solidify that I did trust her. I got up and hugged her.

"I do."

Next - Imagine That
I swear to God that
With a whole lot of love
And a little bit of faith
That we can make it
You just gotta believe that

a dream deferred could make or break the average person. You had to be built differently for the industry. It was hard work, and you were only one song or one meeting away from your big break. I looked around the studio, amazed at what it had become. With the right money, you could almost guarantee that this spot was going to be dope. I played back my song "Soul Dreamer". The LED lights elevated this studio's vibe, and when combined with the orange baffle absorbers and white sofa, the color scheme brought the song to life. It was the start of a project by the same name. I was now ready to work. Hopefully, Dom would agree.

The door to the studio opened, and Dom walked in with his smoke gray double-breasted suit, looking like wealth, with street energy. He was dressed up, but he couldn't hide his dark persona. Definitely didn't pick it up before; I was too worried about what Kareem had going on. All I saw was the lifestyle of the material things he possessed. Seeing that definitely clouded my judgement with a few other things that I was going through at the time, on top of the fact that my song was getting mad love for the first time.

"That's a powerful song," Harvey stated after the music faded. Dom took a seat on the white couch that gave you a front-row seat to the creative possibility. My engineer, Ru, from the other spot agreed to work with me. He was with me when I didn't have access to half of what we were capable of doing in here. I was definitely building my team. I couldn't do it alone, and working with Aonika showed me that.

"Good looking out, Ru. I'll hit you when it's time to work." I dapped him up and waited for his exit. Dom's guards were right outside the door. Couldn't miss them if you tried.

"You wanted to see me?" Dom got straight down to business. I could respect that. He was probably a busy man.

"Dom, I appreciate all of this. I really do. Unfortunately, I can't take your money. I'm going to pay for the studio session, and I'll also help with finding you some engineers. Right now, I'm not looking for a manager or investor. I want to focus on my music, and when I get that done, then I'll decide. You can make a lot of money from this studio. I'll let all the musicians, singers, rappers and recording artists know that this is the place to be. Here is your check and money for tonight's session. Let me know if that's enough to cover."

"We had an agreement. You can't come back weeks later switching up. We were bound by our handshake. That's business, Cashmere." Dom stood tall and placed the check and money back in my jean pocket. He tapped me on my shoulder and sat back down. "That money you gave me for studio time, take your sexy little girlfriend, Jeda, out."

"Jeda? How you know about Jeda?" The mention of Jeda's name caught me off guard. Aonika was with me when we met, so I was confused.

"Let's say I know everything." He looked down at his phone, typing away something. He stood to his feet after putting his phone away. "I found the managing firm I want to use to get you more exposure. They will be giving you a call sometime next week." His guards walked in, holding the door open for him as he exited. Harvey wasn't too far behind. Before walking out, Harvey stopped. "All you had to do was sing. You'll learn sooner or later." He chuckled before the door closed.

I sat for a little while, replaying the conversation back. How was he going to tell me that I had to keep the money? I kept thinking about the guns that were clearly shown when he lifted his suit jacket to put his phone in his pocket. I wasn't sure if he meant to do it or not, but it wasn't much I could say to that. I was pretty sure he had killed people for less, so what was getting rid of me? There were benefits to staying connected, but did I want to put my life into somebody else's hands that didn't play fair? It would always be something, adding on to the deal that was first made. I didn't know what to do.

"Kareem, I tried doing what you told me, but he wasn't for it."

"What you mean he wasn't for it?" Kareem's tone changed up from calm to frustrated really quick.

"I already signed the contract by shaking his hand. It's no take backs." Dom stood on that law. There wasn't nothing I could do about it.

"Man, I'll handle it." Kareem hung up on me. He knew Dom better than I did.

That didn't go the way I was hoping, but hopefully this lunch date with Jeda went better. We'd been texting since our little session in the parking lot. Neither one of us wanted to call. We needed some time to process our next move in life, so texting was a safe place. It was cool for the time being but having to do this more, the distance we would share was crushing. There was a time difference, and with our schedules... who knew.

I pulled into the Friendly's parking lot. I asked Jeda if she wanted me to pick her up. She had a rental, so there wasn't any need for me to. It was nothing like having your own wheels to get from point A to B when you wanted, and she was seeing that for the first time. I was used to her riding with me, being my rider for real. I couldn't stop thinking about her since I felt her lips again. Her touch woke up the manhood in me.

I walked in Friendly's, going straight to our booth. We knew this restaurant all too well. We spent plenty of time here in our high school days. Friendly's was Jeda's first job and my first opportunity of getting a shot with her. She was looking like the girl I met almost four years ago. This time more mature and beautiful than before. I leaned over to give her a hug, almost giving her a kiss too. I thought against that connection. I wasn't sure if after this we would get back on track. Our bodies lingered for a little before I took the seat across from her in the booth.

"Yo, this place hasn't changed a bit." I looked around at what was once our getaway.

"Nope. You know Sheila is still the manager? Once I left this place, I never looked back."

"Is that something you do with everything in your life?"

She set herself up with her comment, and I wanted to ensure that she knew.

"Cash, when I go to L.A., I will always look back. This is where my foundation is. It's where I spent most of my life. If you're going to be here, I'll be here too. You don't think our love can stand the test of time?"

"I don't know. You are the one that's moving." I really didn't want to be frustrated, but the thought alone made me mad.

"We could do anything we put our minds to."

"Hey, you two lovebirds." We were interrupted by Sheila and her over-the-top antics, still as bubbly as she could be.

"Hey, Sheila." If she only knew what was happening, she would have stayed put until we were done trying to fix this broken piece. Whatever we decided, I would have to deal with it, so I changed my tune a little.

"Girl, Friendly's haven't been the same without you. What have you guys been up to? Hopefully, you guys are not still sneaking in bathrooms." Jeda covered her mouth, trying not to laugh out loud. I couldn't help it; I burst out laughing. We used to dip off in the bathroom for a little one-two pump. Sheila was so cool, she used to look out for us.

"Wow, we haven't done that in a while. As a matter of fact, Jeda, come on. Let me get a couple of pumps in before we start eating." We all laughed. I got hard thinking about how I had Jeda bent over trying not to make noise and get caught. We had a couple of close calls though.

"I can't believe you remember that. Nasty self."

"Girl, you know I used to live vicariously through you." Shelia high-fived Jeda and took our orders. She wasn't even supposed to be running a table, but she looked out for us during a busy lunch day.

Talking and laughing with Sheila made our next words a little lighter. It kind of broke the ice for me. Jeda and I shared some good times, and no one could take that away from us, not even the miles separating us from east coast to west coast. We'd come a long way since then. We hadn't fully reached our potential, but we were well on our way. Probably not as one, but in our own individual lives most definitely.

"You really think we could do this?" At times I didn't think so, but I needed to keep reminding her that we could.

"Our love for each other is too great not too."

"I wish I could go with you, Dip." Right now, with everything going on with Dom, it was my way out. That would put a target on my family's back, and I didn't want that. The music scene in L.A. was what I needed, but right now wasn't the right time. Maybe I'd join her soon, but as of now, I was locked into a contract, not knowing when I was going to be released. I grabbed her hands, linking them with mine. "I started my project, with possible new management, so I have to fulfill my obligations. If it wasn't for that, Dip, I would definitely be down to go with you. Plus, Grammy is getting old. I want to spend as much time with her as possible."

"Wait, congratulations. How you going to breeze right past the fact that you started your debut album? First tell me about that, then we can continue talking about our future." I got chills when hearing about our future. I liked the sound of that.

"I had a meeting this morning at a studio on River Street. It was newly renovated. I kept thinking about my dreams, hopes and aspirations all that week. From there, "Soul Dreamer" was born. Not only is it the title of my album, but it's a song that I recorded this morning. Me and Ru were listening to beats, and it flowed from there."

"Soul Dreamer. I like that, babe." It rolled off her tongue, like it always did when she was proud of me. After saying it, she hesitated a little, hearing herself for the first time. I would always be babe, even if we never made it.

"The songs created for this project will be straight from

the soul. That's the heart of R&B music. I was also a dreamer, someone who would do anything in his soul to achieve each and every dream realized. When it comes to us, my dream is that we live happily ever after. To get married and have kids. Us both living our dreams. It seems like a fairytale, but I know we could do it." If I didn't bet on anything else, I could bet on that.

"So you saying we're going to make this thing work?" Tears rested at the brim of her eyes. For once, they seemed to be tears of joy. Her excitement was seen through the clapping of her hands like Mama from *Nutty Professor* saying "Hercules, Hercules, Hercules". I grabbed her hand, bringing her to her feet, sliding out of the booth. I hugged her tight, her arms resting around my neck as she came in for a much-needed kiss.

"Do y'all need a minute?"

"As a matter of fact, we about to run to the bathroom real quick."

"I got y'all. Jeda, you better spill those beans when you come back out here. Like old times."

We practically skipped to the men's bathroom to consummate the next stage of our relationship.

Isolation

An offensive tactic involving one player with the basketball being left alone on one side of the court while their teammates clear out to the other side of the court. This is often used when a player has a favorable one-on-one matchup.

"*W*atch me work." I dribbled the ball, ready to take it to the basket. I spun on Quincy, breaking his ankles as the ball went through the net. "How much is that? I don't hear you talking now. This game right here. You ready to take this ass whooping?" Basketball always took my mind off of everything else in the world. I dribbled, faked to the right, and Quincy went for it. "Bang, Bang." The three-pointer swished right through, making me the winner of the battle of the best.

"Man, I let you win."

"Always says the loser. Stop crying." I laughed as we grabbed our waters and towels from our bags.

"Whatever." Quincy waved me off, rocking his bottle of water until there was nothing left.

"You ready for the season?" I asked, posted up on the metal pole holding the court in the ground.

"I stay ready. They not ready for us this year." He came in for a handshake. "Even if we don't take it all the way, we getting signed. Jim has been wanting me to talk to you. He wants to be your agent."

"Like I told Jim, I'll let him know. Right now, I'm rocking with Liam. He hasn't let me down yet, so I'm cool. I've been putting stuff in motion. I got a lot riding on this, and I can't mess this up. Do you ever think about what you would be if you weren't a basketball player?"

"Nope. That's all I've ever dreamed about. If I didn't have basketball, I'd probably be one of these bums on the street."

"Real talk. So what you gonna do when you too old to play?"

"I don't know. I'll worry about that when I get there. All I know is I want to play ball. The benefits are great, like the ladies and all the free stuff, but ball is my life. It's time for me to take my family out the hood. If I don't, we are never going to break the cycle." The words that Quincy was speaking were true. Sometimes it took that one person in a family to break years of generational curses.

"I hear you."

"Speaking of the ladies." Quincy's eyes landed on two fine sistas walking by. "Hey, shawty, come here. You and your cute friend. Yo, bro, let's see what they about. Come on." I was definitely about to take him up on that offer, but my phone started ringing. *Oh shit. It's Q.*

"Bro, give me a minute, and I got you. Rap with them while I take this call. Let me see where your game at." I laughed, running to a safe space to answer.

"Q, you good? I've been worried about you." Hopefully it

wasn't her husband calling back, assuming it was her husband in the first place. Sniffing could be heard through the phone. It was her, but why was she crying?

I'd been going back and forth in my head since that day. It never crossed my mind that we would ever get caught. Hearing another man's voice on the other end of her line really brought life to our situation. I weighed my options. If I called her back then that would expose us more, leaving her in harm's way, or I could wait for her call, hoping the distance kept her safe. I think both options put her at risk judging from the silence of knowing she was alive.

"Mason, can you come get me and take me to the airport? I can't... I can't take this anymore. Please come get me."

"I got you, Q. Tell me where and I'm there." My heart was pounding for more reasons than one. I left everything, got in my car, and drove off until I got more information. I put her on speaker, whipping my ride like I was in *2 Fast and 2 Furious.* "Tell me where you at, Q? I'm coming."

"No, Mason. You can't come in your car. He has too many cameras. Park your car at the school, catch a cab to me then we can catch the cab to the airport. Wear a hoodie and keep your head down. I want us to get out of here safe, Mason." *Get out of here safe?*

"We gonna get out of there safe alright. Shoot me your address, and I'll be there shortly. You sure I can't drive my car? It will be quicker that way."

"Mason, please get a cab."

"Okay, but you staying on the phone with me until I get there."

"Mason, I can't. I have to go finish packing some of my things. Hurry. Call me when you out front. Okay?"

"Okay."

"I love you, Mason."

I was saying I love you too to a dead line. Qwana had hung up.

I was doing speeding ticket driving. As far as I knew, I was an EMT driver on my way to a 9-1-1 call. I made it to the dorm housing off campus, parked my car, ran in the house and threw on anything black I had, which was a hoodie, jeans, and some black, low-top Air Forces. I even snatched up some dark shades in case. I called a cab and waited for about ten minutes. In between time, Qwana shot me over her address. *Saddle River? That's where all the celebrities and big timers stay.*

I didn't know what I was on my way to, but I knew I had to get there quickly. It was about a ten-minute ride. I braced myself, ready to fight if need be. I usually would have called in the cavalry, but they didn't need to be inserted into this love affair, love triangle, or whatever you wanted to call it. Cash and Kareem would have gladly ridden shotgun.

"You can't go any faster?"

"Sir, I'm going as fast as I can. We are almost there."

I wanted to get mad, but it wouldn't have helped my situation, so I sat back in my seat, taking long deep breaths. Saddle River was all mansions. It's where Rev. Run and Mary J. Blige all lived. Qwana always seemed like she had money, but I didn't know they had money like this. We rode past so many huge houses, I felt like I was on an express episode of *MTV Cribs*. We had to be reaching my destination because the cab driver slowed down. We pulled up to a gate. *How was I going to get through this without setting off the alarm?*

I quickly dialed Qwana's number for some direction of how we were going to get her to this airport without flagging the enemy. *Please answer, please answer.* "Q, how am I supposed to get past the gate?"

"I'm letting you in right now. Slide down in your seat when you come through. It's a security camera on the buzzer. Shit, he might have already seen you. I don't care. Come on,"

Qwana nervously expressed, her voice low and defeated. The cab pulled up to the front door.

"We will be right out." The cab driver didn't care. He knew picking up someone from this neighborhood would probably mean a big tip.

My hoodie was on, but I didn't bother with the shades. I needed to see clearly for our escape into the night. Before I made it to the door, it swung open. Shades covered Qwana's face like I didn't notice the bruises underneath. See, now I dared this motherfucker to catch me in this bitch. He wanted to hit females, let him try me. When we made it from the foyer into the living room, I quickly grabbed her into a hug.

"Ouch"

"I'm sorry, are you okay?"

"Yes, I think I have bruised ribs." Qwana rubbed her stomach to soothe the pain. "I know, I know, but you don't have to worry about it. Dom put his hands on me for the last time. He won't ever get that chance again."

"Wait, who hit you?"

"My husband."

"You called him Dom. I thought your husband's name was Nick?"

"His name is Dominick. Everybody calls him Dom, but I was swept off my feet by Nick, who was an imposter. This is all I'm taking. Let me run upstairs to get my purse and my makeup bag."

I was stuck as she slowly moved up the stairs due to her condition. I needed something to confirm this missing piece. I looked around at the lavish furniture and different paintings that occupied this open space. This living room was bigger than my house. I couldn't believe all this time Q was living like this. I spotted a few pictures, and I'd be damned. *Kareem's boss.* He was in almost every picture that hung around the room. Qwana actually looked happy and in love; it was a montage of the many vacations, exclusive parties, and expensive living they displayed.

I shot a quick text to Kareem letting him know we needed to talk and meet up ASAP. Dom wasn't about to get away with putting his hands on my lady, or any lady for that matter. I was hoping that my cousin was down for the cause. I knew he worked for him, but I didn't know much more than that. Qwana came back, ready to go. I grabbed all of her things, put them in the taxi, and we were on our way. We didn't say much on our way to the airport, both lost in our thoughts. I couldn't believe I was dating Dom's wife, who lived in a mansion in Saddle River. I learned the two most important things about the person I loved in a few hours, after so many years of building a relationship on broken pieces.

I had to break the silence. We were almost there, and I didn't know where she was going or what the plan was. All I wanted her to do was be safe, and I'd handle the rest. "What's the plan, Q?" I pulled her close to me, her back laying on me as I wrapped my arms around her. She flinched a little, but you could tell she wanted to be held while she looked out the window.

"I'm going to get away for a few months. My firm has an office in Georgia that I could work from. I'm sorry, Mason, for putting you in the middle of all of this." She tried to turn but thought against it once the pain shot through her.

"I think you should go to the emergency room."

"Trust me, I'm good. I'm filing my divorce papers in the morning." She started crying. "It probably won't matter anyway. He's crazy, Mason."

We pulled up to Newark Liberty Airport. I didn't want her to go, but I had to so I could handle Dom. I released her from my arms and got out to open her door. I grabbed her two bags, prepared to walk her inside. "I'll be right back. I'm going to walk her inside. Keep the meter running."

"Listen, Mason." Qwana stopped all movement. Her hand touched mine as I grabbed the handle of her suitcase. "Thank you for answering my S.O.S." She found my eyes, even through her dark shades. "I'm going to really miss you. It will be the last time you'll see me for a while. Maybe you can visit?"

"Q, you sound like you're never coming back." My lips met the top of her forehead.

"I promise to call you once my divorce is finalized. Maybe we can finally be together. A girl can still dream, right?"

"What I can promise is to see what's Dom's problem when I catch up with him." She didn't deserve what this grown man dished out by putting his hands on her. I had to let her know as her man, I'd take care of it. I knew she wasn't going to agree, but it didn't matter because I already had the first puzzle piece laid.

"Mason, Dom is dangerous. He owns guns and people that you don't have access to. It's hard to catch him slipping. He's protected at all times; his team will die for him before they let anybody take him out. So please don't."

"You don't worry your little head. I got this. Don't get too comfortable in Georgia without me. Go on before I change my mind. Please, call me and let me know you landed safe."

"I will." I watched her walk away, defeated on so many levels.

I needed her somewhere other than here. It already wasn't safe. I was about to make it even worse by going to war with someone who thought he was untouchable. Everyone around him thought that too, but he'd never met me. I never caught a body before, although I was willing to for her. I couldn't let this slide. I had a gut feeling that this wasn't the first time he put his hands on her. Dom seemed like one of those old heads you had to show better than you could tell. He wouldn't see me coming.

I carried it like the weight I had on my shoulders. I always knew I
was a leader, built and bred from life circumstances.
- Kareem

J had to handle Dom myself. I didn't see it any other
way. He had continued to disrespect my family's
name. It was like a trickle-down effect. First, he got Harvey to
talk me into running for him. Although my choice, the way he
went about it was all wrong. Then he flashed money Cash's
way, preying on his talent. If anybody didn't deserve what
Dom had dished out, it was definitely Cash. Now Mase was
telling me Dom put his hands on Qwana. I still couldn't
believe that was his wife. Mase saw it with his own eyes. It
was such a small world. I didn't know how we got caught up
and entangled in this web of deceit. I had to fix it since it
started with me.

I knew one thing that would make Dom come out of
hiding, money. He was all about his paper. The only differ-

ence was this time it would be about so much more. I looked at the cash sitting on my bed. It wasn't all that was owed to him, but he wouldn't know that. It would be my way in. I hadn't thought past that yet, but I thought it was time. I'd been silent, taking all that Dom threw my way. Time and time again, I felt like a sucker having to take orders from someone who was so far removed from the streets that the little soldiers didn't even know what he looked like. They respected him off of stories alone, and that's not the type of leader I would want to follow.

I hit the button on his contact and the phone started ringing. It was no turning back. "How can I help you, Kareem? I'm actually preparing for a meeting."

"I need to re-up. We been out here working. We won't have any product left by morning. I want to get a jump on it and have everything bagged up tonight."

"Is that right?"

"I only need to re-up for the bottom. We good on the fourth. The fiends loving the new product in the Vill." The crazy part was, they were loving it. We only sold weed in the Vill, and now the drug lovers didn't have to go all the way up the hill to cop. It wasn't all a lie.

"I have a meeting already scheduled with someone at the warehouse. I think you'll be interested in seeing who."

"What that have to do with me?"

"You'll see. Come through at ten, and make sure you're alone."

My rebuttal was met with a dead line. I wanted to see if he could back up what he dished out. Legend said he could, but who knew. It was time for me to test that theory. I was still confused about who he would be meeting up with that I would know. Right away, Cash popped in my mind.

"Yo, you not meeting Dom down at the warehouse, right?"

"Where's the warehouse?"

306

"It's on Bunker Hill, a spot on East 11th Street. Why you ask that? Are you supposed to meet him?"

"Nah, why you so paranoid?"

"Dom is up to something. I wanted to make sure you didn't get caught in the crossfires. If something happens, I want you to know that it was him."

"What you about to do, Reem?"

"I know what I'm doing."

"People that usually say that don't know what they are doing. I'm coming."

"No! Don't come. Go to the studio, cuz, and let me handle this. I'm serious. Stay away from that area. I want to make sure your tracks are covered."

"You got it. Call me as soon as you *handle* what you have to. I'll be in the studio."

"Bet."

I zipped up my duffle bag. I carried it like the weight I had on my shoulders. I always knew I was a leader, built and bred from life circumstances. Never knowing who my father was, to my mother leaving me for the pipe, I never had a firm foundation to stand on, but guess what? I built my own. I liked it like that. That way I knew for sure that I would be able to stand. I didn't understand it as a kid, but as I matured, I got it more and more.

I had a few hours before I had to meet with Dom, I stopped at Friday's and had a few drinks. I had to knock the edge off. It wasn't that I was scared. I had to go up against an army by myself. People pledged their loyalty to Dom, but did they really know him? They only knew the money he put in their pocket. Or the stories of how he became who he was. A change was on the horizon. Either you got with it or you got dealt with. After three rounds of Henny, I found myself sitting in front of my mom's house. I wanted to see her before I headed down the street to the warehouse. I had an uneasy feeling, but I chalked it up to the grey area of the unknown.

I knocked on my mom's door and didn't get an answer. I didn't know her work schedule or even what she did on the side, so I wasn't surprised she wasn't home. She was always on the go, even before the drugs. We would always be at a museum, at a concert or trying food at different restaurants. It was time for me to go see Dom anyway. Once I got in the car, I pulled the gun from up under my seat and placed it in my pants. I checked the glove compartment and made sure that gun was there in case.

I can feel it in the air
My spider senses is tinglin'
Feel somethin', got my radars up

Beanie Sigel's "Feel it in the Air" blasted through the speakers, meeting me right where I was. As he rapped, I felt every lyric as my feet touched the pedal. The lyrics and Beanie's realness was about to get drowned out by the whistles of the upcoming train that I was trying to beat. I was almost to Bunker Hill, and I knew if I didn't beat this train I was going to be waiting for a long time. *Is that my mother?* I looked on as the figure sped ahead, trying to cross before the barriers came down. *That is her!*

"Ma!" I yelled once my car came to a stop before the train passed. She turned around and started walking quickly.

Where was she going?

JANE

$\mathcal{I}$ made it past the train. I heard someone calling my name, and I'll be damned, it was Kareem. I was hoping he wouldn't be anywhere around so I could go through with my plan. I didn't want to die, but if that had to happen to avenge my sister's death, then I was all for it. It was the least I could do for her since I still felt a part of her dying was my fault. I didn't kill her, but she died frustrated and mad at yours truly. My indiscretions were the last thing on her mind. It was the last conversation she had with anybody. Wow, what a way to die. I shook my head as I blended in with the night. I had to get to the warehouse before Kareem.

I didn't want to draw attention my way by running so I walked with speed, trying to make it to the finish line. Little did Dom know, I'd been to the warehouse where he told me to meet him. I'd only been once, but it was the same warehouse that Mason and Jax worked out of. Dom hadn't changed up anything. He was made in China, a carbon copy of Mason, and it was pathetic. He stole Mason's whole life, and

Harvey fit right into what would have been Jax's life. I couldn't respect a man that didn't have his own identity.

"Ma, what are you doing?" I jumped, about to turn on the block the warehouse was on. I stopped in my tracks. I didn't expect Kareem to catch up with me. Any other day, the train took super long, but when I needed it to, it didn't. I needed him to leave and let me handle this son of a bitch. I knew my frustration showed, but Kareem didn't care. He put his car in park and jumped out.

"Why are you following me, Kareem? I have some business I have to tend to, and you're going to make me late."

"Does this business have anything to do with Dom?" I didn't know why he asked a question he probably already knew the answer to.

"Listen, I have to do what's best for my family and if anybody understands that, it should be you. Didn't you say you started selling to help out, right? Well, I'm doing the same thing right now." I was pissed the hell off that I had to answer to my son. Last time I checked, I was the mother and the oldest.

"It's different. Dom is a man, and I'm a man. Let us men handle the problems that transpired between us. I don't need my mother fighting my battles. I'm not ten anymore, Ma. You missed those years." His words stung, but it didn't knock me off course. It actually made me want to off Dom even more. I lost too much on the count of him.

"One day you will forgive me for all the wrong I did and stop throwing it in my face. It's something I can't take back." I wasn't trying to go through this right now. I had to meet Dom. "Now, excuse me while I go to my meeting." I tried walking away, but Kareem blocked my path. If he wasn't my son, I would have kneed him right in the balls, but I wanted grandkids.

"Against my better judgement, I'm going to let you roll

with me. He already is expecting both of us. How you think we should do this?" Kareem blew out a breath, coming to terms with the fact that I wasn't backing down.

"We only have to worry about Dre and Compound. Once we lay them down, our visit will run smoothly."

"I already took care of them. I have something of theirs that will weaken their hard exterior and soften their interior. You strapped, Ma?"

"Of course I'm strapped, son. You thought I was going to strip for Dom or something?" We both chuckled at that thought. I showed him the inside of my purse, and my purple pistol shined in the darkness."

"Where you get a gun from? And you have a silencer? How you get your hands on that?"

"It was a gift. One of the benefits of being on the streets, you knew where to go when you needed something. Let's say a lot of people owed me favors, and now that I'm sober, I'm collecting debt." I didn't plan to use any of the favors owed, but this situation was different, so I had to cash in.

"Shit, shit..." I looked behind me to see what Kareem was looking at. A cab stopped at the opposite corner of where we were at. *Were we in danger?*

"What's wrong?"

"That's Cash in that cab." I turned around, but the cab had pulled off. It was a dead end street, so it would be coming back up soon.

"Cut the shit, Kareem. Why are you guys here? I'm up here thinking you caught me trying to go to Dom, but it seems like you had a plan of your own."

"I told Cash where I was going but told him not to come. I had to let somebody know in case something happened. Of course he didn't listen, like you're not listening right now. Either way, Dom is going to get handled tonight. One way or the other."

"Dom is too smart to not have guards on all sides. Cash better be careful. It's best we all go in together. I don't need anything to happen to y'all."

"Unfortunately, I agree. I can't have my cousin walking into a battle or an arena that he knew nothing about." Kareem always cared about other people, never thinking of himself first. He definitely got his protective traits from his father. "Cash, we saw you. Get out of the cab. Y'all making shit difficult." You could hear the frustration in Kareem's voice. We were inserting ourselves into his little plan, and he didn't like it.

I didn't like it either. Not only was I now liable for one of my grown boys, but now both of them were about to go up against one of the grimiest players in the game. I was surprised that Mase didn't tag along; he was usually front and center. They'd always been inseparable. You couldn't find one without the other. I didn't need any more problems on my hand, so I was glad Mase wasn't there. He was the hot head of the group. Cashmere was quiet. Kareem was laid back, but Mase was the opposite of both. We waited as Cashmere made his way to us. In the meantime, I was thinking how we could pull this off with the added participants. It was more manpower for sure, but were we a match for Dom and his army of men?

"Are you dumb? Didn't I say don't come down here?" Kareem scolded Cashmere.

"I wasn't about to let you walk in there by yourself." Cashmere pointed down the dark street to the warehouse.

"Where Mase?" Cashmere looked at me as if for the first time. I hadn't seen him in years. He did what most people did these days; he looked me up and down.

"Auntie, you look...you look good." It was all he could say. He leaned in to give me the tightest hug.

"Thank you, nephew. We can talk about that later. Where

is your brother?" I asked after he pulled back, ready to focus on the plan before us.

"He didn't answer, but I left him a message."

"We all have to jump back in my car. They're going to know something is up if we all walked down this dark street. I usually drive up, so y'all get in the car."

"What we going to do?" Cashmere wanted to clarify, which I didn't blame him for. If this wasn't your regular day to day, you wanted to make sure you dot every I and cross every T. His life was on the line.

"Sit back and let me do the talking." I looked at both Kareem and Cashmere as we got in the car for them to confirm they heard me. I knew for sure I probably wouldn't have any back talk from Cashmere, but Kareem was another story. We didn't pull off right away.

"Cash, I'm going to give you this gun, but please be careful and only use it if you need to. Do you even know how to shoot a gun?" Kareem reached over and took a gun out his glove compartment.

"No, but I'm not dumb, Reem. I'll manage." Cashmere examined the piece that Kareem handed him. Looking between the two of them, they'd really grown up. Linda and I did everything in our power to give our kids a better life than what was portrayed in this car. Was this more evidence that I failed as a parent? I could hear my sister now going off. I let her baby boy hold a gun. Yes, they were old enough to make their own decisions. I hoped our plan didn't cost them their life.

We pulled off, all in our own thoughts as we made our way up to the front gate. It slowly opened, both guards pulling it apart then closing it. They then made it to the car stalking us to exit. I got out and positioned my pocketbook over my shoulder, tapping it for good luck. Kareem and Mase got out on the driver side. I made my way over. When we all were together, they tried to frisk us, but Kareem put a stop to that. Seeing him take charge, he truly was his father's son.

"Nah, we good. We don't need to be checked. If you don't like it, I suggest you go get your boss. I'm tired of y'all acting like I'm a low-level street hustler. I'm a part of the team, and y'all going to put some respect on my name." Kareem wasn't backing down, and neither were the guards.

"I don't care who you work for. I work for the same person, and my job is to take all weapons upon arrival." The biggest of the two guards who towered over Kareem made him look small in stature in comparison.

"I didn't even think you could talk, but if you don't like what I'm saying, I suggest you do something about it. I'm not letting you touch us."

"Boy, if you—"

"Compound, it's okay. Let them in." We all looked toward the entrance of the warehouse, and Harvey was standing there. He was our saving grace. I could see the lust in his eyes all the way from where I stood. His infatuation with me got us a past the first hurdle. It was no way we were going in without our equalizer.

I guess that angered Compound. He pushed Kareem toward the door. Kareem wasn't no punk, but he understood what we were trying to do, so he took one for the team. Both guards walked behind us while Harvey waited at the door. "Nice of you all to join us. I didn't know this would be a family affair. Jane, I didn't know you were babysitting tonight. I thought you were trying to party with your fine ass."

"Hey, watch your mouth about my mother." Kareem was always protective over me. Like I always used to tell him, "Son, I can handle myself". I spoke it with my eyes. I could use Harvey's flirting to my advantage.

"Thank you, Harvey. Yvette gonna kick your ass you keep

playing with her." I chuckled. In all actuality, it was nothing she could do about his behavior.

We walked down a long hallway to an open space that had a few boxes scattered about. I looked up, feeling someone burning a hole through my body. Dom stared down, smoking what I believed had to be a cigar. He didn't blink. His cold eyes locked with mine. He still looked the same. He didn't age a bit, still black and ugly as ever. I knew him before the money, so it didn't make him cute. The person he had become didn't make it any better either. He didn't move. He looked down on us like he was God. Kareem noticed I was looking up, but by then Dom was no longer there.

"Ma, you look like you saw a ghost," Kareem whispered in my ear.

Seeing Dom brought me back to the day he gave me my first hit. All my problems went away instantly. Little did I know, it was temporary. I would soon find out how a temporary fix could turn into a lifetime of shattered dreams. At the time, I needed it. It numbed the reality that I lost two special people. I tried to bury my old life. I prayed at night, wondering why I kept having to be reminded of the wrong turns I took for so many years. I was glad my sobriety was not predicated on people.

"Well, well, well. To what do I owe the pleasure of having the royal family grace me with their presences?"

We all turned around to see Dom standing there, his deep baritone echoing through the empty warehouse. The dim lights did nothing to illuminate the darkness of his skin. He blended in with the eerie feeling that an empty warehouse brings when caught in between a decision. A decision to live and not die. We all watched as he made his way over to us. His guards walked behind him. Harvey stood on the side of him, still eyeing me like he was watching a porno. It was weird.

"I would like to speak with you in private, Dominick." I

jumped in before anybody had a chance to speak. What I had to say to him, both Kareem and Cashmere didn't need to hear.

"Whatever you have to say, Mary Jane, you can say it right here."

"I told you don't ever call me that." I wanted to pull out my gun and kill him on the concrete where he stood.

"Oh, I forgot. Only Mason could call you that."

Our exchange was halted by shouting coming from a distance. We didn't know where it was coming from. A side door swung open, and everybody had their hands on their guns. Mase walked in with his hands up. Someone held him at gunpoint, the guy stalking his every move. Their clothes were disheveled, like they were fighting. Mason's face was bruised, and somebody's blood was all over their clothes. One wrong move on any of our parts would have pulled the trigger. The guy's hand was shaking, his grip was tight, and he wasn't letting Mase out of his view.

"Boss, I caught him lurking in the back, by the side entrance we use. I left some papers here and had to come back. If I hadn't, he would have walked right in with this." He showed Dom the gun that he confiscated from Mase.

"Good job, Christopher. We can talk about your promotion on Monday. I have it from here."

"Man, fuck you. You better be glad you got that gun!" Mase yelled, angry that he couldn't get the dude like he wanted without risking his life.

"Boss, let me shoot him."

"I might let you if he keeps running his mouth. Stay put. Your bonus will be worth it. I'll add an extra ten thousand if you shoot him in the mouth. Get your aim right. I'll let you know when." His long, dark finger pointed my way.

"Dominick, cut the bullshit. I'm not in the mood for your games."

"Aww... Did I mess up y'all little plan? Was little Mason

supposed to save the day? I'm unstoppable. Can't nobody go up against me!" Dom pounded his chest. "I know Jax told you what I do to people with the last name Cotton."

"No, you tell us, Dominick. Don't leave out the facts. We know you like to lie and manipulate every situation." I needed him to say what I already knew.

"What facts are you referring to, Mary Jane?" Dom looked like he was enjoying our little back and forth.

I looked around at everyone that was present. Each person having a different look on their face, connected by one man's existence. Mason was the glue that tied all of us together. If I really wanted to be free from secrets I still carried, I had to give facts that would without a shadow of a doubt wreak havoc on my family. We'd been through so much, but in order to truly heal, we had to rebuild the foundation. The only way to do that was to piece together the secrets of our past to create something solid.

"The fact that you are a coward and wasn't man enough to fight Mason a fair one."

"What about my father?" Hearing their father's name always sent both Mase and Cashmere in a frenzy. Tonight wasn't any different.

"A fair one? Now you know it wouldn't have been a fair one. He was protected off his name alone. I did what I had to do."

"You killed them, motherfucker! You killed him. You were jealous. You knew you would never amount to half of what he was."

"Wait, who killed my father? Auntie, I thought he died in a car accident?" Cashmere asked, teary eyed.

"Tell them, Dom. Tell them how you killed their father and their mother so you could weasel your way to the top. Tell them."

"Linda wasn't supposed to be in the car, and you know it."

Mase tried to attack Dom, but Kareem quickly grabbed him up before he set off a chain of events. Cashmere had tears falling but kept his composure. "You think I care? She's not here, is she?"

"Why don't you tell them why she got in the car. Don't paint me as a bad guy, knowing you had something to do with it too. Did you forget our conversations, or you were too high to remember?"

"I forgive myself. You're not about to blame me."

"If you weren't sleeping with Mason, maybe your sister would be alive, and Kareem's father would be here to groom him for the throne."

"What the fuck are you talking about, Dom?" Kareem questioned, angry and confused.

"You better stop putting dirt on my father's name!" Mase yelled.

"Or what? What your bitch ass gonna do? You think I didn't figure out that you were messing with Qwana? She was fucking you good, huh, Mason? I taught her everything she knows. Y'all never be together. That's my bitch, and I'm keeping it that way."

"I would fucking—"

"Christopher."

Christopher pulled his gun back out and pointed at Mason trying to make his way over to where Dom was standing. He definitely had some loyal soldiers on his payroll. This time Christopher's hand wasn't shaking. When Mase heard him cock the gun, he stopped in his tracks. His anger fueled him, but his life flashing before his eyes stopped him. Sooner or later, nothing was going to stop him. Dom was on strike two in Mase's book, and he wanted him O.U.T.

"You think I didn't know Jax sent y'all? Percy couldn't keep his fucking mouth shut. I knew Jax would send somebody. He talked Kareem into accepting Harvey's offer, then he got enough information on my wife to have her bump into this fake ass tough guy, and she fell for it. Cashmere, you were a bonus. The weakest out of the bunch. I knew I could pull you right in. Tell Jax he lost again." A cocky laugh could be heard around the warehouse.

"I get it now. You were mad that Mason was getting all the pussy and you weren't?"

Another slow evil laugh cut through the silence of my words.

"He even had your pussy on lock? Did Mason even know that Kareem was his son?"

"Ma, what is he talking about?"

"Yeah, Auntie. What is he talking about?" Mason was curious to know right along with the rest of the boys.

"Oh, she didn't tell you that Mason used to have two of the baddest sistas strung out on his dick. Huh? You didn't tell them that? Huh, Kareem? Did she tell you that your dad is not from Washington D.C.? That you a Cotton, like your half brothers standing next to you?"

"I should fucking shoot you. You lying bastard!" Kareem pulled out his gun and everyone who had a gun cocked it, following suit. My gun was aimed and was ready to fire, trigger finger itching to be pulled.

"Your gun should be pointing at your mother. She is the one you should be mad at. Sorry it had to be me to tell you that your father is Mason Cotton, and your mother used to be on her knees sucking your uncle's dick."

Pop! Pop! Pop!

Gun shots went off. Everything was happening so quickly. Kareem's Glock sent three shots Dom's way, taking cover trying to get me out the way as Dre and Compound let off shots. Before going down, I saw Christopher hit the floor. Mase never had a chance to get away. Kareem had me covered with his whole body, still letting off rounds in the process. A door slammed, the shooting stopped, and nothing could be heard but the aftermath. Smoke filled the air from the bullets exchanged in the heat of the moment.

"You good, Ma?" Kareem moved the weight of his body off of me and looked at himself to see if he was shot. He started examining me when he saw he wasn't hit.

"Maseeeeeee! No!"

Kareem jumped to his feet, and so did I. The scream in Cashmere's voice told me it wasn't good. We ran over to Cashmere as he grabbed Mason up into his arms. Mason was covered in blood. He was shot, but we couldn't tell where. I leaned down checking Mase's pulse, it was there but faint. We had to get him to the hospital. We rushed past Compound's body. Harvey and Dre must have dragged Dom's bloody body out from the looks of the concrete leading to the back door, but they were nowhere to be found. I at least got a couple of shots in. It had to be Dom's blood. We got Mase in the car, racing to the emergency room.

CASHMERE

Stevie Wonder - These Three Words

The one for whom you'd give your very life
Could be taken in the twinkling of an eye
Through your tears you'd ask "Why did you go?"
Knowing you didn't always show
Just how much you loved them so

"$\mathcal{M}$r. Cotton suffered three gunshot wounds to the chest. He lost a lot of blood and went into hypovolemic shock. I'm sorry, Mrs. Harris, there was nothing we could do. We tried everything we could to save him."

I was still stuck on, *there was nothing we could do.* The doctor's job was to save people. Why didn't he save my brother? Why? My body went into shock. I heard nothing but the laughs of my brother. I saw his smile when he knew a girl was looking. I was searching for him, hoping this was all a dream. I couldn't move. Everything was at a standstill, moving in slow motion. After hours of waiting, this was not the information I wanted to hear.

I didn't even know Jeda was there until her hands snaked around my waist, bringing me back to my reality. That's when I heard the cries of Grammy, and Aunt Jane, amongst the many people who showed up for my brother. I knew their cries. We cried the same cry, one of utter disbelief of the cards our family was dealt. Death was a part of life, but why did it keep having to happen to us? Were we cursed for the sins of the ones who came before us? This wasn't fair.

"Babe, are you okay?"

My mouth couldn't find the words nor the gestures to signal that I would never be okay. All my life, I had my brother to talk to, build with, and help me with situations like the one we were in. Who was going to help me now? We still had so much to accomplish together, let alone on our own. Nah, this can't be true. God has to get me out of this dream.

"Aww, baby, it's going to be okay. I'm here."

I don't know how we ended up on the hospital floor, but I cried in Jeda's arms as she held me. Her words and her once soothing touch weren't enough. I appreciated the effort, but I needed my brother. Flashbacks of us growing up kept replaying in my head, from our fights to our victories. We were supposed to make more memories. We talked about getting married and having kids. How we were going to spoil each other's kids, being the best uncle in the world. But how now? Kareem came into view as he sat alone in the corner of the emergency room.

How could I lose a brother and gain a brother in one day? The conversation in the warehouse that led up to the shooting echoed in my ear. Kareem was my half-brother? I finally found the strength to get off the floor and check on my family. We all were scattered around the emergency room. The doctor would let us know when it was time to go to the back to view Mason's body. We were supposed to be holding each other up. I wasn't sure that was possible. Before I was able to walk away, I looked at Jeda, hoping that her words were true that it would be alright.

"Thank you" was all I could muster up. I kissed her on the forehead. As I was making my way over to Kareem, so were Grammy and Aunt Jane. I guess we all felt the same way that we should be together during this time. This was deja vu from twelve years ago. We didn't want to live in our truth then, and we sure didn't want to live in it now. We all found seats around Kareem, sitting in silence for a few minutes. Aunt Jane was the first to speak.

"Are you boys okay?"

I shook my head no, but Kareem had something to get off his chest.

"So you are going to sit up here and not deal with the shit we heard?" Kareem looked his mother dead in her eye. Grammy gasped, never hearing Kareem swear. Her old limbs and broken heart didn't have it in her to even say a word. She looked down, waiting for the exchange. I guess trying to figure out where things went wrong.

"Kareem, I'm still your mother, so watch your tone."

"Are you? All these years, I thought that my dad lived in Washington D.C. Shoot, I even thought for a minute Jax was my father and you didn't know how to tell me. All this time, you were holding out, knowing you were wrong. Why him?"

"Listen, Kareem, we need to talk about this once every-body comes down from the pain of losing—"

"No! Why him?" There weren't too many people in the emergency room, but everyone who was turned to look at us from Kareem's outburst. "You could have chosen anybody else, but you chose to sleep around with your sister's husband."

"You little heifer. I always knew you were jealous of your

sister. I didn't know you would stoop so low." Grammy's anger was evident in each word she spoke.

"Yes, I made a mistake, but it was you, Momma, who turned me and Linda against each other. So don't make me the only bad person in this. You loved her more, talked to her more, but all I got was do good in school or else." Tears flowed from Aunt Jane's truth. Grammy shook her head, not wanting to hear it.

"That was always your excuse so you could go out and be a whore. I really wanted better for you, but you insisted on following after your sister. She was strong enough to handle what came with the streets, you were not. I tried to protect you, but no. You had to run off and cross a line that sisters don't cross."

"What I'm not going to do is be blamed for your short-comings as a mother. I shouldn't have crossed the line as her sister. You shouldn't have crossed the line of being Linda's friend instead of her mother."

"Why, Ma?" Kareem was still stuck on that question. He wasn't about to let his mother get away with not answering.

"Son, I ask myself that almost daily. Mason was my why good girls like bad guys mentality. He didn't look at me as Linda's little sister. He saw me for who I was. You were conceived before Mason and Linda even got married."

"How does that make it better, Auntie?" I was mad at her, but I was more mad at my dad. He played a big part in it too, but we couldn't put him on the stand to testify.

"Before I went off to college, your mom and your dad were broken up. They called themselves taking a little break. It wasn't even supposed to go down like it did. Everything happened so fast that it was too late to take it back." Aunt Jane took a breath that seemed to save her life. Between the tears and her vulnerability, it created a narrative that people made mistakes. I looked at Kareem. One would never know how he felt. He never wore his feelings on his shoulder. The drain of losing Mase was weighing heavy on him while also having to deal with his lineage. This would be too much to handle for the average person, but Kareem was the most put together between the three of us. Aunt Jane continued.

"In mere seconds, a life was created between two young and wild teens. One searching for her identity, the other trying to be a man and survive in a world that didn't want to see us win. Did I love Mason at that time? No, but when you got here, baby, I longed to have a family." Aunt Jane tried reaching for Kareem, but he sat back in his seat, folding his arms.

"So you never were going to tell me?" Kareem's red eyes asked, dissatisfied.

"I never really had the chance to. Once I got ahold of them drugs, my whole perspective changed. I kind of lost my way."

It wasn't that simple, but it was all at the same time. How could one erase the past? I was pretty sure Aunt Jane asked herself all of these questions down through the years, probably never coming to the conclusion that she wanted to. This was the healthiest I'd ever seen her. She paid her dues for the part she played. It was time for a new role. At this point, we were all we had. We could not afford for her to relapse. That would be another battle we would have to fight.

"Did he know?"

"Who, your father?" Hearing Aunt Jane refer to my dad as Kareem's father hurt, but it also brought some relief that I gained a brother. Losing one didn't feel so good.

"The day that I was going to tell him is the day he got into the accident."

"No, he was killed." I had to make that known. Our parents were taken from us, and today's information made me believe my life was built on a lie. A fairytale made into a hood tale that never has a good ending.

"That still doesn't change the fact that he didn't know for ten years. For ten years, you had me calling him Uncle Mason when he was really my father. Ten years, Ma! That's foul, and you know it." You could tell a part of Kareem wanted to get up and leave, but it wasn't his character. As kids, he always wanted to talk through all of our problems, even after we would physically fight.

"Linda and I were starting to build a better relationship. She never really forgave me for hiding my pregnancy."

"Hiding your pregnancy?" I was as curious as Kareem to know what she was talking about as well.

"Your little fast ass should have kept your legs closed. You wouldn't have had to hide nothing. I missed four years of my grandbaby life because you wanted to keep your little secret. You were disgrace then, and you're a disgrace now." I couldn't believe that Grammy spoke those things out of her mouth. I'd always known her to be sweet, never judging someone's situation or circumstance.

"Yeah, you hate me for not being who you wanted me to be, Momma. It's evident in how you always treated me. No longer am I locked under your spell." Aunt Jane shrugged her shoulders, defeated but strong. "I don't have to prove nothing to you or anybody for that matter. We all make mistakes. Unfortunately, some of my decisions hurt my family. The only thing I can do is apologize, hoping one day you all will forgive me."

If Grammy's old bones would have let her, she would have gotten up quicker than she did. She stormed off, but not before stopping to give me and Kareem a kiss on our foreheads. Even with all that had that transpired, she still showed so much strength. We all sat in silence, in our own world, thinking about how our lives changed in an instant. Kareem's phone brought all of us out of our thoughts.

"Y'all better not be calling my phone unless y'all found

him." Kareem sat up in his seat and turned into another person. "Bet. After we get these cops off our back, I'll be there."

We hadn't even thought about that part. We sat around trying to figure it out through whispers so no one could hear us. I didn't know what Kareem planned to do, but hopefully, it didn't bring us more heat. I trusted him. I didn't need anything happening to add on to what the tornado left in ruins. We had to rebuild, and I didn't know where to start. There had to be a starting point though. Mase would have wanted that. Hopes, dreams, and aspirations were important to him, which was a part of living, so I was going to try my best to do so.

I didn't choose the streets; the streets chose me. The only thing I can do is prove that I belong here. My action will speak louder than my words.

- Kareem

*T*was never one to worry about my father not being present. I felt like Grammy did a good job of providing the things most needed in life. It wasn't until now that it hit me after all those years of watching Uncle Mason with Mase and Cashmere. He always treated me how he treated them. Never did I feel left out or ostracized. If he knew I was his child, he would have been the best father he could be. My mother didn't give him that opportunity. She robbed me of crucial moments that could have built a different character within myself. I wasn't a bad dude. I would have been much greater with the guidance of a male figure.

"Yo, Reem." My reflex had my Glock pointed directly at Rick, not realizing he was who he was. I was on the edge for sure. He put his hands up. He caught me off guard, and with everything going on, I reacted. I was prepared to shoot first and ask questions later.

"My bad." I relaxed a little. I gave both Rick and Reese the rundown while Mase was in surgery. I also set some things in motion. I didn't know if Dom was dead, but by the looks of the blood on the warehouse floor, he was sure on his way. One of my shots hit him, if not all three I let off.

"Where he at?" We couldn't really talk over the phone, so I had to wait until I arrived to assess the situation. All I knew was they apprehended the target, and that would lead me to my next step.

Rick and Reese pulled up on Dre trying to sneak all his money and belongings into one of Dom's trucks. They played it cool and followed him back to this big mansion in Saddle River. Once I got past, the gates, I sat in my car, still flabbergasted by today's events. I had made a quick stop before pulling up to the address that Rick gave me. I didn't even have time to grieve or mourn the loss of my cousin. He was my cousin before he lost his life but became my brother after, and that was the shit that bothered me the most. All those feelings and emotions had to wait. Business had to be handled, and it had to be done the right way.

"Follow me. You're going to like what you see." Rick's words intrigued me.

I followed Rick into a massive living room. I looked at the pictures of Dom and Qwana. *Shit.* We had to get a hold of Qwana. I didn't even know where she was or how to even get in touch with her. I prepared myself mentally to have to deal with that. It angered me, but noticing the blood that flowed into the living room gave me some type of satisfaction. A smile broke out as I looked down at Dom's lifeless body. Dre wasn't able to save him. You could tell he tried by the many medical supplies spread throughout the living room.

I walked over to Dom, not caring to attach my silencer. I killed him for the second time. I put two more bullets into his head, making sure that he would never wake up again. That gave me some type of satisfaction knowing the man that killed my father was gone. My first order of business was taken care of. Now it was time to deal with Dre. I had to find Harvey before he had a chance to build another crew for retaliation. The last twenty-four hours had been hell on earth, all by the hands of someone who didn't know their place. This empire was built only for it to be stolen by someone I knew was trusted. I grabbed a chair and sat right in front of Dre who was looking at me the whole time upon my arrival.

"What do you have to say for yourself?" I snatched the tape off his mouth, ripping off some of his mustache in the process.

"Fuck you. You wannabe thug. You better kill me. If not, I'm taking your whole family out." Dre spit at my feet. The red splatter covered my black Timbs. I sent an earth-shattering blow to his midsection watching him fall back in the chair in excruciating pain.

"I knew you were going to play tough guy." I laughed, knowing I had one up on him. All that tough shit was about to go out the window.

"You better kill me now. I'm not talking." Dre uttered from his position on the floor.

"I want the codes to Dom's safes, and I want to know where Harvey at, you dick in the booty ass nigga. I bet you'll tell me when I come back up in this motherfucker."

I stormed out of the house on a mission that I knew would get me closer to cleaning out all Dom's money, not only here but the warehouse and everywhere else. I knew Dre knew all those details, but he wasn't letting up. He had to drop Harvey off somewhere, so I knew he knew that information too. It was cool. That nigga was about to find out about me. Nobody messed with my family. I popped the trunk to my ride. The person tried getting out, but my Glock stopped them from playing with me.

"You can make this easy and walk, or I'll shoot you in your legs and drag you inside. Your choice." She tried screaming one last time before giving up; the tape muffled everything." I couldn't blame her. Every try was a step closer to getting away. She didn't know who she was dealing with because she wasn't going anywhere, no matter how much she tried.

"Look who I have here," I announced as I walked through the entrance of the living room. Dre was back up from the floor. Rick and Reese were staring this nigga down, waiting to see my ammo. They didn't know who or what I was bringing in. Dre locked eyes on my special surprise, and they both started going buck wild once we got in eye's view. She saw his face and body covered in blood, and he saw her tears and the bruises on her face. They both must have known death was near.

"Please, she doesn't have anything to do with this." Dre's softer side spoke, almost turning into a different person.

"Oh, now you saying please? Fuck out of here." I threw his wife to the floor. She was now kicking with a silent scream that would never be heard on the outside. I cocked my Glock and pointed it directly at her head. I had to really think about this. If I killed his wife, he definitely wasn't going to give me the information I needed. As soon as I thought about it, a different plan came to mind. I'd try my hand at it. If not, I'd find another way without them.

"You know what? It would be too easy to kill your wife, so let's see how much she knows. Listen, if you start screaming when I take this tape off, I'm pulling the trigger." With my gun still cocked, I pulled back the tape.

"Please, don't kill me. I'll tell you anything you wanna know."

"Marsha! No!" Dre started kicking, attempting to get loose. Reese put some tape on his mouth, shutting him up.

"Unless you have the codes to the safe and the where-abouts of Harvey, I suggest you don't play with me. I'm not in a playing mood."

"I don't know where Harvey is, but I do know where Dom keeps his passwords and important documents. Please, that's all I know."

"Keep talking." I'd catch up with Harvey sooner or later. Right now, I had money on my mind.

"Upstairs in Dom's office in the top drawer, you should find a black book. It was there last week." She was pleading with her eyes, begging me to believe her. Reese went to go see if what she was saying was true. Reese came back down with a black book and handed it to me. I looked through it and saw codes for a few things. One of these would probably work. We taped her back up and ripped the house apart looking for the safes. An hour and some change later, we had cracked open two safes. One had nothing but papers, and the other had close to eighty thousand dollars. We took everything.

"Your wife has more heart than you. You were loyal to the wrong person, so now it's about to cost you your life. Any final thoughts?" I ripped the tape off his mouth for the second time. He would never be able to utter another word, so he'd better choose his words wisely.

"Fuck you."

Pop! Pop! Pop!

I wasn't about to go back and forth with him. I ended his life, hoping he rotted in hell right along with the nigga he tried to protect. Unfortunately, his wife had to go. This was the part I didn't like. She didn't have anything to do with it, but my brothers didn't either. An eye for an eye reigned true in this situation. I could have taken the easy way out and had

Rick or Reese handle it, but this wasn't their problem; it was mine.

"I'm sorry, Marsha."

Pop! Pop! Pop!

I didn't even wait. I got it over with. Now I had to figure out how I was going to clean this up. I had a few thoughts in mind.

I PULLED UP TO WHITE BOY JOHN'S HOUSE. HE WAS DEFINITELY living large. His pops had money, and you could tell by the security gate I had to check in at. The wraparound driveway was bigger than a go-kart racing track. I pulled up to the door. There was a dude who looked like a butler dressed in black suit attire like he was Geoffrey from *The Fresh Prince of Bel Air*. I pulled behind so many luxury cars I felt I was at a high price auction. The butler opened the car door for me, allowing me to exit.

"Sir, Kareem. Thank you for joining us tonight. You can follow me."

I followed him into this large mansion, not knowing how this meeting was going to turn out. When I called White Boy John to talk with his father, his father agreed right away that he would meet me. I also got in touch with Jax to let him know what was going on. He actually still talked to Scottie from time to time. Scottie B was still supplying the East Coast with that pure white. He was Dom's supplier and he needed to know what transpired. I had to let him know the money wasn't going to stop though.

Mr. Butler escorted me to a conference room right off the living room area. I gripped the duffle bag of money tight as we walked down a long hallway. I was about five minutes early, so I wasn't expecting Scottie to be ready, but him and six other guys sat at the table chatting it up. It was now or never, so I held my head high and proceeded into the room of the unknown. The only reason I knew who Scottie B was from the pictures that hung from the walls of this compound. I was escorted to my seat, and I waited until I was spoken to.

"Nice of you to join us, Kareem." I nodded my head, acknowledging him opening his doors for me.

I looked around the table at the men that sat before me. All of them looked to have been my father's age. Once they knew what transpired, I knew for sure I'd have a permanent seat at the table. My phone started ringing right on time. It was my other key to the kingdom. Scottie looked on, almost confused until I put the phone on speaker and the voice came booming through the speakers. I turned it up for all to hear, and they all sat attentively.

"Scottie, did you miss me?" The smile that spread across his face let me know he was ecstatic to hear the voice on the other end. So was the rest of the table.

"Jax, shut your ass up. Nobody misses you." The room erupted in laughter. That broke the ice in the room. No more were the men seated at the table mean mugging me.

"Let's get down to business, shall we?" Jax got right down to business. He was limited in time, so he ran down the back in the day information that Dom killed my dad. I then caught them up on the death of the grimiest nigga I ever came in to contact with. It probably wouldn't be my last time dealing with a snake like Dom. I now had experience.

"I knew something didn't add up. I always told Mason to watch Dominick. He always covered for him. I'm not going to lie; Dominick made us a lot of money, but knowing Mason's blood was on it doesn't sit well with me. You sure he's dead?"

"I shot him two more times to make sure he will never breathe again." Scottie nodded his head in satisfaction.

"The more I look at you and the more I hear you talk, I see

335

your father. You have big shoes to fill if you want to sit at the table with us." He paused. "How do I know I could trust you?"

"You would have to take that chance. Nothing I say would make you trust me. It's my actions that will show you." I was confident in that and the money I emptied out on the large table.

"We don't take chances. Too much is on the line to do that. Can you handle what comes along with this life? Let me stop you before you answer. Most people nowadays will sit right there and say they are, but when it's time to face a hard challenge, they fold under pressure. That is why the snitching rate rose, people are no longer built to last."

"I didn't choose the streets; the streets chose me. The only thing I can do is prove that I belong here. My action will speak louder than my words. Starting with the eighty thousand spread across this table."

It wasn't much more I could say honestly. I knew what had to be done, and that was that. I never thought I would be here in such a short time. I guess it was always in my destiny to inherit my father's empire. Dom was someone who was holding it down until it was time. The time was now, and I intended to exceed what both of them did. I had to be developed first, not only was I street smart, but I was book smart, and neither of them had that so I knew for sure I would almost triple the profit.

"Sounds like someone I know." I was happy for the comparison, but I was my own man, making my own lane, never taking away the blood I was born from.

We sat around while they gave me the rundown on how everything worked. It was official; they gave me the green light, and I had something to prove. After I gathered all the information and next steps, I breathed a little. To welcome me, we lit cigars, and they talked about old times with my dad and Jax, and we enjoyed the rest of the night. It took my mind off losing Mase, but my heart still ached every time it crossed my mind. These next few days and weeks were about to be really tough, but I was built to last.

"Don't worry about the cleanup at Dom's. We got you covered. Once I introduce you to our clean-up team, you no longer have to go through me. They are now on your payroll." That was one less thing I had to worry about. "Also, we are going to send your brother off nice, the way I know your father would have wanted it. My secretary will be calling you for arrangements. We won't spare no expense to lay him to rest nicely."

I was appreciative of all things. He didn't have to do that, but that's what happened when you were loyal. It hurt to even think about a funeral. It was our reality, and unfortunately, it was something we couldn't change. I had to get home to my family. Now that this was taken care of, I could focus on rebuilding the foundation of what our lives were built on. One thing for sure and one thing for certain, we were going to get through this as a family, as a unit. I rode home, tears finally being released as I thought of the memories of yesterday.

112 - Still In Love

Baby I'm still in love
Said I'm still in love with you
In spite of the things that you put me through
Said I'm still in love with you

"Oh my God, Cashmere. How long have you been sitting in the shower?" Jeda opened the door to the bathroom. I didn't even hear her knock. She turned off the running water as I sat there still in a daze, not wanting tomorrow to come. "Babe, please get up. Are you okay?" I didn't know if it was the water still dripping or the tears. I missed my brother.

Jeda kneeled down on the side of the tub. She noticed I wasn't answering any of her questions, so she stopped asking them. The water was keeping me alive; it was watering death. I couldn't live without my big brother. I kept replaying that night in my head, wondering if we could have done anything different. I wished I wouldn't have called Mase and left a message with the warehouse address. Maybe things would have turned out differently if we erased my part in the matter.

"Babe, I'm here. Whatever you need. I don't want you to get sick, so come on. Let me dry you off." Jeda grabbed a towel out of our closet. Hearing the concern and worry in her voice gave me the strength to stand up as she brought the towel to me.

"Thank you, Dip. I'm losing my mind."

"You're not losing your mind, Cashmere. You're grieving, and that's okay." She dried me off as I tried to not break down in front of someone who I supposed to be strong for. Once she was done drying the dripping water, she wrapped the towel around my waist for me to step out.

"Did my grammy get out of bed yet?" I asked, wondering who let Jeda in. Kareem had left not too long ago. He couldn't stay in the house. It was making him crazy, so he found peace in building his empire that he felt Daddy gave him. I had to get used to saying that. It came a little easy since he always felt like a brother more than a cousin.

"No. She's still in her room in the bed. I checked on her before I came up. You guys are going to get through this. You guys are one of the strongest families I know."

I collapsed on my bed as we entered my room. Clothes were everywhere along with potato chip bags, candy wrappers, and everything else that gave me comfort in my time of need. Kareem even let me blow it down with him the other night for the first time. The soothing feeling I got helped me to sleep for the first time since losing Mase. I needed something. So many people were in and out of the house that it was exhausting. Kareem wasn't a people person, so he opted out of hosting guests and let me and Grammy handle that part.

Grammy was strong in front of people, but once everyone left, she fell deeper into depression.

"Babe, you want me to put some lotion on your body while you relax?" Jeda questioned, bringing me out of my thoughts.

"I don't know." I shrugged my shoulders, feeling defeated. I wanted to go to sleep and forget about all this, hoping that I would wake up and it was all a dream.

As I laid on my stomach, Jeda jumped up and grabbed the lotion. She released my towel and started lotioning my body, starting with my back. It felt so good as she added the massage feature of her soft hands touching my skin. I was thankful that every day she came to make sure I was good. If Jeda wasn't in school, she was with me at the house. Tomorrow we would be coming up on a week of losing Mase. Tomorrow was also his funeral, and I wasn't ready to say goodbye. It wasn't fair. Why did God have to take him away? What had our family done so bad that we continued to have to bury people before they even got a chance to fully live?

Jeda's hands were magical. "Babe, turn around." I turned on my back and she began to lotion my chest. It was feeling so good that I started to get hard in the process. I didn't want to think about sex, but it was probably what I needed to relax. I guess Jeda saw that and started massaging my shaft. A part of me felt bad for wanting some until I thought about it. Mase would have jumped head first in some pussy and wouldn't have apologized. I cracked a little smile, knowing I was about to make my big brother proud by getting some. It was weird, but I knew that would have been his strength if it was the other way around. So I sat back and enjoyed this much needed nut.

It definitely helped that I busted. I felt a little lighter. I had the world on my shoulders, and I was tired of carrying it. It was becoming too heavy, and I no longer had the strength to keep lifting. Jeda laid in my arms as we sat in silence, listening to each other's heartbeat. Her breathing matched mine as we looked into the darkness of the room. Jeda was allowing me to process it all. She was patient with me, but for how long? She would be leaving me soon, and that was another transition that I would have to endure that I wasn't ready for.

"I don't want to go." I was dreading tomorrow. Every time I thought about it, it made my heart hurt.

"I know, babe. I know. I wish I could change that, but I can't. I'll be there every step of the way. Whatever you need."

"I need my brother, Dip. Like... like I don't want to see him lying there. It's not like he's asleep and I could use tissue to play in his ear or nose to bother him like when we were kids. Or go get some syrup or ketchup to pour on his face as a prank like he and Kareem always used to do to me. I was always the first one to sleep, so it was always me who got it." I had shed so many tears that at this point I had no more to give. Thinking back on those memories did hurt, but it also made me chuckle at all the good times we had.

"Those memories are going to keep you going. Hold them close to your heart. Each day, replace the pain with all of the good times you guys shared. It will make it a little easier as the time passes." Jeda kissed my lips.

"I don't know what I'll do without you, Dip. You're going to be leaving me in a couple of months, and I don't know if my heart would be able to take it." I was open, always been the type to never hold in how I felt. Before all of this, Jeda and I were friends, trying to see how we could make the impossible work. Each day she showed up for me brought me closer to my decision to love her forever.

"You don't want me to go?" The sadness in her voice was met with the question she proposed.

"I don't know. I know how important this is for you, and I

would never want you to pass up on a great opportunity. I have to learn how to navigate with you in another state, on another coast, I guess." My intentions were never to sound selfish, but after the words left my mouth, that's exactly how it sounded.

"I'm… I'm sorry, Cash." Tears erupted from the confines of her eye duct. It was as if she was holding it the whole time. It felt like she put my tears, my hurt, and pain before hers, and that made me love her even more.

"What are you sorry for, Dip? I'm trying to piece together my life as I know it. Do I want you to stay? I would be lying if I say I didn't, but I understand that you have to live for you. If you stay, your hopes, dreams, and aspirations will die, and we don't need any more dead things around here. What I can say is, you're my girl forever. One day, you'll be my wife, so forget about this friend talk. Whether you go to Cali or not, you are going with a boyfriend. I may not be able to be there every day, but you're mine."

"What are you saying, Cash?" We lay face to face on the pillow, barely seeing each other's eyes in the darkness but having a knowing of love that transcended from our souls to each other's heart.

"What I'm saying is, no matter where you are and how far I'll be, I want us to be together, never apart. It's going to take some getting used to, but I know for sure we can manage. We both are going to be busy, but we have to make the effort to keep our connection strong."

"I love you, Cash, and there is no other person I would rather be with." We kissed passionately as she slowly mounted me. We sealed our agreement with a loving making session that wiped away all of our fears, even if it was for the time being. We connected on another level, and before you know it, we were knocked out.

Knock. Knock. Knock.

I heard a light knock on my door. Grammy never came upstairs, so it had to be Kareem. I looked at the clock, and it was almost 2:00 a.m. I grabbed my robe real quick to see who was behind the door. Before opening the door, I made sure Jeda was covered up and asleep. She was so beautiful as she slept that I thanked God right then for keeping us connected despite the many things that could have torn us apart. I opened the door and was happy to see my other big brother standing there.

"You good?" Kareem's eyes were red, but it wasn't from crying. They were low too, so that meant he'd probably just got done smoking. As the thought invaded my mind, the smell of the devil's lettuce met my nostrils with a whiff before noticing the blunt in his hand. Kareem held it up, inviting me to come join him. It was my way to bond with him, so I took him up on his offer.

"I'll meet you on the porch. Let me throw something on." I opened the door a little more for him to see Jeda laid in the bed, and he already knew what was up. I threw on some shorts and made my way downstairs. I checked on Grammy who was knocked out, so I closed her door back. I made it downstairs, and Kareem was lost in his thoughts, not even realizing that I had come down.

"You good?" I asked as I sat next to him.

"Right after we spark this blunt, I'll be even better." He lit it, took a puff, and let the feeling take over, feeling relieved after each toke.

"How you been holding up? You've been on the move; that's probably helping out a bit, but it's those private moments when you get to thinking. That's what I'm talking about." I was worried about all of my family, but this affected Kareem and me the most. We spent most of our lives together. Mase and Kareem didn't always see eye to eye, but they loved each other with everything in them.

"You know I don't like to talk about my feelings."

"Bro, you have to. At least with me. We gotta help each other through this tragedy."

"What am I going to say, Cash? That it's my fault that Mase is dead, or that I wasn't man enough to protect my family?" Kareem dropped his head, passing the blunt. I took a pull, still trying to learn to inhale and not choke.

"None of this is your fault. How was we supposed to know that Qwana was Dom's wife? Or that Mase was going to show up? If it's anybody's fault, it's mine. I was the one who called him, letting him know where we were at." Now it was my turn to drop my head.

"You were trying to protect me. That's the only reason you called him. If I wouldn't have gotten caught up with Dom, trust me, none of this would have happened. I made it right though. It's not going to bring Mase back, but it makes me feel a little bit better that the people who killed my brother, our brother, are dead."

I wouldn't have wanted it any other way. I didn't question him about it. I knew that he handled it. We had our lives mapped out, never realizing that it wasn't our choice how it would turn out. All we could do was make the best of what was given to us. Kareem was the control freak, so I knew that was what bothered him the most, that he couldn't control the outcome of Mase's demise. You could hear the conviction in his voice. It was something that he would probably carry for the rest of his life if he didn't talk about it.

"Reem, the longer we beat ourselves up, the longer it will be to heal and move on. We won't forget him, but you know Mase; he would want us to live our lives. I can hear him now." The tears I didn't know I had more of started falling.

"I know you always looked at me as one of your cousins;

now you're going to know me as your big brother. Never taking away what you and Mase had but building something that will help us through this next phase of our lives is my goal. I promise we are going to get through this, me and you." Although his tears didn't fall, I could see them building up. His words held weight. Kareem's word was always his bond. We smoked, talked, and chilled until we saw the sun come up.

Today was going to be the day where I would be the glue to hold us all together.

- Kareem

The windy weather hulked my face as I opened the door to the funeral limousine that held the people that meant the most to me. The damp air matched the rain that was on its way. The forecast called for it on one of the saddest days of my life. We sat in silence the whole ride. My mom sat twiddling her fingers. She never got a chance to say goodbye to Aunt Linda and my father, so I knew this had to be hard for her. Cash sat holding Mase's jersey, looking out the window at life going on, while ours felt non-existent. Today was going to be the day where I would be the glue to hold us all together. I was sure I'd have my chance, but it was about them getting through the day, knowing that they were left in good hands.

I stepped out of the limo, reaching and helping my grandmother out. Cash made sure to help my mom out as we waited for direction from the funeral assistant. We decided to have a private funeral. After hearing of Mase's passing, Rutgers had a vigil. Seeing so many people touched by his gift was amazing. His teammates dedicated their season to him. His boy Quincy promised they were still going to take it all the way in his honor. Coach Patterson spoke and had everyone in tears. The love shown was real. He would definitely be missed. Today wasn't about his career. It wasn't about his player ways. It was about laying to rest a son, a brother, and a grandson.

The service was really nice, and Mase looked good. Seeing him laid there like he was asleep was heartbreaking, knowing he would never wake up. Cash took it the hardest, but everybody expected him to. When Qwana walked by during the viewing part, it crushed me to see her lose it the way she did. She couldn't even stand. We set her right on the front row with us. We were able to get through the service. The whole time, I was wishing for it to be over. Now we had to bury him, and watching my brother go into the ground brought me to my knees. I lost a part of me as "Ashes to ashes, dust to dust" sealed our reality.

A few of Grammy's church members cooked us some food and brought it to the house. We all sat around, talking and trying to laugh to keep from crying, and we were doing pretty good. Grammy had long gone in her room, and Mr. Patterson and his wife had left. Qwana didn't say much all evening, but it was good to have her around. When we got up to clean, Qwana joined us. I needed her to say something. She was low key making me nervous. It was like she had something to say but didn't know how to say it.

"Qwana, you good?" We were gathering the many soda cans and plates that sat around, left by people that probably didn't even know Mase. Cashmere looked on, thinking the same thing I was. He kept looking her way, waiting for her to interact with the rest of the room.

"I'm waiting for him to walk through the door. To see his smile or smell his cologne. I always wanted to see where he grew up, but not like this." Qwana stopped what she was doing, realizing that she will never get to experience it with the person who connected us all in the first place.

"I've been waiting for his call since I scrolled to his name, ready to hit the talk button. I called his phone multiple times to hear his voicemail, so I understand where you are coming from," Cashmere let us know.

"I'm waiting to wake up to some good smelling breakfast one random Saturday. That boy knew he knew how to throw down in the kitchen." I always admired Mase's skills in the kitchen. It was always his thing, so I never had to worry about eating a good meal.

"I notice you didn't eat, Qwana. You want to make you a plate before we put everything up?" Cash offered.

"I haven't been able to keep down much food these days." Qwana looked down and rubbed her belly. A sadness came over her. "But we're going to be alright."

"Who?" I looked toward Cash, as he had the same look of confusion on his face as he looked toward me.

"I'm pregnant." The tears she tried holding on to spilled down her face.

"With all due respect, pregnant by who? You were married," I asked as Cash embraced Qwana. Either way, the child would be fatherless.

"It's Mason's. We... we got careless the last few months. Most of the time, we were happy to be together. I stopped having sex with Dominick almost a year ago. He had problems performing, and his diabetes was killing him slowly. That's when it started going downhill. Mason officially became my everything. I had checked out emotionally a long time ago. If he wasn't cheating, he was always out handling business.

"Wait, so you're saying I'm about to be an uncle?" Cash's eyes lit up as he held onto Qwana's shoulders, waiting to confirm the good news, hoping to have a part of Mase in the form of a niece or nephew.

"You are about to be Uncle Cash in a few months." Cash hugged her tight, thanking God for the blessing. With everything going on, some good news was what we needed.

"Are you sure?" I was excited, but I had to confirm once more before I got my hopes up. Their whole relationship was a sticky situation. At the end of the day, she was still married, and knowing Mase, he always made sure to strap up. That I knew for sure.

"At first I thought it was stress. It happened a few times where my period skipped a month. Then I started to get morning sickness. When I got to Georgia, it became clear to me. I took three pregnancy tests, all confirming what was growing inside of me. I was gonna tell him the day he got killed. We were supposed to be together. I was going to get a divorce." Another wave of tears soaked her face.

"We got you." I joined them. I wished it didn't happen this way, but it did. Mase would have been a great father.

"We have another Cotton on the way!" Cash declared, pounding his chest.

"Man, this baby about to be spoiled." We all shook our heads in agreement.

A knock stopped us from basking in the good news. I was not up for any more company, so whoever this was, was about to get turned around. Visiting hours were over. Cash was the closest, so he took the initiative to see who it was. Before the person could answer, he opened the door.

"Harvey!"

CASHMERE

One year Later...

*T*he Labor Day weekend weather was set as the sun shined bright on us while we sat in the backyard barbecuing. The music was playing on full blast as we rocked to the sounds of Yung Joc "It's Goin' Down". We were all finally getting to a place where our days weren't dark and reminiscent of the people we'd lost. I always wondered if I'd ever see light at the end of the tunnel. With all the great things going on in my life right now, it had to be nobody but God allowing my brother to look down upon me.

"Cashmere, I know you heard me." Grammy slapped me on my arm, taking me out of my thoughts.

"I'm not going to forget about you, Grammy." I chuckled a little. Grammy was being dramatic. "I've only been gone three months. Did you forget I still talk to you every day? Even if it's for a couple of minutes."

"I know, but why did you have to move so far?" Grammy pouted for the thousandth time today.

"You know why, Grammy, so stop." I grabbed Jeda's hand, happy I made the decision to move with her to L.A. Jeda's smile was so wide. She even got the glow and sparkle back into her eyes. I would miss my grandmother for sure, but I knew this was the right decision.

"Now, Grammy, you know he does whatever Jeda tells him to do." Laughter erupted at Kareem's smart comment.

"Yeah, aight." I joined in, silently confirming how much of a hold my future wife had on me.

Jeda and I did the long distance relationship for a couple of months. It worked, but as I got familiar with the lay of the land in L.A., I saw the many opportunities this new territory could bring me. Aonika's album dropped, and it received rave reviews from critics and fans alike. Word got around about my writing and producing skills, so my calendar was a book. I tried my hand at UCLA, and I got in, so not only was I living my dream, I was getting my education as well. I would be starting in a couple of weeks. We were all moved in and ready to start our life on the west coast.

"When I need a break from this little guy, I'm sending him right to you." Qwana knew that I wouldn't mind it at all. Holding Mason in my arms for the first time was a feeling I couldn't quite understand.

"I'm taking him with me when I leave. Right, fat boy? Uncle Cash taking you right with him." I took Mason III from his mother and planted fart kisses to his little belly.

I was going to miss my family. This was our last little hurrah before L.A. became my everyday for the next few months. I was planning on visiting when I could. I didn't want to miss too many moments of this little guy's life. Soon, he'd be having more flight miles than the average adult. Come the new year, I should have enough songs for my debut album with my new label Universal Motown Records. Still couldn't believe they signed me to a multi-million-dollar contract. They liked the songs I had already plus the title, so I was good money.

We never expected life to be what it was. We were trying to make the best out of it. I didn't know what this new chapter of my life had in store. If all these good things were a sign, I was moving in the right direction. I looked around at the many faces, all of us encountering things that should have broken us. Yet we were standing around, listening to music and laughing, enjoying the seconds, minutes, hours, days, months, and years we had left.

RESPECT WAS EARNED, NOT GIVEN. IF THE STREETS DIDN'T teach me nothing else, they taught me that. I knew this takeover wasn't going to be easy. I didn't realize how bad I needed it. Not only was I running and supplying half of New

Jersey, I was doing it with a 3.9 GPA. I got accepted to medical school. I'd be starting in a few weeks. The adrenaline I got from counting my money in stacks made me fall in love for the first time. Once we disposed of the waste or the weak links in our organizational structure, it was easy like Sunday morning. Harvey wasn't the threat I thought he would be. He claimed he didn't know anything, and a part of me believed him. That's why he was alive today. He bowed down and kissed the ring, so he now worked for me. He stayed out of my way, and that kept him breathing. We watched him like a hawk, so nothing would slip past me.

"You burning up that chicken on the grill, boy?" I didn't know when grilling became my thing. I wanted to enjoy the party with the rest of the people. I didn't see how Mase did it. I missed him, especially in times like this. I always smiled, knowing he was laughing at me and clowning me for burning this food.

"Ma, you're the only one that wants chicken anyway." I looked at my mother, not being able to see her eyes from the big sunglasses she had on. Our relationship was growing stronger. She didn't like what I was doing in the streets, but she understood though. As long as I stayed in school, she was okay with it. It was like we picked right back up where we left off.

"Get that girl chicken off the grill so she can be quiet." Grammy looked at my mother and rolled her eyes. Grammy still hadn't let up on her verbal wars with my mom. Most times, my mom let it go. She'd snap at everybody else but Grammy.

"Whatever." My mom shook her head.

"Mr. Patterson, don't get him to cook at the restaurant. Y'all will be closed down before y'all even get a chance to open." Cash had jokes.

Mr. and Mrs. Patterson still decided to go ahead and open

the restaurant. It was a little cool spot that they found in Paterson on 10th Avenue. It seated twenty to forty people. It was called "The Majors: Soul Food Restaurant." It wasn't opening until the Spring, but they got to work on the property.

"I bet I could cook better than you; the only thing you could do better than me is sing." We all laughed, knowing that to be true.

I was living life in the fast lane, and I didn't plan to slow down. The house was paid off, my mother was healthy, my brother was doing good, and my nephew was here. I was making more money than I could handle, so there was no need to complain. Complaining wasn't going to change anything, anyway. We all embraced this season, not sure how long it was going to last. I was going to ride it until the wheels fell off. Our lives were built on broken pieces, and it was time for all of those pieces to come together so we could finally have a firm foundation to stand on.

THE END

LETTER TO MY SON:

Dear Davion,

When we found out that we were having you, I knew then I had to make something of myself. Seeing you when you were born pushed me further into the man I would soon become. My first attempt at doing that was when I enrolled in college to show you that education mattered. In doing that, I became the first one in our family to graduate college with a bachelor's degree. All I kept thinking about as I walked across that stage was, I hope I made my son proud. That same year, I followed my dreams of starting my own entertainment company to show you, you can do anything you put your mind to. Not only did you assist me in performing to a sold-out crowd, but you also got to hear my story from *A Place Called Broken*. Showing you that broken people can be put back together.

Then you watched me find love, being open to what comes with parents who are not together. I hope that you'll be a better husband, a better father than I'll ever be by my actions, not my words. It was your love that got me through some dark days, son. I got up plenty of mornings because of you. You kept life moving for me, and I thank God for you each and every day!

I wrote this book for you. It might have taken me eighteen years, but I did it. I dreamed about, talked about, started, and never finished, but once I finally put my mind to it, mission accomplished! Always remember I'm rooting for you in everything you do in life. Even when I'm long gone, let this be your reminder: "Don't be good; be great, and when they say you can't, show them you can!"

Love you, Son,
    Your Dad

ACKNOWLEDGMENTS

Singing: Lord, I'm amazed by You. Lord, I'm amazed by You, how You love Me. God, I just want to say thank You! Thank You for the many blessings you continue to add to my life! Without You, I'm nothing. Without you, I wouldn't even be writing this. So I give honor to You, my provider, my keeper, my everything.

To my wife, thank you for believing in me. It made it much easier knowing you were by my side, listening to every idea, talking me down off the ledge, and encouraging me not to quit. You are my rock! O-Boogie wit' the hoodie, you're a great kid, and I'm so happy that God assigned me to help you grow in life! The sky's the limit, and I know for sure you're going to reach your full potential! Dayjah, remember, I'm your uncle now, so you better put some respect on my title. LOL. Thanks for being a great niece and rocking with me from the beginning.

Momma, I made it! You are the definition of strength and perseverance. You've overcome so much, and I pray God continues to keep his hands upon you. I'm a momma's boy, always. Brooooooo! To my dance machine of a brother, Mr.

Kid Fatigue himself, you were my first kid. Keep shining, bro. I pray I make you as proud as you made me to be your big brother. To James "J.W." Durham, thanks for being a Father when I didn't have one! Paging Dr. Tomicka McMillion to the stage. That's right. We got a doctor in the family! I'm so proud of you. Every day, I aspire to be like you! I wouldn't be who I am without you. I'm forever indebted to the part you played into shaping me into a *Strong Black Man*.

Stephanie Primus, I didn't know real friendship until I met you. You play so many key roles in my life that if I had ten thousand tongues, I couldn't thank you enough. Love you, buddy! Kita, thank you for giving me one of God's greatest gifts, my son. To Zahyir, thanks for accepting me as your stepfather and trusting me to be the example you need in life. I love you, kid, and there is nothing you can do about it.

To the first friends I ever knew, shout out to my cousins! Tiffany, Jada, Quana, Will, TJ, Janell, Jatasia. RIP T-Ripp. To my older cousins, Stephanie Brown-Cobb, Jermaine, Shae, Towanda, Theia, Nicole, Kareen (Gotti), Keshawn (Diddy), RIP Son-Sun, Star, Tonya, Chris, E. RIP Pep. To Shakera, Shanique, Rodiegar, Shamar. To my aunts, Aunt Lilly and Aunt Diane, I love you both. Uncle T, RIP Aunt Juanita, Aunt Felicia, RIP Aunt Val, RIP Aunt Katie, RIP Aunt Candy, we miss you all like crazy! Kia Farrish, Thanks for loving me since I've been little and thanks for always including me in family memories, I wouldn't be connected with my other side of the family if it wasn't for you.

To my support system, they are some praying sistas, Naimah and Cleo. I thank God for y'all ministry and friendship down through the years. Kendra Virgo, thanks for being a great friend. We are now almost twenty years in. I love you. Brit-The-Grit (Brittany M.), I appreciate you. To Shamaya Mickens and Shaquana Hinton, thanks for reading the book before the world got the chance to. To my boys: Juan, Chris,

Alex, Elder Carter, Elder Bert, my brother-in-law Rasheed. Ericka Monique Williams, we came a long way! We have been rocking for twenty plus years and counting. Thanks for always believing in me. This wouldn't be possible if it wasn't for you.

To Quasheara (Tee Tee), Laquanda (Nea-Nea), Kiara(B9), Kathy Bruce, Rhonda Tombiling, Lori McQueen and countless others who continue to cheer me on from the sidelines. Thank You!

Author B. Love, I can write pages describing the wonderful person you are. People need to know who you are. Not only are you an author with multiple #1 titles, but you are a master teacher, encourager, and an all-around amazing person. Thank you for taking on this project and making it what it is. I'm forever indebted to you. I pray that God continues to take you to heights unknown. Latisha Burns, you were truly sent from God. Thank you for believing in my story. The polish you put on it made it shine so much more. Author Karen Williams, you told me I could do it! Thank You! I pray I'm half the writer you are. Author T. Styles, your mentorship and The Elite Writers Academy helped me become a better writer and storyteller. I will always be a fan of yours. You are one of the reasons why I fell in love with Urban Lit.

Last but not least, to the dopest book club ever! You guys have become my family, I read thousands of books trying to keep up with y'all. I look forward to our nights together, talking about love, life, and everything in between. Thanks for rocking with me. To Danielle (D-Major), Shanequa (BK), Stephanie (Steph), Shanay, Mary, Anna, Andrea (AD). RIP LOU! I love y'all for real!

ABOUT THE AUTHOR

Lamartz Brown is a renowned brand marketing guru, business coach, and founder of Life Lyrics Entertainment. Lamartz was born and raised in Paterson, New Jersey. He attended Berkeley College and graduated magna cum laude with a Bachelor of Science in Business Management.

He may have a sixth-sense for business, but Lamartz's two biggest passions are writing and helping young people in his community. Through his work and his books, Lamartz strives to help youth realize their potential and become better adults who will succeed in life.

Lamartz founded Life Lyrics Entertainment as a platform through which young and aspiring producers, filmmakers, and writers can reach a wider audience with ease. With his books, Lamartz aims to bring some new and fresh stories to Contemporary Urban Literature lovers. Lamartz's inspiration is real-life issues and stuff that people don't like to talk about – taboo topics spiced up with a unique twist.

Lamartz is a warm and genuine person who believes that there is still some beauty left in the world. When he's not writing or helping people, Lamartz enjoys being a loving husband and father.

Social Media:

https://www.facebook.com/LifeLyricsEntertainment

https://twitter.com/LifeLyricsLLC

https://www.instagram.com/lifelyricsentertainment

ALSO OUT:

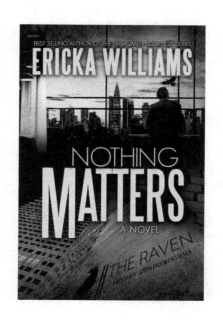

CPSIA information can be obtained
at www.ICGtesting.com
Printed in the USA
BVHW080853070921
616214BV00014B/699